FROM THE AUTHOR OF GIVE ME GRACE

LEXA DEAN AND THE WELLSPRING

BETHANY A. PERRY

Lexa Dean and the Wellspring

Published by: Cloaked Press, LLC
PO Box 341
Suring, WI 54174
Cloakedpress.com

Cover Design by:
Carmilla M. Ravensworth
carmillacreates.carrd.co

ISBN: 978-1-952796-33-3

Also by Bethany A. Perry

The Reclamation Series:
Reclamation
Reclamation 2: Revolution
Reclamation 3: Reconstruction

Give Me Grace

Perry Poems
(with Robert Perry)

To my mom: my first, most loyal, and biggest cheerleader, and one of my best friends.

THE ARTiFACT

CHAPTER 1

Feet soft in the sand, sand just like Earth's—mostly silica, fully annoying—Lexa crossed the cavernous underground chamber, avoiding the nine statues lined up against the chiseled stone walls. Nine was an odd number for these eight-limbed aliens, but she'd come back to it. Right now, the carved relief at the head of the room held all her attention.

That, and the dirt crawling up her nose.

She sneezed, holding it inside.

"You'll blow up your sinuses, little Lexa. Never hold in what's better on the outside."

It may have been a lie twentieth century grandmas told kids to scare them, but Lexa still apologized to Gram under her breath, forehead tight with guilt.

The man behind her whispered. "Bless you."

Sniffling, she approached the relief and pulled a stiff-bristled brush from the pocket of a satchel hanging across her body. "Thanks, Devin." She glanced over her shoulder, enough for him to see the side of her face but not enough to make eye contact. "Now maybe shut up for a second. Let me focus." She turned back to the relief and swiped dust from one of the lines of text. "What do you think this says, Savannah?"

A small nose poked out of Lexa's satchel, its felt tip brushing the palm of her hand.

She stuck her hand in the bag and scratched her cat behind the ears, then raised her voice an octave. "I can't read Gexcorian, Ma."

Lowering her voice again, she whispered, "Not my strongest suit either, Van. But I'm pretty sure this says, 'straight ahead to the treasure that will finally buy you a new ship so you can stop fixing up the same old busted one and get away from Earth for good,' don't you?"

"Isn't that why you brought me?" Devin asked, approaching the relief. He pointed at the words framing the carved picture and translated. *"Kneel and be calm, my people, for your queen is your salvation.* So, pretty much what you said." He lay one muscular, tanned arm against the face of it and smiled at Lexa.

His bright white teeth shone even in the darkness of the tomb and, staring at the lock of brown hair hanging over his forehead, Lexa considered ripping his shirt off and—

Savannah meowed and nipped her finger, her teeth digging into the pad with sharp pricks.

Lexa closed the flap over Savannah's head. Savannah was right. Besides being an inconvenient time, the sand, the horrid, horrid sand, would get in places she was certain she didn't want to imagine. Instead, she slid a paper from her hip pocket—notes she'd scribbled about this tomb. "That diadem is behind this relief." *It has to be.*

A rush of warmth spun her stomach and sent her heart into overdrive. The moment before she uncovered a new treasure, the anticipation, was a feeling almost better than the dopamine dump sex delivered. The high, the sense of purpose, the knowing she was right, it was a chemical soup she could live off of for years.

She folded and pocketed the paper again. Sticking the end of the brush between her teeth, she gnawed the faux wood and studied the stone in front of her. Some of the pictograms didn't line up, so, like the text suggested, she dropped to her knees to get a closer look. The lights embedded under the pink skin of her arms raised with a thought, the light reddish-beige, and she leaned in.

Devin knelt next to her. He grinned in the light, his face a bit like a jack-o-lantern. "I forgot about those. Neural link?"

"Mm-hm," she said, glancing at him. "Something else we stole from the Ummal about 150 years ago, in the mid-2000s. Right after first contact with the Truscians changed everything."

He chuckled. "If there's one thing I know about humans, it's if we want something, we'll work together, even temporarily, to beat it out of our common enemy."

Lexa smiled, still considering the stone. "Gram said it wasn't like that at first, but it didn't take us long, did it?" She leaned forward. The light outlined a cut in front of her. She sat back, ass in the sand, and considered the cut, carved stone.

Devin ran his finger over the words. "Says here, *our love for our queen is as endless as stone*, but it's sideways, and it cuts off the next sentence…" He trailed off, looking over the stone. After a few moments, his eyes brightened, and he pointed. "Here it is. But it's not going the same direction." He leaned up, fingers splayed, laid them on the stone, and pushed. It didn't move. "Hm. Not that."

She slapped his hands away. "You need to be careful." She sat up on her knees, adrenaline rushing through her face and wetting her armpits as it raced through her. Having someone along in a tomb was outside her norm, and here he was trying to get himself hurt. Or worse. "That could have killed you. If you do that again, I'm making you leave, whether or not your superior linguistics are helpful." Which wasn't his only talent with his tongue. But that was beside the point.

"A stone doesn't seem—"

"Traps. You never know what might set one off. Let me think." She stared at the stone while the adrenaline cooled and the fog in her brain coalesced into a thought.

Much as she'd hate to admit it, his idea to push on the stone made a certain kind of sense. But if she couldn't push it…

Using the bristly brush and a small knife she dug from a side pocket of Van's bag, she teased sand out of the cut all the way around a cube about 30 centimeters square. With the sand out of the way, there was enough room to squeeze her fingers around two sides.

She slipped her fingers into the gritty grooves and nodded to Devin.

He did the same, on the other two sides.

They pulled.

It slid out, sand spraying them in the face. With a grunt, sand now sticking to the sweat on Lexa's upper lip, and Devin's brow, they turned it, matched up the pictograms on either side of it, and slid it back in right side up.

At the top of the relief, a stone section surrounded by kneeling penitents slid sideways with a great grinding crunch, yet more sand cascading onto their heads.

She sneezed aloud this time.

"Bless you," Devin whispered again.

They both turned their eyes up to the newly-revealed alcove.

The diadem sat inside, made for a head which wasn't as much human as it was octopus.

Savannah spoke with a muffled *brrt*.

"You'd expect a queen's crown to be better protected," she replied. She reached to relieve the hidden alcove of its treasure and waited to see if anything would spring from the wall to kill her.

It didn't.

She exhaled. What she now cradled in her palm was the very symbol of the Gexcorian's entire civilization, spoken of with a reverence that quivered through their lips like a prayer. In their minds and hearts, it shone like the brightest diamond, the most precious gem in all existence.

In truth, it was covered in dust and honestly? A little underwhelming.

Devin shook his head, sand raining from his ear-length hair. "So that's what's so important to the museum?"

She shrugged and shoved it in the bag with Van. "They can't all be the find of a century," she said, wishing it could be.

"You'll find it one day, Lexa."

"What?"

"The origin of life. Like you talked about."

She pointedly put her back to him. "Listen, it's bad etiquette to bring up pillow talk anywhere other than the pillow. OK?" She didn't try to keep the annoyance out of her voice. Why'd she even tell him that? She was way past starting to wish she'd left him on the ship and come alone with Savannah, and considered how to dump him off after this job while turning back to the paper.

Eight statues should be here, just like the number of Gexcorian limbs.

"We're not done here yet," she said. "This diadem has to go to the museum, and they pay dick. The true treasure is still hiding. The one that'll really change things for me." She looked at the nine statues. "So which is the extra?"

The cat was silent. So was Devin.

Lexa huffed and crossed to the statues. She stopped next to one who stood a bit apart and took out the brush again. With a few gentle strokes, she teased some of the dirt away from its blobby face. Its mouth open wide, two rows of teeth inside the round orifice, it seemed to scream at something ahead of it.

"He's one ugly son of a bitch," Devin said, shuffling up next to her. He knocked on one of the man's limbs. "Hard as a rock."

Normally, Lexa would respond with something along the lines of, "That's what she said," but right now, this statue held all her attention. She found herself less and less sure he'd been carved. Nose almost pressed against its face, she ran her hand along one of the limbs. Its rough surface bumpy, almost scaly, it felt like real Gexcorian skin beneath her fingertips. She knew. She'd had the pleasure once.

OK, maybe twice.

Some dirt sifted onto her head.

She glanced up.

Just in time to see one of those underground Gexcor creatures she'd nicknamed Gex-rats scurrying, upside down, along the ceiling. It extended its wings and leapt at her head seconds before she had time to process what it was.

With a shout, she swatted at it, turning the lights up in a flash of surprise. This rat must have been hungry because instead of scampering back to the dark, it changed direction mid-air and flew at her face, its eyes squeezed shut. It sank its front claws into the soft flesh of her lower arm like twelve tiny, serrated knives, the pain immediate and exquisite.

She sucked in through her teeth and shook it off. It turned in mid-air once again.

Savannah hissed. Devin shouted and covered his head with his arms, falling to the sand with a grunt and a poof of dust.

Lexa dropped the paper and unsnapped Van's bag.

The cat leapt out before the rat made another attack. It squealed as Savannah chased it off into the dark, silent and smooth as an oil slick.

Devin's voice shook. He stood, sweat glistening on his upper lip. "Do you think it's smart to let her go like that? Those things are strong and fast." He took out a hand-held flashlight and shined it into the dark after them, the beam jittering.

Lexa didn't bother answering. Instead, she snatched up the paper and turned back to the statue, trying to work out if it was supposed to be there.

The squealing stopped in an abrupt crunch.

A grin lifted half Lexa's mouth, and she met Devin's eyes for no longer than a moment. Without a syllable, she spiked her brow with a pointed "I told you so" expression. She knelt in the dirt, knees not a fan of the hard, rocky floor under the sand, and examined the skin of the Gexcorian's lower extremities, searching for chisel marks that didn't seem to exist.

Something shuffled in the shadows.

Devin turned his light toward the sound, the beam steadier now. "How much longer, doc?"

With slow precision, Lexa folded the paper and slid it back into her pocket. If this statue wasn't carved, the alternative wasn't pretty. She clicked her tongue through her teeth, eager to make sure her cat didn't run afoul of a trap. "Savannah." *Click, click, click.* "Vanny, time to come back."

Out of the dark, another Gex-rat flew at them. Raising her already-scratched arm between her face and the winged rat, Lexa ducked and ran into the statue. It overbalanced.

The rat flew past.

The statue seemed to squeal almost out of the range of Lexa's hearing as it fell, slowly, slowly. Watching its screaming face, its outstretched limbs, she leapt for it, trying to grab onto it and keep it from falling while Devin jumped back, the flashlight beam following the Gex-rat back into the dark.

She wasn't fast enough. The statue toppled, smashing on contact with the floor. Shards of shimmering stone flew everywhere. Ichor spilled from the broken statue and pooled, as though it were bleeding. And it stank of bubbling tar.

She covered her face and turned away, stomach knotted. Too late, she remembered why she had run into it.

The Gex-rat flew at her again and embedded all twenty-four of its claws into her shoulder.

She screamed, her voice echoing, and tried to grasp the rat. It dug in, shooting red pain straight up her brain stem. Teeth clenched, she spun in a circle and slammed her back into the wall next to the now-vacant pedestal, leading with the rat. She hit it dead on, and it went limp and dropped.

Devin's flashlight beam stayed on it. It must have been the light that annoyed it, and it shook itself with surprising alacrity. It jumped five feet directly in the air—and directly at Devin's face. It embedded its claws on either side of his head.

Shouting, he dropped the flashlight and swatted at the thing. He tripped over his own feet and landed on the pedestal.

Savannah came dashing back from the darkness, blood in her whiskers. She growled at the rat still hooked to Devin's face. His screams almost hit the same high pitch Lexa'd heard when the statue fell. Van lowered into pouncing posture, her back legs bouncing her butt, and some centuries-old mechanism clanked in the ceiling.

What was about to happen hit Lexa as Savannah leapt.

There was no time to do anything for Devin but, for once, her reflexes were faster than her cat's.

"Savannah, no!" She snatched the cat out of the air and fell back with her as a glut of some blackish, stinking fluid poured onto the pedestal, catching Devin and the Gex-rat in the waterfall. The fluid smoked on their skin and Devin's scream would likely haunt Lexa's dreams for months.

The fluid ran into his eyes and down his throat, blanketing them both in steaming offal. Devin wailed and the Gex-rat flapped its wings, trying to get away.

But as Lexa watched, lying ass in the dirt with an arm wrapped around her cat so hard they almost melted together, the movement of the wings slowed, almost like it was in slow motion, until it stopped. Devin's screams bubbled like he was gargling the stuff, until they too died out to nothing.

Once the whole mess quit smoking, Lexa stuffed Van back in the bag and stood. Absently checking her pocket to make sure the paper was still in place, she inched toward the pedestal.

She'd never smelled something quite so vile, not in a hundred different tombs. Scavengers like the Gex-rat died inside all the time, and they always stunk. But this was…this was something else entirely. It burned her nose-hairs.

Devin's top half and the Gex-rat lay on the pedestal, a moment frozen in time. They screamed, much as the Gexcorian had, into infinity.

Lexa found her brush lying in the dirt about a meter and a half away and, with tentative care, tapped it on the Gex-rat's body.

Solid as a rock.

Devin's lower half was still unblemished, and his legs twitched as the life oozed out of them, his heels scratching in the dirt in an uneven staccato. The sound died away and left Lexa and Savannah in a heavy silence.

Bile creeping up her throat, Lexa backed away and stared at the stone fragments of the statue that used to stand here. Had the same thing happened to him? It was likely. Those traps she'd warned Devin about had gotten him anyway. A slick feeling in her gut telegraphed her own guilt at being too slow to save him.

A breeze ruffled her hair.

Shivering, she glanced up.

The ceiling had opened in a door, and she could make out glimmers coming from the other side.

Still looking up, she slid the paper from her pocket once again and unfolded it, her heart hammering her ribs. She examined the door in front of her, maybe one meter by one, and compared it to the crude drawing she'd made of this section of the tomb.

Yep, that was it. That was the way into the throne room, the chamber all the lore either said didn't exist or was forbidden. To the queen's final resting place and the myriad of other treasures this tomb promised.

Though Devin's death didn't make her want to run away from this, it put a hitch in her step. But now that he'd given his life for the treasure waiting in that throne room, she owed it to him to finish. As hard as her stomach clenched, turning her gut to stone almost as surely as the black offal that killed Devin, she couldn't back away now.

She'd just have to be sure never to lead someone else into a situation like this.

Lexa mumbled under her breath, lights ebbing and flowing as she pulled herself up into the hole. She chattered to her cat to try and block out what she was leaving below her feet.

"Of course it would be in the ceiling. These assholes have no sense of up and down. It's those damned tentacles, Van."

The cat didn't say anything.

With a grunt and a kick of her legs, Lexa inched through the hole, her abdomen finally clearing the lip. Should be smooth sailing from here, as long as she didn't set off the trap again. Were *all* those statues down there actually dead men instead of effigies? Thinking of Devin down there as one of them didn't do anything for her mood. The lights ebbed again, and not because of the exertion of getting up here. What had happened to him…she wouldn't have wished that end for anyone.

By the time she slid all the way through the hole, her abs burned like she'd done a thousand sit-ups. Something Gram used to have her do every damn day. Just like most millennials, Gram'd been into shit like yoga and vitamins and saving the planet. She should have been grateful when the Truscians came along and reversed climate change in less than a decade with their carbon-cleaning tech—not that'd it'd reversed the damage already done—

but instead she'd been wary like she spent most of her life being. Authority never sat well with Gram.

Lexa brightened the lights and checked out the room, the central figure doing more than pulling her eyes. It tugged at her heart and she moved her feet without thought. Speaking of authority, the power this figure exuded was more than she could put into words. Gexcorians had tried with their songs and their paintings and their statues and prayers, but even dozens and dozens of Gexcorian centuries later this woman had a hold on them that rivaled Earth's many faces of God.

And as she sat on her throne atop its dais, Lexa could see why. Her tentacles surrounded her in a cloud of twisted limbs, each tip pointed outward like it was the head of a snake, ready to strike.

Maridoxia. The queen to end all queens.

Breath caught in her chest, Lexa approached the throne, climbing each stair one baby step at a time. They'd covered their queen in whatever substance it was that turned the Gex-rat to stone. Each tooth gleamed inside her open mouth like a tiny shard of obsidian.

Lexa paused, hand on Savannah's satchel. "How do you reckon they got her mouth to do that after she died? They did wait till she died to bury her, didn't they?"

The cat meowed.

"I'm not so sure, either." She shivered, eyeing the queen and doing her level best to steer her thoughts away from Devin and failing. That they seemed to have shared a fate somehow felt…out of place.

Still holding her breath, Lexa crept up the final two stairs, the thick dust muffling her footfalls. The oddly-shaped throne didn't invite an easy way in. Of course, it didn't look anything like a chair Lexa would sit on. Why would it, with her piddling two legs? No. These people had grand, extravagant chairs that held each of their eight limbs in a reclined posture, almost like a cradle with eight little indentions.

Her notes didn't mention any booby-traps here, but then they didn't mention the one below, either. And though the strange term led her to thinking about alien boobs, she was in no way in the mood for it now.

She slid the paper from her hip pocket one more time. Scribbled in the corner was a crude picture of Maridoxia on her throne. The third limb from the top on Lexa's right should hold the artifact she was looking for. But she couldn't just reach in and grab it. In her cramped style, she'd written something that looked like "cross-over butts."

She eased the paper back into her pocket and turned up the lights. Leaning in and focusing on the tentacle to the left that mirrored the one she wanted, she counted four of the little things she thought of as suckers. She pressed, and it slid in as smooth as greased butter.

What had just happened to Devin wasn't enough to dim the rush, it seemed. She tingled while she switched sides, careful to avoid the pointing tentacles. "Cross-over butts. Sure, Lexa."

The opposing tentacle had flopped down, the inside of it as shiny as the perfectly pointed little teeth.

She wiped her sweating hands on her pants and held her breath again. "This is it, Van," she whispered through her teeth. "This is the one that gets us a new ship and a new life. Never to see Earth again."

Or her deadbeat mother.

It would buy Lexa's solitude.

She reached for the palm-sized artifact stuffed inside the queen's tentacle but before she laid a finger on the artifact, she noticed something out of the side of her eye. Not movement, exactly. A puff of dust, settling.

Her wide eyes snapped back to the queen's face and her breath stuck in her throat. She raised her arm and lit the effigy.

The two rows of pointed, obsidian teeth glinted in the light. It flickered with her pounding heart and it made it look like the frozen teeth were moving, slow as tectonic plates.

Lexa backed up, ready for anything. Maybe another turn-you-to-stone trap, maybe something worse.

And it was a good thing she had. The ceiling above the queen fell in jagged pieces in a semi-circle around her like eight stalactites had broken off and buried themselves in the steps.

She backed fully off the dais, eyes fixed to the queen.

Who was moving.

With the grinding of stone like boulders rolling in rushing water, her limbs moved almost imperceptibly. Her face still frozen in that death masque, her tentacles, even the one that Lexa had broken open, pushed her above the throne and she towered three meters over Lexa, bearing down on her like a glittering cloud of volcanic ash. The grinding sound grew louder, promising Lexa that when she reached her, she'd pulverize Lexa's bones as she stood frozen in the queen's entrancing gaze.

That gaze glued Lexa's feet to the ground. Meeting this walking statue was enough to convince Lexa she might have made the last mistake she was going to make in a string of some real doozies.

Until Savannah meowed. She could tell something was wrong, and she meowed half a dozen times, each call more desperate than the last.

Lexa unstuck her feet and backed up until she was standing in front of the hole she'd climbed up.

She could just jump down and run out and forget about this artifact. Her buyer could come up with something else. But this had taken years of research to find and now, the life of a man. She couldn't turn back now, not when it had already cost so much.

"Thanks, honey," she said, scratching Savannah between the ears without taking her eyes from the moving statue. It continued its slow crawl toward her, the stones flaking off like a landslide each time she moved. The tentacles beneath looked like they might still be alive. This was more than any run-of-the-mill trap.

It took Lexa over a minute to realize she'd been hearing a sound all along. Ever since she crawled up into this room. A Gexcorian scream, one that was at so high a frequency it could pierce her eardrums. And it was getting louder.

Lexa nodded to herself. Time to get out. She turned to sit and put her feet out the hole.

Glass tinkled.

Against her better judgement, she glanced over her shoulder.

The stone queen had brought down her open tentacle and the glass artifact, shaped like a bulging teardrop with eight Gexcorian pearls embedded in the rounded body, had fallen to the ground.

Dammit, that thing was going to bring her at least nine hundred thousand bucks. She hadn't had a job this luxe in forever. She had to pick it up. If she was fast, she could beat the queen's resurrection.

Unclipping Van's bag, she snapped the flap closed and laid it in the floor. "Stay put, Van. Mom'll be right back."

Maridoxia inched closer, the crushing sound of mountains moving echoing in the still chamber. Lexa peered through the tentacles, raising her lights again, and caught a glimpse of the artifact lying in the dirt. Her research had referred to this thing as the Cynosure. If the diadem was the most precious gem in existence, the Cynosure was existence, itself. And each of those pearls were worth almost a hundred thousand on their own.

Crouching, she scooted around the queen. If she timed each movement to the movement of the tentacles, she could keep out of her line of sight. But when Maridoxia brought the next tentacle down to propel her forward, the scream continued to get louder, and it felt more and more like Lexa and Savannah weren't the only things breathing in this room.

The ancient queen had come back to life to protect her treasures.

Lexa's eardrums vibrated from the strengthening scream. She checked the bag to make sure Savannah wasn't trying to claw her way out.

But turning her head was a mistake she shouldn't have made. One of the stony tentacles came down on her head, ripping at her hair and coming to rest on her shoulder.

Her scalp screamed where the hair caught in the tentacle. It pulled at the tiny hairs near the base of her neck and tried to drag her down just by the sheer weight of it.

With a grunt, she shoved it off of her shoulder. She had to stop this living statue and here she was without her hammer and chisel.

Another tentacle swung at her face, with a lot more alacrity than she expected. It almost took her nose off at the tip.

She leapt back, her feet landing half in and half out of the hole. She teetered on the balls of her feet, holding her breath and pinwheeling her arms. Next time she talked to Whiskers, she'd kill him for ever bringing up this place. If the place didn't kill her first.

If it did, she'd haunt his ass until the heat death of the universe.

Three more tentacles slammed down in front of Lexa. Maridoxia was definitely getting closer. Her teeth had almost met, and stone fell from her limbs like a waterfall. Soon she'd be as real as any living Gexcorian.

Lexa put her back to the queen and dropped through the hole.

Lifting her arms as she dropped, she snagged and gripped the side of the hole behind her head. Her arms screamed with the exertion, triceps ready to rip right off her bone and fly away. Lexa had continued the yoga practice even though Gram was long gone, and now it paid off, as she swung by her precarious grip. Lifting her knees, she rocked back and forth enough to get her momentum started.

When one tentacle dropped next to the hole, Lexa counted to seven. A bad luck number for them. Good luck for her. It might be enough.

She gave herself one final push and swung her legs up into the hole with everything she had.

Feet together, they connected with the queen's face.

The shock of kicking solid stone traveled up Lexa's legs and almost knocked her back through the hole. She hung on and, much like that Gex-rat, changed directions mid-air by shifting her hips. With a thump, she landed next to the hole and rolled away, trying to catch Maridoxia in her peripheral.

A stone fell to the floor, the sound of its fall resounding in the chamber with a clang large enough to wake all the dead soldiers, and a small spray of pebbles sprinkled from the ceiling. A prelude.

Lexa crawled to Savannah, covering the bag with her body, and waited for the stone shower to be over.

Some of them felt like boulders as they bounced off her hip, her shoulder, the hand covering her head. White stars lit up the inside of her head after that one, and she almost lost track of time as the stones rained. She floated, unsure if the next stone would break her head right open like a rotted melon.

The rockfall eventually ended, the last few stones bouncing around her as she looked up.

The queen's face lay staring right into hers.

Sucking a painful breath over her teeth, Lexa sat up and scooted back so fast she caught her pants on a sharp rock that drove itself painfully into her ass cheek. With her breath coming in shallow gasps, she waited for the queen to stand up and start coming for her again.

Didn't happen.

Raising the lights, she scooted back toward the face.

The head was still stone. It hadn't turned to real skin and probably wouldn't get the chance.

Her kick had separated the head from the body, and it lay there, black ichor oozing from the stump that used to hold the neck up. It smelled like the fellow below, like bubbling blacktop on a searing summer day.

She exhaled through her teeth, staring at the Cynosure a few feet away just waiting to be picked up. "If I never see another Gexcorian, Savannah, it'll be too soon."

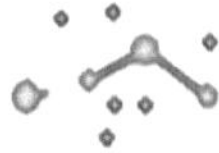

"Doctor Dean."

"Doctor Wiscious."

The comm screen flickered and the furry-faced alien chuckled. "Still have trouble with my first name?"

She shrugged. "Got your artifact for the museum, Whiskers."

He smiled, showing pointed teeth almost like a cat's, and tapped buttons out of sight. "The Galactic Historical Record committee will be thrilled, Lexa. That Gexcorian diadem will be an invaluable addition. Did you get the proper paperwork? You know the GHR requires it."

Lifting a stack of stamped, inked, and if she was being honest, a little smelly and wet, papers, she waved them next to her head. "All signed and sealed. The diadem is yours, legally and officially. You can feel free to put it in the museum. The Gexcorians were only too happy to have such an important piece of their cultural heritage in the most prestigious museum in the galaxy." She flicked a few switches and fought a swallow. Lies of omission were still lies, as Gram had been fond of reminding her, but it's not like this was the first time. "I'll drop it off with the gallery when I get back to Earth."

Whiskers snickered, one of his ears flicking. It swiveled toward the screen. "When are you going to come visit me? It'd be lovely to have you over for dinner again. I'll make some of that Earth food you're so fond of."

Leaning back in her chair, she wondered how long she had to talk to him to make it seem like she had nothing to hide. How quick could she get him off the line? "Or some of your weirdo fish food. You know I've never been afraid of trying new things."

"Twice." He laughed.

She joined him, watching his ears flick. A lot like Savannah's. "Gotta try everything twice. Soon, Whiskers. Soon." Wiggling her fingers at him, she shut down the screen with her other hand. A perfect closing line, with just enough personality in it to keep him from suspecting that lie.

Shoving her hand in her front pocket, she fingered the teardrop and flicked on the autopilot. The eight light years back to Earth wouldn't take too long, but it would take long enough for a snack. A shower. Maybe a nap.

But first, another call. To ease her anxiety, she reached over to Savannah, who lay in the co-pilot's seat, and scratched her between the ears. Once she was calm enough and had enough of the conversation planned out, she dialed her buyer.

On the second ring, the screen brightened. The scowling face of a Truscian filled it. He sniffed through the nose located on what a human would call their forehead, his smoke-colored skin glistening, giving it a swirling effect. "Ms. Dean."

"Doctor, if you please, Qesson."

He sniffed again. "You're calling later than my lady expected."

Lexa flashed on Devin again. This time, though, not as she'd left him, but the last time they'd been in the ship together. Under the stars in the greenhouse, her blue galactic roses offsetting the smell of sex.

She shook her head to try and get rid of the image. It faded, if slowly. "Sometimes tomb crawling takes a little longer than expected. Does she still want it, or should I find anothe—"

"Your agreement was with Lady Jenierien. If you contact another buyer, there will be consequences."

"Good. I'll see you in—" She checked the readout. "Five hours, provided the light speed lanes are clear."

Qesson let a chuckle pass through his nose, nasally and high. His skin flushed orange. "You do not set the meeting times, I am afraid. Milady will see you no sooner than the day after tomorrow."

The hand in Lexa's pocket clutched the Cynosure, its pearls smooth in her palm. Another day with this beauty? Who was she to complain? "Fine. Fine. I'll see you then." She blew him a kiss and switched off before he had a chance to respond.

Once the screen was shut down and locked closed, she pulled the teardrop out of her pocket and held it up to the window, distant starlight shining through it. "She is going to love you." She smiled, letting the nervous energy she'd held back during her calls flood her shaking hand. Devin's sacrifice wouldn't be in vain. Her new life was just around the corner.

CHAPTER 2

Lexa let herself in the back door of Gram's house. The cute 84 square meter one-story was over 200 years old, probably more, and it had seen a lot of changes. Most recently, Lexa had hired a contractor to come out and give it modern lights and an air filtration/circulation system. And thank the universe. Summers in the old American South were still the worst, but the inside of the house was cool and dry and comfortable.

Gram would have hated it.

Savannah shot to the bedroom as soon as Lexa opened the bag. She knew they were home, which was funny because they hadn't been here in months. But it had been on a trip home that Lexa found the starving black kitten sleeping on the patio in the sun and adopted her.

"Don't get too comfortable, Savannah," she called. "Gonna be putting the for sale sign out front before long." She glanced around the kitchen. Gram's twentieth-century range was still here. All the other appliances had been updated to at least this century, but that range was something she just couldn't bring herself to get rid of. How many cookies they had made in that oven, filling the house with the bitter scent of chocolate chip, how many meals had Gram taught her to make on it. Even its faded yellow color made her smile.

She spoke under her breath. "Smile or not, it's time to move on."

But when she slid under the cool sheets of Gram's bed, and realized it had been eighty years almost to the day since Gram died, she snuggled down with Savannah and listened to the roof creak. The wind whistled through the trees outside, the summer breezes warm and happy as they blew in through the open window.

And she sighed, drifting into dreamless sleep.

The hot sun came early, and after massive amounts of coffee she wished she could just inject straight into her veins, Lexa left Van curled up in bed so she could tackle the overgrown yard. There were so many ways to do this that didn't involve manual labor, but there was something about pushing the mower around the way Gram had taught her that cleared her mind. The sweat poured down her body, rolling in rivulets down her back, her hands slick on the handle of the mower and the smell of green firmly embedded in her nose.

Probably because she insisted on using a mower that was designed to look, sound, and operate just like an early 21st century model, she didn't hear the small ship in the drive. She didn't see anyone approach the house as she rounded the far corner, pushing the cacophonous mower and getting her mind good and clear of all the bullshit it kept trying to remind her of. Her failed relationships—all of them, not just boyfriends and girlfriends— her half-assed commitment to getting artifacts into the museum and the way she sold as much as they displayed, Devin, the way Gram had refused even a single DNAging treatment. Damned stubborn millennials.

"Alexandra!"

The shout permeated the scream of the mower's whirring blade and Lexa shut it down, already knowing exactly who stood behind her, calling her by her full name. She unwrapped her white-knuckled fingers from the handle and pawed sweat off her forehead. "Mother."

"I'd hug you my love but you're filthy."

Digging her heel into the ground, Lexa turned as slow as gravity would allow. "Mother."

Her mother stood there in the sun, gently glistening like a rose petal. Her espresso-colored hair shone, full and cascading over her shoulders and down her back. Her slightly pink skin glowed, the smile on her red lips stretched tight across skin that belonged on someone a century and a half younger than her age. She and Lexa could have been sisters. Maybe even fraternal twins. She smiled, white teeth peeking out. "I didn't know you'd be here. It's a pleasant surprise."

"What are you doing here?" Leaving the mower sitting, Lexa marched past her and flung the back door open. The cool air inside assaulted her hot skin, and she suppressed a shiver. To say her mother's unannounced visit shredded Lexa's nerves like a cheese grater over knuckles would be the understatement of the year. Maybe of the century.

Her mom caught the door before it slammed home and followed her in. Not that she'd been invited. "I thought I'd come see Mom's old place again before I left for my next whirlwind tour of the galaxy."

Lexa drew water from the sink and leaned on the counter, making eye contact as she drank. Her mother's eyes, a touch lighter brown than Lexa's own, widened with childlike innocence. Clutching the glass to keep from punching her, Lexa scowled. "Get a good look. I'm selling it."

She'd be a liar if she said the look of surprise and anger that covered her mom's youthful face didn't fill her with joy.

"Alexandra, you cannot do that!"

With a shrug, Lexa sat the glass on the cleaning circle and pressed the cycle button. A small force-field, for lack of a better term, popped up around it and sterilized the glass. When it was done the force-field popped out of existence with a warm puff of air. Lexa put the glass away and made eye contact again with the woman who'd considered a baby at sixty less a miracle of science and more a burden to be dumped off. This was a conversation Lexa'd been daydreaming about for months, years maybe, and it was finally time to let the anger fly. Decades of resentment crystallized on her tongue. She spat the words. "I can and I will. Gram left it to me."

"I grew up here, too, Allie, you forget." She crossed her arms, flinging her hair behind her back. The six necklaces draped on her breast clacked against each other. "This house is just as much mine as yours."

"Tell that to Gram's will. It's my house. I'll do what I want." She took one large step and filled her mom's personal bubble, her stomach in a hard knot. "Once it's gone, if I never see you again, it'll be too soon."

"What's all the shouting?"

As if Lexa couldn't *be* more upset, her eldest sister, Juniper, flounced into the kitchen with that ditzy look on her face, her golden hair almost sparkling. Had she even opened a book in the last hundred years? Doubtful.

Lexa exhaled, releasing her tight abs, and stepped away from their mother.

Juniper repeated her question.

Mom answered before Lexa could inhale. "She thinks she's selling your grandmother's house."

Lexa ground her teeth, the squeaking deafening inside her head. "It's my house, Mom."

But Juniper spoke over her. "She can't do that!"

Before Lexa could think to ask June how she got in the house, a man almost as tall as the ceiling walked in from the living room. "Let's not fight, Junie. Paisley, you may look like someone in her Earth twenties but you're almost 158. We must remember your blood pressure."

Mom deflated. "I thought the doctor said we didn't have to worry about that as long as I kept up treatments."

The stranger with his large blue eyes and shock of black hair shook his head, a somber expression lowering his pale brow. "DNAging extensions can only work for so long. They are the fountain of youth, but they are not a cure for mortality. The better care you take of yourself, the longer I will be able to guide you through the wonders of the galaxy."

Lexa frowned. "Who are you?"

When he turned to her, the full gaze of those piercing blue eyes landing on her, she took a step back without thinking. He had to be closing on two meters tall and something about him made her want to climb him like a huge, hunky tree.

He smiled, perfectly straight white teeth meeting his lower lip. One hand stuck out, he approached, ducking under the light fixture. "Forgive my bad manners. Reid Stuart. Paisley and Juniper have hired me to accompany them on their next trip around the galaxy. Our first stop is about four light-years away but we're planning to go much further than they've ever been. Isn't that right, ladies?" He smiled down at them both.

Inhaling, Lexa backed into the counter again and rested on it. "Are you a doctor?"

He chuckled. "No, nothing of the sort. I am more a personal assistant than anything, and I take detailed notes."

A frown drew her lips down so far it hurt. "All of you can get out. I didn't invite you in, I didn't open the door for you, and you're not welcome in my house."

Paisley frowned back. "You have an extra room, Alex. We'd like to stay the night before we head out and—"

"Lexa. My name is Lexa. You know that. She knows that," she said, jabbing a pointing index finger toward Juniper. "You all fucking know that. Have the decency to call me by name at the very least."

Her mom approached, hands out. When the pad of one finger alighted on her cheek like a bird's foot, Lexa didn't flinch. Not on the outside. But on the inside, she revolted, her stomach slippery and nauseated.

Mom caressed her cheek. "When is the last time you had a treatment? I can see the lines beside your eyes." She lowered her voice. "I know you miss her. I do, too. You're ninety-seven, as old now as she was when she died. It's not a slight to her memory to keep up your treatments."

Lexa closed her eyes. If Paisley wanted to press her buttons, all she had to do was bring up Gram. One of them would have to relent and Lexa hated to be that one. But if everything went like it should with Lady Jenierien and her purchase of the Cynosure, Lexa would never again have to put up with the mother who abandoned her for her recaptured youth. So she caved. "You can stay. For one night." She opened her eyes, narrowing her lids and catching and holding eye contact. "The house is going on the market next week."

"Dip the spoon in, just like this."

"Gram, it says one tablespoon." Lexa stared up at her, her face wavering in and out of focus. One thing was clear, her smile.

She clacked her dentures together. "One tablespoon, one tableschmoon. You do it like this." She plopped the cookie dough onto the wax paper, licked off the spoon, and started over.

Lexa laughed. A deep, belly laugh. "Now you're getting your spit all over the cookies!"

Gram stuck her tongue out, the lines around her mouth both deepening and disappearing at the same time. "You can pry my cookie dough from my cold, dead hands."

Laughing again, Lexa licked off her own spoon.

But—cold, dead hands.

She glanced up at Gram again. "Wait, what are you doing here Gram? You're dead."

And this time the belly laugh came from Gram. Her mouth open wide, she threw her head back and laughed. "Just came to check in on you, little one. How are you?"

Lexa's eyes flew open.

The wind sighed through the window, billowing the curtain she didn't tie down well enough.

Her heart rate came down from the ceiling as she lay on her side, staring at the dark window with her eyes wide open, the wind drying her wet cheeks.

From the hollow of Lexa's knees, Savannah chirped at her and stretched, her claws digging into the back of her thigh.

She raised her voice. "I was sleeping nicely, Ma."

Voice lowered again, Lexa whispered. "I haven't seen her in a dream in probably years." She slid from between the cool sheets and hung her legs over the side of the bed. Her feet hit the floor and she wiggled her toes, the hardwood cold on the soles of her feet. Gram had had carpet. She'd loved carpet. But the house would never sell with hundred-year-old, stinky, matted carpet, so out it came.

The curtain flapped again. She pinned it back and peeked into the driveway.

Her mother, sister, and their hunk of an "assistant" had come in a small ship, a rental they'd brought in from town. Their big ship, the last one Lexa had seen them leaving in, likely sat in space dock. At least they hadn't come barreling down here in that beast and asked to park it on the damn lawn.

A single light burned inside the ship. Reid slept out there, no room for him in the house. Not just because there were only two bedrooms, and Mom and June were sharing the other one, but also he was just too damn tall for the couch and even the floor barely had enough room for him to stretch out.

The thought of fresh outside air as opposed to the air in Gram's old bedroom crowding in around Lexa and her still-wet cheeks latched onto the lingering threads of the dream and pulled her toward the door. If Reid happened to still be awake and she happened to go say hi…who knew what might happen on a warm summer night like this.

She slipped out of her pajamas, threw on a robe, and eased out the front door. The screen door closed with a tired rasp.

The occasional lightning bug lit up next to her face, the freshly mown grass cool between her toes. She knocked on the side of the ship's open door, the metal clanking against her knuckle.

Someone rustled inside. "Just a second." Followed by a huge thump. The ship swayed on its landing struts. Reid spoke again, somewhat muffled. "Sorry."

Grinning, Lexa peeked inside.

Reid lay mostly in the floor, one long leg caught in the hammock he'd strung across the cabin. His face pressed to the ground and one arm caught under him, he tried to grin. "Miss Lexa. Pleasure to see you again. Just um." He wiggled. "Give me a sec."

Chuckling, Lexa stepped into the little ship, not much bigger than Gram's car, really, and let her robe fall open a crack. "Your foot's tangled. Let me help you." She grabbed the hammock with one hand and his leg with the other. Giving him a sharp tug, she freed his foot and held onto his calf.

"Stronger than you look." The one side of his mouth not mashed into the floor turned up in a grin. "You can put me down now."

"As you wish," she said, releasing his leg all at once.

It flopped to the floor, spinning him one more time. His face firmly planted in the deck, all Lexa could catch was a muffled "ow."

She grinned, watching him untangle his legs, his sleeping shorts exposing what looked like miles of skin. As he finally righted himself and stood, she bit her lip and watched his muscles work. "You're human?"

He smiled and took note of her open robe with his eyes. They traveled up and down the slit, all the important bits hidden behind it. For now. His bright blue eyes twinkled. "Why?"

"No reason." With two large but swinging steps, she crossed the cabin. She swayed one hip and bumped his with a light touch. Thank creation he slept with no shirt. He had abs on top of abs and pecs that belonged to a gymnast. "My mother and sister hired you from…" She let the last word hang in the charged air between them, licking her lips and letting her wet mouth hang open a touch.

He stammered, shifting his hips to touch hers. Probably without realizing it. "They uh. Yeah. I work for the Litmus Agency. We specialize in showing tourists only the best intergalactic destinations. The ones that've passed the tourism litmus test, if you will." He trailed off, his white teeth flashing again. "Sounds silly when you say it out loud, I guess." He chewed his lip, one hand creeping up to her waist. He didn't reach inside her robe, though. Not yet. "What about you? You're an exoarchaeologist, right? I bet you know some really stunning places."

Lexa laughed, soft and under her breath. Flick all the right buttons and he'd be putty in about five seconds. "Oh honey. The best places I know are underground and covered in dust. But I didn't really come out here to talk about that." She pressed against him, her robe falling further open. Their skin flush, she slid an arm around his tight waist and smiled up into his eyes.

His cheeks were already red. Aliens could be a trick sometimes but damn it was easy with humans. "What, um." He licked his lips, his eyes sparkling. One rough hand finally slid inside her robe and clutched her bare waist. "What did you come out here for, then?"

She rose up on her tiptoes, gripping the back of his neck and pulling him down to her.

The arm around her waist stiffened and he pulled her almost off her feet as he met her in the middle.

Swinging her other arm around him, her robe fully open, she pressed all her skin into his and arched her back as he continued to lift her. Her fingers clenched in his hair and pulled him into a rough kiss that might have left her lip bloody.

Whatever was left of the dream floated away like the gossamer strings of a spiderweb.

When he stopped to take a breath, hard against her already and breathing like he'd run a marathon, she smiled with one side of her mouth and her eyes half-open. "Close that door and I'll show you."

CHAPTER 3

Morning brought a screaming alarm before coffee, and Lexa woke with a start, alone in her bed. She'd left Reid sweating and happy in the ship and claimed her own bed once again. Great lay or not, no one slept in the bed with her except her cat.

She had a few hours before her appointment with Lady Jenierien. Running Mom, June, and Reid off would almost certainly be harder than she hoped, but luckily they had a travel window to catch. Authorization to travel the light speed lanes was restricted and if they didn't go in their window, they'd fall behind on their itinerary before they'd even begun.

Abandoning her youngest child was totally OK with Mom. But missing her flight lane? Perish the thought.

It was close, but when she sat down her ship at the dock in Proxima New York, a city 100 miles inland from the watery grave of Manhattan Island, she was left with just enough time to hop on her mini-bike and zip through its crowded streets to Jenierien's manor.

When she arrived, she parked on the sidewalk next to a shining silver wall at least four meters high. A guard with light brown skin and freckles sat inside the gate, sipping her steaming coffee. She glanced over the lip of the cup at Lexa and pressed a button, her deep-set dark eyes disinterested.

"*State your business,*" she said, through the speaker.

"Lexa Dean. Here to deliver some flowers." She popped one of her electric blue galactic roses out of the bag and held it up. She tried on a flirty smile, but the gate guard maintained her neutral expression.

Couldn't blame a girl for trying.

"Credentials," the gate guard said, her voice robotic. What Lexa could only describe as a backward siren let out on wail.

That little siren never failed to twist Lexa's stomach. She clenched her teeth and positioned her ID next to her face.

A red laser nodule the color of fresh blood popped from the wall of the guard booth and flashed.

This was the worst part. These lasers, terrifying tech invented by none other than humanity, could kill you in an instant if your face didn't match the living organism algorithm. Or, you know, if it malfunctioned. Lexa closed her eyes and the laser's beam passed over her face, warm as it crawled over her lips. It depressed her eyelids almost like fingertips rubbing across them, tickling the lashes.

When her hairline tickled, she opened her eyes again and watched the laser shut down. It turned green.

The guard spoke again. *"Please pass through the gate."* It clicked open.

Before passing through, Lexa eyed the screens behind the guard—each of twenty of them showed almost every square inch of the yard and house. About the only thing missing was the section directly behind her little booth. "A delight as always," she said.

The guard snorted into her coffee and watched Lexa slip through the gate.

Lexa entered a large courtyard. Well. Large for 22nd century standards. Overpopulation was on the rise again, now that DNAging treatments were almost universal and people had begun to age backward.

Though as she made her way through the ridiculous courtyard, fruit trees and marble statues at every turn, pearls lining the pathways, she remembered why she was here. Despite all this new—free—tech, the barrier between rich and poor had only grown. Turned out there were many, many, many fortunes to be made in space colonization.

And as always, in theft.

The front doors, seven meters tall if they were a centimeter, opened as she reached them. The relief carved into them showed her a pretty picture of Truscians and Earthlings sitting down to dinner, last supper style, with Lady Jenierien in the center of the table. Draped in rich cloths, more pearls—real ones embedded in the wooden relief—and gold leaf were pressed into the whole thing.

Lexa paused inside, where Qesson, who she'd made the appointment with, stood, wearing a grey five-piece suit. He sniffed and folded his two clasped hands in front of him.

"Ms. Dean. Welcome back. Lady Jenierien is very excited to see you." He bowed.

She nodded. "Qesson. Wish I could say it's good to see you again."

He sniffed again, the large almond-shaped eyes below his nose blinking slow. "This way, if you please."

She fell in behind him as he shuffled away, all four of his feet moving in time, giving the impression of only two legs. "Qesson. You're from Truscia, right?"

He glanced over his shoulder with one eye. "Yes of course."

"Why do you insist on waiting on Jenierien hand and foot? Couldn't you, I don't know, do anything else?"

Qesson nodded and they mounted a marble staircase gilded in more gold. "Indeed. But Lady Jenierien and I have an understanding."

"Which is?"

"None of your business." He stopped in front of another ornate door, one set of legs stopping just after the other. He snapped all his heels together and rapped on the door twice.

A muffled voice came from inside. "Better be important."

Qesson's eyes glowed red, and he leaned through the door. Truscians always said, *"It's only matter if it matters,"* but it was weird to see them pass through solid doors nonetheless. A shame Lexa couldn't do that trick. Would make exoarchaeology that much easier.

He leaned back through and raised up on his long set of legs, towering over her with his mouth drawn into a frown better than any human could put on. "Do you have what you promised?"

Her stomach jittered from his attempt to intimidate her, but she put on her best "don't fuck with me" face, brows spiked, mouth flat. "Would I be here if I didn't?"

He nodded his bulbous head and eased the door open. "You may enter."

As she slipped past him, his cold, campfire-colored skin rippling, she could have sworn she heard him mutter "good luck." And when she entered the room, she saw why.

The woman in front of her was a vision. Her starkly pale skin, all of it, glistened as though it was lit from inside. Her perfect cheeks lifted in a smile, sparkles shining on her eyelids. She wore not a stitch of clothing, and every centimeter of her was tight and youthful, even though Lexa knew she was far beyond Lexa's own 97 years. The DNAging treatments rich people could afford were still far and away better than what people on her level got access to.

Lexa sucked in her belly and pushed her shoulders back. How could you not, in front of such beauty?

Sitting in a chair that was more like a throne and surrounded by a bubble of sparkling water, Lady Jenierien chuckled. "Lexa Dean. My favorite thief. How are you today? Did you bring me something lovely?" She extended a hand beyond the water and held it out, palm up, fingers dripping.

Eyeing the bubble bath, a term that had meant something completely different to Gram, Lexa took two lunging steps forward and leaned as far as she could before placing the Cynosure in Lady Jenierien's hand.

She lifted it, letting the light fall through it, and Lexa couldn't help but notice the way her breasts perked up when she stretched. Joining her in that bath flitted across her mind. Just for a moment, though. It'd be a bad idea to get involved with such a woman, no matter how irresistible she might be when naked.

The smile that lit Lady Jenierien's face told Lexa all she needed to know.

"It's perfect, my dear. Just perfect. Wherever did you get it?" She caressed one of the Gexcorian pearls.

Lexa shifted, arms crossed. "You know that's the only secret I keep from you, ma'am. Where your little treasures come from." She held out the blue rose. "I hope a galactic rose will do in its place."

And now Jenierien stood and stepped out of the bubble, her whole body glistening and smelling of lavender and vanilla. As she stepped down from her dais and the bubble of water drained into a grate the floor, Qesson appeared from nowhere and wrapped her in a towel.

Lexa remembered to breathe.

Jenierien took the rose from her, maybe not watching herself well enough. She gasped and with wide eyes, glanced at her finger.

A single drop of blood beaded on one of the thorns.

"Watch yourself, milady." Lexa gave her half a smile. "Galactic roses have very sharp thorns."

The lady chuckled under her breath and smiled. "Quite like you, I should think." Still smiling, she brought it to her nose. She inhaled all the way to the bottom of her lungs, her chest straining the towel. "Grown by the light of the stars. It's perfect. Your usual payment?"

Flashing on the damned Gex-rats, the eight-limbed angry queen, the statues, the falling damn ceiling, Devin's feet scratching on the gravel as the life left them, Lexa shook her head. "I'm gonna need a little more this time. This thing is pretty valuable to the people I stole it from. You can see it's got eight pearls."

"I have many more pearls than that just in the garden."

"Yeah but those are from Earth. These aren't."

Jenierien's red lips curled. "If I knew where they were from, that may make them worth more."

Lexa frowned. "Maybe I'll take it back, then. Sell it to someone who—"

"You'll do no such thing." She clutched the Cynosure. "I'll give you…five percent more than usual."

"Twenty."

"Ten." Her flinty eyes sparkled, cheeks rosy.

Lexa tried to distract herself, especially when Jenierien dropped the towel and inched closer, her eyes still sparkling. She swallowed. "Eighteen."

"Fifteen." It fell from her silky lips like a lover's whisper.

Lexa backed into a pillar. "Fine. Fifteen."

Lexa stepped out Jenierien's gate and into PNY's humid afternoon. She leaned on the sheer wall next to the guard booth and exhaled like she'd just taken a long, deep drag off a smoke. The tension alone in that sale would be enough to wind her up for days; last night with Reid may as well have been a week ago.

Eyes burned into her. She could feel it.

She glanced at the guard booth.

The woman stared through the glass, a slight smile on her lips, the kind people usually weren't aware they were wearing.

Lexa began to smile back, wondering if the two of them could fit in that booth together. Before she got a single syllable out, her communicator went off.

She frowned at the guard and turned away. One click of a button on what looked like a watch around her wrist and she spoke to the air in front of her. "Nice to hear from you again, Whiskers. Is everything OK with the diadem?" She straddled her mini-bike and flipped on the screen, linking it to the communicator on her wrist.

Whiskers's furry face filled the screen. "It's not about that. Where are you?"

She waved a hand vaguely in the air. "The pristine streets of PNY. Why?"

"I've just entered Earth's atmosphere. Send me the coordinates of your ship. I will meet you there immediately."

"Why do you—"

He hung up.

Despite the humid heat radiating from the sunny streets, a chill worked its way straight up Lexa's spine. Shivering, she sent him the ship's parking details by text.

The ramp to the back bay of Lexa's ship lowered with a few more clanks than she considered strictly necessary as she waited on her mini-bike, foot lowered. Once the ramp touched the ground, she went to start up it but stopped with her foot halfway off the ground.

A cat-like creature stood in the bay, smiling down at her. He strolled on two legs to meet her. "Lexa, how lovely to see you."

"Whiskers." She stood, the bike between her legs, and greeted him. He rubbed each cheek on each of hers. Something she considered a very European greeting.

With a grin, he dropped to four legs and followed her up the ramp. He squinted as she raised the ramp, watching the sliver of daylight disappear behind the closing door. Once it'd disappeared, he turned to her.

Only now did she notice the bag strapped to his waist. A long, plastic tube poked out the top.

"Is that a map in your pocket or are you just happy to see me?"

He stood on two legs again and pretended to pat pockets he didn't have. The only thing he wore, besides his fur, was the bag. "Both." Those sharp, pointed teeth poked out of his mouth again.

The resemblance to Savannah was sometimes uncanny. It brought a smile to Lexa's face each time she met with him. But he'd come a long way to see her, and the curiosity was eating her alive.

She turned and walked deeper into the ship, and Whiskers followed.

"What's so important you flew all the way to Earth? Your office on Fauborix is almost as good as the actual museum. I'm always happy to meet you there" She stopped amidst her tomato plants, the close air of the greenhouse surrounding them both. Water *drip-drip-dripped* somewhere out of sight. The moment stretched and Whiskers swiveled his ears, the tip of his tail twitching.

Lexa broke the odd silence. "Whiskers? You're not as chatty as usual. Everything OK?"

He started, like he was coming out of a trance, and glanced around the room, giving each corner a small, furtive look before shifting his eyes elsewhere. "Do you have somewhere private?" His tail twitched again and he caught it in his hand, twisting the tip through what Lexa considered his "fingers."

"The ship is mine, it's all private." Her voice came out even, but his clear nervousness seeped into her bones, bringing back the shiver she'd had on the street after he called.

"Somewhere without…" He glanced up. "Without windows."

She took his arm and without another word, led him through the plants, all edible, even the flowers, past the engine room whose exhaust kept the greenhouse warm, and to her small bunk. Most of her ship didn't have windows because the cost of vacuum-resistant windows added up, but this room was the smallest on the ship, its contents pressed right up against each other. Not cramped, but only enough room to walk between the bed and side table without knocking everything on the table into the floor. She sat on the bed and patted it.

If he was human, he would have been wiping his brow at this point. Lexa's nerves jangled and screamed in alarm. It took all she had to keep her face neutral. Inviting, even.

Whiskers perched on the edge of the bed and lifted the bag around his waist. "I brought it here to you because it could not be zipped." His used his prehensile tail to lift the flap of the bag, and one hand slid the tube out of it. Inside, something had been rolled up.

Lexa'd seen enough of them to know. "A map? What kind of map can't be zipped? That Dysling teleportation tech works on all inorganics. Even non-living tissue."

"I've never seen anything like it." He opened the tube and slid the rolled map out, catching it before it hit the bed and smoothing it flat with one hand and his tail. With the other hand, he sat the tube aside.

Lexa leaned over it. The paper didn't look much like paper. "Looks like leather or something," she said, trying not to breathe on it. "And old."

"The GHR has dated it. It's at least thirty-seven thousand Earth years old."

"Bullshit!" It was out of her mouth before she even knew she was going to speak.

The bed next to her depressed and without thinking, she reached for Savannah, pulling her into her lap with one motion. Thirty thousand? No way something made of leather or paper survived that long. No way. But as the reality of it sunk in—the fact it couldn't be zipped, the weathered but completely intact surface—she couldn't help but lean closer. She ran her fingers along red, blue, and yellow lines which crisscrossed it. "What is it for?"

"We're not sure, but we've done some research into its origins—origins I'm afraid I cannot currently share—and it seems the site is over…" He cleared his throat and stopped.

She glanced up, her finger pausing over the map's legend. There was a shape inside the lines of the legend that looked almost familiar, but it had faded too much to completely make it out. "Over what?" Her question came out in a whisper.

His answer matched her tone. "Twelve billion."

"What!" The word ripped out of her much like her earlier curse had, and echoed off the walls of her bunk. She squeezed Savannah easily as hard as she had in the tomb when that glut of petrifying fluid had poured from the ceiling.

Savannah clawed both Lexa and the map, her legs flailing as she tried to escape being asphyxiated.

The response of the map was immediate. It vibrated on the bed, the covers rippling under it. Before Lexa had a chance to consider what was happening, the bed itself began to vibrate, reminding Lexa of a silly movie Gram once showed her where a man had put coin money into a slot next to the bed, setting the bed rocking. Lexa's teeth chattered against each other, a bone dance inside her head.

She plowed through the shock and raised her voice over the bucking bed, the only thing keeping it on the ground the fact it was screwed down. "What the hell?"

Whiskers shook his head, the hair on top of it standing straight up. It matched Savannah's bottle-brush tail as she exited the room at a high rate of speed. At least one of them had sense.

The map undulated, vibrating so fast now that the fabric itself almost disappeared. A hum began somewhere near the map and Lexa couldn't tell if it was coming from the map, or if it was the vibration between the map and the bed. She reached out to touch it.

Whiskers bounded over the bed and yanked her hand away. "It will take your fingers off, Lexa dear. Don't you see?"

Mouth still dry, she glanced back at the map. He was right, it vibrated so fast now that pieces of her blanket flew into the air, like the map was a chainsaw. The hum got louder.

She raised her voice, doing her best not to shriek. "What are we supposed to do?"

Whiskers shrugged, still holding her wrist with his furry paw. "Apologize to it?"

A scoff on her lips, she looked back at the vibrating, screaming map. It couldn't be zipped. And now it was throwing a tantrum because it had been scratched.

Could it be?

"Map," she said, trying to imagine what a map of unknown origin that was tens of thousands of years old could possibly be named. "I'm sorry. We didn't mean to hurt you."

And that was it. It was as if a spell had been broken.

It stopped vibrating, pieces of blanket falling around it like confetti as it settled back on the bed.

Lexa leaned over it. A scratch was evident in the corner, and she hoped she could figure out how to repair it. But until then, she brushed the blanket confetti off the top with more care than she'd ever shown any living thing.

A memory hit her at the same time with staggering velocity. Brushing Gram's hair from her cool forehead as she lay in bed, frail and mute and wheezing. Dying.

A tear dripped from her eye onto the map.

The map stilled completely, lying flat on the bed. The rip knitted itself together and even though it was still there, Lexa got the distinct impression it would be gone in a few days. Just like Lexa's own skin would do to a cat scratch.

The spot where the tear had hit darkened, like ink. It spread, forming a shape in the bottom corner of the map. What Lexa's years of education taught her was probably the map's key.

And inside it, something in the shape of a teardrop.

Something with several pearls around it.

Something just like the Cynosure.

CHAPTER 4

"There, that looks good," Lexa said, pointing out the front window. Not that Savannah cared from her position in the "co-pilot's" seat.

Pulling back the throttle, Lexa guided the ship on spit and wishes, setting it down between piles of junk almost a kilometer high. Besides a couple of bumps and one really good knock, she missed all the debris and landed straight on the struts. "Not bad," she whispered to the panel. She scratched the cat between the ears and stared out the window.

Dark as night down here, surrounded by junk and garbage, she hoped no one would mistake her ship for anything less. It certainly looked about like the hunks of junk she parked between, and she was probably the only one who could tell any difference, anyway. But she couldn't very well stay parked downtown if she was going to go through with this.

This was horrifically reckless. Colossally inane on a level even her mother wouldn't sink to. Stealing from Jenierien? Did Lexa really want to burn all the bridges she had—because Jenierien was powerful enough to alight all of them in one stroke—and get herself killed in the process?

Not especially.

But what Whiskers said haunted her.

"Our research indicates this map could lead you to the site I know you've been looking for all your career."

How could it be? The origin of life in the galaxy? And the map to it just happened to fall into her lap?

Whiskers had stopped on his way off the ship. *"I think it best, after you study and catalog the map, that we simply return it to the GHR and forget it exists."*

"You're right," she said. *"It's not worth it."*

A bald-faced lie.

The very meaning of life could be encoded directly into its origins. The meaning of it, the cost of it, and even—if she was very, very lucky—the value of it. She'd worked toward this for decades. If discovering the origins of life didn't make her the richest, most famous exoarchaeologist in the galaxy, something was incredibly wrong with the system. And if she had that kind of fame, maybe her mom could see what kind of mistake she made when she abandoned her. Not that Lexa would be around to notice, or care. But Paisley would have to live with that for the rest of her long life, while Lexa enjoyed total freedom from any of that concern, for good.

Spinning her chair to face a side screen, she pulled up the city's building archive. It might not be as easy to access as other historical records, but she'd long ago bought access through certain intimate favors. Getting back the Cynosure would not be simple, but meticulous planning could make even the most difficult task easy.

Not that Whiskers knew what she was about to do.

"I know what that key is," she breathed, leaning over the map again.

His ears flicked. "Do you?"

She nodded, stomach roiling. "It's a Gexcorian artifact. Very special. Lost for thousands of years."

"Would you know where to look? Would they even give you permission to take it?"

She'd nodded into the distance and with ginger care, rolled up the map. She eased it into Savannah's satchel and ushered Whiskers off the ship with the promise to forget about the key.

Forcing her thoughts away from the lie, she searched up Lady Jenierien's house. All the blueprints Jenierien'd been required to file with the city popped up in front of her.

She scribbled notes on a paper ripped from a notepad. A few pictures for reference, and a question mark.

Next, she punched up the city streets around Jenierien's, inspecting the alleys, the buildings that girded them, and the sewers beneath. Once she was satisfied, she shut everything down, folded the paper, and stuffed it in her back pocket.

She clicked her tongue to get Van to follow her and headed to her quarters.

Savannah, the traitor, yawned and promptly fell back asleep.

In her quarters, Lexa searched the closet. She kept so many choices for just such an occasion, where had she put that…

Ah! There it was.

She pulled out a wrinkled outfit of plain brown. Cargo pants and a loose-fitting shirt with pockets and a popped collar, with "ZPS" on a tag over one of the shirt pockets, and "Burbelle" on a name tag over the other. It also came with a cap, and after she slipped the uniform on over her clothes, transferring the paper to one of the shirt pockets, she pulled her dark brown hair through the hole and settled the cap over her eyes.

The mirror showed her a symphony of brown. She spoke to her reflection. "Just Ms. Burbelle of ZPS Delivery at your door, Lady Jenierien. Nothing to worry about."

With a grin, she headed to the greenhouse.

Back here, the light from outside made it through the glass ceiling, a single shaft of sunlight falling through the scratched window. She squinted at it, then down at her galactic roses.

Kneeling next to one, a flower on a double stem from which one had already been cut, she grinned again. "Something you don't know about these, milady." She snipped the remaining rose from the pair and took it into the dark. Overhead lights came on as she stepped into the room adjoining the greenhouse where she potted plants and cared for any sick ones. A three-legged wooden table leaned in one corner.

She dropped the flower into a bowl and picked up her pestle. "Sorry, baby."

In moments, all that remained of the rose was dust.

She spoke to the air and opened a drawer at her thigh. "You see, Lady Jenierien, galactic roses are sympathetic. Even when they're separated. They tend to absorb whatever their partner does, which is why they seem to live so long without water. As long as the bush is alive, a cut flower will live and thrive for months. But—" she said, emptying a vial of microscopic nanobots into the mortar, "whatever is absorbed by the cut flower also transmits back to the bush. Back to its mated flower." She shrugged. "Don't ask me how. Might as well ask me how the universe keeps spinning when there's nothing more than empty space holding it together. I don't know. But it does. And that—"

She snagged a magnifier and leaned in, watching the nanobots pick up Jenierien's blood now seeping out of the flower dust. She stuck her finger into the bowl and they skittered to it, coating her fingerprint and hiding in the whorls and swirls. Standing, she lifted her finger to her eyes. "That is your blood and soon, it'll be your fingerprint. All because you pricked yourself on one little thorn."

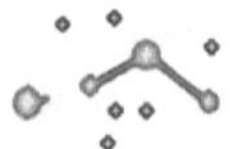

Leaving Van to watch the ship, Lexa took her mini-bike and zipped through the crowded evening streets of PNY. After parking in an alley a block away, she plucked a somewhat smelly and damp box out of a dumpster, popped it back into shape, and stuck it under her arm. If she was supposed to be with ZPS, she ought to look the part as best she could.

Bill of the cap lowered over her eyes, she approached Jenierien's gate.

In the waning light of dusk, a different guard sat at the booth. Good.

She approached and held up false ZPS credentials. Something else she'd paid for with certain favors—man, there was so much more to currency than money—and waited for the laser to decide if it wanted to fry her face off.

The guard barely looked up from a screen in front of him. A movie, maybe. "*Enter*," he said, after the laser shut peacefully down.

She glanced at the screens again. Servants moved through the house but Jenierien and Qesson were nowhere to be seen.

As she passed through the gate, she leaned down into the blind spot behind the booth and slid the box between the gate and the wall. The door remained open enough to squeeze her fingers through for a quick getaway but not enough for anyone to notice unless they knew what they were looking for.

Satisfied, she glanced at the house. The sunset hid behind it and golden streaks of light framed it like some kind of religious painting, made all the more believable given the opulent garden and the Last Supper carved into the door.

Feet light on the gravel, Lexa crept through the garden. The shadows of the day deepened here, and she tried to stay in them. Tried to blend in and become one of them.

Normally when she prowled tombs, the residents weren't alive to watch her. She didn't have to worry much about stealth. But Jenierien could be upstairs right now, watching her on one of her own screens. Waiting to call security or blast her with a hidden laser or goodness knew what else.

Lexa pulled the paper out of her pocket and rubbed it between the thumb and forefinger of one hand.

The door with the Last Supper tableau eased open on silent, well-oiled hinges. Knowing Jenierien, she'd sprung for some of that fancy stuff made of silicone rather than dead dinosaur juice. It was easier to produce and far more effective and long-lived than oil, so of course it was thousands of dollars more a quart. Only the best for those who got rich off the backs of others.

You know, stealing from someone like Jenierien didn't have the same sting as stealing from the dead. Maybe she could turn to cat burglary if this stunt got her fired from the museum.

The hall clock clicked and began to toll.

Lexa's skin threatened to jump off and run away without her.

Holding her breath, she backed against a wall and waited for the clock to finish. As she did, she gazed around the room. It shone with all the gold and sparkling diamonds and crystals. Lexa often saw rooms like this, but usually they were buried beneath centuries of dirt. Shrines to excess, hoards the rich and powerful had taken to the grave.

She frowned. Normally their most precious prizes were kept closest to the dead king or queen or president. She didn't suspect Jenierien would be any different. She pulled the paper from her shirt pocket and unfolded it, slipping deeper into shadow.

What she had assumed to be Jenierien's room from her visits here was dead center of the house. The room had a small alcove in the plans, and it could have been a built-in safe. She'd start there.

The blueprint showed service stairs outside the kitchen, which would likely be better than just charging up the front staircase.

She moved to head that way.

A door opened upstairs and voices floated down. "Milady. You need not go. I will decline the invitation."

"Of course I will still go, Qesson. I was merely waiting for you to finish your evening meditation. Besides, I have not seen Katrina in so long. It will be nice to see if she has acquired enough to make her feel like she belongs." She laughed.

Qesson exhaled through his nose, something that Lexa could have considered a laugh. "She will be thrilled to see you, milady."

"Of course she will. And I'll tell her all about my newest acquisition."

Lexa held her breath. She had to be talking about the Cynosure.

"And will milady be bringing it?"

"Not right now. For now, leave it here. Be ready to retrieve it, though. Katrina only lives a few blocks away. I will signal you if I want you to come pick it up."

They came down the stairs in front of Lexa. If she hadn't been buried deep in shadow, they would have looked right at her as they descended. But studying the blueprints did more than just show her where Jenierien might keep her most precious treasures. It showed her where all the good hiding spots were. And she was in one.

Neither of them saw her.

"Why don't I just bring it?" Qesson asked. "Then at the right moment, I will present it. Katrina—"

"No!" Jenierien almost shouted. "Leave it here."

"As you wish," he said, guiding her through the front door. "If it isn't too much trouble, I—"

The closing door muffled the rest of his words.

Lexa waited, counting to two hundred.

Once she got there, and they hadn't returned, she didn't bother with the service stairs. She took the main staircase two at a time. "Just hurry," she whispered under her breath. "Qesson could be back anytime."

She stopped at the top. She'd seen the door but had never been in Jenierien's bedroom—for better or worse—and her memory agreed with the blueprint that it was around the curve of the banister.

The door didn't have a handle. It had a fingerprint plate. A detail she'd noticed before.

She pressed the finger with the nanobots into the plate and held her breath.

It clicked, and opened.

Hopefully, the safe was as easy to access. She crept into the room and shut the door.

The room surrounding her was a lot like the tombs she regularly visited. It was less dusty, but otherwise, the grandeur dripped from the canopied bed draped in silks. From the chairs covered in gold leaf. From the ceiling adorned in literal rubies and diamonds.

It was a jewel and gem encrusted show, not a room. Did she really sleep in here?

And if she did, how soft was the bed? As soft as her glistening white skin?

Lexa shook her head and took the paper out of her pocket again. Focusing her thoughts, she counted steps to the alcove in the blueprint.

On that space of wall hung a painting in a frame so golden, it made Lexa's eyes hurt to look too long. She jiggled it.

It came away from the wall, revealing the safe behind it.

No fingerprint plate this time. Just an old-fashioned looking combination lock.

Knowing Jenierien, it was probably one of those Truscian locks, one of the hardest in the galaxy to pick, and something Lexa didn't bring equipment for. It could be cracked, though.

What did she know about Lady Jenierien that would help her crack this thing?

First of all, the woman did love to show off her riches. This whole house was dedicated to making everyone else feel small. To making everyone else view Jenierien as the central pillar in a vault full of the most precious items in the galaxy. She took baths on an actual throne.

Stark naked, showing even her blemish free alabaster skin to anyone who came to call. Shining like the crown jewel of a collection that included all the gold left on this planet.

Lexa frowned at the safe. She wouldn't keep something like the Cynosure here. Hidden behind plain steel.

She stuffed the paper in her pocket.

Lady Jenierien would keep something like the Cynosure, something she clearly considered almost as precious as herself, as close to herself as she could.

This whole house was a vault.

Using the velvet-upholstered step-stool next to it, Lexa climbed onto the bed and slid across the silk sheets.

Oh yeah. This bed was as soft and sensual as Jenierien's skin looked.

She inched her hand under the pillow.

Her fingers, enclosed in the cool depths between the pillow and sheets, ran into glass.

She wrapped her hand around it and pulled it out.

The Cynosure.

With a grin, she slipped off the side of the bed.

A soft voice spoke from the door. "Alexandra Dean. I thought I'd never get you in my bedroom."

CHAPTER 5

old glass of the Cynosure gripped in one hand, Lexa chuckled. "Lady Jenierien, I—"

"Looking to sell my treasure twice and make double the amount? I would question how you got in my room, but clearly one of your fortes is getting into places you shouldn't be." She approached the bed, Qesson stuck to her side, his legs out of sync so he more slid than walked. They stopped at the foot of the bed.

"I just want to borrow it back," Lexa said, sliding to the floor.

Jenierien hung off one of the bed posters and swung around. Her perfume wafted in Lexa's direction. "That will cost you," she purred.

Lexa breathed deep, the perfume creeping up her sinuses and into her brain like dust from a tomb. This was a lot more pleasant, and intoxicating. Her fingers relaxed, the Cynosure slipping.

With a wide smile showing each and every pearly white tooth, Jenierien undid a button in the front of her already low-cut shirt and let it hang open. Her creamy white skin glowed in the low light, and the perfume wafted toward Lexa again, seeming to curl around her head like a spell.

And that's what it was. A spell. A trap, designed just like each and every one of those tombs she'd explored, both for the museum and not. She couldn't let this slow her down.

Clenching her fist around the Cynosure again, she glanced behind Jenierien.

Qesson stood at the ready, all four legs spread, hands up.

Jenierien chuckled under her breath. "Do you think anyone comes into this house without me knowing? Even in disguise?" She plucked the brown fabric of Lexa's shirt between two fingers and *tsk*ed. "I am glad I was able to convince you I had gone." She gestured at Qesson. "We thought you were smarter than that, didn't we, my friend?"

He nodded, campfire-colored skin flushing above his nose. "So much so, that I have to wonder if this is a trap, madam. I would suggest you move away and let me handle her."

"Handle me?" Lexa asked. She moved a step away from the bed, flipping through mental images of the blueprints. Not that Jenierien didn't know this room better, but maybe she could find a way out she didn't expect. "You offering to take Jenierien's place in this bargain, Qesson? I've never tried Truscian, better late than never, eh?"

He flushed again, all the skin above and below his nose turning a deep orange. "I—" he stammered.

With a chuckle, and a last, quick glance at Lady Jenierien's open shirt, Lexa broke into a dead run and headed for a hidden door that should lead to stairs.

Jenierien screamed. "No! You bring that back! Qesson!"

Lexa locked it out, a lot like she could lock out falling rock and screaming metal, and sprinted for the hidden doorway, sizing up the wall. The doorway was hidden for aesthetic purposes, so the handle shouldn't be hard to operate.

She hit the wall with Qesson on her heels and Jenierien wailing loud enough to call every servant in the house and maybe even the cops. Lexa shoved the door and it popped open on a spring. She had just enough time to slam it shut before Qesson hit it.

He charged into the staircase as she sprinted down, skipping three stairs at a time.

Gram had taught her to focus on her breath when they would practice yoga in the field next to her house. In the quiet, still, dewy morning, they'd do square breathing and connect their bodies to their minds with the thin string of breath.

She pulled the cool air of this dusty staircase through her mouth, into her lungs, down to her stomach, and back out, turning her body into a single heartbeat that flowed with her mind. And her mind said there was a small window around the next corner.

Tucking the Cynosure into her elbow like a football, she gripped the banister with the other and switched her downward momentum to sideways, feet together.

She crashed through the window and covered her face with her arms as the rest of her followed her feet out the jagged hole. The loose ZPS uniform caught on a piece of glass, the fabric ripping with a *brrrrt*.

The broken glass dug into her forearm, and it shot spikes of heat into her brain.

She fell about half a story, landing feet first. She rolled, minimizing the impact on her feet and taking the brunt on her right knee and left shoulder. The Cynosure squirted from her hand and landed in the gravel, tinkling as it skidded away.

Holding her shoulder, she glanced up.

Qesson stared at her through the broken window, his eyes glowing red. He was about to come through that wall.

She sucked a breath through her teeth, the cold air coming so fast over them they ached. "Get up, Lexa," she whispered, rolling toward the Cynosure. She wouldn't have another chance like this. If she left it here, she may as well burn the map and give up her career.

As Qesson floated through the wall, she snagged the Cynosure and jumped up. Her right knee wanted to buckle, but she kept it to a slight stumble and limped for the gate. Qesson's feet hit the gravel behind her, his breath blowing out his nose like a hurricane force gale. Tucking the Cynosure in her elbow again, she let her legs loose and sprinted for the door, concentrating on her breath again. Stretching both her legs and her lungs to the absolute limit.

She hit the iron door, box still crammed in the side like a door stop, and shoved it with her hip. It flew open. She dashed through, slamming it closed after her. Not that that would slow Qesson for long.

Through traffic, she dashed across the street, headlights bathing her in white light and taillights turning the street red in a soft rain that had begun while she was inside Jenierien's. She ducked into an alley and out of sight.

Horns blared as Qesson crossed the street, and she could only imagine him phasing through the cars as they sped past, scaring the life out of people with his glowing red eyes.

Lexa ripped the buttons on her fake ZPS shirt, plastic clicking to the ground with the rain, and tossed the shirt. Blood flashed in front of her eyes but she didn't have time to stop and see how bad it was. Instead, she shrugged out of the loose cargo pants and shoved the Cynosure in her front pocket.

Now, to get to her bike before Qesson.

And she was willing to bet he didn't know these streets as well as her friends in the city archives.

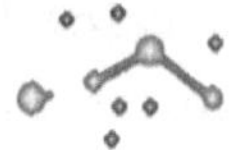

In rain that had hardened from soft to driving, Lexa rode her mini-bike into the back bay of her ship. Soaked to the bone, she closed the bay door. Qesson had only been able to keep up for a couple blocks before she lost him in the tangle that was PNY. She was alone here, in the dark junkyard. She allowed her shoulders to relax from where they'd been resting near her ears.

On her way to her quarters to change, she fought with her front pocket until it released the Cynosure. It shone, even in the darkened ship, and the rain pounded on the metal roof. She considered just crawling into bed and sleeping for a week.

"Vanny-poo?"

The cat didn't answer. Too bad, she was nice to snuggle with.

Stripping off her wet clothes, she crawled under the blankets from the bottom and curled into a ball around the Cynosure, its surface cool and slick. The Gexcorian pearls broke the smooth bubble of the teardrop shape but at the same time, strangely felt a part of it. She rubbed her thumb over one, considering its texture and drifting into sleep.

Savannah mrowed.

"Come on, Van. Get up here and snuggle—"

"Do you have it?"

Lexa froze, all her muscles tense. Whoever invaded her home had managed to catch her not only unarmed, but nude.

Great.

Clutching the Cynosure, she drew the blanket down by millimeters until she could look around it.

In the doorway stood an eight-limbed alien holding two energy rifles and Lexa's own satchel. The satchel moved and a muffled meow came out of it.

The Gexcorian spoke again, his lips undulating with the tones issuing from between his teeth. "Do you have it?"

Lexa glanced under the blanket. "Have what? I don't even have clothes on. Who are you?"

His mouth approximated a smile, edges curling up. He slunk into the room, riding the smooth motion of five flopping limbs rolling in concert. One of the limbs not holding a rifle or Lexa's squirming cat dipped into a bag suspended over his body and pulled out a tattered piece of paper. "You forgot this, when you defiled Queen Maridoxia's tomb." He tossed the paper on the bed.

An exhale whistled between Lexa's lips. She'd ripped her pants in that forbidden room, leaving evidence behind that she'd been there.

And broken their most revered queen into a million pieces of shattered stone.

She spoke through tight lips. "What do you want?"

"You know what I want." He shook the bag. Savannah yowled.

Lexa clenched the Cynosure under the blanket. If she let go of it now, not only would it undo all the work she just did to steal it back, she'd never be able to decipher the map. Letting it go just wasn't an option.

She riffled through the options she did have. Nude, in her quarters at night in the middle of a dark junkyard, there weren't many. But there was at least one. Maybe two.

Inching to the edge of the bed, she let the blanket slip in favor of holding the Cynosure. With her free hand, she reached beneath the mattress, her fingers meeting cool plastic. She gripped the energy pistol and slid it out. "Listen, uh, what's your name?"

"You cannot pronounce it with your human—"

"I'm aware. Tell me anyway."

The Gexcorian squealed and groaned, his throat undulating and the mirror behind the bed wobbling. Savannah yowled again and the bag shifted.

Eyes narrowed at her satchel, Lexa tightened her grip on the gun. "OK, you're right, I can't pronounce it in your language. Is it all right if I translate it to Ferrinogean?"

He nodded. "That is a very good translation. How do you know that?"

Under the blanket, Lexa lifted the barrel of the pistol and took aim for the fleshy sac beneath Ferrinogean's mouth. Energy pistols weren't meant to kill, but they hurt like a son of a bitch. It'd slow him down. Hopefully long enough. "You found the paper, right? I'm an exoarchaeologist. Studied some exoanthropology, too. You'd be surprised what I know about your people." She waggled her eyebrows.

One of his rifles dipped. "Then." He stopped and cleared what passed for a throat, all his tentacles waving like they were in a strong breeze. "Then you know how important the Cynosure is to my people. You must return it."

She shook her head. "I told you, I don't have it."

"Don't lie to me!" His scream rocketed up, piercing her eardrums and shattering the mirror behind her.

Teeth gritted, she resisted the urge to cover her ears and ducked as shards of mirror peppered the back of her head and shoulders. A few sharp pieces sliced her back open, lighting her skin on fire. Some bounced off him as well, opening wounds on his forehead and one of the limbs he stood on.

He stood on two uninjured limbs and gripped the bag with Savannah in it. She yowled.

"Give it to me!"

Despite the slick blood dripping down her back, Lexa grinned. "OK."

She fired.

He twisted, dropping the bag and throwing the limbs over his face.

The blast bludgeoned one of them loose and hit him somewhere in the thick tissue beneath his face. What might be referred to as a torso if these guys were shaped anything like a human. And his scream rivaled the one Lexa heard in Maridoxia's tomb in its intensity.

Back dripping, ears throbbing, Lexa dropped both the blanket and the pistol, and leapt for the satchel. A piece of glass sliced her heel and she grabbed the bag, squirting past Ferrinogean as he reached for her with the injured limb. Some of his black blood splashed her in the face.

He took aim with one of the rifles.

She held up the Cynosure. "Careful now, you don't want to hit this."

He dropped, all eight limbs flopping to the floor with a splat. Forehead lowered, he bowed and groveled, mumbling something in Gexcorian.

Lexa stepped around him and the shards of glass, snatching the blanket from the floor and wrapping it around her chest. "Do you know what he's saying, Vannah?"

A weak meow came from the bag.

She slipped the strap over her head and backed out of the room. "Look," she said, stopping in the doorway. Ferrinogean continued to mumble. "I'll give it back when I'm done with it, deal?"

Of course, not giving it back to Lady Jenierien would come with its own set of consequences. Never setting foot on Earth again was one of them, but did she even want to?

Before Ferrinogean gathered his wits, she slammed the button to close and lock the door to her quarters. She snuck her hand under the flap of the bag and laid the Cynosure next to the cat. And…what was that in there?

Her fingertips slid over what could have been skin, soft and supple and leathery.

Ah, the map. Good. She would—

A low hum from outside caught her ears. As she stood in the doorway, listening, the hum grew louder.

"Shit," she whispered, tying the blanket next to her armpit. "I'd really like to get dressed before the next disaster, you know?"

Van didn't answer.

Stomach tight, Lexa limped into the hall and up to the cockpit. Without stopping to put the bag down, she started the engines. "Gotta figure out that bounty hunter or whatever in my quarters, eventually," she mumbled, bringing up the view screen. She set it to scan above the ship.

The origin of the hum became apparent almost as soon as the picture flickered to life.

Directly above her ship was another. A Gexcorian warship.

This Ferrinogean was more than just a bounty hunter, it looked like. And he had some powerful friends.

Before she could even think about waving the white flag, they started firing.

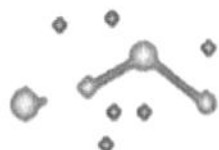

Breath caught in her throat, Lexa dashed through the ship, stopping only to pick up her shoes. The bag with Savannah, the map, and the Cynosure banged on her hip. Blanket gathered in one hand, she felt like film she'd seen of nineteenth century women, their skirts bunched in their hands as they hurried down stairs or trekked across a lonely moor.

As she passed through the greenhouse, ammunition from the Gexcorian warship pounding the roof as loud as the driving rain, she glanced up through the window.

The warship floated above the kilometer-high piles of junk, hovering below the thunderhead which had also parked itself over Lexa's ship.

It was like even the heavens wanted her to return the Cynosure.

She tore the door open between the greenhouse and the rear bay as the glass above her roses shattered. Ducking, pulling the blanket tighter over her already bleeding back, her stomach curled in on itself. She gritted her teeth and mashed the button to open the back bay.

The door to her quarters slammed open. Ferrinogean wailed, shattering whatever glass might be left on this ship.

Forehead slick, she stuck her hand in the satchel.

The Cynosure was still in one piece, thank the universe. Savannah swiped at her hand, all claws and anger.

"Sorry, Van," she said, teeth clenched. "I'll get you out of this as soon as I can." She sat and tugged her shoes on.

Ferrinogean crashed through the ship, wailing.

Lexa's ears rang. "Untied is just going to have to do. Ready?" She patted the bag and sat on her bike.

The bounty hunter hit the wall between the greenhouse and the bay. He wrapped several limbs around the doorjamb and shoved his face between them, his slathering, snapping maw engorged with rage. A guttural shout crawled from the back of his throat but whatever he said was in Gexcorian and Lexa didn't have the wherewithal to translate.

Didn't have to translate that tone, though.

She kicked the bike's engine over and spun it, leaving a track of rubber on the bay floor.

Gonna have to clean that up later.

An absurd thought to have as she sped from the ramp and into the junkyard, the bounty hunter on her tail. She accelerated and he fell behind. Doing her best to remember the lay of the piles, she slalomed through the place, wishing she'd installed some boosters on this bike or a flight package or something.

The rumble of thunder mixed with the growl of artillery and the skin of her ship buckling under the onslaught, screaming into the night.

The wind whipped the blanket up over her legs and she wished she'd been able to stop for clothes. Shit, she didn't even have underwear on.

Her rear tire slipped in the mud, skidding left as she leaned right. She laid her bare right knee on the ground and kept the bike upright at the expense of most of the skin on her knee. Fire raced through her body into her brain and she clamped her lips over the shout that tried to escape her throat.

She had to find somewhere to go.

Clearing another pile of junk, she came face to face with a set of taillights.

The bike skidded, sliding through the mud until it came to rest not one meter from what had to be a garbage scow, picking up trash to take to the recycler.

Without thinking too hard about it, she cut the engine and dumped the bike. Gathering the blanket again and holding the bag close to her body, she sprinted for the scow before it took off. The six by three meter bucket in the rear, where they loaded the garbage, had a ladder in the back. She grabbed it as the scow lifted off. Clinging to a rung, the wind whipping the blanket, she tried to look up.

Rain pounded her in the face, stinging the skin of her forehead and cheeks.

Rather than continue to try and look up, see how far from the top of the bucket she was, she climbed.

The wind whipped the blanket off. It became part of the storm.

Pelted with driving rain, the fresh gashes on her back burning, she struggled up the ladder as the scow lifted higher. Were they leaving the junkyard? If so, she wouldn't be able to hang onto this ladder. Not given the height of the piles.

Satchel hanging around her neck like a 20-kilo weight, arms shaking, she drug herself up the ladder. One rung at a time. Just one rung at a time.

When she reached the top, she looked down into the pitch-black mess of garbage in the bucket. She tried to raise the lights in her arms, but the light quivered, hardly illuminating anything but her forearms. Fingers crossed, she climbed over the lip and lowered herself down, toes questing for the top of the pile. When they hit something solid, she loosened her fingers and dropped in.

She had the luck to land on something soft. Granted, the flickering lights in her arms revealed it to be a moth and rat-eaten mattress, but she could sit on it and try to figure out what the hell to do next.

The sound of artillery and thunder receded and she leaned against the side of the bucket, rocked by the steady thrum of the scow's engines.

CHAPTER 6

"Come on, Elani, let's do this in the morning."

"Jake, the faster we get it done, the faster we can offload it, collect our pay, and get to the weekend."

Lexa swam to consciousness as the man named Jake grumbled, clearly letting Elani win. Whoever Elani and Jake were.

Rubbing her eyes, Lexa stretched. When the air hit her skin, she remembered the fact she was nude except for a pair of untied shoes and a messenger bag full of cat.

She curled back around herself.

Above the bucket was a ceiling filled with neon lights; looked like some kind of warehouse. At least it was relatively warm and it wasn't raining on her anymore. How she'd fallen asleep in the pitch-black bucket with the rain pounding her and the air streaking by as they flew out of the junkyard was a mystery even she might not be able to untangle.

Someone climbed the ladder.

Lexa gritted her teeth. The next few moments could get…interesting.

A woman's head cleared the lip of the bucket. Her deeply bronze skin and smooth black hair stood in sharp contrast to her golden eyes. They landed on Lexa.

The woman gasped, her soft pink lips as round as her wide eyes.

Her glowing golden eyes were the only giveaway she wasn't human. Lexa grinned, and her mouth hurt. She lifted her arm to wave and her bicep screamed.

With a grimace, she lowered her arm and covered her bare breasts. She tried to think of something good to say to explain what she was doing here, Gexcorian blood covering her face and her own covering her back. But when she opened her mouth, three words croaked out. "Hi. Um. Help?"

The woman glanced down. "Jake, grab me some coveralls."

"Is there someone in there?"

Those golden eyes met Lexa's. "Yes. And I need you to get me some coveralls."

His voice receded. "If it's a homeless person, we have to report it. You know they're not allowed to squat in junkyards. It's dangerous. If we get caught with one, we could lose our license."

Jaw bunched, Elani glanced down. "I'm aware. Just get me the coveralls."

He continued grumbling but didn't object again.

Elani climbed up another rung. "What are you doing here?"

Before Lexa could speak again, Savannah began meowing, yowling to be let out of the bag. She scratched at the flap, and her claws stuck in it.

Jake spoke from below. "Is that a cat?"

"Here," Elani said, tossing a pair of coveralls to Lexa. "Put these on and then you can explain just what is going on."

Lexa stood and tried to smile, but everything hurt, now. There was hardly a piece of skin she hadn't injured in the last hour, or a muscle she hadn't put under strain. All she'd done to get the Cynosure back crashed in on her at once. One hand on the coveralls, she fell to the mattress.

The woman gasped. "Oh my god! She's bleeding, Jake get the first aid kit."

"Now we've got to play doctor to a vagrant—"

She leapt into the bucket and crawled to Lexa. "Jake, just get the kit." Leaning over Lexa, Elani helped her roll over and lifted her so she didn't put weight on her back.

How bad must it have been for this woman to react so violently? Was her back a living approximation of ground burger?

An image of Gram cooking real hamburgers on the stove, something Lexa hadn't had since she was probably fifteen, assaulted her. Gram smiled, and Lexa could almost smell the beef smoke. Her mouth watered. She tried to arrange her tongue to make words again. "Hey, you got any food? Elani, right?"

The woman smiled, her wide, almond-shaped eyes framed by dark lashes, the edges folded with small crow's feet. "Elani Reihana. And you are?" She slid Lexa's shoes off and pushed the legs of the coveralls over her feet.

"Lexa. Lexa Dean." She tried to smile. It felt more like a grimace stuck to her cheeks and she ended up just baring her teeth to this vision in front of her.

Jake poked his head over the top of the bucket. "*Alexandra Dean? The exoarchaeologist?* Holy shit, Elani." Dark, round eyes set deep in rich russet-colored skin inspected Lexa's body, pausing on her face.

Lexa exhaled through her nose. "Archaeology a hobby of yours, Jake?"

He nodded, averting his eyes as Elani slid the coveralls past Lexa's ass and up over her breasts.

Lexa's arm screamed when she stuck it in the sleeve, and she remembered her trip through Jenierien's first floor window. She groaned.

"I know," Elani said, voice low. "I'll get you cleaned up. But first let's get you dressed and out of this filth."

Jake spoke to the air over Lexa's head. "Should I call someone, Doctor Dean?"

"No one I can… No. If you just help me out of here, I think I can cover it." Leaning on the side of the bucket, she stood. The bag pulled her back down before she could take a step and she collapsed.

Elani caught her, clutching her injured arm.

Fire ignited in Lexa's brain and she shouted, both falling on Elani and trying to disentangle herself from her arm at the same time.

"Lexa, you're injured. You need help."

Lexa shoved at the arm harder. "Just show me the door."

Which was the last thing she remembered saying, before her knees buckled again.

The gentle rocking of a ship in flight lulled Lexa as she rolled with it. Eyes closed, she sniffed the air.

Fresh air flowed in through a window, helping to dissipate the garbage scent.

So, she was still in the scow, but they were flying close enough to the ground to open the windows.

She pushed the sleeves of the coveralls back and felt her arms, fingers questing over a myriad of bandages. Elani must have given her some painkillers, too, because it didn't hurt to touch them.

She poked a soft lump somewhere near her abdomen.

"Mrow?"

"Hey, Savannah. Glad you made it." She smiled, her eyes closed, and relaxed into the mattress, idly wondering whose room she was in. Whoever it was had the most comfortable bed she'd been in in ages. Breathing deep, she held the air in her lungs until it wouldn't stay in anymore, and released it through her lips like a pinched balloon. Sinking back into sleep, she drifted and rolled with the rocking.

The back of her mind tickled. Just a little, like one of the feathers in this faux-feather pillow sneaked out and brushed against her ear with the slightest touch, like the whisper of a lover.

It was enough to make the hair on her arms stand up.

With no more preamble, she sat straight up. "Shit! Van, where's the bag?"

The cat stretched and stepped off, curling up on the mattress. Her eyes accused Lexa of being inconstant.

Lexa panted, jumping out of the bed. The bag had to be here. It had to. Those junkers couldn't have taken it. They just couldn't.

Her eyes landed on it where someone had laid it at the head of the bed on a shelf behind the pillow.

She leapt for it, catching the strap. Ripping it down from the shelf, she knocked off a small crystal bauble that fell to the floor and broke into about a hundred pieces. "Damn," she whispered, pawing through the bag.

Her fingers hit the map first, and she had a moment to register that it was still warm, as though Van was crammed into the bag with it.

Moving across the bottom of the bag, breath caught in her throat so tight she almost choked on it, she waited for her questing fingers to find what she was looking for. The prize she'd almost died for about five times already.

Her fingers hit smooth glass.

She gripped it and pulled it from the bag. When it glimmered in the low light, she collapsed back onto the bed, displacing the cat again.

Before she had a chance to exhale, someone rapped on the door. A soft knock, polite and sorry to be interrupting.

"Dr. Dean?"

"Yes, Jake?" She glanced around. So this was his room? Or did they share it? Hm.

"Is everything OK? Can I come in? I brought you some food and water."

Seeing as she was still fully clothed in the coveralls, she nodded. "Yeah. Please." She sat the bag, map and all, back on the shelf.

The door slid open and Jake walked in, tray balanced on one arm. "Hey, you're up. How do you feel?"

She got a better look at him than she had earlier. The pain had obscured everything but his wide, round eyes. Most likely human, short, neat twists of his curly black hair stood out in all directions. His round eyes, a richer brown than his skin, smiled easily. If he was getting DNA treatments he could be anywhere from twenty-five to a hundred and fifty. There was no way to tell.

He turned his back to her, setting the tray on the table amid the bedside detritus gathered there.

Not a bad ass, either.

Turning back to face her, his lips stretched in a wide grin. "This your cat?" He sat on the end of the bed and scratched Vanny behind the ears.

Which flattened. She backed away from his hand, her tail poofing to three times its size.

He pulled his hand back and clasped it inside the other one. "Not too friendly?"

"She's met a lot of unkind people, aliens, dogs. She's not terribly fond of strangers." Lexa shooed her across the bed. "Sorry."

He nodded and exhaled, staring at the wall.

In the silence, Lexa glanced at the tray he'd brought. Clear water, beading sweat on the glass, and some squares of cheese. Also a few nuts, probably his ration for the week, knowing what they paid junkers. She crunched one between her teeth.

"If you don't mind me asking," he said, turning those bright, dark eyes on her, "what were you doing in the back of the bucket? You could have been crushed."

She smiled and her mouth hurt. "It's a long story. But thanks for helping me."

"Does it have to do with that?" He pointed.

With a start, she realized she was still gripping the Cynosure in one hand, now warm from her grip. She stuck it in the pocket of her coveralls and took a cube of cheese. "You said archaeology is a hobby of yours?"

He nodded, sliding one leg onto the bed. "You bet! On my days off, sometimes I go out to the Valley of Kings just to look around. It's so—"

The comm blipped. *"Jake. You with Lexa?"*

He reached behind her and touched a button at the head of the bed.

Her leg rolled into his. Leaning on her, he nodded. "Affirmative. What's up?"

"I think she needs to see something. Can you bring her up here?"

He clicked his cheek and touched the button again, severing communication. "Ready to see the cockpit of our little home away from home?"

She glared at Savannah. "Don't break anything."

The cat stretched.

Lexa grabbed a handful of the food and followed him out of the room. She'd kick herself later if she didn't ask. "So are you and Elani…"

Jake chuckled. "Elani? And me? Haha no. You know she's Ambran, right?"

"So? You could be her soulmate. I just met you, how do I know? Besides, I heard some of them do casual dating before they locate their wayward half."

He shrugged. "Sure they do. But, well. No. And no. Not Elani and me." With a smile, he glanced over his shoulder. Those dark eyes danced. "Why? You wanna…"

She snorted, not filling in the blank for him. "Too soon to tell, Jake."

His smile didn't fade. Hand extended, he stopped to let her pass. "Right this way, Dr. Dean."

Lexa took one step down into the cockpit and grabbed the rail when her ankle went out from under her.

Jake grabbed her from behind and kept her from going ass over teakettle down the next two stairs.

"Sorry. Must have hurt my ankle, too."

Elani spoke from one of the three seats in the cramped cockpit. "How did you get all those injuries?"

Lowering into the chair in the middle, behind the two in the front windows, Lexa shook her head. "Doing something ill-advised." She stuck her hand in her pocket and fingered the Cynosure.

One eyebrow raised, Elani glanced over her shoulder. The way she eyed Lexa, her golden irises pulsing, wasn't full of as much suspicion as Lexa thought it would be. She'd met few Ambrans, but their ability to see energy fields was legend. She thought maybe Elani could see her lying, but she also wasn't about to tell the truth.

Either way, Elani said nothing and turned back around. "We're just about to make our approach to the recycling center. But while we were at cruising altitude, I took a look at the news." Pointing to a monitor with one hand, she turned up the volume with the other.

"…*WFLG drones captured this footage last night. As you can see, this is a Gexcorian warship. The first ever recorded to enter Earth's atmosphere.*

The council is currently working to make contact with Gexcor and verify their target, along with…"

But Lexa didn't hear the rest. As soon as the broadcaster said the words, "Gexcorian warship," her ears started ringing. She stood, hand on the back of Elani's chair, and looked down at the monitor in front of her, sound from the broadcast fading.

There, on the screen, large as life, was a shot of her ship in the junkyard. She could just make out the mini-bike speeding away, and the warship stopped firing its guns.

She exhaled.

But as the last of the breath escaped her lips, the Gexcorians let loose again. Her ship, and most of the junk piles surrounding it, disappeared in a flash of heat so bright, she squinted at the screen.

When the smoke cleared, the ship, Lexa's ship, her home, was gone. Gone.

Into dust.

The broadcast cut back to the newscaster. Next to his head, a three-dimensional hologram of Lexa's ship turned, showing the whole thing in detail. "*WFLG has not yet determined the owner of the ship but we will bring you that breaking story as it develops.*"

Lexa's mouth went dry. She shifted her eyes to Elani and Jake.

They both stared at the screen.

"*Lady Filhelmina Jenierien has extended a reward for information in the sum of two hundred thousand dollars. The Gexcorians have as well, for a reward totaling half a million dollars. We'll sit down with Lady Jenierien later today to learn what she knows about this occurrence.*"

Lexa sat in the chair again, so hard her tongue got caught between her teeth. Blood, coppery and slick, filled her mouth.

Elani spun around. "Lexa? Are you OK?" Her golden eyes wide, she glanced at Jake and nodded.

He flipped the screen off. Silence fell over the cabin, nothing but the low hum of engines and wind slipping through the open windows.

The garbage smell crawled down Lexa's throat and threatened to bring up the cheese and nuts. Something told her they'd be significantly less pleasant coming back up. Her eyes flipped between Jake and Elani. That reward would be a fortune to junkers like them. "Are you going to turn me in?"

They glanced at each other. Something passed between them, and Lexa had a moment to wonder if Jake had been telling the truth when he said they weren't soulmates. They certainly seemed to possess an unspoken language.

Elani turned her eyes back to Lexa and pushed an errant strand of hair over her ear, her nails chewed to the quick. "No. But it's not safe for you to stay on the ship. Once we park at the recycling station, I'll show you the best way to leave without being spotted."

"That's the best we can do," Jake finished. "I'm sorry."

CHAPTER 7

Savannah opened her eyes a crack and stared at Lexa where she leaned against the inside of the door.

"Shut up," Lexa said.

She still hadn't worked out whose quarters these were, or if they shared them, but that mystery was so far in the back of her head right now, she could hardly see the shape of it. Or know why she cared.

She'd done it. Burned her bridges not just with Jenierien, but with anyone who was within Jenierien's reach. And her reach was long.

Whiskers might even know by now.

Would the GHR kick her off the staff? It's not like they paid her regularly, just by-the-job freelancing. But still, it was a job.

Flopping onto the bed, scaring the cat, she exhaled and stared at the ceiling.

Fwap fwap fwap.

Van patted at something.

Fwap fwap fwap.

Lexa rolled her head, hair catching on the duvet cover, and watched Savannah paw at the strap for her bag.

Its slow, inexorable slide to the bed mesmerized Lexa. She didn't want to stop it. She wanted the bag to fall. She wanted it all to fall. That ship was all she had in the world that mattered, next to her cat, even if it was old and busted and barely hit light speed without feeling like it was going to fly apart at the seams.

The map rolled out of the bag and onto the bed with a soft thump.

Van hissed and backed away from it, her tail as big as a bottle brush.

Brow furrowed, Lexa reached for it. It wasn't warm anymore, but it had been. Earlier. What was different?

The bottom corner of the map unrolled and flashed the teardrop shape at her like a strip tease.

Of course. The Cynosure. It had been in the bag with the map, and the map warmed to its touch.

She tugged the Cynosure out of her pocket and sat up. May as well see what this thing did.

Snagging the map, Lexa stood and looked around the room. The only surface besides the bed was the night table Jake had put the cheese and nuts on. She tossed a cube of cheese in her mouth and moved the food to the bed. "No touchy, Van."

She kicked something with her shuffling foot and whatever it was tinkled as it slid across the floor.

Oh yeah. The crystal figurine she broke. If they had let her stay on the ship, she might have offered to replace it. As it was, she'd probably never see Elani or Jake again after the recycling center. Hell, she might not see free air again after that. It was only a matter of time until the cops, and then every news station in the sector, got her name.

Smoothing the map with ginger care, she held the Cynosure above it. It was the legend, the key to the map, but if there were instructions on how to do this, she—

The map started vibrating, but not like it had in Whiskers' office. Then, it had been trying to kill her. Now, it raised up in the center, pointing at the Cynosure.

And the Cynosure warmed, almost alive and pulsating. The pearls moved under her fingers, matching themselves to a shape forming on the map.

Eyes narrowed, Lexa studied the shape on the map and turned the Cynosure until the pearls aligned with the dots.

She sat it on the map.

The map relaxed back to the table, and all the light in the room sucked into the Cynosure. If there hadn't been an open window, it would have been pitch black in here.

As it was, Lexa felt for the table to be sure she was still standing next to it in the dim room.

Before her pupils could adjust, light exploded from the Cynosure. It focused into a single beam and projected something onto the ceiling.

Lexa stared up at it, heart pounding in her temples, fists clenched so tight she'd have to peel her nails out of her palm later.

On the ceiling was the vision of a woman. No, seven women. They ran, all holding hands, as a man with a bow and arrow gave chase. On his belt glimmered a sword made of stars, a nebulaic cloud shining on the hilt like a gem.

Falling to her knees, watching the story unfold on the ceiling, Lexa whispered a snatch of Tennyson to herself.

Many a night I saw the Pleiads, rising through the mellow shade,
Glitter like a swarm of fire-flies tangled in a silver braid.

As the words trailed from her lips, one of the sisters fell. She screamed.

Lexa tried to catch her. "Electra!"

But the disappearing Pleiad had faded.

The light drew back into the Cynosure. As it did, the room came back into being. Sun streamed through the open window, warming a spot in the floor.

Savannah jumped from the bed and laid in the spot.

Someone rapped on the door. "Lexa?" Elani asked.

Lexa grabbed at the Cynosure and the map, hands shaking. Even in all the years in school and in the field, she'd never seen a map do that. Her cheeks cold, she reached up to one of them and discovered it was wet.

She stuffed the map and Cynosure into the bag and slung it over her head. "Yeah. Time to go?"

The door opened, and Elani nodded, arms crossed. She pressed her lips together and leaned in the door. "Time to go."

Lexa scooped up the broken figurine. Snatching her limp cat from the floor, she shoved the cat in the bag and followed Elani down the hall. "I don't know whose this is, but I'm afraid I accidentally broke it." She held out a large broken shard in her hand. Funnily enough, it was some abstract crystal piece that reminded her, in a non-specific way, of the Cynosure.

Not that the shape of a teardrop was unusual. Cultures all across the galaxy incorporated them into their art one way or another.

Elani stopped and paled, her light brown skin ashen. She pushed a swath of black hair from her brow. "Oh no. That was…" She glanced up and stammered. Her golden eyes flitted around Lexa's head.

"Are you reading my energy?" Lexa frowned. "Some cultures consider it rude to peek."

She shrugged. "I can't help it. I see it," she said, holding her hand in the air palm out and patting at the air surrounding Lexa's face, "like waves of color surrounding you. I can't turn it off like some can. It's just always there, the way you see the color blue."

Lexa stared into her deep eyes, mesmerized by the way they glowed. "I thought the golden eyes thing wasn't super common anymore." She stepped closer.

"It's not. Neither of my parents had it. But here I am anyway." Half a sad smile touched her lips. "Here I am anyway."

As much as Lexa could see the secrets hiding under the sand, she could see pain hiding beneath that smile. Behind the eyes, Elani was a bigger mess than she wanted to admit. And Lexa couldn't remember being so drawn to someone.

She shook her head and started walking again, turning down the hallway toward the cockpit.

Elani grabbed her upper arm. "Not this way. I'll take you out the back and sneak you off. So the dock workers don't see you."

Lexa kept walking, pulling Elani along. She spoke over her shoulder. "I don't want to do this, I just want you to know that."

"Don't want to do what?"

Tugging her down the steps into the cockpit, using Elani's hand to help steady her on that tricky ankle, Lexa grimaced. Undoubtedly Elani could sense the energy coming off her. She tried to think sunshine and flowers thoughts, and slid the knife out of the side pocket of her bag.

"This." She pointed the knife.

Elani's hand popped off Lexa's arm. "What— Why?"

"I need a ship. You have a ship."

"For what?" She backed into a panel, flipping a couple buttons with her shoulder blades. Her eyes dimmed.

Lexa's stomach crawled to her toes. "I don't want to hurt you or Jake. But I need the ship. I have to…I have something very important I have to do."

"I can see that you believe that," Elani said, nodding and looking around Lexa instead of at her. "I can see that."

Footsteps sounded in the hallway and Jake approached, talking. "Elani, did you get Lexa out? We're all offloaded, ready to— What's this?" He stopped in the door, eyes wide.

Lexa backed between the two chairs in the front and aimed the knife at him.

Exhaling from what sounded like her toes, Elani sat in the third chair. "Looks like we're being hijacked by your archaeologist friend."

Jake stammered, tripping down the steps, and gripped the back of Elani's chair. "Why?"

Finding her voice again, Lexa unstuck her tongue from the roof of her mouth. "I'm truly sorry. I don't usually steal from the living. I'm having a weird couple days. But I need to locate something, and I need to go now before Jenierien finds out where I am. And the Gexcorians who blew up my ship."

Eyes alight, Jake smiled. "Find something? Like treasure? Like something from a tomb? You need to dig something up?"

She shrugged, bile coating the back of her throat. "Something like that. I guess." The hard metal corner of the drive panel dug into her back.

Elani nodded. "Something like that." Her eyes floated around Lexa. "Something you're incredibly excited about but can't tell us." Her brow furrowed. "Why can't you tell us? Did you steal something from these Gexcorians? From Lady Jenierien? That's a high ransom." She narrowed her eyes and met Lexa's.

"Stop reading my energy. I told you it's rude."

Elani's eyes widened.

Jake jumped into the copilot's seat. "Elani, get up here and steer. Lexa," he said, swatting at the air next to her, "move."

She stared down at him. "You don't understand. I'm stealing the ship." Her stomach bubbled.

"Oh no. I understand. You're stealing the ship, and we're coming with you."

Squeezing past her, the heat of her warming Lexa's cold skin, Elani nodded. "I'm the only one who this ship listens to anyway." She sat and turned those eyes to Lexa. "So, where are we going?"

Lexa stared at the screen beside Elani, where her ship and all her belongings had turned to ash before her eyes under the onslaught from the Gexcorian warship. She looked between the two people in front of her, their fingers on the controls, flopped into the third chair, and tucked the pocketknife away. What more did she have to lose by rolling with it?

THE CHASE

CHAPTER 8

Sitting in the back of the cockpit, Van purring and warm in her lap, Lexa watched black space pass by, the stars changing position. In the quiet, she tried not to think about the last person who'd come with her to look for treasure, but something in the cockpit rattled in a rhythm like his feet had against the floor of the tomb.

Lexa petted her cat, letting the motion sooth her, and wondered if she could get rid of these people. It was worth a try, and the sooner she started, the better.

"Hell. I thought my ship was bad at light speed. I feel like I'm going to chatter my teeth out of my head."

Elani patted the drive panel. "Don't listen to her, baby." She glanced over her shoulder, eyebrow raised. "Just be glad she can make it to space. She couldn't always."

"But I wanted to go to Mars on our time off one time and visit the ruins under Olympus Mons," Jake said, settling his feet onto the panel in front of him and crossing his ankles. "Spectacular, what they found there."

"Those aren't burial mounds," Lexa said. "It's just magma vents. The similarity to pyramids is simply a trick of nature."

Jake shifted in his seat, shoulders slumped.

"You might supposedly be the expert," Elani said, cocking a brow over her shoulder, "but that doesn't make you right." She glanced at Jake and jutted her chin.

Lexa couldn't fathom what that chin jut meant. Not only was she the expert here, she *was* right. Sure, there were conflicting studies, but the people who thought they were burial mounds were just dreaming. She'd been there and seen for herself.

She widened her eyes at Elani and stared out the window again, running her fingers down Van's back.

The cat blinked up at her and stretched.

"Hey Vanny-fanny, how was your nap?"

Van's eyes blinked slow and her rough tongue curled out of her mouth as she yawned. Eyes half-open, she hopped down and sauntered to Elani. She twisted around her leg.

Elani reached down to pet her and Lexa waited for the swipe. If she even gave that much warning.

It didn't come. Instead, the cat jumped onto the console in front of Elani and stretched again.

When she let Elani scratch her between the ears, Lexa's mouth fell open. Now not only were these two horning in on her investigation, her cat seemed open to the idea.

Teeth clenched, Lexa stood and paced. "How far are we?"

Jake, his tone dull, glanced at a screen to his right and spoke over his shoulder. "Twenty minutes from Yophiethea. Where are we landing?"

"Request access to the northeastern continent. Where's a radio? I'll call my friend, Nylah. She's a cartographer. I've got to figure out how to use this map or it's worthless."

Elani pointed over her shoulder but Jake interrupted.

"Map?" He spun his chair so fast his feet flew out. Wide eyes alight again, he beamed. "You have a map? Can I see it? What are we looking for?"

Brow creased, Lexa tried to ignore his enthusiasm. It was hard. It wanted to bubble up inside her and make her stomach light, her head fuzzy in that fun way serotonin caused. She clenched her teeth against it and stalked down the hall without answering.

CHAPTER 9

Lexa, freshly-changed into some of Elani's clothes that almost fit, sat on a bench with she and Jake in the waiting room at Yophiethea's premiere university, waiting for Nylah to join them. Savannah had stayed in the ship, making herself right at home.

Gape-jawed, Jake stared around the room, his eyes glazed.

Lexa leaned into Elani. "What's his problem?"

She smiled and glanced at him, her eyelids low. "That trip to Mars was the only time he's left Earth. He's always wanted to see something like this."

"Like this? A waiting room with potted plants and unforgiving wooden benches? Pretty sure you can get that on Earth at any doctor's office."

Elani bumped her. "Come on, you know what I mean. This isn't like Earth and you know it."

She did. If nothing else, the busts and portraits of Yophiethea's notable academics set this waiting room apart. No boring, two-armed stuffed shirts here. Instead, ape-like people with five appendages greeted them, solemn as academics tended to be. "Fine. You've got a point. But we're not here for a tour."

Without looking at her, Jake stood and walked to a painting. Hands behind his back, he craned up at it.

"Lexa Dean," a voice said from the door. "What a singular pleasure. And you brought friends?"

Lexa joined Nylah in the doorway and hugged her. Though she was about half as hairy as an ape, her silky hair still tickled Lexa's skin where it escaped from her sleeves.

Nylah's unique neon-green eyes smiled. In a traditional Yophiethean greeting, Nylah rubbed the sides of her face against the sides of Lexa's. Once Lexa made introductions, Nylah repeated the greeting with Elani and Jake.

Jake laughed and hugged her tight. "Thank you! I'm so happy to be here!" He let her go and pointed to one of the paintings. "Can you tell me much about this man? I'm sorry, I can't read your language. I didn't know we'd be coming or I would have tried to learn…anything." He bounced on his toes.

Elani took his arm. "Not now, Jake. Lexa has important things she needs to ask her friend." She glanced at Nylah, her eyes flashing. "Don't mind us. It's Lexa who needs to speak with you."

Nylah bowed at the waist. "Why don't you all follow me to my office. Maybe before you leave I can give you a tour, at the least," she said, extending one long arm toward the hallway.

Following Nylah across campus, Elani had to tug Jake more than once.

And not that she cared, but Lexa was glad to see the sullen look she'd accidentally put on his face on the way here had disappeared. He seemed too nice—and too cute—to upset like that. Not that she cared.

"I wasn't expecting Earth company, please wait here while I get you some chairs," Ny said, opening the door to her office. She gestured at the circular room.

Lexa walked in and sat on the edge of Nylah's desk. "Sure. But get this one one of yours." She cut her eyes at Jake.

While they waited, Jake sat cross-legged in the middle of the office floor and stared around. Books lined the walls in piles, scrolls sat haphazardly on top of them, and the sections of walls not blocked by books were covered in maps of the stars. The smell of musty pages laid over the air like perfume.

Lexa smiled. The smell, and the feel of a professor's office, crammed to bursting with books, were two of her favorite things about all those years in college.

Elani sat next to Jake and curled her knees up to her chest. "You said Nylah is a cartographer?"

"Best in the sector, probably the galaxy," Lexa said, crossing her feet and resting on her hands. "Stellar maps are her specialty. There's no one else I'd rather bring this to." She patted the bag with the map and Cynosure tucked inside.

Jake grinned. "Are we gonna get to see it?"

She shook her head. "I don't think that's a great idea."

Jake huffed, but before he could go on, Lexa interrupted him. "There's a lot of people who want this, and I hardly know you. The less you know about what they want and why, the better."

Elani crossed her arms over her knees and pulled them in tight. "Debatable."

"I don't want you getting hurt over it." It was out of her mouth before she knew it was coming, and before she knew how to take it back. Cheeks hot, she crossed her arms and stared at the floor. She couldn't just let that hang out there. So she spit out the first thing she could think of. "Or stealing it."

Jake inhaled.

Elani scoffed. The point five seconds of eye-contact Lexa made was enough to tell her she wasn't going to like what was about to come out of Elani's mouth.

Nylah came through the door, carrying three chairs and walking on two feet. One of the chairs was something a Yushhanio like her would find comfortable. Something like a chaise-lounge with armrests on either side and one above the head. She sat it behind Jake with a grin.

He popped up like he was on a spring and climbed into the chair, lips stretched from ear to ear. "This is great, thank you!" He went about trying to get comfortable and mostly failing, wide smile plastered on his face as he did.

Elani sat in her chair next to Jake and rested her chin in her palm, her gaze cool and fixed to Lexa.

Lexa let her breath out and leaned on Nylah's desk. At least Ny's return had blocked the dressing-down Elani was probably about to give her, and if her lucky streak kept up, she could get out of here to read the map before Elani got a chance to tell her what was on her mind. What was written all over her face.

"Thanks for the chairs, Ny, but there's something I'd like to show you in private. Can we leave these two here and go to the map room?"

Nylah narrowed her eyes. "I suppose we could, can I not look at it here?"

Elani exhaled through her nose. Jake didn't notice, he was still trying to figure out how to sit in a chair not made for humans.

On the way out the door, Lexa tried not to make eye contact with Elani again and failed.

Nylah flipped on the lights in the cartography room, the central projector looking sort-of like the ones they used in old Earth planetariums. A thousand points of light hit the ceiling, walls, and floors. "You've never come to see me with other people in tow. What's the occasion?"

Scowling, Lexa stalked to the table next to the projector and sat. She had slightly more luck sitting in this Yushhanioan chair than Jake, but only because she had practice. "I don't want to talk about them."

With a shrug, a much larger production than a human shrug, Nylah sat next to her and smiled. "Have it your way. What is it you've brought me?"

Before reaching in the bag, Lexa angled her chin at the door. "Is that locked?"

"Why ever for?"

"Lock it."

With a frown, Nylah did as she asked. "You're behaving very strangely, love. There's no decorous way to ask this, but are you here against your will? Are these two somehow forcing you to speak to me?" She leaned close and whispered. "Do you need help?"

Lexa pushed her lip out and exhaled, the warm breath tickling her nose hairs. "Yes, but not for the reasons you think. Nevermind them. They're just…" She trailed off, looking for the words.

"Jake is adorable. Most humans try to pretend they don't enjoy something when it's very clear they do. Even when you're intimate." She winked and nudged Lexa's shoulder, her silky hair brushing the skin on Lexa's arm.

She moved away. "Don't even. Never once have I tried to hide how much fun I'm having with you."

"And yet you only call me when you need something. I'm beginning to think you're not serious about me." As she spoke, each of her appendages worked a machine next to the projector, and the room filled with gossamer strands of light. They surrounded them, solid as spiderweb.

Lexa shivered, remembering what else she could do with all those appendages. "Since when have I not been serious?"

Ny snorted and touched a couple gossamer strands. She used another appendage, one more like a foot, to tug on the sleeve of her denim-like shirt. "You don't have to lie. We both know I'm just a…" She trailed off, flashing her neon-green eyes at Lexa. "What's the Earth word?"

Lexa shrugged. She knew damn well what word Ny was searching for, and it hadn't been in popular use on Earth for at least a century. But when some species learned the language, they learned all of it. Like, *all* of it.

Ny snapped two fingers together. "Booty call! Haha, that one." She smiled, showing a few rounded teeth.

Suppressing a grin, Lexa reached in the bag and pulled out the map. "Tell me about this."

Nylah took it with one hand but continued to smile sideways at Lexa with her human-like mouth. "I see you're not interested. Is it the Ambran? I saw the way you murmured with her. You know they hardly get involved outside their soulmates. Silly beliefs of theirs."

And there she'd come full circle back to her unwanted companions. To the pull she'd felt from Elani as soon as she laid eyes on her, to the way the two of them barely knew Lexa but wanted to travel to the ends of the galaxy with her, and the way that made her stomach do some kind of jitter she'd never experienced.

Again she shook her head. "Look at the map."

Nylah ran her hands along its rolled-up length. "I've not seen a map made out of such material in longer than I care to remember." Her smile dipped. "This is very old, Lexa. Where was it discovered?"

"Not sure. The GHR found it and passed it on to me."

"Official business, for once? Interesting." With one hand, she unrolled it and with two others, she placed it in the center of the table next to the projector. The gossamer strings surrounded it, lighting up wherever they passed through it. Nylah looked up. Her brow drew together. "It's not showing us anything. Are you sure it's a map?"

Reluctant as she was to expose the Cynosure, Lexa had no choice. Her stomach knotted, she drew it out of the bag, its smooth surface cool to the touch. "It has a key." She held it up, one of the gossamer strings going through it, shining white light through the Cynosure and refracting off the pearls. It struck Nylah in the face when she turned to look.

Her mouth dropped open. "It's gorgeous. Where did you find it?" She reached for it.

Lexa aimed her forehead at the map. "Not information I'd like to share. Just watch what it does." Rather than hand it off, she held it close to the map.

Like it had before, the map reached for the Cynosure, almost as if it yearned for its touch. And the Cynosure responded, warming in her hand before she laid it down. Once it touched the map, they both settled to the desk and the same scene projected onto the ceiling, the strands of light slashing through it.

Nylah leapt into her chair and began to move all five appendages, manipulating different strands with each. Bursts of light sped away from her hands and feet, and the strands themselves intersected the scene of the sisters being chased by Orion at every point a star would be. Still working furiously with the strands, pinpointing as many stars as she could, Nylah cleared her throat with a growl and dropped her voice to a husky, reverent whisper. "Lexa Dean, what have you brought me?"

Lexa watched Nylah and the sisters in equal parts awe and fear. The scene was bigger, brighter, and overwhelming in this room. She shivered and felt for the other chair she knew was only a few steps away. When she found it, she collapsed into it and threw one leg over the arm. "I don't...can you tell me what it's for?"

"First," Ny said, "let's see if we can at least get you a location." She manipulated more strands, light shooting away from her and surrounding her in a spiderweb of stars. All five of her appendages grabbed the web in a circle, and she pulled them close to her body. The stars she'd pinpointed came with it, and she stopped them in front of her face, the blue light of the sisters shining in her eyes. "I've never seen a map like this." Her voice came out in a breathy whisper. "This is incredible. There are no words."

Chewing her lip, Lexa leaned forward over her leg and squeezed until her stomach hurt. "Do you know where I need to go?"

She shook her head. "No. But I have an idea how we can find out. To your other question…" She trailed off, the light from the stars shimmering over her face. Opening all of her hands, she released the strands and let them float away from her. "It's precious. It's incredibly precious. What can you tell me about it?"

"That it might—" She stopped. How much to tell Ny? Should she be involved in this any more than she already was? The Gexcorians had already blown up her ship. What would they do to Ny if they found out she'd even laid eyes on the Cynosure? It wasn't likely to be good. But Lexa also needed to know. She needed to know how to read the map, she needed to know, without doubt, what she was headed toward. And she needed to know what she might run into on the way. "It might lead to something more groundbreaking than anything I've ever found," she finished, hoping the answer wasn't too vague for Ny to accept.

But Nylah knew her too well. "A secret treasure, huh? Interesting. Is it valuable?"

"Very."

She gazed up at the scene of the sisters, floating in the web. "What do you need to know, besides your destination?"

"How do I read this thing?" She gestured at the map, not that Nylah was looking.

But Nylah nodded. "I believe that when you bring it to the location shown, the way forward will reveal itself. You must go when all seven stars are visible, and it must be…" She trailed off again, reaching for the projector with one foot. Her toe clicked the off button, and the room fell into darkness.

Before Lexa's eyes had a chance to adjust, the backlighting came up. Just enough to see by. She snatched the Cynosure from the map, its surface still warm, and shoved it in the bag. With a gentler touch, she rolled up the map and slid it into the bag again, hoping the two wouldn't get too warm in there together, touching. It seemed like they weren't too bad when the map was rolled up. What an odd pair.

Elani and Jake flashed through her mind. Odd pairs. She was surrounded.

Nylah tapped her on the knee. "Did I lose you?"

Head shaking, Lexa stood. "Do we need books?"

"Charts. Yes. Let's go back to my office."

Elani and Jake sat much as they had when Lexa and Nylah had left, though Jake seemed to have figured out how to make his oddly-shaped body fit in the chair. He beamed when they entered. Elani watched with her swirling golden eyes, but with a brow that remained flat. Her eyes narrowed as Lexa sat on Nylah's desk again, and she crossed her arms.

"Do we know where we're going?" Elani asked.

Lexa shook her head. "It kills me that you keep saying 'we' like this is a team effort."

Jake snorted. "You're the professional, Lexa. We're just along for the ride. But it's been amazing so far!" He winked at Nylah.

Nylah smiled. "Do tell me you'll have time to take a tour of the university, Lexa. Jake here would enjoy that very much, I'm sure."

He jerked. "Yes! I—"

"We don't have time for that." Lexa cut her eyes at Jake. "But you can stay here and I'll go on without you, if you want."

His smile fell a tick, but he shook his head. "You're not leaving us behind now. Not when we're just about to find out what your map says."

She turned back to Nylah, ignoring the fact that Elani had been mostly silent after her dig about the 'we' thing, and shrugged. "What does the map say?"

Nylah rooted through her desk, grunting. "Like I said, it's a strange map. Not like anything I've ever seen. I think it will tell you your next destination when you get there. But where is there, that's the question." She stood, eyes searching the office. "Ah," she said, charging to the opposite side of the round room. She pulled a chart from under about seven books, stabilizing the listing pile with two appendages and unfurling the chart with another. "This should tell us something…" Eyes wide, she searched the paper, turning it around several times. The circular parchment seemed to be giving her trouble, as her eyes narrowed and her brow drew down over them. She pursed her lips and grunted again. After a few more moments, she tossed the chart down and grumbled. "Useless. Let's see…"

She crossed the room four or five times, pulling increasingly dusty charts from under increasingly deep piles. None of them satisfied her, and she started cursing before she was done.

As she did, Jake leaned on the desk and joined Lexa in watching. He didn't say anything, but his enthusiasm radiated off him in waves, even in silence. No wonder Elani enjoyed his company.

Lexa fought off the feeling his effervescence attempted to give her. She didn't want to feel good. She wanted to feel alone. But dammit, it was catching.

Which caused a bigger letdown than necessary when Nylah flopped in her chair, dust flying off her, and threw up three of her hands. "I don't bloody know. None of these charts are helling helpful." She shook her head and rested her forehead in one palm.

"I can't believe I'm saying this, but I don't have what you seek." Nostrils flared, she let out a deep exhale. "I am so sorry."

Frowning, Lexa spoke from between her clenched teeth. "What do you mean, you don't have a location?"

"That's what I mean. I am, for once, at a loss."

Lexa flapped her mouth up and down. She never considered Nylah wouldn't be able to help.

Elani crossed her arms and approached Nylah's desk. "What can you tell us?"

"I can tell you the angle you need to see the Pleiades from." She flopped a chart on the desk and pointed to a system marked with symbols すばる. "This is an Earth map of the stars. This is not the correct angle." She lay another over it. "This is close. It's in a system sixteen light years from here. Not a long trip. But it's still not right. I recommend you begin…" Chewing her lip, she leaned over the maps.

Elani leaned with her, resting her fingertips on the polished desk. "The Lautrolin system?"

Lexa snorted. "What do you know about stellar cartography?"

Ignoring her, Elani leaned further over the maps, conferring with Nylah in a hushed voice. Her rich dark hair fell over her shoulder, brushing the old maps with a feathery sound.

Stymied, Lexa shifted from foot to foot, watching them confer. Her stomach clenched and she crossed her arms over it. It was bad enough coming to Nylah but at least that she was used to. She could come here, ask for help, get laid, and leave. No problem.

Getting help from Elani, when Lexa had to continue being in her presence, with Elani petting her cat and intruding on her thoughts, was the last thing she wanted. And yet she stood here, waiting on Elani to come up with an answer to her burning question. *Where do we go?*

Ny stood up straight. "Head to Kepler 444. The library at Port de Playa should have the information you need."

Jake snorted. "A library? Doesn't Port de Playa thrive on tourism?"

Lexa met his eyes. "What, people don't go to the library on their vacations?"

"Not really," Elani said, facing them. "I mean, our vacations are a little unorthodox but I understand not everyone vacations at historical sites. Most people like the beach."

"More sand. My favorite thing." Lexa held her hand out for Nylah, who rounded the desk and pulled her into a hug.

Hair tickling her ear, Nylah leaned into it and whispered. "Don't be so sour. You could have a lot of fun with these two, if you decide to." She leaned back and smiled. "Good luck!"

Beaming, Jake shook her hand while she still hugged Lexa with the other two. "Can we take that tour now?"

"Not now, Jake," Lexa said. "Let's go."

CHAPTER 10

Book covers rubbed against each other, leathery whispers in the vaulted space. Surrounded in hushed lighting and even quieter patrons, what there was of them, Lexa and Elani crept through the stacks.

The librarian ahead of them glanced over her shoulder, her red hair tied up with what looked like knitting needles, and pitched her voice low. "You said you're looking for reference material for the Pleiades?"

Lexa leaned forward and matched the librarian's tone. "Yes. And your star maps."

She smiled. "The cartography room is on the fifth floor. A good friend of mine would have loved to see it." Head lowered, she kept walking. "I'll take you up there after you're done with the books." She stopped and pointed to a shelf.

Elani slid a book from the shelf. *The Seven Sisters.* Why do we need this?"

Lexa took it from her and opened it, scanned the table of contents, and turned to the section about Orion. "See, here. The hunter. That's what I saw." The map and Cynosure hung heavy in the Savannah-less bag at her hip. No cats in the library. She turned to the librarian. "Can we see the maps?"

"Right this way." She swung her hips as she walked ahead of them and spoke over her shoulder again. The smile in her voice obvious, she slowed. "I wish I could have told my friend about traveling the stars. She'd have gotten a kick out of it." She chuckled to herself.

Elani, eyes glowing gold, the amber in them swirling like the clouds of Venus, frowned. "You miss her."

"Something fierce." She stopped at the top of the stairs and pulled a key from her pocket. "Ring the bell when you're done and someone will pick you up. Do you need anything else?" The key flashed when she held it next to the door, and the door opened itself.

Lexa started up the stairs.

Elani didn't follow. "You'll see her again," she said, taking the librarian's hand. "She misses you, too."

Tongue stuck to the roof of her mouth, Lexa snagged Elani's other hand. She'd never seen an Ambran so willingly give out energy readings, and while Lexa'd told her it was rude to read someone's energy without asking, she was curious what Elani saw when she looked at her.

No way she'd ask.

"Come on, Elani. Thank you." She nodded to the librarian and tugged Elani into the map room.

The librarian, tears standing in her eyes, pulled the door closed.

"You have to stop doing that," Lexa said, tugging her arm.

Elani shrugged. "I've never been able to help it. My peers always hated me for it, and my mom said they were just jealous they couldn't do it." She shrugged again and picked at her shirt. "I wish I could turn it off like they do."

Sighing through her nose, Lexa walked to the map table and flipped on the light inside it. The last thing she wanted was to start psychoanalyzing her new "friend." She laid the book on the table. The map light shone from under it, projecting a rectangle of shadow onto the domed ceiling above the table. "I want to look for a planet where we can see this scene"—she pointed to the scene in the book where Orion chased the sisters and the seventh fell—"from exactly the angle I saw on my map. Like Ny pointed out to us."

"Show me your map, maybe I can help."

Lexa clutched the bag close and shook her head. "No one touches this map but me."

Lips pressed together, Elani crossed her arms and headed toward the racks of star maps. "Fine. You want to start with Lautrolin, like she said?"

The tone in her voice laid heavy over Lexa's ears. It wormed its way down her backbone and over her heart. Why would it bother her that this practical stranger was upset?

Nevermind the fact that she still felt that undeniable pull. That Elani had seen her in her worst moment and hadn't judged or asked questions. She'd simply helped dress her wounds and let her sleep in her bed.

"Look. It's old, and valuable, and kind-of a secret. It's probably best if you don't—"

"You can check this one in addition," Elani interrupted, pulling two map drives from a rack of them.

Lexa took the files she held out, twisting a toe. "Is cartography your hobby, like archaeology is Jake's?"

"I picked it up." She shrugged, not looking at Lexa. She slid one of the files into the map reader and stood back. "Star view from the surface of Lautrolin 3a," she said.

The machine beeped. A male voice spoke in a hushed library tone. "*Northern or Southern Hemisphere?*"

Leaned over the book, Lexa chewed a nail. "Southern."

A four-dimensional model of the night sky on Lautrolin 3a projected itself onto the domed ceiling. In the dark room, with its cool air, Lexa could almost believe they were standing on the surface of the planet, looking up at the stars. But, the view was wrong. "Not it," she said, removing the file. The dim lights came back up and she held her hand out for the next file.

Elani handed her one.

They went on like that for what had to be fifteen minutes. Inserting a file, viewing the stars, and Lexa passing on to the next one. Elani didn't say a word the whole time, but every time she handed Lexa a new map, she stood a little closer. By the time they found the right one, a formerly-inhabited world in the Birkishni system, they stood leaning on the table side by side and staring up at the Pleiades as the disappearing sister flickered in and out of existence.

The warmth of Elani's shoulder touched Lexa's. "Why does it do that?"

"Do what?" She turned her face toward Elani's, breathing into her ear.

But Elani kept staring up at the flickering star. "Vanish."

Lexa's shrug moved both of their shoulders. She shifted her arm and leaned on her hand behind Elani's back. Those golden eyes were unreal, and she wanted them turned to her again. "The Greeks thought she fell from the sky when Troy was conquered. Grief stole her from her sisters."

"How sad," Elani whispered.

It took everything Lexa had not to brush the hair away from Elani's ear and kiss her shoulder. She talked herself up, working up the courage to touch such a creature—one who'd already seen her naked anyway—and lifted her hand to do just that.

Elani turned those eyes on her, a tear dripping from one and sparkling yellow and orange like a sunset as it trickled away from her eye.

The breath bound in Lexa's lungs.

Brow furrowed, Elani opened her mouth and drew in a breath. The irises of her eyes swirled.

Before she could ask Lexa what she was doing, or ask her to stop, or any of a hundred other rejections, Lexa snatched her arm from behind her and removed the file from the machine. The lights came back up. She cleared her throat. "So. Next stop, Birkishni system."

"Lexa, what—"

Lexa rang the bell to call the librarian.

Stepping out of the library and back into the sunlight blinded Lexa. She squinted, the heat of the close yellow star seeping into her skin and beating off the pavement. The nearby ocean crashed to shore, Port de Playa's version of seagulls screaming on the breeze flowing in off the water.

Certainly a place some might consider paradise.

Lexa glanced at Elani, who smiled at the sea, shielding her eyes and watching the tourists as they sunned.

The question was out of Lexa's mouth before she thought about it. "What's it like?"

Elani shrugged, like she knew what Lexa was asking about without seeking clarification. "Energy holds the universe together. It doesn't flow through the air, it *is* the air. It's the connections between the birds, the ocean"—she faced Lexa—"between us."

Throat dry, Lexa swallowed over a click. She licked her lips and tried again, trying to unstick her eyes from Elani's. "Between us?"

Nodding, Elani took a step toward her and reached for her hand. Her voice almost a whisper, just loud enough to be heard over the surf, she leaned in. "There is energy between all living creatures, Lexa. All life is held together by it. The illusion your eyes show you is separation. I can't help but see the truth." She gripped Lexa's hand. "We're connected."

Lexa ripped her eyes away and glanced down at the dock, Elani and Jake's scow like a rusted eyesore parked next to the pristine beach. On the edge of her lips was the admission that she'd felt a pull to Elani from the moment they met.

Frowning, stomach churning, Lexa stared down at the scow. A few people seemed to mill about by the lowered bay door. "Can I ask you something?"

"Sure."

"How do you know…" She trailed off, staring down at the people outside the scow. One of them was Jake. The other two looked like… "Crap."

Elani followed her eyes. "Crap?"

"Those are port cops. What is Jake telling them?" She caught Elani's hand and jerked her down the sidewalk at a fast clip. "What do you think they're asking him?" Her stomach roiled, the fuzzy feeling that'd floated around her navel when Elani mentioned the energy between them turning into a cramp that wanted to double her over. By the time they reached the dock, she was practically running. She let go of Elani and pushed past the cops.

"Jake, honey." She grabbed his hand and pulled him into her. Hanging off his arm, she gave the cops what she hoped was a dazzling smile. "Hello gentlemen, what are you speaking with my husband about?"

"This is your husband?"

She eyed the cop. He looked human but there were at least eight species from other planets that looked human. Although, humans seemed drawn to law-enforcement, and Port de Playa was an Earth territory. "Just married." She giggled. "We're on our honeymoon!" Laying on as many exclamation points as she could, she pressed her breasts into Jake and bounced up and down on her toes.

Behind the port cops, Elani faded into a shadow. Her eyes amber pinpricks against the dark.

Jake, not someone Lexa'd taken for being super-quick on the uptake, squeezed her hand and surprised her. "Honey, did you find what you were looking for at the beach?"

The cops watched them, the other one clearly Truscian. His smoke-colored skin blanched in the sunlight.

Before they could get any more suspicious, Lexa spread the icing on the cake and planted a huge kiss on Jake's lips.

Jake didn't waste a moment. He wrapped one arm around her and squeezed her hand, tucking into her waist and kissing her back with wild abandon. Turned out traveling and alien planets weren't the only things he was enthusiastic about.

When he let her go, she had to work to catch her breath. What a kiss. He was cute, sure, but she hadn't seen any of that in him. Another taste couldn't come soon enough.

She glanced past the port cops, who looked just about ready to leave now they'd seen that, and caught Elani standing in the shadows, eyes hooded.

Something socked Lexa in the gut.

What were all these feelings floating around her head? She had to ditch these two. The sooner the better.

As the port cops walked away, inspecting ships on their way down the dock, she waved Elani over. "Listen. I don't think it'll take long for the authorities to realize this ship was the one I probably escaped on. Were you the only scow in the area?"

"That time of day? Yeah," Jake said. "We're the only ones who work at night."

Warm pressure on her hand woke her to the fact she was still clinging to him.

She let him go and backed up, glancing at Elani again.

Her face didn't read anything. She simply squinted her eyes at the sun and waited for Lexa to finish trying to run them off.

So she did. "I think I should go the rest of the way on my own. They're going to ID your ship and find us. If you get back to Earth, without me, you can just deny everything. Without evidence, they can't do anything."

Jake nodded. "I guess that's true. But—"

"But nothing. You've got to stop following me." Lexa crossed her arms.

Elani stepped onto the bay ramp. "They already know, Lexa. Before we left for the library, I ignored a call from our boss."

Jake jumped. "What? What did he say? Elani!"

"Sorry, Jake. He left a message." She dug in her pocket and came out with a fob no bigger than her palm. She clicked it and a holographic representation of a man Lexa could assume was their boss popped into being. In the sunlight, he was washed out and hardly visible. But the tone of voice couldn't be mistaken.

"If I find out the two of you were involved in whatever happened at yard twelve, which is your *yard, it'll be the last job you get from me. I'll turn you in for the reward money myself."* It abruptly cut off and the hologram disappeared.

Stomach in her toes, Lexa turned to the scow and inspected it. "Once those port cops call it in, you guys are sunk. Jenierien will be on you before you can even get out of the system."

Jake grabbed her. "What are we going to do?" His eyes bobbed between her and Elani, the note of desperation in his voice tugging Lexa's heart as he tugged her arm. "Elani? What are we going to do?"

Elani's mouth flopped up and down. "I don't. I don't know." She closed her eyes. "I can't look at you. Jake, you have to take a breath. Your energy hurts my eyes."

Oh, these two were both hopeless.

Lexa pushed Jake away from the ship. "We're going to the Birkishni system. Go. Find us a ship that will take us there. I have enough money to pay for it. Just book it." She grabbed Elani's hand. "Come with me. We'll get clothes, Savannah, whatever we need for the trip."

They stood and stared at her, slack-jawed.

Looking between them, she sighed. If she couldn't get rid of them, they were going to have to help. "Go, now!"

CHAPTER 11

Lexa dropped Van's bag on the bed and opened it. The cat crawled out, stretched, and yawned up at her. The end of her tail flicked.

"Sure you couldn't have found something nicer?" Brow raised, Lexa looked around the room. This single room was probably bigger than her entire ship—the one the Gexcorians had blown up—every surface shining and clean, the bed large enough for a platoon, even a nook in the corner with a table set for four. And a large picture window that currently looked out on the pitch-black interstellar medium.

Jake chuckled. "I did try to book two suites, one for you ladies so you could have some privacy, one for me, but they only had the one berth. I guess they're all full."

"And they're going to Birkishni?" Lexa flopped on the palatial bed and laid back. The hammered metal ceiling shone enough to see herself in.

"Seems like, yeah. I spoke to a tour guide and told him where we were looking to go. He showed me the cruise itinerary, they're headed there next. Something about the black beaches in blue starlight." He pointed at a panel. "I can pull up the itinerary."

She waved her hand and sat up on her elbows. "I believe you. Tour groups don't go there much, but I'll take it. I have heard the beaches are lovely. Black sand. No life, so it's perfect."

Elani finally spoke from a corner where she'd perched on a gilded chair. "No life? But there's beaches?"

Lexa sighed and sat all the way up, watching as Savannah explored the corners of the room and likely searched for a place to go to the bathroom. "I'm not a climate scientist. The life is gone now, that's all I know."

Looking at her hand, Elani spoke so low Lexa hardly caught the words. "Were there people?"

"More than likely. There are archaeological sites. Good call. Let me pull up a map." She walked across the room to a blank panel and punched a few buttons. As she stared at the map of the third planet in the Birkishni system, the one they'd identified in the library, she spoke over her shoulder. "Anyone got any ideas about a litter box?"

"I got it, Lexa." Jake found a golden trash can low and wide enough to work. "I'll get some litter from the ship's main fabricator. Be right back."

The doors whooshed shut after him.

The silence between Lexa and Elani could have stood on its own as a living creature. It hung in the air like fog you couldn't see or breathe through.

Whatever. Lexa had always been good with silence.

Savannah bumped against her leg.

"Shit. You need food too." She knelt. "For that matter, so do I."

"There's a dining hall, I think." Elani headed for the door without a sideways glance.

"Elani, wait."

She stopped and looked over her shoulder, one brow raised.

"Jake told me you guys aren't. Like. You know."

She waited, brow still cocked. She'd gathered her thick black hair in a ponytail and it hung half over her shoulder.

A shoulder Lexa would still like to taste. If she could get close enough again to do it.

Come on, Lexa. For once, there are other things to worry about.

"He told me you're not soulmates. Or together, or whatever. Don't your people date?"

With a turn so slow glaciers could have matched the speed, Elani faced her. "Does this line of questioning have a point?"

Lexa stepped back and bumped into the bed. She overbalanced and fell onto it. "Are you mad at me?"

"For what?"

"Kissing him."

"Why should I be? You both enjoyed it." She cleared her throat. Though it looked like it pained her, she gave Lexa a wide smile. "Immensely."

Lexa couldn't help but meet her smile. "Yeah, that was a bit of a shock. Not gonna lie. But." She stood and crossed to Elani, hands out, palms up. "I like you, too."

Elani backed up a step. "You think I don't know that?" The irises of her eyes swirled.

"Stop reading me."

"I told you, I can't turn it off."

"You can't turn off the energy you see," Lexa said, closing the last few centimeters between them. "You *can* control whether or not you interpret its meaning. Right?"

"You." Elani swallowed and started again. "You know a bit about my people. More than most."

"You're secretive," she said, pulling a breath in as far as she could get it. Elani's scent came with it—freshly cleaned skin, something that smelled like rose petals crushed into her shampoo—and her head swam. "I didn't spend thirty years in college learning only about dirt. To understand why people bury the things they do, and how, you have to understand the people. Your people keep a lot to themselves, but there are some—like you—who wander into the galaxy looking for their soulmates."

"Those of us whose reincarnations aren't born on Kuarpa have to be found."

"What if they don't want to?"

Elani backed up a step, her mouth hanging open. "What?"

"What if they chose to reincarnate elsewhere in the galaxy to get away? What if they don't want to be found?"

She shook her head. "Why? Why wouldn't they want to know where their home is?"

Lexa flashed on Gram's house, in the middle of a bunch of fields and woods, standing alone with its "for sale" sign in the yard. Her throat tightened and she crossed her arms. "What if it isn't home anymore?"

Elani took one small step toward her and laid a cool hand on her crossed arms. "Why are you asking me this?"

Staring into her swirling eyes, Lexa felt the pull again. She studied it, let it tug her in. It gripped her midsection, holding her heart like it was cradling it, and her stomach ached for something she couldn't grasp in her hands. The back of her throat hurt, her eyes stinging.

Before she had any more chance to think about it, she grabbed Elani's hand and stepped into her. And before Elani could protest, she gripped the back of her neck and kissed her.

But Elani shoved her with her other hand, breaking the seal of their lips before Lexa could get a chance to enjoy it. "No, Lexa. You don't understand. I can't."

"Why not?"

"I—"

The doors whooshed open and Jake stopped halfway through, a small bag full of plastic pellets in his hand. "Uh. Sorry. Should I come back?"

Stomach in free-fall, Lexa backed away from Elani and shook her head. Why on Earth was she even still in the same room with these people? A solitary corner was suddenly the only thing she wanted. Probably forever. What was happening?

Jake poured litter in the box and glanced up at them. "You guys hungry? They're serving lunch."

Before Lexa could speak, Elani stepped into the hallway. "That's a wonderful idea."

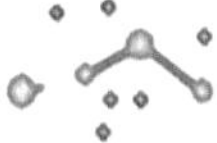

The dining hall filled with people. Each table was laid with gold flatware, the crystal and brass centerpieces almost too big to see over. The server complement was at least as big as the passenger manifest. People who hired a ship like this liked things to be comfortable. Like a Gexcorian chair, they wanted everything around them to cradle them, hold them in a comfortable position, and then be spoon-fed by a platoon of attractive, thin people.

Probably about twenty passengers, both human and not, filed in and took seats around the room.

Lexa sat with Elani and Jake, across the table from them both, arms wrapped around herself and legs crossed. The chilly room surrounded them all with the cold breath of separation.

Separation. Elani said it was an illusion. What did that even mean?

The last of the passengers filtered in, and even though a centerpiece sat between Lexa and the door, the sound she heard traveled down her spine like goose feet.

Teeth clenched, she stared across the room, her eyes so wide they dried out.

"Junie, if they run out of vegetarian offerings, I will not stay on this ship."

"Mom, everything is vegetarian now."

"That's not true, it's—"

"Paisley, please. Your blood pressure."

Lexa spoke out the side of her mouth, teeth pressed together so hard they squealed. "Jake. What did you do?"

"Sorry, what about?" He leaned on the table, eyebrows raised, and lifted his lips in half a nervous smile.

"This ship. You—"

Elani slid into the chair next to her and laid a hand on her arm. "I'm not doing this on purpose, Lexa, but there's too much anger coming off you to avoid it."

She stood so fast, the chair fell over. "I should fucking hope so!"

Everyone in the room stopped. Even the crew. Every eye in the room landed on her.

She lowered her voice. "Shit." Looking down at Elani and Jake, their wide eyes fixed to her, she whispered. "They're all staring at me, aren't they?" But she didn't wait for their answer.

She couldn't have, anyway.

Mom leapt to her feet. "Allie! What are you doing here? Come to join us on our family vacation?" She crossed the room in bounds, Juniper trailing her like a satellite. Reid towered over everyone at the table where he still sat, his mouth hanging open.

Before they reached her, Lexa sat so hard she bit her tongue. Her mouth filled with the metallic taste of blood and she ground her teeth together, arms folded over her breast.

"My little baby, I'm so happy you're here!" Mom grabbed her shoulder and wrenched her back to standing, then threw her arms around her. "I can actually hug you this time, since you're not so sweaty and stinky." She chuckled, rubbing Lexa's back. "What made you decide to come?"

Puking in her own mouth might be preferable to speaking to her mother. And now she was stuck on a ship with her until when? At least Birkishni. Hell.

Jake popped up beside them. "You're Lexa's mother? Hi, my name is Jacoby Harris. I'm a friend of your daughter." He stuck out a hand and grinned wide, all his teeth showing through his warm smile.

Paisley shook with him. "My Allie has friends?"

Lexa spoke through her teeth, blood rushing to her face. "Lexa."

One of the crew approached the table. Another picked up Lexa's chair and slid it toward her. "Shall we set more places for your table, Mr. Harris? Is your party being joined?"

Juniper took Jake's other hand without asking and pumped it up and down. "Any friend of Lexa's is a friend of ours. Especially one as handsome as you." She kissed the back of his hand and sat at the table.

Finally, Reid got up from where they had all been about to sit and weaved through the tables. He flushed. "Lexa. Didn't expect to see you again. At all." He bowed at the waist. "And you have guests?" He nodded to Elani with a smile and shot Jake eyes that could have killed a normal man.

Yet Jake was anything but, especially now. He smiled at Paisley and Juniper, bowed to Reid, and extricated his hands from Lexa's pushy relatives. He laid the fingers of one hand in the small of Lexa's back. Not hard, just enough to let her know they were there.

The support almost weakened Lexa's knees. The only feeling she knew when she saw her mother was anger. A tight stomach, clenched teeth, and a frown that could leave cramps in her cheeks. She hadn't had anyone between herself and Paisley since Gram told her if she was going to leave, to not come back.

Lexa was seven at the time.

And Paisley had left. Again.

Lexa gripped Jake's arm.

He smiled at the crew. "One moment, please. Paisley? Is your last name Dean, as well?"

She shook her head, sitting next to June and picking up a long-stemmed glass that one of the crew promptly filled with something clear and bubbly. "That was my mother's maiden name. I'm Paisley Parker." Lips pursed, she sipped from the glass.

Jake laughed, a good-natured light thing that broke the tension with the rest of the diners.

They all went back to their food.

"Alliterative," he said, smiling. "I think it would be lovely to have your company for lunch. Lexa and Elani, however"—he glanced at Elani and gave Lexa the smallest of pushes in her back—"need to run back to our room. We had a long journey getting out to Port de Playa and they're still tired."

Elani popped up and took Lexa's hand. "If you'll excuse us." She tugged.

Stomach hollow, Lexa let her pull her away from the table. The anger and shock had begun to wear into something else. Something she hadn't felt in so long she couldn't place it. But it warmed the hole in her center and she loosened her teeth, centering herself on the feel of Elani's fingers laced between hers.

She glanced over her shoulder one last time before the doors slid closed, and saw June had seated herself next to Jake. And was currently hanging on his every word and giggling. Reid's piercing blue eyes followed she and Elani as they left the room, only breaking contact with hers because the door slid closed between them.

Sagging, she gripped Elani and let out a quiet sob. "Where's the nearest airlock?"

"Why?" Elani tugged her hand and started the walk to their berth.

"Because I'm gonna throw myself out of it. Take care of Savannah for me."

Elani chuckled. "Let's get back to the room. I'll help you calm your energy."

Lexa stopped and looked in her swirling golden eyes. "You can do that?"

She shrugged. "Yeah. It's tricky and about the extent of my abilities manipulating energy. But I'd be happy to do it for you." Sweeping her hands in front of Lexa's face without touching her skin, she hummed. Maybe a song, but it was too light for Lexa to make out. She continued over Lexa's shoulders, never touching the skin, but holding out her hands, palms facing Lexa, and sweeping them down her arms. Her brow furrowed in concentration.

That feeling warming Lexa's center crawled outward. Still struggling to put a name to it, she closed her eyes and swayed to the sound of Elani's humming. "That's lovely. Can all Ambrans do that?"

"I thought you studied."

"Your people are secretive about this stuff. I told you that." And though she meant it to come out harsh, it flowed out of her lips without barbs, without the tang of anger. Her teeth stopped hurting.

Elani grabbed her hand again. "Come on. Let's get back to the room."

Jake came through the doors holding two trays with metal domes over them. "The crew is so nice."

Lexa laid with her back on the bed and her feet hanging off the side, Elani lying beside her. She watched him through slitted eyes as he balanced the trays on his arms.

He sat them on the table in the window and removed the domes. Steam billowed out and beneath it were plates full of fragrant food. "They were only too happy to send me with a doggy bag for you guys. We can eat the rest of our meals in here if you want, Lexa."

She sighed. "While that sounds nice, you don't know my mother." She sat up on her elbows. That warm feeling still encompassed her center and now that Jake was back in the room, it seemed to expand. Had Elani done something to her mind as well as her energy? Regardless, she went on. "If I ignore her, it's just going to get worse. She'll find this room eventually and ring the doorbell until I lose it. No," she said, lying back on the bed again and swinging her feet, "I have to talk to her. At least once or twice."

Jake sat on the bed next to her. "That was so wild, right? Of all the ships in the galaxy to pick, I pick the one with your mom and sister on it!" He laid back too, and the three of them stared at the ceiling together.

Lexa considered the reflection of the three of them. She found something about being surrounded by them oddly comforting. "Thanks for helping me out. I don't know why I couldn't… Anyway, thank you."

Jake turned to face her. His large brown eyes sparkled. "Of course."

Elani laughed. "He's nothing if not good with people." She stood and held a hand out. "Let's eat some of this food."

Lexa took it and joined her at the table. Her mouth watered at the scents coming from the plates. The spread Jake brought was impressive even for luxury cruise standards. Tucking in, she realized she hadn't eaten since before they landed at Port de Playa. And she hadn't eaten like this in years.

They ate in silence, Lexa facing the window. She let them think she was staring out it but what she was really doing was watching them in the reflection. The way they spoke without speaking. The way Jake would point out something for Elani to try, and she'd take the smallest nibble at it, a smile spreading across her face as she chewed.

"How long have you been on Earth, Elani?"

Elani chewed a single chocolate chip and half-closed her eyes. "Six years, I think. In Earth time."

"Long enough to start using Earth time," Jake said, pointing to a piece of pie sitting all by itself. He spooned some whipped cream onto it and pushed it toward her. "We don't get paid the greatest, so I haven't been able to show a lot of this kind of food to her."

Lexa pointed her fork between them, not missing the way Savannah, from her perch in the windowsill, followed it with her eyes. "Are you *sure* you two aren't—"

The doorbell rang. A soft and unobtrusive chirp, it let them know someone was outside the door in the politest way possible.

Eyes rolling, Lexa threw her napkin to her plate. "Oh, good. It's starting sooner than I expected."

Jake half-stood. "Let me get it."

She held up her hand, palm out. "No. I'm better now. I just have to deal with it until we find a way out of here. Sit. Eat."

Jake sat and ate.

On her way to the door, Lexa planned the next few sentences, and how her mother would respond. It was always easier with her if she worked out the conversation beforehand. It's why she'd been so flustered in the dining hall—no prep.

The door slid open.

Reid smiled, his electric blue eyes wide.

Lexa looked around him. No, he was alone.

She contained the eye roll. "Hey there, Reid. How are you?"

From the table, Jake spoke around some food. "Oh hey I meant to tell you, this is the tour guide I spoke to, I told you about earlier."

Smile pasted to her mouth, Lexa glanced at Jake and back to Reid. Her stomach clenched. She hadn't had time to plan this conversation yet, even though she should have seen it coming. "I didn't know," she said, eyes somewhere near Reid's belly-button.

"Neither did I," he said, taking a step into the doorway. "Did you follow us here?"

Lexa stepped back. "What? No. Pure coincidence."

One side of Reid's mouth turned up. He matched her step backward and leaned down. Voice lowered, he whispered near her ear. "It's OK if you did." He leaned back and took her in with his eyes. "It's good to see you again."

Jake called from the table. "Why don't you invite him in for some dessert?"

She wasn't sure, but Lexa figured her face hadn't turned this red since the last time she was actually on Proxima Centauri B, where the light itself was red. "Come in, Reid. I do have a couple questions for you." She walked back to the table on stilts. She'd started to maybe get used to Elani and Jake, they were at least personable, but to have someone in her personal space who she clearly had never expected to welcome back to it was…uncomfortable to say the least. It rubbed her the wrong way, like a polyester and wool blend sweater.

But she couldn't sit here with her teeth clenched the whole time, so she shoved a piece of Elani's pie into her mouth and tried to smile around the too-large bite. When she swallowed a bit of it and felt she could speak without spewing whipped cream everywhere, she spoke around the mouthful. "Do you get any news channels on this ship?"

Elani scooted over next to Jake and let Reid sit next to Lexa.

He smiled and shook his head, surveying what was left of the food Jake had brought. He picked up a shortbread cookie and took a bite. "This cruise is for relaxation, not for news. The Litmus Agency is focused on the comfort of our guests and I'm afraid the news is a proven stressor. We don't allow stressors on our tours. We don't allow phones, either."

"Do you receive notices from Earth regarding, I don't know. Important happenings?"

"Why? Did something happen?"

"No." She sipped her coffee. It'd been warm when Jake delivered it, but it was inching past lukewarm and closer to cold, now. "I just wondered what would happen if I needed to know something or check in. Just, in general." She shrugged, her stomach doing back-flips, and tried to swallow down the nervous jitter in her voice. If they didn't get the news, not even as alerts, they wouldn't know about her ship and the price Jenierien had put on her head because of the Cynosure. So that was a plus.

She tried to relax.

But Jake and Elani had stopped murmuring between themselves and just ate, watching Lexa and Reid in turn. And Savannah had run off somewhere, probably under the bed.

Lexa tried to eat more but it was difficult to chew, and none of it wanted to go down her tight throat. Her shoulders started to ache. She released them, lowered them from where they'd been creeping up next to her ears.

"Well," Reid said, standing. Which took forever, heavens, he was tall. "I should go. It's been good to meet you, Elani, and Jake. And Lexa"—he took one her hands and kissed the back of it— "it's absolutely delightful to have you on this star cruise with us. I'm sure it's some much needed time off from your important work." He bowed at the waist. "If you'll excuse me."

Stunned into silence for a moment, Lexa almost missed her opportunity. But before he left, she jumped up and joined him as the door slid open. "Can I speak to you for a second?"

He smiled, wider than he had since he'd walked into the dining hall with Paisley and Juniper, and motioned to the hall.

Lexa let the door to the berth close before she faced him.

He put one arm around her waist. "Come to my room. It's private."

She leaned back. "Maybe I will, after my friends are asleep." Extending a finger, she ran it up his chest. "Do you know exactly where we're landing on Birkishni?"

Leaning further into her, his lips brushing her extended neck, he nodded. "I can find out. Why?"

With one hand, she grasped his arm and unwrapped it from her waist. With the other, she pushed his chest. "Find out, and I'll tell you later."

She winked and disappeared back through the door, back to Jake and Elani, before he had a chance to respond.

CHAPTER 12

Jake snored softly, shifting in his sleep, his bare leg warm against Lexa's. Elani matched his shift on her other side, sighing, hair covering her face when she rolled over. Lexa hadn't planned on all of them piling into the same bed, but there was only one in this room and it hadn't really been a conscious thing. After dinner they'd changed into some extraordinarily revealing pajamas—Jake had picked them up from the ship's store but claimed they were all he could find—and fallen into bed together. Savannah had even joined the warm pile, curled into a ball between Lexa and Elani.

Much as she hated to, Lexa folded the covers down with a soft rustle and climbed out from under them. The only one who shifted was Van, but just long enough to crack one annoyed eye and cover her nose with the tip of her tail.

Lexa made a kissy-noise at her and crawled from between her itinerant companions. Maybe they'd be gone soon. Maybe they wouldn't. Before slipping away, she covered them back up so they wouldn't get cold and wake, wondering where she was. She considered getting redressed, but these revealing pajamas were, unfortunately, perfect for where she was going. And though the ship's air was a little nippy, right around 20 degrees Celsius, she didn't think she'd freeze to death if she walked around in these short shorts and tank. On the way out the door, she glanced at her shoes, but decided she'd be quieter barefoot.

She padded down the darkened hallways, the ship seeming to rock its passengers to sleep in the night. Or maybe that was just her tired body. Goldilocks planets didn't have the same rotational intervals, meaning longer days and nights than Earth, so the clocks were set to run on 39 hour days. Something close to average for everyone.

When she came to the door she was looking for, she held her hand up to the bell and hesitated. How entirely necessary was this? She could just find her way to a good site once they landed, as long as it wasn't too far away.

Fuck it. She rang the bell.

Reid's tired, puffy eyes lit up when the door slid open.

Arms crossed, hands cupping the cold skin above her elbows, Lexa looked past him and dropped her voice to a whisper. "Are you alone?"

He stepped back and motioned for her to come in. "You caught me at a good time. You here for that landing info?"

"You look like you were asleep." The door slid closed behind her. She glanced around the room. A small suite, it had a couple things their single room didn't. Its own fabricator station, for one. For another, a large screen where she could access not only the news—maybe her face hadn't been broadcast across the *whole* galaxy yet—but also a phone. Employee perks, probably.

He slid his hand up her back.

That was one way to get what she wanted. Human men were pretty agreeable to anything—up to and including murder—right after getting laid. Or she could just tire him out and wait till he fell asleep before hopping on the transmission waves and seeing what was what out there. News from the Gexcorian search for her, from Jenierien, from Earth, had taken up a large part of her brain since leaving Earth.

She faced him, smiling. She hadn't planned on sharing space with him again. But whatever.

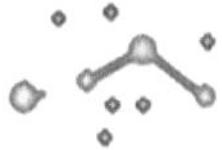

She lost count of the number of times she almost accidentally fell asleep while waiting for Reid to hit REM. Every time her eyes tried to close, she reminded herself she had a warm cuddle to get back to, including her cat, and forced them open. The cool air of the ship dried them out, and when she sat up and glanced at Reid, watching his eyes roll behind his lids, the lids themselves cracked just enough to show white, she could barely blink.

She crept across the room. The silent door between the bedroom and the living area slid closed, locking off Reid's light snoring. She pressed up against the door and listened, waiting to see if she'd wakened him with her movement. But his snoring went on, uninterrupted.

She clicked on the tube and surfed through the frequencies until she found the news.

Nothing about her. She curled up on a small couch that wasn't as comfortable as it was pretty, and watched until her eyes slipped closed again.

Jerking up, she flipped the channel. The display asked for a phone number.

Hm. Who could she call? Who *should* she call?

Oh, right.

She dialed the number and hit send.

. . .

The screen asked for a passkey. Damn. She didn't know Reid well enough for that and hoped she never would. But after the run-in with the cops in Port de Playa, she needed to know if the Gexcorians were still after her and just what the hell was going on. Standing to pace, she turned the remote for the TV over and over in her hand, running her finger along the uneven edge on the back.

The uneven edge which was a different texture than the rest of it.

She glanced down.

Taped the back of the remote were five numbers. 28144.

A smile crossed her lips. She bit her lip and typed in the numbers.

The screen beeped and dialed.

Chuckling, she dragged a chair in front of the screen and turned the volume down. The last thing she needed was Reid waking to find her using the off-limits "stressors."

The line picked up. "*Lexa. What time is it where you are?*"

"Hey Whiskers. Don't worry about that. Listen—"

He pressed his face against the screen. Which, on her side, gave her a twenty-centimeter closeup of his pink nose. "*What the hell happened?*"

Shit. She crossed her arms, goosebumps racing up them, and fought to keep her tone even. "What do you mean?"

"*The Gexcorians broke a century-long treaty with Earth and attacked your ship. They, and Lady Jenierien of Proxima New York, are offering a reward for information.*"

She shrugged, her stomach in her toes. "Is there more? What's going on? Have the Gexcorians released a statement?"

Backing away from the screen, he shuffled papers out of sight. They brushed against each other like a pile of autumn leaves rustling. "*Yes. What did you steal from them?*"

"Nothing."

"*If that's true, we have some things to speak with them about. If not, I don't want to know. Does it have to do with the map? Do you know where you're going, did you work out how to read it?*"

With a quick glance at the door to the bedroom, she nodded. "I can't say much right now, Whiskers. But yes. I found the key to the map. I have a destination, but I'm not sure what I'll find there. It's—"

He raised a hand. "*Don't tell me. Call me when you find what the map is trying to take you to. Until then, I think it's best the less I know. I'll inform the GHR you are on schedule.*" Leaning in, he looked side to side.

Lexa leaned to match him.

Voice lowered, he whispered into the mic. "*You must hurry, Lexa. The humans and Gexcorians are not happy with each other. There is an ongoing inter-galactic incident and I'm not sure how long we can keep a lid on the fact that you're on GHR business. This is going to get messy. Can you return the item to Gexcor when you're done?*"

She envisioned Jenierien's twisted features, her curled brows. Qesson's red eyes as he floated through the wall to chase her. Ferrinogean, the Gexcorian bounty hunter, shattering the glass in her quarters with his scream. "How messy?"

"*At best, we might be able to keep you out of a Gexcorian prison. Since it's official business.*"

She shivered. Cold, wet, and full of eight-limbed hardened criminals. Delightful. They wouldn't need good-old fashioned shanks to tickle her with, they'd just use their hands. Especially considering the fact stealing the Cynosure hadn't been official business. That would be a planet full of people pissed at her, a new record if she wasn't mistaken.

Whiskers went on. "*At worst, Earth might see war.*"

She bit her lip so hard she drew blood, slick in her mouth and tasting metallic. "They're not prepared to fight a people like the Gexcorians. We could be decimated."

"*Exactly.*" He lowered his voice again. "*So, can you return it?*"

Lexa grimaced. "Sure."

"*Then that's all I want to know. Good luck, watch your ass, and hurry.*"

He clicked off.

CHAPTER 13

Passing the time proved more interesting—and infinitely more fun—than Lexa had assumed it would. Sightseeing across the stars, games where Lexa, Elani, and Jake meshed together as a perfect team and wiped the floor with all the other teams, fancy dinners, and now dancing, it almost seemed like a real vacation. And they'd avoided Paisley, Juniper, and Reid pretty successfully on the large ship.

Tonight, Lexa leaned on the deck railing and stared out at the stars. In one hand a champagne flute dangled. In the other, her shoes.

Jake leaned next to her, elbows on the railing, and faced the deck. "Some party."

"I didn't come here to party. I hate you for making me wear these shoes," she lied. The truth of it was, she'd had more fun on this cruise with them than she'd had in decades. Still, she considered pitching the heels off the rail. They'd just bounce off the clear dome and right back into her face, but the last time she'd worn shoes like this to a museum function, she'd about broken an ankle and had sworn off them. Plus the ankle she'd injured in her escape from the junkyard had only just gotten to feeling better. Not that Jake wanted to hear any of that as he shoved them at her earlier this evening.

"We've got to look nice for the party. Birkishni is still a few days away. If we hide in our quarters now, people will start to wonder. You said yourself, we have to go out there."

Dammit if Jake wasn't right, even if he threw her own words back at her in that persistently good-natured tone of his. Blending in was still the best way to keep a low profile. She pushed a breath out through her teeth and past her extended lower lip. Her bangs fluttered.

And Jake chuckled, his voice deep. "You don't hate me." One warm hand caressed her bare shoulder. "You look really nice with your hair down. It's longer than I thought it would be." He twirled a lock between his fingers.

Eyes on his face, she turned sideways and took a sip of the champagne. Maybe having a good time wasn't such a bad idea, after all. She'd enjoyed that kiss on Port de Playa, at least. The champagne bubbled in her nose and warmed her throat, while something else bubbled in her stomach.

Smiling, Elani glided off the dance floor. Whatever rando passenger she'd been dancing with didn't follow, and she spun a few circles on her way to Jake and Lexa. Eyes wide, she smiled and brushed her thick, wavy black hair out of her face. "It's been ages since I danced." Without a word, she plucked the glass from Lexa's hand and sipped. "Thirsty work, dancing." Her sweaty brow almost glowed, her cheeks round and flushed. She twirled to the rail and leaned on it.

They all faced the dance floor, Elani and Jake on either side of Lexa, and they must have cut quite the trio. Elani and Jake both cleaned up pretty well and Lexa thought, in this no-back glittery dress Jake picked specifically for her, she looked OK, even though the last time her pasty pale skin had seen ultra violet had been…

How long? A while, anyway. She should take advantage of the fact they had a cure for skin cancer more often. But there was always some tomb to crawl, some artifact the museum wanted, some money to be made while she was at it.

A smile crept onto her mouth. She handed the glass off to Jake and snagged Elani's hand. "Dance with me." She tugged, dropping the heels to the ground with a *clop*.

Elani followed after her, not a word of protest crossing her lips. In fact, she grinned and let her eyes flash, throwing her hair over her shoulder.

No sooner had they stepped onto the parquet dance floor together that the fast-paced tune turned slow. The lights dimmed with the slowing tempo, turning everything a soft purple. Lexa almost fled. But Elani tugged her hand and pulled her in, her arms resting on Lexa's exposed back. Hell, everything about this dress exposed Lexa's skin. Which, normally would be fine. Why did she shiver now?

They danced, slow, in large circles. Elani led, Lexa along for the ride. And she tried not to stare into Elani's eyes, glowing in the low light, their effervescent gold lighting her eyelashes, turning them gold, too. She wanted to try and kiss her again, did she ever, but Elani had not reacted well to that last time and they were stuck together for now. Lexa cast around for conversation.

Elani beat her to it. "Why is it such a bad thing your family is here?"

Lexa sighed and looked around the room. Paisley danced with Reid, her arms tight around his waist, her head laid on his chest. Not for the first time, Lexa wondered if "tour guide" were the only words in his job description. She clenched her teeth.

"Whoa," Elani said, slowing and stepping back. "Every muscle tensed just then. And, not that I'm spying, but your energy took a hell of a hit. What's going on?"

"Besides me not wanting to talk about it, nothing." She pushed back and started to walk away, the high of being so close to Elani waning fast.

The music livened again and Jake leapt onto the dance floor. He grabbed Lexa's hand in one hand and Elani's in the other.

"Come on, we should all dance!" He lifted his arms and walked them back onto the dance floor.

Much as Lexa wanted to resist, the upbeat music made it hard. That, and Jake's usual enthusiasm, only turned up to eleven. His cheeks shone as he smiled, bright blue and yellow lights shining down on them. Elani smiled too, from ear to ear. Her usual serious demeanor the perfect counterpoint to Jake, she now drew Lexa into that boundless enthusiasm with her own.

Jake spun them both away from him and stepped across to dance with Elani, their feet moving in a complicated little rhythm together, kicking out in time to the strong beat. Something that resembled music from Earth's 1930's, if Lexa wasn't mistaken. They bounced up and down and Jake twirled Elani around himself, then released her to spin off on her own.

Which was when he stepped to Lexa and held out his hand.

In the moment, her heart already racing, she didn't even consider not taking it. She just did.

With surprising but gentle strength, he gripped her and they spun around the dance floor, his hand firm in the bare small of her back.

Breathless, she took a moment to lean into his ear. She raised her voice over the hopping music. "I don't know what I'm doing!"

He smiled back, all his teeth showing, and glanced at Elani. "Just trust us." He released her and she spun to Elani, noticing as she did they'd cleared their own little swath on the dance floor.

Elani caught her and stepped in front of her, both of them facing Jake. She linked the fingers of her left hand through Lexa's left, extended her arm, and positioned herself on Lexa's right side, Lexa's right arm draped over her shoulder. "Follow me," she said. When she stepped in time, Lexa did too, and they shuffled to Jake.

He drew them both against his body and swung the three of them in a circle together, and a laugh bubbled up and out of Lexa's throat before she knew it was happening. Smile wide, she backed up when he let her go and watched him physically lift Elani from the dance floor, swinging her legs around his waist and popping her back on her feet. Lexa applauded with the rest of the people crowded around the edges of the dance floor, and laughed as Jake and Elani danced circles around each other, their feet swinging with abandon.

But then he approached Lexa again, hand outstretched, and she faltered. "I can't do that!" She pointed at the center of the floor, where he'd picked Elani up.

He just smiled and tugged, his other arm stretched toward Elani. She joined them and met Lexa's eyes. "Trust us." It was hardly above a whisper, but Lexa felt it in her bones with a tingling loss of inhibition.

The music pumped along, coming to a crescendo, and when they reached the center of the dance floor, Jake's strong arms lifted Lexa as he'd done Elani. Lexa tucked her feet together like she'd seen Elani do and her loose body followed Jake's movements when he swung her around his waist. But instead of putting her back on her feet when she got back around, Elani grabbed Lexa's ankles and for one heart-stopping moment, Lexa fell, weightless. Her heart flew up into her mouth, her stomach right behind it, and Jake dropped to his knees, Elani doing the same. Lexa landed in Jake's arms, Elani still gripping her legs, and when they finished their controlled fall, Jake threw both arms out and raised them to the ceiling, wide grin stretching his face to its limit, chest heaving.

As the crowd applauded, long and loud, Jake, Elani, and Lexa laughed.

Lexa's whole body buzzed, her lungs pulling in deep breaths, and she laughed until her stomach hurt.

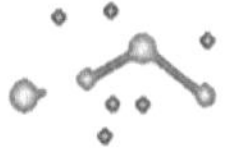

A day out of Birkishni, Lexa led the two of them down a long hallway in the below decks. She stretched her legs and charged down the hall, Elani and Jake following like orbiting satellites. She searched for the door to the launch bay, some notes she'd scribbled on the ship's stationary clutched in one sweating hand.

Jake caught up to her. "Are we going to get in trouble for doing this?" His eyes wide, he glanced around the hallway as though it were full of people and not dead-of-night quiet.

"Not if we don't get caught." She turned left down another hall and continued. They were close.

"And if we do?" Elani flanked her.

"Clearly we got lost on the way to the pool."

"A swimming pool under the stars?" Jake asked, breathless. "How did we miss that? I've always wanted to—"

"We're out of time. We're almost at Birkishni and we've got to continue avoiding Jenierien and those damned Gexcorians who blew up my ship and maybe, just maybe, find what's at the end of this map." She tapped Savannah's bag where it hung on her hip, Van, the map, and the Cynosure all crammed inside.

"Can I see the map?"

She snatched the satchel away from Jake's questing fingers. "You absolutely cannot. I already told Elani. No one touches this map but me."

"Why?"

Pushing a hot breath out her nose, nostrils flared, Lexa stopped in front of a door. This voyage had been fun, but it was time to put her game face back on. "This is the door."

Elani moved to push the access button.

Lexa caught her hand. "No. Not that way." But she didn't let her hand go.

"What do you mean? This is the door, right?"

Tugging Elani's hand, Lexa stuffed the paper in her pocket and grabbed Jake's. She pulled them down the hall and around the corner. "If we go through that door, someone will see. The panel will store our info and it'll be no problem to find out we were in the launch bay. Especially once one of their skimmers goes missing. They'll figure it out eventually once they check the passenger manifest, but why make it easier?"

Elani raised her brows, forehead creased. "What do you suggest?

"Here." Lexa dropped their hands and tugged at a panel near their knees. It came away from the wall, revealing a tunnel. "This way." She crawled in and stopped far enough in to let them creep into the tunnel after her. "Shut the panel, Jake," she said, watching as he slid in last. "This is the avionics access network. It goes everywhere on the ship. Should be just a couple junctions till we reach the launch bay." Once Jake shut the hall lights out, she crawled away.

Their scuffling hands and feet let her know they followed. It was close in the tunnel, and only had two strings of green LED work lights lining it, so when Lexa fell over a conduit crossing the tunnel and smacked her face on the floor, she wasn't surprised. In pain, her front teeth feeling like they had almost gotten knocked out and her tongue bitten, again, but surprised? No. What did surprise her was she'd forgotten her sub-dermal lights.

She stopped and rubbed her face. "Dammit." Her tongue throbbed, saliva rushing to fill her mouth. She swallowed.

"Let me lead," Elani said, crawling close. She sat beside Lexa, squeezed between her and the wall, her *"let me take care of you"* aura taking some of the sting out of Lexa's mouth. "I can see better in the dark than you."

Lexa wiped her lips and rubbed her fingertips together, checking for blood. Her lower lip stung. "Like, see see? Or see energy?"

"Does it matter?"

She considered. "Not really." Rather than turn up her lights, she let Elani do the leading and pressed her palm to her lip, hopping on one hand as they crawled.

Jake wiggled up beside her. "Need a hand?"

"No, I'm—"

It quickly became apparent he hadn't really cared what her answer was.

He slipped beneath the arm not on the ground and helped her balance. The two of them side by side was a tight fit, but Elani warned them about conduit as she came to it, either on the floor or ceiling, and they made it to the launch bay without incident. And Jake was warm, which was nice in the chilly tunnels.

Elani stopped before pushing the panel out at the launch bay and put her hand on it.

Lexa released Jake and inched up next to her. "What are you doing?"

"Checking the room."

"Oh. Is that—"

"Stop speaking. I have to concentrate."

Lexa's mouth snapped shut. She sat and stared at the woman in front of her, her brow drawn. Elani's sharp tone set her sideways, but she couldn't figure out if she was mad or not.

It didn't feel like mad but it didn't…not.

Still mulling the feeling, she followed in silence when Elani gave the go-ahead and slid out of the tunnel.

The launch bay, a cavernous room, housed four silver and black skimmers. They all shone like they had never been used, not a single dent or ding in their metal skin.

"I got the coordinates of the beach we're landing on. We're going to need to take one of these down the beach a few clicks, which should get us out of sight of the tourists." She walked around the craft and honed in on the fourth, which was clearly bigger than the other three. "I think this one has a berth. If we're going to steal it when we're done, I'd like it to have a bed in it." She punched a button near the docking door. "Let's check it out."

Jake let out a squeak. "What if we get caught?"

Lexa stopped, halfway into the craft, at least mildly surprised that was his question, and not how she got the coordinates. "You honestly think Jenierien or the Gexcorians aren't going to eventually track us to this ship? You did well, not giving my name, but come on. It's not like we were exactly sneaky. And their flight plan is filed and set with Light Speed Control."

The inside of the skimmer smelled like a new car. Fresh leather, shining faux-tile floor, perfectly polished walls. She could almost see herself in them.

She unsnapped the bag and let Van out. "Go find a cozy corner, girl." She shooed the cat.

Savannah stuck her tail straight in the air and walked into the shadows.

"Jake, go check and see if there's a berth. Elani, help me find spare fuel." She headed back to the door.

Elani grabbed her arm. "I don't know about this. Jake's right. If we get caught, it could be bad for us. Our jobs are probably gone already but getting caught stealing could ruin our chance at new employment."

Lexa bit her lip. She'd resigned herself to them sticking around. But that didn't mean they wouldn't, and shouldn't, leave her the first chance they got. So she gave it to them. "Listen, you don't have to do this with me. I've already paid for this tour. Why don't you two stay on the cruise, and I'll just slip away. Enjoy yourselves. Who knows when you'll get another opportunity like this? And then go back to your jobs." She smiled, her lip stinging again. She licked it and smiled wider, doing everything she could to mean what she had just let fall out of her mouth.

Biting her own lip, Elani eyed her. "Maybe. Maybe that's best."

"Sure." Lexa bent to go out the door.

"Maybe it isn't. Lexa, are you sure?"

She stood back up, narrowly missing hitting her head on the hatch door. Gripping Elani's hand, she turned back to her and stared in her eyes. And did her best to lie her ass off without getting caught by this walking lie-detector. "Yes. You're right. I can't endanger your whole livelihood. It was weird having you help, anyway, much as I appreciate it."

The pull tugged her again. That feeling she got when she stared into Elani's swirling eyes. Like they were pools of molten gold she could slip into and never resurface. Melt away her life and her ego and every bit of desire for anything but her. For a fleeting moment, she wanted to take back the last two minutes of conversation.

Instead, she stepped through the door and back into the bay. "Let's load up some spare fuel."

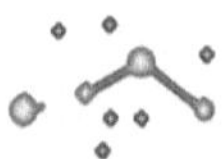

"Attention honored guests, we have landed at Birkishni Beach. Please let us invite you to swim in the ocean or stargaze from the black sand of Birkishni. Do let us know what we can do to make your evening more comfortable."

Lexa lie on her back, staring at the shining ceiling again. Jake and Elani bustled, getting ready for the beach.

"Thanks for getting the suits, Lexa," Jake said.

She sat up on her elbows. Only his shadow visible on the other side of the room divider, he changed clothes. "If you're going to stay and do the tourist thing, the least I could do was make sure you could really do it." The side of her mouth turned down, watching the way his biceps tightened and stretched when he slid the shirt over his head. Even his leg muscles stood out in the shadow and Lexa had to take a moment to wonder if they set the thing up with backlighting on purpose for this exact reason.

He poked his head around, his hair tousled. "Sure you won't stay with us?"

"She's got to go, Jake." Elani walked out of the bathroom, her deep blue swimsuit visible under the shifting, iridescent fabric of the translucent sari she'd tied over it. The skin of her abdomen peeked out, a lighter brown than her face and arms.

Lexa wondered what that skin might feel like. How soft, how warm. Her cheeks prickled with heat as she considered it.

Head shaking, she slid off the bed and looped Savannah's bag over her shoulder. "Listen. Thank you two for, uh—" she faltered, the pair of them watching her with open expressions. When she made eye-contact with Elani, Elani pinched her lips together. The sliver of skin disappeared beneath her crossed arms and Lexa picked up where she'd left off. "For being a huge pain in the ass and not leaving me a moment's peace. Enjoy your trip."

Before she could march to the door and leave them with that, Jake grabbed her in a hug. His arms around her, warm as he'd been in the avionics tube, enclosed her in a feeling she hadn't succumbed to in so long she couldn't remember the number of years. All she knew was the last time she felt it, Gram was alive and smiling.

Her gut rolled. She hugged him back and closed her eyes.

When he let her go, she staggered a step and glanced at Elani.

Rather than attack her with another hug, Elani took one of her hands and cupped the back of her head with the other. "You're a singular person, Lexa Dean, and I'm grateful we crossed paths." She held her eyes.

The nervous butterflies that'd taken wing in Lexa's stomach stopped flitting, and she swallowed, a sense of calm laying over her like a sheen. "You doing this?"

Elani smiled. "I'm not trying to. But I guess I am." She squeezed her hand and dropped it. "We better get down there before they come looking for us."

Jake picked up their towels. "Black beaches? I've only ever seen that in Hawaii and Iceland."

They walked out of the room and fell in behind some other passengers, chatting about the black sand on Earth and why it was a different kind of sand here on Birkishni. Truth be told, Lexa didn't know as much about this planet as she pretended. No active archaeological sites equaled about a week's worth of study sixty years ago. No reason for more.

On cue, as they passed the open launch bay doors, Jake pointed a finger. "Lexa! Is that your cat?"

Lexa jumped and spun, watching the bay as though Van had just run in. "Oh shit, there she goes. I'll catch up to you!" She dashed into the bay and the rest of the passengers gave her a wide berth as they walked out the lowered bay door onto the sand. Lexa called for Van, circling the bay. The large skimmer was still there, and two of the others. The fourth was missing; someone must have taken it out. Lexa approached one of the smaller ones. "Van? Vanny-fanny?" She knelt and looked under it.

Feet stopped on the other side. "Need some help?"

"No thanks, just trying to catch my cat before she runs out on the beach." She chuckled, standing. "She's not a fan of water."

"I'd be only too happy to help," Reid said, rounding the side. He stopped and leaned on the skimmer. "You spent one night with me on this voyage. I thought you were going to come back?" One finger extended, he ran it down her arm. "Is it that guy you're with?"

She stammered. "I uh— No. It's…"

It's that I spent every moment of this trip with people I don't need to be as attached to as I am.

Backing up, she called Van again. "Savannah?"

The cat meowed from inside the large skimmer where Lexa had left her.

Reid approached it. "How did she get in there?"

In two large steps, Lexa flew across the bay and ran into the small ship. It rocked. "Wait. Let me. She doesn't like other people. She might run, and then I really will lose her." Which was all true, and the sweat popped under her arms as she covered the door panel with her hand.

"Are you sure?" He glanced around and leaned toward her, voice lowered. "There's a berth in there. It's pretty private, if you wanted to—"

"Reid! There you are. Junie and I were looking all over for you."

Lexa had never in her life been happy to hear her mom's voice. There was indeed a first time for everything, just like they said. She pushed Reid's shoulder. "Go, Mom needs you. Me and Savannah will be fine." And before he had time to argue, she punched the door button and let herself into the ship. The last thing she saw before the door closed was Paisley, sliding one arm around Reid's waist with startling familiarity.

Lexa was quite sure she didn't want to follow that thought to its conclusion.

She shuddered.

Savannah approached, yawning, and meowed again.

Scratching her behind the ears, Lexa sat the bag down and grabbed a handful of food from the pocket. She scattered it on the floor. "Not exactly what we're used to, but I think it'll do for now. When we get home, we shouldn't have to worry about any of this anymore."

She raised her voice an octave. "I don't care, Ma, as long as I'm with you."

"Nice of you to say, Van."

Her eyes stung. What the hell? Why?

She wiped them and shuffled to the cockpit, which was little more than two seats, two yolks, and a simple panel to fly with. The extra fuel would get her to the nearest port, where she should be able to pick up some money and a better ship. And go wherever it was the map was about to tell her she needed to go.

The ship powered up with a whine and the mooring skids released the bay floor.

She backed it out and pointed it down the beach.

CHAPTER 14

exa gave it about ten clicks before using the skimmer's land-assist feature and setting down on black sand between night-darkened rocks. The ghostly computer-generated image of the beach below her was a lot more accurate than the equipment they had in the twentieth century. Hell, it was more accurate than the instruments on her blown-up ship.

The skids settled into the sand, and she shut down the craft. "In or out, Savannah?"

Van ran to the door.

"OK, but don't get lost. We're looking at the map and getting out of here before they realize we're gone."

Van chirped. She bolted out the door as soon as Lexa opened it.

Lexa stepped out and her foot sank about 15 centimeters into the sand. More sand. Super.

No wonder Van liked it, though. It was like the biggest litter box ever created.

Chuckling, Lexa walked down the beach to where it was packed by the shifting, slightly glowing water. Leaving Jake and Elani was…weirder than she wanted it to be…but standing alone on this beach, staring up at the Pleiades as she'd never seen them, she tried to capture a sense of correctness, a sense that everything was as it should be.

Did she get there? Not really. But she was close enough to get on with it.

The map settled to the beach much the same way Lexa's feet did, a few tendrils of sand falling over the sides and snaking down the face of it. Almost as if it was cozying into a comfortable bed.

Jealous, Lexa slid her shoes off and dug her toes into the sand. Now this, this was different from Earth sand. A similar feeling, sure, with the microscopic granules slipping between her toes, but it didn't stick to her skin the way Earth sand did. It slid right off as though she were made of glass.

The serene sea shimmered, the blue glow of the water coming from the seven sister stars hanging in the night sky above it. They had to be within two lights years at most, and took up so much of the sky they were almost like six suns.

Six. That was odd. Where was the seventh?

Chewing her lip, she slid the Cynosure out of the bag and lowered it to the map once again. The map did the same thing as before, rising up to meet the glass teardrop like they were two lovers, aching to come together after a long absence. It yearned and stretched for the Cynosure, almost vibrating in its desire to touch it, and when she lowered the Cynosure far enough and they came together, the glass warmed in her hand and shone, as though it were lit from inside.

She lowered it to the ground and stepped back, staring at it with a smile she was barely aware of. She licked her lips and tasted sea salt.

The sand rippled under the map, undulating like water, and the light exploded from the Cynosure, reaching up into the sky and bathing the entire beach in blue light.

The light striking her eyes as painful as bright noon on unprotected pupils, Lexa covered them and stepped back again. From between her fingers, she followed the light as it stretched and expanded to lay over the stars in the sky.

Backing up, Lexa stumbled over a rock. She fell, her ass hitting the sand with a sigh. Leaning on her elbows, she stared up at the scene before her.

The seven sisters floated in the sky, overlaid on top of the blue stars pinned to the black cloth of the night. The seventh star flickered, the one named Electra reaching for her sisters even as she fell away from them. She screamed, as she had when Lexa watched this scene unfold on the ship, but this time, Lexa's mouth was too dry to scream with her. Her throat locked, all the breath gone from her lungs. She'd never seen a map like this. As though it were a living, breathing thing.

The seventh star shone brighter, brighter, brighter still, till Lexa had to cover her eyes again. Electra almost reached the outstretched fingers of her sisters, all of them straining together to help her. Her teeth gritted, eyes closed, she reached for them with every breath she had.

It wasn't enough.

The star didn't wink out this time like it had from Earth all those millennia ago when the myth was created. It didn't wink out. It fell, a flaming ball of exploding star, screaming directly at Lexa's face.

She shouted, covering her eyes again and curling into a ball in an attempt to protect all the important bits. Teeth clenched, stomach one hard knot, she waited for the world to end.

And waited.

She opened her eyes in slits and peeked around her knee.

The exploding star sat just above the sand, glowing, and the size of a marble.

Lexa tried to stand but her legs wouldn't do the work of supporting her. Instead, she crawled, lifting one hand to shield her eyes from the fiery floating star. Crouched next to the map, she reached out to touch it.

Her hand recoiled before it even got close. The map was hot. Maybe not as hot as a star, but hot enough to burn if she laid a single skin cell on it.

The Cynosure glowed red, the pearls pulsing with blue light.

The mixture of red and blue turned the star floating above it all purple, and it dropped closer and closer to the map until it sank right through it and disappeared under the sand.

And the point on the map where it had gone through brightened, a constellation appearing as though it had always been there. A constellation Lexa recognized.

Reaching out a hand again, she inched closer and closer to the map, waiting for it to burn her.

The Cynosure lay on it, back to its reddish-iridescent color, the color calling to mind the skin of a Gexcorian.

Both lie there, quiet and cool.

She slipped the Cynosure back in her pouch and lifted the map from the sand.

Beneath it, the sand was smooth as glass. As though the heat had fused it into one solid chunk.

After rolling up the map and stuffing it back in the bag to get cozy with the Cynosure, she laid her hand on the patch of sand. It was solid, and smooth. A lot like onyx, white lines flowed through it, swirling in the deep black and reflecting the blue light of the sisters still hanging in the sky.

Lexa glanced up at them. The seventh had returned.

Smiling, she stood and headed back to the ship, clicking her tongue. "Savannah. Come on baby, time to go. Mommy's got our next destination and—"

One of the skimmers blasted across the beach, cresting the hill she'd parked behind so she'd be out of sight.

She tried to hurry through the sand and get to her ship before they got here. The last thing she needed was one of these damn tourists seeing her out here and watching her take off with the ship. If she timed this all right, they wouldn't know she had left the planet until she'd been gone for a few hours. And she'd disabled the locator beacon last night after they loaded up the extra fuel.

The sand was still greedy with her feet, pressing between her toes and pulling them down beneath the surface.

She snagged her shoes on the way and slipped one on before the ship landed. But before she could get the other on, the ship's engines started blowing up black sand, blasting Lexa in the face.

Eyes closed, teeth clenched, she shielded her face with her bag and waited for the engine whine to die, her arms taking the brunt of the sandstorm.

Once the engines powered down, she opened her eyes and lowered the bag, brushing it and her arms. Since she hadn't beaten them to her ship, she'd wait and give them a dressing down for blasting her like that.

Before their bay door opened, another ship flew over the hill. She prepared herself for another sand blasting but this one landed far enough down the beach, it caused little more than a stiff breeze. At least whoever was piloting that one had two brain cells to rub together.

Lexa turned back to the first ship, fire ready to spit out her eyes and off her tongue.

The rear door opened, a ramp lowering onto the sand, and a figure stood at the head of it, outlined in the light coming from behind them. Lexa couldn't make out any features, other than the fact that it appeared to be a human or humanoid woman with hips that swayed and shifted as she waltzed down the ramp.

She was almost at the bottom of the ramp and into the sand when the back of Lexa's mind told her to run. Told her she knew that hip sway.

"Lexa Dean. How lovely to see you again. You should make it harder to follow you."

Another shape appeared at the top of the ramp, four feet walking in a unison that made them almost look like two. His eyes glowed red. "Lady Jenierien is right, Lexa. You really should."

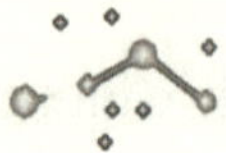

Not that she wanted to take her eyes off Jenierien and Qesson, but Lexa had to know who was landing down the beach. Whoever it was could either be a good distraction and get her clear of Jenierien before this all went super sideways, or—

"Allie, dear!"

—or it could be Mom.

"Mother, wait, I have to adjust my suit."

And Juniper.

"Ladies, let me carry the umbrella and towels, here, Paisley, give me that please."

And Reid.

Good lord. Could this be any worse?

Jenierien smiled, her lips curling up so far they seemed to almost touch her ears. "You have something of mine, I believe."

Lexa shrugged, one shoe still in her hand, and shifted her feet in the sand. Mother and the others were coming closer, she could hear their chattering, and Savannah was nowhere to be found. "There are others who say it belongs to them. They blew up my ship to find it."

Qesson chuckled, breathing out his nose. "Indeed. I watched as they did so, and I saw you ride away from the destruction, only to find yourself on the back of a garbage scow." He folded his arms over his chest.

"I thought I lost you in town."

"Did you? Why ever would you have thought that?"

Stomach clenched, Lexa tried to scoot toward her ship. She clicked her tongue but didn't dare call any louder for Van. Either her cat would get the message or she'd have to start considering how to get out of here and come back for her later. And Paisley and crew kept coming closer.

"Look," she said, addressing Jenierien again but still keeping one eye on Qesson, "I tried to tell you before. I'll give it back when I'm done."

Jenierien almost purred. "To me, or the people you stole it from? They're quite desperate to find you, you know."

Lexa started to sweat. She couldn't get around the implication that Jenierien knew quite well who was after her. And the million-dollar question—how Jenierien had found her here.

"Qesson," Jenierien said, tilting her head toward him. One strand of pearls out of the six roped around her neck swayed. "Please do bring our other guests. I'd love to make their acquaintance. Officially."

He nodded and disappeared back up the ramp.

"Allie, dear, who is this you're talking to? I saw you leaving the other beach, and I thought, with all the studying you did, you'd know the best beaches. So we followed you down. This is quite nice, isn't it Reid?"

Lexa glanced over her shoulder. Her mother and her satellites stood just behind her, Reid setting up an umbrella that made little to no sense at night, and laying down beach towels, while Juniper gazed out at the ocean. She removed her outer clothing and stripped down to her barely-there swimsuit, not paying a stitch of attention to Lexa, Jenierien, or anyone else.

Though she did turn back to Reid and wink. "Come on, sweetie, let's go in." She reached out a hand to him.

And that's when Lexa thought she might throw up.

Reid, to his credit, cleared his throat and glanced at Lexa. "Is the water safe?"

She shrugged but before she had a chance to answer him, someone shouted from inside Jenierien's skimmer. Someone who should not be here but who Qesson was nonetheless dragging down the ramp. Lexa's desire to know how Jenierien found her disappeared in a puff of smoke.

One head in each hand, he held his struggling hostages by the hair.

Elani on one side, Jake on the other.

"Would you like to introduce me to your accomplices, Dr. Dean?" Jenierien turned to Elani and Jake.

Qesson pushed their heads until their knees buckled and they knelt on the ramp before Jenierien.

Jake whimpered. Elani didn't make a sound. But her eyes watered, the tears lining her lids glowing gold and orange.

"Leave them out of this, Jenierien," Lexa said, teeth clenched. She tried to breathe around the lump that sprang up in her throat, seeing her friends pressed into the hard metal of the skimmer's ramp. "They didn't know. They had nothing to do with what I did. With what I've done."

Jenierien leaned over Elani and extended one long finger. With her nail curved up, she hooked it under Elani's chin and jerked.

Eyes narrowed, mouth twisted so tight it was almost gone, Elani stared up at her. She scowled and spoke through clenched teeth. "How do you live with that energy?"

Digging her immaculate fingernail into Elani's chin, Jenierien drug her upwards. Qesson didn't let go of the handful of black hair he had, and so Elani ended up in a half-crouch, half-standing position that looked like hell on her back. Jenierien's lips twisted into a smile that was almost as much a grimace as it wasn't.

"Usually quite well while I roll in piles of wealth and never want for a single thing in my life."

"You want that thing Lexa has pretty bad though, don't you?"

Qesson ripped at Elani's hair.

She screamed.

Lexa and Jake shouted in unison, Lexa moving closer to the ramp. Jake flailed his arms at Qesson, trying to snag him with a fist.

"Stop this, Jenierien. We can work something—"

The rest of what Lexa had planned to say to smooth-talk Elani and Jake out of there was cut off by a ship descending from the atmosphere behind them. The wail of its engines as it hovered over the ocean, spraying water 20 meters in the air, drowned out even the room for thought in Lexa's head.

Ears covered, she bent so she could face both the ship and Jenierien.

Oh, that ship looked familiar.

Her stomach hit her toes, the hair on the back of her neck stood up so fast it stung, and all at once pressure socked her in the bladder.

Juniper was still in the water, and every single person on the beach stood transfixed as the Gexcorian warship approached, guns lowering from its belly.

Lexa whispered to herself. "Shit."

CHAPTER 15

The first few shots went over their heads. Warning shots.

Lexa didn't hesitate. As soon as they began firing, she grabbed a handful of sand and threw it directly into Qesson's face.

With both his hands full of Jake and Elani's hair, he couldn't deflect it, and took the whole handful directly to the eyes and nose. Coughing, he let go of Lexa's friends and shouted.

Sprinting for her ship, Lexa shouted over her shoulder. "Get on this ship, everybody, right now!"

As she slammed into the side of it, skidding in the sand and gripping the hull for support, she caught sight of her cat out of the corner of her eye, making a beeline for the open side door.

The people weren't nearly as smart as the cat. Elani and Jake were just now picking themselves up off the ramp where Qesson had dropped them, and Juniper was still in the water as though continuing her swim right now was the most normal thing in the world. As if a warship wasn't bearing down on them, laying a shadow over the entire beach larger than their three ships put together. Paisley and Reid both stood, watching the ship, their mouths open, eyes wide.

Paisley clasped her hands to her breast and turned to Lexa, shouting over the whine of the approaching engines. "What do they want?"

Lexa shook her head and shouted back, straining her voice and inhaling what felt like a kilo of sand. "Does it matter? Get in the damned ship!"

Rather than listen, not really her strongest suit at the best of times, she spun back to the ocean and cupped her hands around her mouth. "Junie! Come back! We have to get off the beach!"

And as if to illustrate the point, the Gexcorians fired again.

Three shots hit the ramp of Jenierien's ship, sending sand into the air along with Jenierien, Qesson, and Jake. Elani, the only one who seemed to be listening to anything Lexa said, leapt off the ramp before the shots hit. She rolled away from the blast, skidding through the sand and ending up at Lexa's feet.

Hand outstretched, Lexa reached down to her. "Thought you were going on vacation?" She hauled her to her feet.

Elani shrugged. "This isn't vacation?"

Lexa grinned. "Get Jake and the others to the ship and start her up."

"What about you?"

"I'll be right behind you."

Before dashing off, Elani kissed her on the cheek, her lips soft and partially open.

Cheek warm where Elani had kissed her, Lexa held one hand over the spot and charged Qesson before he could get up. She'd never tangled hand to hand with a Truscian but she'd heard about it. The only shot she had was to catch him by surprise. If he got all those feet working again, she could just about give up any chance she had of outrunning him.

Landing on him, the sand cushioning some of the blow, she angled her forearm across his forehead and cut off the air coming into his nose. "Thing about you guys is, you can't breathe through your mouth." She grinned, wrapping one leg around two of his and pressing the other knee into his gut.

Qesson struggled, his nose creating suction against the skin of her arm as he tried to inhale. His free legs flailed, slapping her in the back, the shoulder, the side. One of them drew blood when it hit her in the arm, stinging and burning before it slipped off and tried again. His eyes narrow, he stared up at her. They glowed red as a ruby in the sunlight, boring into her like the laser on Jenierien's front gate.

Before Lexa could adjust her grip and stop him from phasing, she found herself floating toward the sand. She'd never had a Truscian go through her before, and she'd never been sure they could do it to organic material, but if she'd had any questions about it, she wouldn't after today.

Her skin tingled where they touched, alternating freezing cold with burning hot so quickly she could hardly tell the difference between the two. The pain where he'd torn her skin receded until it became noise, just like the rest of her skin. Buzzing like static. As his face touched hers and then passed through it, her nose plugged and her ears rang, blocking out the next round of shots coming from the Gexcorian ship. Instinct kept her from inhaling, and her lungs burned with the need to take a breath.

The worst of it was her mind. As Qesson passed through her, his mind almost touching hers, she lost all sense of self. She floated, nothing more than a spark of light on a darkened beach, no more than a speck of barely conscious thought, unable to comprehend its own existence.

She didn't know how long her face lay in the sand, how long she breathed it through her nose. But the first thing she became aware of, almost like being born, was the sound of Jenierien's shouting.

"Qesson! Q! Wake up! Get my Cynosure! What are you doing?"

Light came to Lexa as though it had not been created until this moment. Bathed in blue, she spun her face in the sand, some of it getting between her parched lips, and stared at the figure next to her. At first, it wouldn't come. She didn't recognize him. She didn't recognize what he was—person, water, rock—none of it made sense.

And he lie on the sand, staring at her, his eyes wide and unblinking. His mouth slack, his limbs flopped like dead fish in the surf.

The surf.

She was on the beach.

She was on the beach and she needed to get up and get on the ship.

Dragging her tingling limbs up, she got to her hands and knees and wobbled, drool stringing from her mouth into the sand.

Water washed over her feet. The one without a shoe—where was the other shoe?—sent her a message. The water was cold, foamy, and silky. It caressed her foot and washed back out to sea.

It was enough to get her moving.

Qesson still lay on the sand, but it looked like he was getting control of his limbs, too, as Jenierien screamed in the background.

"Come on, Lexa," she said to herself, working her heavy limbs to standing. "You got this. Get on the ship."

Someone stopped next to her and wrapped a hand around her bicep. "Let me help you," Reid said.

Head fuzzy, she looked up at him.

He smiled, blue eyes round, and dragged her across the sand toward the skimmer. A dimple creased his cheek.

Placing one foot after the other, she got her legs working and pushed off his chest. "I got it. Are Mom and June on the ship?"

"Paisley got on, Juniper's still in the water." His voice shook and he clutched her arm.

Lexa stopped and spun, and saw it wasn't the tide coming in. The waves, topped in white foam, flung themselves at the shore as the ocean undulated beneath the massive engines of the

Gexcorian ship. June popped up and disappeared beneath the waves, clearly trying to swim back to shore and failing. The sound of her screams almost didn't reach Lexa's ears through the pounding of the intensifying surf.

"Shit. Get on the ship, Reid. We gotta get out there to her."

With a nod, Reid ran ahead.

"Get them to open the back bay door," she shouted after him. She couldn't run through the sand as it ate her feet, her legs still dragged through it like lead weights. And somewhere back there, were Jenierien and Qesson. Was Qesson moving again? She didn't have time or mental bandwidth to look. She dragged one foot after the other, trying to keep them both from sinking into the sand and failing. It was like running through mud.

The engines of her skimmer hummed and the back bay door approached her, opening. White light from inside hit her eyes and she squinted, eyeballs stinging. What had Qesson done to her?

Jake shouted from inside. "Lexa! Do you need help?"

She waved him off, eyes still mostly closed, and dropped to her knees again. Her legs shook too much to carry her weight, but she inched through the sand toward the door.

A hand wrapped around her ankle. "No you don't."

Without glancing over her shoulder, she pulled the bag from around her neck and flung it at the ship. It landed inside the bay door and Reid snatched it before it slid back down the ramp. He slung it around his own neck. After confirming its safety, Lexa glanced over her shoulder and kicked Qesson in the face with a sandy shoe. Her heel connected with his nose.

He clapped his free hand to it and fell over, still holding her other foot. It twisted her around and she fell in the sand again, struggling to free her leg. Blood spurted from his nose, red as a human's, and dripped to the black sand.

Jenierien shouted. "Q! Lexa what have you done!" Her feet pounded the sand. Looked like she wasn't willing to get her hands dirty unless she had no option. And with Qesson struggling for breath and finally releasing Lexa with a rasping all the way down the top of her foot, Jenierien didn't have an option. If she wanted the Cynosure, she'd have to do it herself.

A weight slid off Lexa's shoulders. There was no way Jenierien could beat her, physically. Mental mind games were her thing, but this was Lexa's.

Lexa climbed to her feet again, the salty sea filling her nose, tinged with the afterburn of the skimmer's engines as it sat hovering over the beach. "Elani, point this thing at my sister." She tipped an imaginary cap to Jenierien, who held her skirts in both hands as she struggled through the sand toward Qesson.

"I'm going to get my treasure back, Lexa. Do not doubt that," she said, teeth clenched. She dropped to her knees next to Qesson.

"Yeah, not today," Lexa said, finally finding purchase on the metal ramp of the skimmer.

Elani gunned the engines once she was aboard and they shot across the foamy water, angling for Juniper.

Lexa stared down at the tumultuous surface, watching for the bobbing head of her oldest sister. "Elani, can you see her?"

Shouting to be heard over the engines and the air rushing past the open door, Elani spoke over her shoulder. "I have a fix on her energy, one second." The engines throttled down and they slowed, lowering over the water. "You need to hurry. That warship is closing pretty quick."

"Radio them. Tell them if they blow us up, they'll lose their trinket to the ocean forever."

The radio clicked on. A Gexcorian wailed through the speakers. *"Give it back, now!"*

Well Lexa knew that voice, didn't she? But as she looked over the edge of the door, the sound assaulting her ears faded into the background. Her focus, all of it, was now on her sister bobbing between fifteen foot swells. And losing her fight against the tide.

June paddled limp arms, bobbing up and down with lazy kicks. Her energy waned, right before Lexa's eyes, and she slipped below the surface.

"Shit. Hang on June, you bitch." Hooking her foot around the door's strut, Lexa hung off the side of the ramp. "Lower, Elani!"

A high-pitched squeal sounded though the speakers, Gexcorian tongue. *"We are here to collect what belongs to us,"* Ferrinogean said. *"Allow me to remind you what happened when we last met."*

The ship rocked with a gun blast. Clearly Ferrinogean didn't care if he had to retrieve the Cynosure from the bottom of the ocean, as long as Lexa was dead before he did.

And Lexa was too far from June to reach her. She glanced over her shoulder. "Reid."

He stood, plastered to the wall of the ship, and stared at her with wide eyes.

"Get over here and help me. Bring that rope from the locker next to you."

He didn't so much as twitch.

Lexa screamed. "Jake!"

Jake ran the length of the ship and skidded to a stop at the head of the ramp.

"June is under the water, I've got to go in after her. Grab that rope and tie it to my ankle."

In record time, Jake did as she asked.

She dove off the ramp. The cold water enveloped her, and her entire body turned into one giant goosebump. She shivered, reaching through the water for June. Something brushed past her hand and she clenched her fingers closed.

But it wasn't June. The surface of it was not human skin. It was like pliable sandpaper, and it pulsed beneath her fingers.

This planet was not supposed to have life. So what the fuck was that?

Skin, human skin, bumped into her arm.

She clutched again and got a handful of June's arm. Tugging, she swam back to the surface, lungs burning for air. The unforgiving surf tried to keep them both, sucking them into the next rolling wave.

The rope around her ankle pulled her up out of the water foot-first. Her leg tightened from her ankle up, her hip screaming like it was about to be pulled from its socket. Someone grabbed both of her feet and hauled her into the ship.

Reid reached past her and clutched June, pulling her past Lexa and into the boat.

Lexa let go of her and grabbed the person hauling her up.

Jake's hands like a steel vise, he didn't let go of her legs until she lay firmly on the deck. Once she was all the way up, the bay door closing on smooth hydraulics, Jake hugged her to him and covered her lips in an urgent kiss, clutching the skin of her back in his fingers and squeezing her shoulder with the other hand.

Skin tingling again, but for a wholly different reason, she kissed him back. It was just as exciting as the kiss they'd shared on the dock in Port de Playa, just as unexpected, and twice as much fun now that she remembered to enjoy it while it lasted.

His tongue slipped into her mouth for a brief moment and back out, and he pulled her closer. "Jesus, Lexa. Never scare me like that again."

It was a damn good thing she'd been sitting. Her head swam. Water dripped from her hair and clothes onto the deck and she sought for words.

"Lexa," Elani called from the front, "you better get up here."

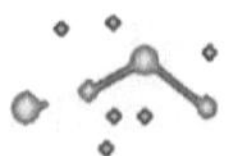

Another gun blast rocked the ship.

"We don't have guns," Elani said, flipping switches and angling the ship's keel toward the Gexcorian's. Blasts buffeted them, bouncing off the hull. "We won't last against them and we can't outrun them. Not in this thing."

"I know. Give me a second to think." Lexa flopped into the copilot's seat.

"Allie honey, are we going back to the cruise ship?"

Lexa rolled her eyes and stared out the front window. She licked her lips and tasted Jake. Whew.

But now was not the time to get lost thinking about that. Besides the fact her everything was still tingling and half-paralyzed after her trip through a Truscian.

And the sea was still rolling. In fact, it was getting worse.

Her hand had brushed something underwater, something moving. Something with skin. Was it alive? How could it be when they'd told her in school this planet was lifeless?

Had they been wrong?

At least she didn't have to wait long for the answer.

Paisley shouted. "What the hell is that!" She pointed over Lexa's shoulder out the front window.

Elani leveled the ship off so they could see the whole scene unfolding in front of them.

Something had broken the surface of the water. It leapt into the air, toward the loud-ass Gexcorian ship, rising, rising, rising from the water like it was never going to stop.

It hit Lexa that the water had not been unsettled because of the Gexcorian ship's engines. It was because something as large as the ocean itself was surfacing.

This planet very much had life.

The creature continued to breach the surface, its rough hide falling in reverse as it lifted into the air.

Lexa pointed. "Elani, fly us closer to the Gexcorians."

"Closer?" Paisley shouted, charging up to the cockpit. "Alexandra, you can't be serious!"

"Fuck off, Mom. Elani, get us in there."

Despite Paisley's interference, Elani never hesitated. She pushed the accelerator, jerked the yoke, and glided them closer to the Gexcorian ship with a confidence that radiated off her like rays of pure sunlight.

Lexa clenched her teeth and gripped the bottom of her seat so hard her knuckles ached. Elani got them so close to the hide of that sea creature, Lexa was sure they would just land on its back and surf it to the atmosphere.

But they never touched it. Lexa could only assume Elani's ability to see energies kept them the right distance from it as it finally finished its breach. They closed in on the Gexcorian warship, which continued to fire.

"That's it, just a little—"

Elani nodded, easing back on the yoke and bringing them in to coast right up next to the Gexcorians. She took the skimmer higher, crossing the midplane of the enormous warship. She called over her shoulder. "Hold onto something!"

Lexa leaned in, the scent of Elani's skin hitting her nose and mingling there with the smell of Jake. Her stomach churned. "Do you know what you're doing?"

Grin lifting the corner of her mouth, Elani nodded and flashed her eyes at Lexa. They swirled so fast it mesmerized her. "Yeah, I got this."

Lexa nodded and leaned back, gripping the seat belt. "Strap in you guys, it's going to get—"

The Gexcorians started firing again, buffeting the ship with their small cannons.

Someone ran into the back of Lexa's chair and held on, pulling her backward.

She looked up into Reid's wide blue eyes, her bag still across his neck.

He screwed up his brow and stared out the window. "Why are they shooting?"

"Oh, you know. Little of this, little of that," she said, following his eyes.

All the ship's guns had moved into position, all of them aiming at the skimmer.

"Elani," she started.

"I hope you're all hanging on!" She slammed the yoke forward into the control panel.

The skimmer nose-dived.

Spacecraft were all fitted with what they called shock absorbers, which kept the riders from feeling the weirdness that was space travel. In space, the ship could be flying upside-down, if you could call anything in space right-side-up, but its occupants would never know.

This wasn't space, though, and the shock absorbers didn't work quite the same way they did in space.

Everyone fell forward.

Lexa and Elani had strapped in, but the rest of the ship bumped and knocked as its passengers ran into each other. Juniper shouted, Jake answered with an, "I got you," and Reid fell over the chair, ending up practically in Lexa's lap. He hung onto her waist with one hand and the back of the chair with the other. Lexa's bag swung between them as the ship plummeted toward the creature.

Its hide was the color of Earth sand, a light brownish-tan surface that rippled with its breathing. Rivulets of water still ran down its sides, splashing into the ocean in waterfalls. It would have been incorrect to say it was a whale, and it didn't have tentacles like so many other sea creatures and aliens Lexa had encountered, but it looked almost like a mix of squid and whale. As they neared its surface at breakneck speed, Lexa found she could almost see through the pulsing flesh, the organs beneath it undulating. She held her breath, spit stuck in her mouth because she couldn't swallow.

The Gexcorian guns had followed them down, but rather than hit the small skimmer, they hit the creature with most of their shots, puncturing the skin in half a dozen spots.

It rolled, and on its side Lexa caught sight of a giant flipper, easily three times the size of the skimmer. It rose out of the water, the ocean drenching both ships.

Lexa gripped Reid back. He was closest. "Let's get the fuck out of here, Elani!"

"Not yet," she said, still diving. The enormous flipper angled out of the water, aiming directly for both ships. It would crush this skimmer like a beer can. "Not yet."

"Elani," Lexa said, teeth stuck together. It would probably take a crowbar to pry them apart at this point. Her voice jittered. Reid clutched tighter.

Before they crashed headlong into the creature, Elani twisted the yoke and brought them alongside it again. The Gexcorians continued firing but their thrusters were lit. They were backing away.

A ship that large and lumbering didn't have half the maneuverability as the small skimmer, though, and getting out of the way of the flipper didn't happen.

The creature hit the Gexcorian ship with a glancing blow, taking out one of the thrusters in the process and denting the side of the ship.

As they flew under, Lexa stared up and could see right into the ship. They weren't going to space anytime soon.

"I don't want to see what happens to them, just get us out of here," she said.

Elani nodded, yanking the yoke back again.

Reid fell backward and into Lexa, crushing her own elbow into her ribs and flattening her face with his solid, albeit sculpted, abs.

The ship shot straight up into the atmosphere.

THE SEARCH

CHAPTER 16

Elani climbed into the bunk, no more than a mattress and some walls, after Lexa. Door closed, she leaned against one wall and stared at Lexa in the dark, her eyes making their own dim light. "Are you feeling better?"

Flipping on the bunk's small reading light, Lexa held her head with her other hand and leaned on the opposite wall, the pillows between them. "I think so. I do not recommend phasing through a Truscian."

"I thought they were only able to phase through inorganics?"

"So did I. We thought wrong." Eyes closed, she breathed through her nose. Her skin had stopped tingling, the taste of Jake had faded, but the headache she had wanted to pound her eyeballs out of her head. Their escape on Birkishni had been nothing short of miraculous. When Jake had taken the helm once they left the atmosphere, Elani tugged her hand and brought her to the bunk. Lexa knew why.

"Are you going to tell me?"

"Why they blew up my ship and followed me to Birkishni?"

"Eventually I need to know. So does Jake. You kind-of owe us that."

Head pounding, heat flashed into her cheeks and tightened her throat. "You're kidding me, right? I accepted your help on Earth because I really had no choice, being unconscious and all. I tried to dump you both in Port de Playa, I tried to leave you on the beach in Birkishni. What I owe you is a swift kick in the ass on your way to leaving me the hell alone."

Not that that speech helped her headache. It pounded more than ever. But who cared. She was right. She didn't owe them shit.

The bedsheets rustled. Elani leaned into her, her warmth touching Lexa on the shoulder, pressing into her side and leg.

"That's unfair, Lexa."

She shook her head, eyes stinging.

"Look at me, please."

Lexa cracked an eye. She and Elani now sat nose to nose.

She swallowed, her throat clicking.

One hand lifted to Lexa's shoulder, Elani hummed a little. Her brow creased, and she hummed a little louder, something like a lullaby maybe.

The pain in Lexa's head dulled. She couldn't feel every nerve ending in her skin anymore. It was almost enough to make her cry with relief, and her jaw relaxed. Her teeth throbbed from being clenched for who knew how long. "Thank you." She smiled.

"Please tell me," Elani answered, whispering.

"You poked your head over the top of that garbage scow's bucket and I was lost. Do you know that?" She met Elani's eyes again.

"Lost?"

"To you. Don't tell me you don't feel drawn to me. Because for the love of creation, I can't escape this feeling. I've never, ever been pulled in by someone the way you pull me. From the second you laid those golden eyes on me."

Elani cleared her throat. "I told you—"

"You can't. Why? Waiting for your soulmate?"

One side of Elani's mouth turned down. "Something like that."

Lexa blew a breath out her pursed lips. "Great. So I just pour my heart out to you and you—"

"That's not it, Lexa, I—"

Sliding away, letting Elani's warmth seep away from her side, Lexa reached for the door. "It's fine. You don't have to explain. I just. I don't feel this way about people, and I thought. I don't know. I didn't know how to bring it up but." She stopped, sighing, and stared at the door. "Why won't the two of you just leave me alone?"

"That thing I did with your energy just now? That I did before? My 'golden' eyes, as you call them? You know those are all recessive genes on Kuarpa, right?"

Lexa looked over her shoulder. "So you said. Well, you said it wasn't normal or whatever. Recessive?" She turned around and drew her knees to her chest, crossing her arms over them.

"Manipulating energy is looked down on. It used to be something we could all do, but we bred it out when we learned how dangerous it can be. Whole nations became enslaved by rulers who manipulated their energies. The world tried to destroy itself, just to be free of it." She cast her eyes down. "We're secretive because we're ashamed. Our past is…less than perfect."

"It's not like humans are saints." Lexa slid closer. "You think you're some freak of nature? And people, what? Are they afraid of you?"

She shrugged. "I'm something of a…what would you call it on Earth? A piranha?"

Lexa smiled. There was no way learning Earth languages was easy—and so many of them—and a simple mistake like that was easy to make. "Pariah. It's pariah. And you can manipulate energies like these people no one wants to talk about?"

"Oh, no. Not like that. It's been diluted by purposeful breeding. But in some ways, yes, I can. I've always been able to. When we met, I felt the pull you spoke of." She slid closer, her legs slipping over the sheets in a soft whisper. "And I'm sorry if I did that to you. You were so helpless, lying there nude in the trash.

All I wanted was to protect you, and I'm afraid I may have covered you in my own energy." She lowered her eyes. "That's probably what you felt."

Though Lexa had felt it again and again since then, she locked that behind her lips. Elani didn't want to hear it. Her whole posture, that little story, it screamed "don't tell me about how different I am."

Instead, Lexa reached in the bag she'd gotten back from Reid with a little prodding. "Here, this. It's this." She pulled out the Cynosure, its surface warm from lying in the bag next to the map. By the time she slipped it into Elani's palm, it was cool again, the pearls smooth.

Eyes wide, Elani held it up to her face. Her fingers traced the teardrop shape, running over each pearl in turn. Leaning, she held it next to the reading lamp and let the light shine over its surface. Her voice dropped to a reverent whisper. "What is it?"

"It's a Gexcorian holy item. I might have stolen it."

When Elani looked at her, brow drawn, Lexa shrugged, her mouth trying to smile and failing. This kind of guilt had never accompanied her this long after taking something. Probably a side-effect of being shot at.

"And Lady Jenierien? She put up the reward, right?"

"I sold it to her."

"Then why doesn't she have it?"

"I stole it back. Then ran into you."

"Jesus, Lexa." She handed it back to her, her finger sliding off the pointed side of the teardrop. "Anything else?"

She slid the Cynosure in the bag and brought the map out a few millimeters. "It goes with this map."

"Can I see it?"

Shaking her head, Lexa pushed the map and Cynosure back to the bottom of the bag. "I. No. I don't think that's a good idea right now. But it did tell me where we need to go."

"How far?"

"Further than we can get in this ship. We need somewhere to shake off the Gexcorians and Jenierien, and find a ship that can take us deeper. And get rid of my mother and sister. And their tour guide."

"He seems to like you."

She chuckled, stomach bubbling again. "We had a." She cleared her throat, that pull still tugging her. It might have been Elani's doing but it was still there, even if she wasn't doing it on purpose. "Just a casual thing. Once or twice."

Elani laughed. "I shouldn't be surprised, yet here I am. What about your mom and sister? Why won't you speak to them?"

"My mother could get eaten by a Dysling warmonger pig and I wouldn't give it a second thought." She clenched her teeth again, the squeaking inside her head louder than her thoughts.

"Why?"

"When she started getting DNAging treatments and aging backward, she thought having another kid was a good idea. But she left me with my grandmother when I was a baby so she could travel the galaxy with my much older siblings and her boyfriend of the week. Gram raised me till she died, and I couldn't care less if I never see Mom again." She frowned, meeting Elani's eyes.

Elani frowned. "My parents, they're wonderful, but they. Well neither of them have…what I do…and they never tried to hide me away. But they never didn't. Does that make sense?"

"Perfect." She slid one hand up Elani's jaw. "I'd never hide something as beautiful as you in the shadows."

Elani laid one hand over Lexa's and stared into her eyes. Her tongue snuck out and wet her lips. They gleamed in the low light.

"I'm sorry," Lexa whispered.

Matching her tone, Elani whispered back. "For what?"

Lexa couldn't pull her eyes away from Elani's glistening lips. "Trying to kiss you without permission. Before."

Elani bit her lip and shook her head.

Lexa's stomach floated somewhere in a soup inside her midsection. If she looked down, she might find she wasn't attached to the bed anymore. It was like zero-G had taken over.

The moment stretched like elastic, Elani leaning closer, so close Lexa couldn't see her lips anymore. She stared up into her eyes.

They swirled like hurricanes. "You're forgiven. This time." Her lips brushed Lexa's, velvety and smooth.

The door opened without a knock. "Lexa, Paisley and Juniper— oh. Sorry." Reid stopped.

Stomach crashing to her toes, Lexa turned and glared at him. "Reid, you have impeccable timing. Has anyone ever told you that?"

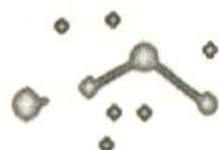

"This thing hits atmo like it's on greased ball bearings," Elani said, angling the nose of the skimmer up. "We should be sliding into the traffic lane in minutes. Everybody ready?"

Jake strapped in next to her and took up the co-pilot position, hands on the yoke in front of him. He flipped some buttons and nodded.

Elani flipped buttons to match.

Watching them from one of the jump seats in the back, Lexa shook her head. There they went again, speaking without speaking. Jake was human, but did they have some kind of telepathic connection? It was certainly something she'd like to dig into, at some point, if she was going to stick with these two.

"Lexa," Mom said, from two seats down, "what kind of shopping do they have on Kuarpa? I'd love to get some new clothes, since all of mine are back on the cruise ship. If we're going to continue with you to some of your dusty archaeological sites…"

"I don't think that's a great idea, Mother." Heart pounding, she tried to pretend like her mom didn't just call her by her chosen name and not whatever the hell she felt like. She leaned forward, collarbones pressed into the seatbelt. "You guys saw what happened on Birkishni. I have some bad people after me."

Between them, June smoothed her hair. "If the places you're going are half as wonderful as that beach, count me in."

Lexa's mouth fell open. "You almost died!"

"I didn't know you cared so much." She smiled down her nose.

"I—" She stopped. Did she?

Dammit. Yes.

"Listen, guys, what's going on right now is high reward. But it's also very, very high risk. If you're with me, I'm worried you might distract me. Any number of things could go wrong." She grimaced, unable to believe she was about to say this. But she was, and it was the truth. "If something happened to you because of me, I wouldn't be able to forgive myself. I don't know how you'll get there, but please go back to Earth."

Reid leaned around both of them and caught Lexa's eye. "Lexa, if that's really your wish, and Paisley agrees, I can take care of it. My company has an office here, I can get the ladies everything they need." He smiled and winked, straight white teeth shining.

"Good," Lexa said, sitting back and closing her eyes. The ship slipped through the atmosphere and she rocked with it, almost falling asleep. Paisley and Juniper had commandeered the bed, so the little sleep she'd gotten on the way here had been filled with a lot less sex than she wanted. She cracked one eye and watched Jake copilot the ship into the traffic lanes.

"I can get you a ship, too," Reid said.

Jolted out of her daydream, she sat up so fast she caught her collar bones on the seatbelts, stinging the skin beneath them like a carpet burn. Teeth clenched against the pain, she scowled around June and Mom. "That won't be necessary."

"I didn't mean to eavesdrop, but I heard Elani and Jake talking earlier. She told him you guys need a ship that will get you deeper into space. I can get you one." He winked again. "No charge."

She doubted that. Her stomach curled and she leaned back, easing the pressure from the safety belts. "I really don't need that. You take my mom and sister home, and we'll call it even."

Paisley sniffed. "I really would love to come with you, Lexa. We could finally spend some time together as a family."

Socked in the gut, still, Lexa couldn't answer. Her mother being this congenial was something she thought impossible. But the need to tell her she'd never treated her like family before warred with the softer side of her. The side that seemed to have a bigger and bigger voice since she'd met Elani and Jake.

She pressed her lips together. "It's just not safe, Mom. When we land on Kuarpa, get you a ship, and get home."

June chuckled. "Right after we get some new clothes. I cannot go all the way back to Earth in a swimsuit."

Just a few hours ago, June nearly drowned—or got eaten by an alien sea monster, pick your poison—and now all she could think about was her clothes. She was truly her mother's daughter. Protecting them might get Lexa killed. But more importantly, it might get them killed.

Lexa leaned back and looked out the window, watching space turn into sky.

CHAPTER 17

A woman with deep brown skin, jet black hair, and wide brown eyes opened the door. She could have been human.

"Mom," Elani said, ducking her head.

Elani's mom's face lit up. She threw her arms open and crushed Elani in them before Elani could twitch.

Lexa bumped Jake with her shoulder. "You ever been here before?"

He shook his head, his smile wide. Leaning close enough to Lexa's ear to tickle it with his breath, he whispered. "She didn't want to come back here. Like. Ever."

Shivering, Lexa faced him. She could really do with another kiss. Or six. "Never?"

"Who are your friends, honey? Please, all of you come in. What a surprise! Atnold!" Elani's mom spoke quickly and in a high-pitched tone that would make dogs roll over and die, sweeping the door wide and ushering them in.

Arms crossed over herself, Elani led Jake and Lexa in. She perched on the edge of a chair, leaving a couch for Lexa and Jake to share.

Jake sat and Lexa sat almost on top of him. Kuarpa was about three degrees Celsius cooler on average than Earth. She snuggled up to Jake for warmth and looked around for a blanket, laying the bag with Van in it in the middle of her freezing legs.

"Are you all going swimming?" Elani's mom smiled at them, hand out. "Pleased to meet you. Yrciel Reihana."

Lexa half-stood and shook it, shivering. "It's a long story, but I've already been." She chuckled, teeth chattering. Until this moment, she'd forgotten entirely that Elani and Jake were dressed in swimming clothes. And her own clothes were still damp next to her skin.

"Oh goodness, you two are human," she said, glancing at Jake and back to Lexa's shivering frame. "Let me bring you a blanket." She walked away toward the hall, still talking. "We always knew Elani would make it to Earth someday, so I learned what I could about your people. You always…" She got further down the hall, her voice dwindling, and the words stopped making sense.

Lexa glanced at Elani.

She tried to smile, her eyes dull, and ended up answering Lexa's glance with half a grimace. Poor Elani looked like it had been a lie when she said coming home was fine with her. But it'd been either stay with her mom, or Lexa's.

"…and I said to her, my dear Elani, if it's Earth you're headed to, make sure you take plenty of shorts! You humans do like things warm." She handed them the blanket.

Lexa took it with a smile and spread it over she and Jake's legs, the warmth of him immediately filling the blanket and thawing her frozen skin. The scent of cinnamon floated up from the blanket and in the time it took Elani's mom to call for her dad again and sit on a chair opposite the one Elani perched on, Lexa's eyes started to droop.

"It's lovely to be here, Mrs. Reihana," Jake said, smiling around at the room. He held a hand out to Elani.

Without a word, she squeezed between him and the arm of the couch, sitting outside the blanket. "We could probably use a change of clothes. And Lexa needs some shoes. Do you think I could—"

"Elani, why don't you and I go down to the shops and pick up some things for them and for dinner. It's been so long since you were home," Yrciel said.

Elani stammered. "No, it's uh. What about my. Um."

"You still have some old clothes here. Put them on and let's go shopping while your friends take a nap," a man Lexa presumed to be Elani's father said, walking into the room. "Atnold Reihana," he said, leaning over to shake Jake and Lexa's hands. He tugged Elani from the couch and smothered her in a hug.

When he let her go, Elani didn't look any happier. If anything, her eyes rolled like a wild animal caught in a trap, and she looked ready to bolt at the first sign of an opening.

And Lexa wanted to rescue her. But at the mention of a nice, warm nap, all she seemed able to do was lean into the back of the couch and fall half asleep. Her body still needed to recover from the Truscian experience.

"Jake," Yrciel said, standing.

Even from this oblique angle, Lexa could see his wide smile. "Ma'am?"

"Have you eaten Kuarpan cuisine? My findlesni loaf is the best in the East, if I say so myself."

"Mom. My friends do not need findlesni loaf. Please."

He leapt up. "I'd love to try it! Lexa," he said, reaching a hand out, "let's get you somewhere warm to sleep. You've had a long day."

Enfolding her hand in his, she followed Elani and Jake down the hall.

Elani opened a door about three down and sighed. "Oh it's just like I left it. That's…surprising." She led them in.

Jake chuckled. "This is your room?"

"Shut up."

Lexa followed them in and glanced around. When she was still living with Gram, she couldn't have been more than thirteen, one of her friends was obsessed—*obsessed*—with unicorns. They filled every millimeter of available space in her room. Pink and blue and purple and white, ceramic, glass, marble, stuffed, they were everywhere.

Young Elani might not have been quite that obsessed with glass sculptures, but it was close. All colors of the rainbow, they littered every surface, including extra shelves that had to have been installed just for a collection of them. And like the one Lexa had broken in the bedroom on their scow, most of them were shaped like teardrops.

Twisting a foot, Elani flushed, her brown skin tinged with rose.

Lexa didn't think she'd ever seen her quite this far off her footing. She reached for Elani's arm, hoping to impart some kind of brief comfort or acceptance. "I see you're a fan of glass sculpture."

"I—"

"Elani, dear, please hurry." Yrciel popped in the door, blankets in her arms. "Jake, darling, come on down the hall. I'll show you to the guest room." Without asking, she handed one blanket to Elani and tugged Jake from the room.

"Jake, wait, take Van." Lexa pulled the bag off and handed it to him. "I don't trust her with...all this."

He smiled at Elani, blew them both a kiss, and followed a chittering Yrciel out.

Elani's bed wasn't flat like Earth beds, it was more like a rounded nest with a bow in the middle long enough for a person to fit right into. Or maybe two or three; Elani's parents had a large house and this bedroom was easily the size of half of Gram's whole house. Lexa sat on the bed, her clothes still stinking of salt from the Birkishni ocean. "Is it really OK that we're here?"

Arms wrapped around herself, Elani shrugged. "Where else were we going to go?" She sat with Lexa, and their legs rolled into each other, the raised edge of the bed pushing them together. "Sorry you had to see my room and." She exhaled. "I don't know."

Lexa cupped her cheek and tugged with a gentle pull.

Elani faced her, laying her hand over Lexa's.

"I don't mind," Lexa whispered. "I kind-of like it. A glimpse into young Elani. Fan of blown glass and a lot of pink."

A smile curved Elani's lip. "Thanks for that."

Returning the smile, Lexa caressed her cheek with her thumb. "Can we finish that kiss, from earlier?"

"It's probably better if we don't."

"Why not?"

"Because. Because I." She sighed, not pulling back. Her grip on Lexa's hand tightened. "Because I want to."

The weirdest feeling overtook Lexa. Not just the pull, that was a low-grade feeling she'd gradually grown accustomed to when she was around Elani. This bubbled in her stomach, light and airy, and she had no name for it. "Then why not?"

Elani closed her eyes, her long lashes almost resting on her cheeks. "I want to tell you, Lexa. I do. But I can't. Not yet." She opened her eyes a crack, and gold light flooded out of them. "Promise me you'll wait. Wait for me to tell you."

That strange feeling in her midsection didn't abate. But she pulled back and nodded. "If that's what you want, I'll wait."

The sound of the Reihana car faded, leaving Lexa alone in Elani's silent bedroom. The air just as cool as the rest of the house, she stripped off her damp clothes, curled up in the soft, nest-like bed, and covered herself with the blanket, head to toe. Breathing into the space between her knees and chest, she tried to get warm enough to sleep.

Elani's door creaked. Jake whispered. "Lexa? Are you asleep?"

She lowered the blanket enough to see him, her mouth still beneath it. "You wouldn't think a couple degrees Celsius would make that much of a difference but I am so cold."

"Me too. Scooch." He flapped his hand.

"I'm not dressed."

"Oh, perfect. Skin contact is even better for warmth."

Before Lexa could protest—if she wanted to—he stripped and slid under her blanket, his skin a warm, dark umber kissed with gold in the sunlight filtering into the room. One arm around her, he snuggled down and threw the blanket over both of them. "Better."

The warmth didn't just come from him, especially when he hugged her tighter and snuggled his face into the hollow of her shoulder. That muscular physique she'd seen behind the screen on the cruise ship was just as tight as she imagined.

She frowned. "Question."

He didn't lift his head. "Mmm-hmm."

"Are you sure you and Elani aren't together? You're not her soulmate or anything?"

"Yes I'm sure. No I am not." He peeked up at her. "That's not the first time you've asked me that. So I'll repeat what I asked you the first time. Why? You wanna…" His infectious smile widened his shining cheeks.

The heat curled up in Lexa's gut unfurled and spread slowly down each limb, out to her fingertips and toes. She tingled. "Did she tell you that? Because you guys are closer than a lot of married couples."

He straightened out, pressing almost all of his skin against hers, their eyes level. "We're friends, Lexa. I've never asked her if I'm her soulmate but I can promise you, I am not."

Lexa's hands moved without her command, sliding down his chest and abs until she got to his waist, where they stopped. Well, almost. Her fingers played in the top of his pubic hair and against her leg, he moved without moving.

An ache started inside Lexa. If he was half as good at sex as he was at kissing… The fact was she needed to know. Right now.

"Yes Jake. I wanna." She gripped his cock and threw one leg over him, sliding as close as she could get without slipping him inside.

His bubbly smile covered his entire face, eyes wide and smiling. "Good. Me too."

"I know."

He laughed, deep and long. Before she could say anything else, he cupped her cheeks and kissed her longer than either of the other two times. His tongue danced in and out of her mouth and she responded, exploring his mouth with the tip of her own. Hips sliding closer to hers, he rocked in a rhythm, one hand sneaking down to her hips to pull her back and forth with him.

Not that she needed the encouragement. The kiss pushed her into a cloud where she floated, the only part of her that existed anymore the desire to have him inside her. That was all she was. Tingling desire and need.

When he finally pushed gently inside, filling that need with his warmth, she was almost afraid she wouldn't last but a few seconds. She'd not felt this kind of need in…years, honestly. All the sex with all the people and aliens and whoever, it was great. Fun and exciting, every single time. But it was a transaction. She did it for information. She did it for favors. She did it to get off.

But this. This. This.

This needed to last forever.

Chattering voices woke Lexa from the best nap she'd had since she couldn't remember when.

Jake shifted against her, still sleeping, his fingers loose where they'd fallen asleep with them entwined.

Still warm, Lexa poked her head out of the blanket. Hers and Jake's clothes lay in a pile by the bed.

She climbed over him, skin sliding across his again, and entertained the thought of a super-quiet quickie. But best to see where Elani was and what was going on out there first. See how much time they might have. Letting that go for now, she oozed out of bed and instantly regretted it. Her skin froze. She almost pulled the blanket with her, but it would have been the height of rudeness to awaken Jake that way. Instead, she rifled through Elani's drawers until she found something to wear.

Leaving Jake sleeping, she slipped out of the room and padded down the hallway. The voices murmured from somewhere else in the house, and she stuck close to the wall, trying to figure out where they were. The house had more rooms than four of Gram's.

As she crept down the hall, she considered what she'd tell Elani. The fact she had enjoyed Jake as much as he apparently enjoyed her—she went to sleep holding his hand, for the universe's sake!—came as much a shock to her as anyone else. But it was clear to them both it shouldn't be just a one-time thing. It might even become "a thing," a regular rendezvous she was already looking forward to. Yet that didn't change the pull she felt for Elani. The way that airy feeling crowded her stomach, made her heart flutter. The way she never wanted to be apart from Elani, the way she wanted to hold her in her arms and never let go. It didn't erase the pain of not getting to finish that kiss.

How to wrap all that in a neat little box?

She rounded a corner and the voices got louder. Pots and pans clanked. Must have been the kitchen. She stopped to listen.

"I really don't think you need to cook for us, Mom."

"Nonsense. Your friends have never been to our home. Have they even been to Kuarpa?"

"I'm not sure about Lexa. Jake hasn't. He's barely left Earth."

"Poor boy. We'll be sure he gets the full Ambran experience."

Elani snorted. "Not necessary. He knows all about it."

An interesting way for her to respond. What did she mean by—

"Anyway, lovely daughter, you should have called to tell me you were bringing your soulmate home. I would have been better prepared."

Lexa stopped breathing. Her *what?*

"Can you not bring that up in front of them, please?"

"Why ever not? I knew it would be a human, just like you said when you were little. You have such a gift. I don't understand why—"

"Just don't, OK? I haven't…we haven't had the talk yet."

What? No. *What?*

"Do you think they won't believe you? I know our neighbor Sheeni's son matched with a human and they couldn't take it. When she found out her son would have to wait for the next life to be with his soulmate again, that the human had flatly denied his very existence, I can't tell you how much frozen cream I took her."

"It's not that. It's just not the right time." Elani sighed so loud, Lexa could hear her clear out in the hallway. "It's complicated. Can you let me handle it? Please? Don't say anything."

Lexa backed down the hallway, every bit of her colder than she'd been earlier. She couldn't feel her toes.

Yrciel chuckled. "If you insist. But at least tell me…"

Her voice trailed off as Lexa got further away.

Hell, fucking hell. She knew it. She *knew* it. Elani and Jake were soulmates, just like she thought they were. And he didn't know because she hadn't told him yet. Breath coming in short, sharp bursts through pinched lips, she rushed back to Elani's room and locked the door. "Jake."

He stirred but didn't get up.

Sitting on the bed, she shook him. All thoughts of a quickie gone. Probably forever. "Jake. You gotta wake up. Get dressed. Shit. Shit shit."

"Whoa," he said, one hand coming out from under the blanket. "What's wrong?" He lowered the blanket from in front of his face and gave her that sunshiny grin. "What's going on?"

"Elani is back and I overheard her and her mom talking and." She stopped, unable to continue in the brightness of his wide brown eyes and stupidly pretty grin. "You need to get dressed and get back to the guest room. This,"—she pointed between them— "never happened."

The smile faded. A crease formed between his brows. "What do you mean? Why not?" He fully frowned, something Lexa hadn't seen on his face since they'd first met. An expression she hated to be responsible for, but had no choice. "Do you mean we can't do it again?" He gripped her hand and held her eyes with his. "I thought, I mean I thought we both wanted to… Was it me? Did I—"

Without thinking, she ran a hand up his shoulder and gripped the back of his neck. Her stomach jittered. "Believe me a hundred percent. It wasn't you. I don't think I've enjoyed sex with someone as much as I did with you in a very, very long time."

If ever.

"Then why—"

The doorknob rattled, followed by a light knock. "Lexa? Are you asleep? Dinner is ready."

She cleared her throat and slapped one hand over Jake's mouth. "Yeah um. Just give me a minute."

Elani spoke through the door again. "You can wear some of my clothes. Just check the third and fourth dresser drawers. My winter clothes should be in there."

"You got it!" She tried to sound bright, happy. Hopefully Elani wasn't spying on her energy through the door, or she'd see Jake in here too. And stars above, she could not be caught with Elani's soulmate in her bed. Nude, for the love of creation. "I'll be right there, go on to the dining room. I'll uh, I'll bring Jake with me!"

"Thanks, Lexa." At least it sounded like she was smiling, which was something she hadn't done since they arrived.

Lexa counted to a hundred, eyes closed, hand warm in Jake's. After she was reasonably sure Elani wasn't at the door anymore, she handed Jake his clothes. "I'm sorry. I really am. But you've got to go. And if you tell Elani, I'll never speak to you again."

He sat up, blanket pooled at his hips, and met her eyes with a serious gaze. Something Lexa didn't even know he had. "Can we talk about this?" He ran a hand down her arm. "Please?"

"It's for the best if we don't. Once dinner is over, I think we should get the hell off this cold planet."

CHAPTER 18

"Lexa Dean. Just when I keep thinking you've had enough of me, you show up again." Reid smiled through the phone screen, straight teeth shining. It was sunny wherever he was.

Standing in the Kuarpan equivalent to a phone booth, Lexa pushed the folding door with her back to keep it closed. The rain came down in sheets out there in the dark, almost freezing. Cars whizzed past on all sides, the street corner crowded with people.

"Need a favor, if you would."

He greeted this with a lascivious smile. "It'll probably cost you."

Without warning, she thought of the cruise ship. How she'd "paid" for the use of the phone there. How it'd been fine or whatever, but ugh. Not like Jake. It was going to take some time before casual sex was fun again.

She kept her lip from curling by sheer force of will. "We need to get off this planet discreetly. I don't want any of this traced back to Elani, or Jake. And I need to go forward, not back to Earth. Can you help me? I'll pay you."

He waggled his eyebrows.

"Money."

His face fell. But he nodded. "Yeah, sure. What can I do?"

"You get that ship booked for Mom and June?"

"Not yet. They wanted to sight-see a bit here on Kuarpa. They've asked me to call your 'uptight Ambran friend' about six times now, to see if she'll give them a tour. I told them I don't know how to get a hold of you but"—he looked over his shoulder—"they don't believe me." He narrowed his eyes and leaned forward. "I guess I still don't have your number. Are you at a pay phone?"

"Yes. It's best if we just keep this all as hands-off as possible." Some near-freezing rain seeped in the door, wetting her back in a line. She leaned back harder, one foot braced on the opposite wall, sealing it out again. "When are you getting the ship?"

"I can get it right now, if you need."

"I do. File your flight plan for Earth."

He smiled. "Where are we really going?"

"I'll tell you once we leave orbit. Gotta make some more calls." She wiggled her fingers at him. "I'll call you in an hour to find out the dock address."

"You got it."

She hung up on him before he could hit on her again. Was she like that? Did people see her on the screen and think, *"Not her again, asking for sex?"*

Teeth clenched, she dialed again.

"Alamay Fix's office."

"Is Fix in, Stev?"

The secretary looked up. "Oh hey, Lexa." He squinted, curls on the top of his head bouncing. "Where are you? Is that a phone booth?"

"Some street corner. You look warm."

He chuckled, the beach hut on the screen behind him filled with warm, red sunlight and reflections from what was surely an ocean. "There are advantages to having your office in a tropical paradise. Especially if it's not on Earth."

"Yeah, no mosquitoes."

Stev laughed, the pale skin of his face reddening across his cheeks. He pointed at the screen. "Exactly. Hold on, I'll get

Alamay." The screen went blue, a pattern of swirls repeating on it like an acid trip, the words "please hold" swirling with them.

She waited, pushing the door tighter. Her back was already soaked, her socks wet inside her shoes. Shoes she'd had to buy, none of Elani's fit her. And warming up when she got back was going to be impossible.

Before the screen flickered back to life, she thought of Jake sliding into bed with her, his skin warm on hers.

"Lexa! So good to see you! Well, 'see'," Fix said, hooking her fingers around the word. Her painted purple lips raised in a wide smile, her brown skin rosy. "Where are you?"

"You're the third person to ask me that in five minutes. I need a favor, Fix. I can pay, if you need it."

Fix nodded, lip drawn up in half a frown. "Probably won't need that. What is it I can help you with?"

"I need covert passage to"—she looked at the notes Elani'd scribbled, once they went through the star maps at the library to be certain —"Grissom 845a."

"845a? That's pretty far out. The very edge of the Grissom telescope's range, in fact." She smiled, almond eyes curving up at the corners.

"Can you get me out there?"

Fix scratched her head, tight curls of her afro waving. "How fast?"

"The fastest route you've got, as long as it's discreet."

"Someone after you?"

Pressing her lips together, Lexa glanced out the side of the clear booth. The rainy street called PNY to mind, the night she escaped Qesson. Well, "escaped." She licked her dry lips. "I just need to get there, without detection, as quick as I can."

"Give me a sec, love." Fix clicked a button and Lexa went back on hold. Some of the blue swirls mixed with gold. The same colors of the lights on the cruise ship dance floor when she, Elani, and Jake had cut a section of it out for themselves.

Dammit. At this point, she'd drop them both if it would do her any good. Leave them here on Kuarpa and be done with it. She wasn't used to guilt floating around her navel; betraying someone she thought of as a friend was something she hadn't experienced since before Gram passed. After all, that's why she didn't have friends. Couldn't betray what you didn't have.

Her feelings about Elani as more than a friend aside, sneaking away in the night or forcing them to stay here just wasn't… Something in her didn't want that. Until she could sort out what that was, she was probably stuck with them. Besides the fact she'd tried to get rid of them umpteen times already, and it never worked out.

The screen beeped. "Lexa, you have a ship?"

She nodded, stomach twisting. "Not sure the make or registration, but I wouldn't tell you if I knew."

Stev laughed in the background. "We love you, too, Lexa," he shouted.

Fix chuckled at him over her shoulder. Smiling, she turned back to Lexa. "I've got what you need. Can I transmit you the coordinates and times?"

Lexa shook her head. "Pay phone. Can you show me?"

"What, are you going to write it down?"

"You know I like pen and paper, Fix." She tugged her small notebook from her front pocket. "What's the info?"

Fix read it off. "Can you make it in seven hours?"

Lexa considered. Get Jake and Elani ready. Meet Reid, Mom, and June at space dock. Get everyone on the ship and out to the coordinates. It was going to be close.

But she nodded. "No problem. I owe you, Fix."

"Yeah you do." The smile disappeared from her voice. "Four thousand."

The blood drained from Lexa's head, making her dizzy. "Four *thousand?* I thought you said you didn't need pay."

"That was before I knew what you needed. I can't just let you use it. I have people to answer to, too."

"Fine. I'll transfer it before we leave."

She hung up, chewing her lip. Once she returned the Cynosure to the Gexcorians—if they let her live long enough to give it back—she wouldn't have enough left to repay Jenierien. This damn site better deliver, or she was royally and truly fucked in the wallet.

CHAPTER 19

"Are you sure you brought enough stuff?"

Lexa stood on the space dock, a pile of suitcases taller than her stacked next to the open door of a large luxury craft. Arms crossed, she peered out the dock windows at it.

A long storage bay stretched away from the dock and met the main living section of the ship. Berths and other rooms like the greenhouse were individually separated and spread around the cockpit like the petals of a blooming rose. Extending at intervals along the length of the loading bay—or the stem—were what Lexa would have called the rose's thorns. Guns, if she had any guess. A lot of these fancy luxury craft didn't come armed, but depending on your destination, that could be a foolish idea. And knowing what they'd gone through on Birkishni, it seemed like Reid hadn't taken the chance. And if that chance should arise and they lost the battle, two runabouts currently moored to the sides of the stem, shaped like leaves. Along the stem was the ship's designation, scrawled in rolling script. ISM *Auriga*.

"We had to get new *clothes*, Alexandra. You got some too, I see." Paisley stopped at the bottom of the ramping bay door, hands on her hips. "They don't fit very well, I must say."

She tugged at the front of the shirt. "Borrowed them from Elani. Are you going to help load this?"

June walked up the ramp, a long, golden skirt wrapped around her waist, nothing but a string top covering her breasts. "That's what servants are for." She disappeared inside.

Elani, arms crossed, looked around the dock. "Where is Reid, anyway? You said they were all coming?"

"I did. He did. Whatever. I don't know." She blew out a breath through her teeth. "Let's start loading this shit. We don't have time to waste waiting."

Jake lifted a large suitcase and stuffed two little ones under his arms. "Can we leave without him?"

"He has the start codes." Lexa didn't make eye contact. It'd been so hard to look at either one of them. She couldn't imagine traveling with them would get any easier, not for a while. But they were soulmates. She had to let them be, even if she couldn't leave them behind. Without another word, she lifted two suitcases and dragged them inside.

Behind her, Jake and Elani carried a few more, Elani murmuring something about blue energy. Once inside, they took the bags to Paisley's berth and dropped them there.

She shouted before they got out the door. "That one is not mine, Allie dear. Could you please take it to your sister?"

Jake and Elani backed out.

Teeth clenched, Lexa grabbed the bag her mother pointed at and hauled it up. All the good will Paisley had built before disappeared in a flash. "Thanks, Mother. I appreciate you considering me 'the help.' You're something else, you know that?"

"What else are children for if not to help out?"

"You're fucking kidding." She dropped the bag in the floor. "What are children for? You seem to be confused on that front. Let me tell you what they aren't for." She stalked across the room. "They are not for you to abandon at the first hint of a great piece of ass and a trip across the galaxy. They are not a trophy for you to show off, something you can show people to prove how young you still are. They are not objects." Finger pointing, she ended up in Paisley's face, her finger jabbed into her chest. "You're on this boat with me because I had no other choice. And if you're not careful, I'll jettison you into space as soon as we leave orbit."

Mouth gaping, Paisley stammered. "I didn't…"

Lexa didn't stay to listen. She kicked June's bag on the way out the door and charged into the hall before her mother could say another word.

Arms crossed so tight across her chest she could barely pull in a breath, she charged back toward the dock. But as she closed in on the bay door, the tops of Elani and Jake's heads came into view where they stood outside the ship.

Face to face, they leaned toward each other. Elani ran her hands across Jake's face, millimeters away from his skin, following the curve of his forehead, over his nose, under his jaw, and then sweeping across his shoulders and out. Much like she had done to Lexa in the hall of the cruise ship when they discovered her family aboard. She soothed Jake, humming, and he leaned closer and closer until their foreheads touched. Eyes closed, he gripped her arms and swayed.

She closed her eyes, too, but kept humming.

Lexa covered her mouth. Spying on such an intimate moment turned her stomach to snakes. She backed into the darkened hallway until she couldn't see them anymore. Before moving again, she kicked the wall and exclaimed, "Watch it, wall."

By the time they came into view again, they stood apart, each bending to pick up bags again. Like the energy-healing bonding had never happened.

She could only imagine what it must feel like to have your soulmate heal your energy like that. What kind of insane, gravity-defying pull it must have. Considering she almost felt like she'd left her body the couple of times Elani had done it to her, she couldn't imagine how intense it must be for Jake. And she couldn't imagine how down he must have been to need it.

Of course now would be when Reid would show up. Sunglasses covered his bright blue eyes, a hat drawn low over his brow. "We ready?"

Lexa gestured. "Help us get these bags. Where the hell did they buy so much crap?"

"I couldn't go with them to the shops." He gave her a lopsided grin. "They were unsupervised."

"No wonder." They hauled the rest of the bags in and shut the door.

Reid chuckled. "Who's flying this thing?"

"We will," Elani said, gripping Jake's arm. "Can you show us to the cockpit?"

He held out a hand. "Right this way."

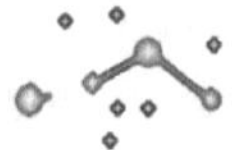

The *ISM Auriga* did just what its title suggested, guiding them through the blackness of the interstellar medium. And this ship was unlike Lexa's, or Elani and Jake's scow. It was made for sight-seeing. Nestled in the center of the flower, a dome of giant curved windows covered one full wall of what could only properly be called the bridge—rather than the cockpit—because of its size. The pilot and copilot sat in chairs suspended in the middle of the bubble, with a third chair on a tier below them, all at the end of a long catwalk. Lexa thought of it as the captain's nest. And there was an observation deck suspended above the pilot and copilot, complete with luxury seating and a fabricator for all the passengers' needs.

Lexa sat there with her mother and sister, occasionally glancing through the grated floor at the tops of Elani and Jake's heads. They watched the display, the ship on smooth auto-pilot, and said little. Jake seemed in a better mood, though. The last few hours they'd spent at Elani's had been full of avoided glances and low energy. So much so, Elani's parents had both commented on it. After Elani told them Lexa considered it rude to peek, they stopped mentioning it.

Lexa got the feeling they were still peeking anyway.

No doubt, Elani wanted to ask about it. But she hadn't, and she'd have to pull Lexa's tongue out to get her to tell her.

"Alexandra, dear, can you tell us where we're going? I'd hate to be inappropriately dressed."

"You're fine, Mom. Where we're going doesn't have a dress code."

"Still."

Juniper sighed. "Why bring us if you're just going to give us the cold shoulder?"

Without moving her head, Lexa cut her eyes at her sister. Her bronze tan glowed in the low light, the light blonde hair on her head shining in a small spotlight that cascaded over the seating area. "Why are you even here? Don't you have at least a boyfriend or something? Kids of your own? You could get any man you want. Human or not."

June's mouth pinched closed.

"Even I know not to ask that question," Reid said, turning from the fabricator. He set a drink in front of both Paisley and Juniper, and laid a hand on June's shoulder. "That's highly insensitive of you."

Lexa's brows dipped. "How can it be insensitive? No one tells me what's going on in your lives. You left me with Gram and pretended I didn't exist. I did the same. If you can't be bothered to tell me, I can't be bothered to care. Sorry I asked." She stood and leaned over the rail, stomach churning. She shouldn't feel bad for something she didn't know about. It was ridiculous, and yet, as Elani would say, here she was.

A twinge of regret for ever seeing the map clenched her teeth. This whole trip had been nothing but a mess. She stared down at Elani and Jake and their silent communication.

She turned to leave.

Paisley spoke up. "Where are you going?"

"To find my cat. The only person on this ship worth talking to." *And the only one who will care I'm around.*

"I'm sorry, Lexa. We should have told you."

Mom's use of her chosen name for the second time stopped her in her tracks. She faced her mother. "What?"

"Junie came on this trip with me because her family…they're gone."

June covered her face.

Reid pulled Lexa's chair next to her and sat in it so he could hug June to him.

She sank into his chest, silent sobs wracking her shoulders.

Lexa's stomach thought about throwing up the clam chowder she wolfed down after they'd gotten underway. Ambran cuisine was fine, but nothing about it was warm. And the ship was still chilly, because she didn't want Elani to be uncomfortable. She'd set the environmental controls at 20 degrees Celsius like they'd been on the cruise ship.

Paisley looked over June's head at Lexa. "Why don't we just talk about where we're going?"

She glanced out the windows. The black of space was no longer a blank canvas. In front of the ship sat a colossal ring, the edges like that of a bubble, or crystal ball. It reflected light back at them from what few stars lay behind them, shining like a lens flare.

"I don't have to tell you." She stood again and sprinted down the stairs. She forgot all about the embarrassment, the pain, the wish she could leave Elani and Jake behind, and dashed down the catwalk to them. She stood on the platform between their chairs and panted. "We're here."

Jake's mouth open, he reached for her. "I've never seen one of these, I thought they weren't real."

Everything forgotten but the enormity of what was in front of her, she took his hand and squeezed. "They're real. And this one is stable."

Elani grabbed her other hand. "Stable? Do you mean we're…" She trailed off.

"Yeah."

"We're what?" Paisley shouted down.

Lexa looked up at her. "We're going through it."

June joined their mother at the railing. "Going through what? That bubble thing?"

Elani lowered her voice. She stood and leaned into Lexa's ear. "That's what you see? A bubble?"

"Yeah. Like a crystal ball. Or a fish-eye lens. A kind of shining, circular distortion in space." She turned to her, their faces centimeters apart. "Why? What do you see?"

Still looking at it, Elani whispered. "So much energy. It's pulling it in at the same time as pushing it out. It's folding all the energy in all the colors, even the ones that don't exist, around itself. It's like…" She trailed off, staring and slack-jawed.

Jake stood too, the two of them forming a warm cocoon around her.

In that moment, gratitude that she'd brought them this far overwhelmed her. Despite what had happened at Elani's, despite the fact one day—hopefully later rather than sooner—Elani would find out about Lexa's betrayal, having these two with her filled her with a happiness she never expected. Had never felt.

"Lexa, what is it?" Impatience tapped its foot in June's voice.

Elani answered before Lexa could. "It's a wormhole," she said, still staring out at it. "And it's one of the most beautiful and terrifying things I've ever seen."

A wolfish, daring grin spread Lexa's cheeks. "And we're gonna fly right through it."

CHAPTER 20

*I*t comes on slowly. I look left and right, my eyes too big for their sockets. They pulse with my heartbeat, like they will pop out of my face and land on the ground, the light reflecting off the wet, squishy insides of them.

The air is thick. Not like fog. Not like humidity. It is solid. I could use a knife to cut a piece of it out and eat it, the color of iridescence. It would taste like eating my own tongue, and the person on the other end could hear me speak the words.

Words. They existed once, but now they make no sense. Someone—I don't know her name but she has shining brown skin and golden eyes to match—she tries to speak to me. But if she is speaking a language, any language, I cannot recognize it. Her tongue sneaks out and wets her lips, and the saliva there turns pink. Is it the color of her lips beneath? Or the light shining down from above? From everywhere.

We are going too fast. My forehead pulls away from my eyebrows, like the wind pushes me back while I fly toward the end. The end of what? Everything? Maybe the universe. Maybe myself.

Where? Where is this?

My chest is so heavy. I must remember to breathe. I must force my chest up and down, up and down, so it doesn't turn inside-out. There are a thousand people singing here, voices raised in a discordant harmony of song that pounds the depths of my soul. It's turned inside-out anyway, but yes…my body is still here. It's racing.

That voice! It comes from all around me. I can breathe again as it speaks. It's a man? What is a man, I don't know if I can picture it? But it is one.

And he is soothing, like fresh air. An opening into the world I knew, something to hold onto.

The racing ends.

In its place, whispering. Hands tickling, touching, gripping. My skin tingles.

Breathing, loud in my ears. Is it mine? Or is it theirs? The air fills my lungs, it must be mine.

Voices again, overlapping. A shouting, singing realization of shattering. Blue.

It's blue.

The sides of the tunnel appear and I am tumbling through it. There are others, but are they going to the same destination? Do they know where it is? Do I? The tunnel turns, its sides slick, colors of purple and orange and green interfering with each other. Overlapping. The sound of them sharp but soothing, a slow beat like a human heart.

Before my eyes, the stars flower. The flower opens, it is the center of the universe. And it is beautiful. I can touch it. I created it. I made it matter, and so it is matter.

Who am I?

I am.

The flower folds in on itself, re-sealing its secrets in the depths of the bloom. But they are there, I have seen them, and I will always remember them.

CHAPTER 21

Lexa woke, floating in space. The stars pinpricks in the distance against the black cloth of interstellar medium. One red one glowed brighter than the rest.

With a start, she sat up, hand pressed against the cool glass. Something held her, kept her from standing.

She glanced down.

Both Elani and Jake clutched her, both also laying at the bottom of the glass dome. Their eyes wide, they searched her face, and she didn't have words for either of them. Her mouth flopped like a dying fish in the sand.

From above, Paisley spoke, but her voice came from a thousand kilometers away. "That was worth the cost of admission and then some. Juniper, where are you?"

Lexa shook her head, trying to rid her ears of the cotton.

Elani used Lexa's arm and shoulder to pull herself up and the three of them slid further down the slick side of the bowed glass. She buried her face in Lexa's neck and clutched the other side with her hand, encircling Lexa in something that felt equal parts hug and lifesaver, like the ones they would toss to drowning victims on the ocean. She spoke into Lexa's hair. "I have never seen so many colors in all my life."

Her eyes met Lexa's.

They were no longer golden. Not only. They swirled with the iridescence Lexa had seen in her fever dream, whatever trance the wormhole had put her in. And they glowed so bright, Lexa almost wanted to look away.

"Elani, your eyes…" She put a hand up to her face.

Elani closed them. "I don't feel the same."

Jake sat up and folded both of them in his arms. So warm. "I don't think any of us do. And how did we get down here?"

"Lexa," Reid called.

She cranked her neck and looked up, finding him leaning over the railing of the observation balcony.

"I think you should get up here."

Lexa tried to stand. Her feet went out from under her, the glass too slick and rounded. She chuckled. "How do we get out of this bowl?"

Jake scrambled to his feet, bent at the waist, and duck-walked to the lower seat's platform. "Here." He stuck out a hand.

Lexa grabbed it and let him pull her, the muscles in his arm standing out, until she could catch the platform.

He did the same for Elani, and hoisted her up onto the platform with one arm, her legs pin-wheeling, until she got her midsection over the lip.

Then he reached to help Lexa.

One look in his eyes told her he hadn't had Elani fix his energy so much as let her slough off the worst of it. The rest of the positivity she'd seen so far on this trip, since they boarded the same ship once again, was his effervescent personality. And it was quite clear from the way he squeezed her waist and inhaled her scent deep into his lungs when he pushed her up to the platform that he very much was not about to never mention it again.

But he did her the favor of not mentioning it right then, and simply helped her onto the platform.

Elani and Lexa both turned around to help him up.

"There needs to be a ladder or something," Elani said, staring into the bowl with her hands on her hips.

"If we see another spaceport anytime soon, I'll have one put in," Lexa said, staring down with her. The stars beneath, above, and in front of them almost seemed to increase in brightness.

"Lexa," Reid called again.

"Yeah, coming," she said, still looking at Elani. Everything slowed, and the energy Elani said she could see seemed to flow out of her, like it'd done in the scow bucket, and covered Lexa in a sheath of warmth. Standing between Elani and Jake, holding both their hands, the reasons she never let anyone close after Gram died seemed as far away as Earth.

Savannah meowed.

"Oh shit, my cat," Lexa said, dropping Elani and Jake's hands and tripping up the stairs to the pilot and copilot seats. She hurried down the catwalk, clicking her tongue. "Come here, girl. Are you OK? You made it through the wormhole?"

Van warbled, showing Lexa her butt instead, and flicked her tail in the air.

"Oh so now you're mad. Are you out of food?"

"Alexandra, please," her mom called.

She rolled her eyes and chased the cat to the stairs going up. Van stopped at the bottom and licked a paw. "Yeah Mom. One sec." She picked up the cat and stroked her. "I would not have taken you through that if I knew that's what it was like," Lexa said. "My first time, too." She kissed her on the head and sat her down when they reached the top of the stairs. Elani and Jake followed, their feet clanging the metal staircase behind her.

Why Juniper had been the only one to not say anything after their trip through the wormhole became obvious as soon as Lexa looked up.

She lay on the floor of the observation deck, her cheek pressed into the metal grate, her legs partially on the carpet that lie beneath the chairs, couch, and table. Drool slid from her mouth, and her forehead raised off the metal from a goose-egg she must have gotten from falling. Her eyes open but unfocused, shifted back and forth while her mouth moved. No sound escaped it.

"Juniper?" Lexa knelt next to her sister, hand on her shoulder, and lowered her voice. "Junie? Are you OK?"

Still silent, June shook her head the tiniest fraction. She didn't make eye contact, but Lexa was relatively certain she was responding directly to her question.

Lexa sat back on her heels. "Reid, pick her up. Let's take her to her quarters. I want a better look at that hematoma."

"Is she going to be OK?" Paisley's voice shook.

"She's fine, Mom. I think she hit her head when we came through, that's all."

She got under June's other arm and she and Reid helped her down the stairs. Juniper at least moved her legs on her own, even if they didn't fully support her weight. It was a bit like someone who'd had too much to drink, which Lexa suspected June had done more than once in her life.

Paisley trailed them. "Where are we?"

"We made it through the wormhole," Lexa said, stepping off the last stair and turning them toward the quarters. "By my calculations, we should be next door to our destination star system."

Elani stepped off the stairs behind them. "Could we see the map?"

"I don't think—"

"Alexandra, correct me if I'm wrong but we all just risked our lives coming through that thing with you. I'd like to know why."

Lexa opened her mouth to argue.

The image of the universe opening before her like a flower intruded, reminding her there was more to existence than being mad at her mother. And Mom was right. They'd come along because she forced them. She literally asked for their help to get her here.

"Elani," she said, "get Savannah's bag. It's time to show you all what we came for."

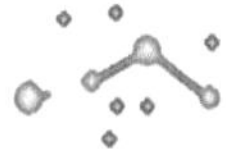

In the petal Juniper had taken for her berth, one of the outer ones with a wall of windows, they all gathered, Savannah included. Although Van radiated "I just happened to find myself in the same room as you" energy and curled up at the foot of June's bed, her back to everyone. Juniper also lied on the bed and Reid covered her, rubbing her shoulder. The hematoma on her forehead wasn't bleeding, and the handheld scanner in the first aid kit showed Lexa a minor bump beneath. No concussion.

Not that she cared, but…OK maybe she cared a little.

Paisley sat on June's other side, her back to the window.

Elani and Jake—Elani's eyes already returning to normal—shared an oversized chair almost big enough to call a love seat. Apropos.

Lexa flipped the top of Savannah's bag open. Hands shaking, hopefully imperceptible to the rest of the room, she pulled the map and Cynosure out of the bag. The glass of the teardrop warm, she held it up. "This is what the Gexcorians want." Starlight shone through it, reflecting into her eyes. Lowering it, she held up the map. "It goes to this. Key"—she held up the Cynosure—"map. Together, they've led us to this system. And should take us to the origin of all life in the galaxy. I hope."

The light from the pinprick she'd seen on Birkishni shone through the back of the rolled-up map. That was new.

Paisley crossed her arms. "And where are we?"

Lexa blew a slow breath out from between tight lips. She checked the stars, looking for any shape she recognized. Even the galactic bar in the center of the galaxy looked different. Why shouldn't it? "We're in what some cultures refer to as the Sanctum. What Earth astronomers simply call 3kpc."

Elani covered her mouth.

Everyone else stared, faces slack, eyes blank. No recognition of the fact they'd traveled over twenty-thousand light years in what felt like minutes. Hours, at most. Except for Elani, they must not have known the distance.

Hesitating, Lexa stared out the window at the strange stars. Stars she'd only seen in photos from long-range telescopes. Stars that were so far away, they hardly had names. Only a little-known constellation, Ophiuchus. The serpent bearer, who had appeared in the center of the map she now rolled open on the floor.

Savannah sat up.

Lexa cut her eyes at the cat and held out a hand. "Don't even think about it."

The tip of her tail swished.

One eye on the cat, the other on the map and Cynosure, Lexa held up the teardrop again. "You can see here, the map is glowing. It didn't do that on Birkishni, not once the location had been revealed. It stopped glowing. I don't know why it's doing this, but—"

"Lexa," Paisley said, leaning over Juniper, "I'm impressed you can read the map. It makes no sense to me. But it's gorgeous. How does it know?"

She shrugged, laying the Cynosure on the map. Like all the times before, the map reached up to greet its friend, maybe its lover for all she knew, and the glass warmed in her hand before they met. Starlight from the open ceiling shone onto them both, a large concentration of red from the nearest of them, and the light focused and radiated onto the map. "I think…" She trailed off, staring at the amplified starlight on the map's surface. The way it moved, like light shining through the tide.

When Savannah had scratched it, the map reacted. Until Lexa apologized to it, it had thrown a true fit, trying to shred Lexa's sheets. And the pearls of the Cynosure moved when they were together, aligning to meet some pattern only the Cynosure and the map knew. And the thing couldn't be zipped. Wasn't that enough evidence?

"I think it's alive," she said, her voice low. She ran her hand over the map without touching it, much the same way Elani did when she was feeling energies.

"I've never seen energy like this," Elani whispered, as though she'd heard Lexa's thoughts. "It is alive, Lexa. They both are. But moreso when they're touching." She crawled into the floor and knelt on the opposite side of the map. "When you showed me the Cynosure before," she said, flicking her eyes at the others, "it was not like this. It is beautiful, no question, but it was not alive like it is right now. It came alive when you lowered it to the map, and their energies…" She trailed off, her mouth raised in a smile Lexa wasn't sure she meant to have. Her eyes unfocused and she stared over Lexa's shoulder. Still smiling, but now like she meant it, she met Lexa's eyes. "They resonate like soulmates."

Lexa forgot to breathe. The pull from Elani crushed her gut, pulled her like a hand gripped her she couldn't see. Tugged her toward Elani's swirling eyes, toward the energy Lexa knew for a fact she was pushing on her. She had to be; nothing was this magnetic without being on purpose.

Before Lexa's hollow, gut-punched center could react, Van leapt from the bed and pounced on the map.

Light exploded from the Cynosure, bathing the room in red, like they'd all been covered in blood. It practically dripped from the walls, and it was so bright, it shone out into space.

June screamed and covered her eyes. "Make it stop!"

Eyes closed, Lexa shooed her cat. "Van, get!" She flapped a hand in the direction of what she thought was the map. Red light streamed through her closed eyelids, and she covered them with the other hand to try and mitigate it. At least the map didn't try to vibrate its way through the bulkheads.

Sweeping her hand across the floor, she connected with the Cynosure, the glass now hot. So hot, it seemed it may begin to melt any minute now. Her flailing hand hit it, sending it skidding away. The glass tinkled against the floor, and the light dissipated.

Opening her eyes cautiously, she squinted around the room. Everyone sat with their eyes covered, and Jake had jumped in the floor with Elani to cover her eyes with his own arms.

Elani peeped over his forearm. "Is it over? What happened?"

Lexa rolled up the map, the shake in her hands definitely visible to everyone else this time. "The map doesn't like Savannah. She scratched it the first time they met." She looked around for the Cynosure. It must have scooted under June's bed. Face on the cold floor, she searched for it in the dark space beneath the bed. Nothing there.

She sat back on her heels. "It's not there. Anyone see it?"

And though they looked for a good 15 minutes, no one could find the damn thing. It was like it disappeared.

For all Lexa knew, it could have done just that. When Reid suggested maybe that flash was the Cynosure destroying itself, either to keep others away from the site or because that's what it was supposed to do once it had revealed the location on the map, Lexa couldn't deny it made a certain kind of sense.

But the Gexcorians were not going to be happy.

Chair drawn up to the observation deck's railing, her arms crossed over the cold metal and chin resting on them, Lexa stared out the front windows at the red star nearby. They'd popped out of the wormhole not far from it, but without light speed lanes or the specialized equipment to find one, it'd take a few days to hit the star system.

Feet echoed off the stairs.

Lexa didn't turn around.

Whoever it was sat in silence. Whether they waited for her to speak or also just wanted to watch the system come closer, they said nothing for several minutes, the silence between them as empty as the space outside the windows. The mystery of the universe surrounded them both, the red star lighting up its heliosphere with pinks and reds and orange slowly shifting like a sunset, pushing invisible solar winds out into interstellar space.

But the silence had to be broken.

"Lexa," her mom said softly.

Lexa didn't turn, but for the first time in a long time, longer than she cared to recall, her stomach didn't clench at the sound of her mother's voice. She had no words for Paisley, but she hoped she'd take her silence as assent.

She did. "Can I ask you something personal?" The quiet in her voice almost reverent.

There were so many ways this could go wrong, but right now, Lexa didn't want to look too hard at them. She sighed out her nose and nodded her head, a slow up and down bob, and turned to face her.

"Why aren't you keeping up with the treatments? It won't take long for your aging process to progress too far to stop. Maybe a decade or less, considering your age. And you…" She trailed off and broke eye contact, staring out at the stars. A tear trickled down one cheek.

Lips pressed together, Lexa watched her struggle and waited to see if she had more to say. When it was obvious she didn't, Lexa turned back to the stars. "Gram never got a single one."

"I know."

"Do you know why?"

"Because she was a stubborn old woman."

"Old? You're sixty years older than she ever was. You're one to talk about old."

"Fine." Paisley sighed. "She was stubborn though. You know that."

Lexa nodded, her chin digging into her arm. "That wasn't why."

"She told you?"

Facing her again, Lexa crossed her arms over her stomach, the backs of them cold from the railing. The only good news about her relationship with Jake and Elani falling apart as quickly as it'd come together was soon she could turn the ship's heat back up and leave it. "We lived together for seventeen years, Paisley. She was all I had. She was my best friend. Yes, she told me."

Paisley brushed the tear on her cheek away with the back of a finger. "Would you tell me?"

"So she didn't?"

"Tell me? No. We weren't close. Not like the two of you. You were better off with her than me."

Stomach tight, Lexa squeezed her arms harder. "You don't know that. You never gave it a chance. You got some random donor to give you a baby and then decided you didn't want her after all."

Lips pinched together, Paisley dragged her chair across the carpet, the legs scraping on the fibers louder than anything else in the room. She stopped next to Lexa and sat. "That's not how it went." Her voice so low, it was almost a whisper.

Staring at the bulkhead across from her, Lexa nodded and swallowed back tears, her throat burning and eyes stinging. "'If life has no end, what would give it meaning?' That's what she said to me. As she lay there dying, wheezing out her last breaths, and you halfway across the sector, that's what she said to me."

Paisley sniffed. "If you agreed with her, why did you ever get treatments at all?"

"Seemed like the cool thing to do at the time." She stood and considered how hard she would drop to the glass if she leapt over the railing. Probably only hard enough to get a bump like June's. Artificial gravity was good but you couldn't get up to full speed like on a planet. Pros and cons.

"If I pay for it, would you start getting treatments again?"

"I—"

Static crackled and screeched from the pilot's chair, the sound loud enough to make Lexa wince as it invaded her eardrums. Without another word to her mom, Lexa rushed down the stairs.

She collided with Elani at the bottom, and they grabbed each other rather than fall down. Elani's hands warm on Lexa's cold arms.

Her golden eyes inspected Lexa's face. "You OK?" And before Lexa spoke, she shook her head. "I'm not reading you, I promise. It's all over your expression."

Lexa grabbed her hand and tugged her toward the pilot's chair. "Fine. What is that sound?"

"The radio. We must have left it on."

They approached the chair and the sound grew in intensity and volume. Lexa's eardrums vibrated when it oscillated to a higher frequency. She clenched her teeth and tried to find the button to turn it down.

"Let me," Elani said, sneaking past her. She kept Lexa's hand in one of hers and worked the radio buttons with the other. The volume diminished.

Exhaling, Lexa sat in the copilot's chair. She squeezed Elani's hand. "Thank you. That was unbearable."

Elani met her eyes. "Anything I can do to make you feel better." She smiled. For a long moment, they sat, staring into each other's eyes, breathing in the newly reestablished silence.

Until the radio crackled again.

"Dr. Alexandra Dean, you have something that belongs to us."

CHAPTER 22

The PA broadcast the Gexcorian's message throughout the entire ship. It echoed down the hallway, from which Jake came running. Reid and Juniper followed not far behind. While they stopped at the stairs, Jake rushed down the catwalk and joined Lexa and Elani at the nest. He gripped Lexa's shoulder, and removed his hand almost as fast.

"Sorry," he said, speaking to her. "Who is that? What do they want?"

She gestured to the air. "The Cynosure. It's the Gexcorians."

"How did they find us? Are they here?"

Holding her breath, stomach tight, she sat at the co-pilot's seat and flipped on the valdar—vibration and laser detection and ranging. This was something else humans had borrowed from aliens, but it worked in a similar way to radar or sonar.

The screen was empty. Not even a rogue asteroid.

She exhaled, but her stomach remained tight. "I don't see them close, but they have to be on this side of the wormhole. You can't send a message this fast through space, and you can't transmit through a wormhole."

"Dr. Dean, surely you haven't forgotten me so soon."

She fingered the knob for the radio. They were here. They shared the same space, even if they weren't on the valdar yet. Thank the universe this ship was fast. Maybe they could outrun them to the system.

And then what?

She clicked on. "Ferrinogean. Good to hear your dulcet tones again. You guys get your ship fixed?"

Jake bounced on his feet behind Lexa. Elani reached over to the arm of the co-pilot's seat and gripped it, and energy flowed from her to Lexa, at least in thought if not in reality.

But it calmed Lexa, either way.

Ferrinogean laughed through the comm, sounding for all the world like the laugh bubbled underwater. *"You did extensive damage to that ship, Lexa. We had to get a new one. Faster. Stronger."* He laughed again. *"It's not long before we catch you. You still have it, don't you?"*

The bravado in his voice couldn't hide the tremble when he asked about the Cynosure. His fear dripped through the radio.

Lexa clenched her teeth. Knowing the Gexcorians, they were unlikely to give up pursuit at this point. They were nothing if not determined. Look at how Maridoxia had continued trying to kill invaders, even after death. If Lexa told them she didn't have it, they'd blow up the ship the moment they caught up.

If she told them she did have it, they'd continue to follow, but wouldn't blow her up *immediately*. They'd give her some warning first. Probably.

She flipped to transmit. "What would I do with it?"

"You've already sold it once. And stolen it twice. Who is to say you haven't sold it again to get that new ship? Seeing as how we exploded your previous ship into dust, the price of a new ship isn't…cheap."

Lexa worked through all the possible responses she had but couldn't land on one that made enough sense to give him. All the things that'd happened since they last encountered him on Birkishni crowded her thoughts, bunched up in her throat, and turned her stomach. Everything was so much more complicated, she'd almost be willing to give him the Cynosure back—if she had it—if it would make all these emotions stop.

She buried her face in her hands.

Jake leaned over her and clicked the radio on again. "We'll only negotiate face to face, and we won't speak to you at all again until we see you at the coordinates I'm transmitting to you now." His arms surrounding Lexa, he extended his fingers and they flew over the console. A series of rapid beeps transmitted to the Gexcorian ship out there in the mysterious dark.

Seconds, loud ones, passed.

Lexa tried not to breathe in, but his scent swam up her nose anyway. Slightly woody, a little musky, and a whiff of earthy soap. Her stomach didn't ask before it lodged itself in her throat. Her heart pounded below it, both of them trying to suffocate her.

"We will meet you at those coordinates. If you do not present the Cynosure, we will be forced to take physical action."

The transmission faded and the panel went dark.

Mumbling another apology, Jake crumpled to the floor between the two chairs. His voice low, he whispered to the deck. "We don't have it."

Lexa almost reached out to grip his shoulder. Instead, she heard Elani's mom asking why she didn't mention Elani was bringing her soulmate home.

She glanced at Elani. "We don't. But you did the best thing we could hope for right now, which is buy us some time."

Elani leaned over the arm of her chair and did grip Jake's shoulder. But she spoke to Lexa. "How do they keep finding us?"

Lexa shrugged. "Maybe the Cynosure transmits a signal when it comes alive. Last time they showed up, it was after I'd used it."

"And the first time?"

"They followed me to Earth. Not hard to work that one out."

"But how did they find the wormhole? How did they get through? Aren't there guard patrols?"

"Yes, and we got through the patrols because we had the access code. Maybe someone gave them the code, too."

Jake raised his knees and rested his chin on them. "They were so quick. How were they so quick?"

That one, Lexa didn't have an answer for. She cast around for it, but the only thing she could think of was maybe Fix tipped them off. Or whoever Fix had gotten the info from, though Lexa doubted that person knew who the codes were for.

Someone walked out onto the catwalk, their feet softly echoing off the latticed metal path.

Lexa peered around the side of the chair.

June stared out at the stars, their light reflecting in her eyes. "Well sister, if we're going to die when we get there, we may as well enjoy the ride. Tell me about those." She pointed at a large red star cluster and lifted a brow. "This isn't a side of the galaxy I'd ever bet on seeing, and dammit I'm going to enjoy the ride."

Truly, what else could they do?

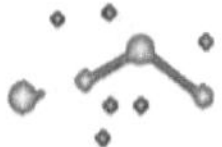

The med bay wasn't as unwelcoming as some others Lexa'd seen, but it still reminded her of the doctor's office on Mars where she got her DNAging done. Every time she walked in there a wave of sadness mixed with anxiety and surgery nerves hit her, mingled with the hope she wouldn't have to come back for another fifty years and the knowledge these cheap treatments only lasted about thirty, tops.

She rifled through the trauma tray, plucking out the few instruments she'd need and the electronic bandages—tech that'd been a gift from the Gexcorians, of all people.

"Is this really necessary?"

She spoke over her shoulder. "June, you hit your head really good. I know the scanner didn't show a concussion, but sometimes those things are wrong and these bandages"—she raised them and flapped them in the air, their little flexible circuits slapping against each other like real latex—"will help that hematoma heal in record time. No bruising, either." She faced her sister, frowning. It hurt her face. "If you want me to give you this tour of the stars, you're going to have to let me patch you up. Besides, I know you want to look your best when we get there."

Not a single line appeared next to her mouth when she smiled. "Always."

"Here." Lexa set everything on the small rolling table next to June's patient couch. The bay held three couches, each adjustable and each comfortable enough to sleep on, with sparkling clean white padded seats. "Let's check again with this scanner. It's a little better than the one in the first aid kit."

June closed her eyes and pursed her lips. Chin tucked, she leaned forward.

This close, the high cost of her treatments was obvious. Tight over her brow and cheeks, her skin showed almost zero blemishes. She hardly wore any makeup and her complexion didn't need it. Even her eyebrows were perfect. It wasn't just DNAging she was getting done.

Anger, and no small amount of jealousy, floating around Lexa's temples, pressing in on her skull, she cast about for something to say while the scanner did its job. What she landed on wasn't what she intended to say, but, "What happened to your family?" was out of her mouth before she knew what was happening.

To her credit, June didn't flinch. If she had, they'd have had to start the scan over. But tears rolled down both cheeks, her eyes still squeezed closed. "An accident."

"But you were OK?"

"I wasn't with them. It was just me and Doug and our daughter, Ayan."

Completely sorry she began the conversation, the need to finish it overwhelmed Lexa. June didn't mention them before, she simply cried. If she wanted to talk about it, or was willing, was it right to stop her? Wasn't that what the one counselor Lexa saw after Gram's death said? That talking about it helped? Not like she'd gone back after the government-mandated three visits, but it was something like that.

So instead, she asked a few questions. This scanner was thorough but it was slow as molasses. "How old was Ayan?"

"Eleven."

Not even old enough to begin DNAging. You had to be a fully-developed adult—25—before they would let you fuck with your DNA.

"Shit, June. I'm sorry. That must have been—"

"Bullshit? Horrific? Unfair? All that, yeah. More." Her fingers twisted together. "I miss them so much, Lexa. So much." More tears rolled out from under her closed eyelids. "Ayan was going to be an exoarchaeologist like her famous aunt."

Ah, fuck.

The scanner beeped so loud, Lexa jumped, her stomach a knot. It clattered to the ground and she cursed. "Sorry, June." She wasn't sure if she meant about dropping the scanner, or June's family, or bringing it up, but it seemed like June took it to mean all three.

She flapped her hand and wiped her face with the other. "No. It's fine. My assigned grief counselor told me to talk about it, and I haven't. I went out and found the Litmus Agency a week after I scattered their ashes into the sun and scheduled this trip with Mom. It was my idea to come out to Gram's," she said, voice hitching.

Lexa stood with the scanner, results forgotten in the wake of what she knew June was about to say.

"I wanted you to come with us. I wanted you to know about Ayan." She met Lexa's eyes, her lashes wet and stuck together. "I know we weren't close. And I'm sorry. I wish it was different."

Laying the scanner on the couch next to June, Lexa grabbed her hand and squeezed. "I'm sorry I never called. I'm sorry I didn't even know she existed. I didn't think you knew *I* did."

June chuckled and pulled a fob from her waistband. "Do you want to see a picture?"

Unable, unwilling, to say no, Lexa nodded.

From Juniper's palm, a holographic image of a little girl popped to life. She had on a wide-brimmed khaki-colored hat, khaki shorts, and a polo. There wasn't a millimeter on her not covered in dirt, and she knelt next to something out of frame. She clutched a hand shovel in one hand and the smile across her face lit up the picture from the inside out.

June's smile wasn't as bright. "I used to plant alien artifacts Doug would bring home, just trinkets, in the back yard and let her dig them up. Just like her Aunt Lexa."

Lexa's eyes stung. Burned. A dam inside threatened to burst. Such a bright face—that smile, that upturned, button nose. Dirt caked on it, just like Lexa at that age. She'd known what she wanted to do, too, from the time she was four years old. She dug so many holes in Gram's backyard, Gram almost broke her ankle more than half a dozen times.

The picture, mercifully, flipped to another.

A tall brunette man, Ayan on his shoulders. A wide smile showed all his straight, white teeth, his white skin red from the sun and flushed from carrying Ayan up high. The picture was so good, Lexa could make out sweat glistening on his brow and a small puff of cotton candy stuck on the edge of his mouth. This picture moved with them for the briefest of moments, the two of them repeating the same laugh, over and over and over again until June quietly shut the display down.

"I don't know what to do without them."

Lexa met June's wide, naked eyes. Her mouth flopped. As much a diversion as anything, she formulated another question before the tragedy of it all forced her onto the couch next to June. "What did Doug do for a living?"

June smiled. "He was a Shadow. The best in the business."

"Aren't they like bounty hunters?"

"No." June's eyes hardened. "No, he was the best tracker in the sector. Maybe even the quadrant. No one could top him, and he only took on the most difficult cases. Things the police couldn't solve. In fact, they sent him an intergalactic case a week before he died. He was so excited about it. Some Ambran."

Lexa choked. "An…Ambran?"

"An abuse of power, he said. He couldn't tell me much about his work. But he picked up the trail fast. Said he almost had it licked. And then…" She trailed off, her eyes drifting down. "Does that say I don't have a concussion?"

Lexa followed her eyes to the scanner and checked the results, the readout upside-down. "You're clean. Just let me put these e-bands on."

June nodded. "You're the boss."

Chuckling, Lexa stuck the first one on. It lit briefly, tiny lights inside mimicking the look of a circuit board. She unwrapped the second one and went to stick it on.

The ship rocked and she missed, sticking it in June's hair. "Shit," she said, hand on the med couch. "The fuck was that?"

Jake sprinted past the open door of the bay. "Lexa!" His voice Dopplered away, following him down the hall.

June tweezed the e-band out of her hair with two fingers, nodding. "Go. I've got this."

Breath caught in the back of her mouth, Lexa followed Jake to the bridge.

CHAPTER 23

A robotic voice sounded from the PA. *"Halt your progress and prepare to be boarded."*

Eyes wide, Elani watched Lexa and Jake run down the catwalk. "It's the Gexcorians again. They closed in fast." She pointed to the valdar screen.

Lexa skidded to a stop behind the co-pilot's chair where the display flickered. A dot moved toward the *Auriga*, blinking when the screen refreshed.

Jake made a bunch of noise back there, and Lexa braced herself for the inevitable collision.

He ran into her, smashing her midsection against the chair.

She winced. "Bowl me over next time, Jake."

He gripped her shoulder. "I'm sorry, Lex. I didn't mean to hurt you."

Boy, if that wasn't a loaded statement. She could hear it in his voice, the regret. Not just for this.

It was like a tiny child pushed a sharpened ice pick straight into her heart, pushing pushing pushing until it popped and spilled hot blood everywhere.

"You didn't hurt me. You're good." She met his eyes, hoping he could hear the meaning behind the words like she'd heard in his.

He opened his mouth, his eyes wide, and stepped around her. "That's good." He slid into the co-pilot's chair and fiddled with the valdar knob. The picture sharpened.

Lexa leaned between both of them and nodded her forehead at Elani. "Flip the radio on."

The click of the transmit button echoed against the glass, ringing in Lexa's ears.

"Ferrinogean. Back so soon? I thought we told you not to contact us again until we got to the system."

"I am altering the deal."

Another gun blast rocked the ship.

Jake punched buttons. "I can't see what the damage is from here. Lexa, get down in the other chair. See if you can tell how bad it is."

Lexa slid between them and skipped the three stairs to the lower station. She sat, bringing up the display for the first time. It glowed blue. She checked the main readouts.

Radio.

View.

Damage.

Valdar.

Weapons.

Ah. This was tactical. That made sense. She flipped on the weapons, the viewer, and the valdar. On the valdar touch-screen, she tapped the Gexcorian ship. The weapons display alerted her it was acquiring target. She couldn't feel the ship turning, but the stars moved, and that was enough to tell her the display wasn't kidding.

Once they finished the turn, she didn't need the view screen anymore.

The Gexcorian gunship sat in space off their starboard side. It filled the entirety of the window on the right side, their own guns not hidden like the *Auriga*'s. That was OK. This ship was just as deadly. Lexa had counted seven thorns protruding from the stem. Reid had done well, choosing a comfortable ship that could stand its ground.

She flipped to transmit. "You don't want me altering the deal, either." Stomach in knots, pressing on her bladder, she fired the smallest gun she saw on the display.

The shot bounced off their hull.

Which reminded her.

Her eyes flicked down to *damage*.

Not too bad. No breaches. Nothing that would need repair.

Yet.

She glanced up at Elani and Jake. At this angle, she could see their feet and the bottoms of their chins. They both faced the Gexcorian ship, lips drawn tight over their teeth. Their expressions almost mirrored one another.

Not like she had time to think about the soulmate thing, but she should have known. She did know. She just wanted what she wanted, and damn the consequences.

And for the first time in 97 years, that sat sideways in her head…and in her heart.

"I will be coming aboard to accompany you to the system. We must be allowed to verify the Cynosure is safe."

Oh that was going to be a trick.

Jake popped up and ran away.

Lexa couldn't blame him. She wanted to do the same. Her bladder agreed.

"Listen," she said, leaning close to the radio, "I can't let you on board. I'm telling you, it's here, it's safe, and you'll see it when we reach the system. If you don't back off, I'll shoot it into space and you'll never see it again."

The *Auriga* rocked with another blast.

A yellow warning lamp illuminated in front of Lexa.

Stomach now in her toes, she checked it.

One of their guns had been shot right off the ship. The way the stem was designed, this wouldn't affect the living environment, which was why it was only yellow. But in Lexa's mind, it was red. Red red red as blood.

She glanced up at Elani.

Who leaned between her knees and held a hand out for Lexa.

She took it, the pull so strong she almost lifted from her seat, and squeezed. "We're going to be all right."

With the other hand, she flipped to transmit once again. "I'll meet you at the docking port."

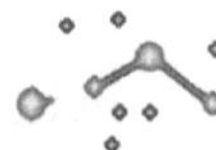

The Gexcorian ship latching on rocked the *Auriga*, her frame shuddering when the gears screwed in tight. Lexa could only imagine the way it looked in space. Like a carp with its mouth around a fishing rod. Only they were the ones caught on the hook.

Before holing up in Paisley's room with her and Juniper, Reid had shown Lexa to the weapons locker. Lexa'd taken an energy rifle and now pointed it at the docking bay door as it lowered.

Ferrinogean stood at the mouth, six limbs in the air in a gesture Lexa knew well.

He gurgled. "This is supposed to put you at ease. I come unarmed."

Lexa snorted. "You come with eight arms. But I don't see any weapons. Elani." She jerked her chin at the Gexcorian. "Search him."

Elani did, not that there was much to search. Ferrinogean carried one bag strung across his body like he had when Lexa first encountered him, and that was it. In the bag? Gexcorian food.

Ferrinogean's lip quivered. He squealed in Gexcorian before switching back to his not-terribly-shabby imitation of English. It just had to get through his pointed teeth, so sometimes the plosives had a hiss to them. "Show me the Cynosure before my ship detaches."

Lexa lifted the gun. "No. You altered the deal, this is mine. Your ship gets the fuck off of mine, and I don't shoot you right now."

At least her voice came out like she meant it.

The fleshy bit beneath his mouth wobbled and he entered the *Auriga*, sealing the door to the gunship behind him.

It detached and The *Auriga* shuddered again.

Stomach churning, acid gurgling up her esophagus, Lexa stepped back. "I guess we'll get you settled in an extra berth. I don't have anything as humid as you'd like, so you're just going to have to make do."

One of his limbs landed on her shoulder and gripped, his suction cups digging in. "The Cynosure."

She stopped, staring forward, and gritted her teeth. "If you don't remove your hand from my shoulder, I will shoot you out the nearest airlock and be done with you. I'll even throw in your precious and the two of you can spend eternity floating through space together."

He peeled his limb off, the suckers making small popping sounds and tearing at her skin. Stinging pinpricks along the front and back of her shoulder.

She tried to relax, tried to play aloof. What would he do when they eventually had to reveal the Cynosure had destroyed itself? Blow up the ship and everyone in it, most likely.

Teeth still clenched, she stalked down the long hall toward the berths. Elani followed behind the two of them, her gun still trained on the bounty hunter. "First," Lexa said, "let's get you in a berth. Then we can discuss the precious."

Ferrinogean grumbled but followed willingly enough, and they reached the bend in the hall where they could choose to go to the inner or outer bunks. She chose inner and turned the corner to the stairs.

Jake ran smack into her.

Her arms pinwheeling, she fell backward.

Jake caught her in his steel but gentle grip, the same grip that'd dragged her from that Birkishni ocean and the brink of drowning.

Her breath lodged in her throat. Too much about his touch was magnetic. A hole opened in her center, and she grabbed him back. For at least a moment. A moment that stretched for maybe a second, but lasted for years.

"I'm sorry," he said, again, meeting her eyes. "I keep running into you."

"It's OK, Jake. Really. You didn't do anything wrong." She could tell him that a hundred times and he probably still wouldn't believe her. There had to be some way to let him know. Some way to convince Elani to tell him they were soulmates so he could stop wondering why Lexa cut off something that had just gotten started. Something that was over before either of them wanted it to be, a feeling she couldn't deny when he let go of her and took part of her with him.

He stammered before spitting out words. "You may follow me. I'll show you where we're keeping the Cynosure."

Ferrinogean snapped to attention, his suckers popping across the floor. "Thank you." He squealed in Gexcorian.

An excited phrase that Lexa roughly translated to, "I can't wait."

Mouth open, Lexa turned back to Jake. "Are you kidding? We can't—"

"I assure you, we can." As Ferrinogean passed, Jake dropped Lexa a wink. "While you guys were chatting over the radio, I was making sure the safe was ready."

So whatever he was taking them to, that's what he'd leapt up to go do while she was trying not to get them blown up. Intrigued, she reached back for Elani and they followed Jake and Ferrinogean to one of the innermost berths.

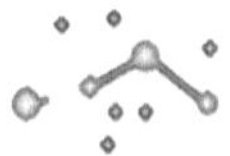

Jake stopped at a door covered in shadow. This deep inside the ship, the simulated night hours were almost as dark as the real thing on Earth. "I need you to know," he said, hand hovering over the door plate, "we are keeping it in a safe. The safe is sensitive, and it's surrounded by a variety of security measures. Step only where I step."

For once, Lexa couldn't tell if he was being serious or not. He was certainly putting on a good show for the bounty hunter.

Ferrinogean held his breath, stilling his waving limbs and bringing them all in next to his head, curled around his face like a flower, except for the few he left down to "walk" on. He nodded.

Palm sweating, Lexa gripped Elani's hand and pulled it into her stomach. Right now, that touch was the only thing keeping her inside her own skin.

Elani didn't seem to mind. She still held a rifle in one hand but she let Lexa keep the other, she even stepped into it so Lexa didn't pull her arm so hard.

Universe knows, Lexa was trying to pull it from its socket.

They followed Jake and the bounty hunter inside the darkened room.

Jake raised one light in the center of the room, illuminating a grey metallic case Lexa recognized as the first aid kit.

Oh, boy.

Ferrinogean vibrated, much as he had when Lexa pulled the Cynosure from Van's bag back on her now-destroyed ship. His voice a low whisper, he squeaked. "May I view it?" One limb reached for it with tentative hesitance.

Jake waved his arms. "No!"

Startled, Ferrinogean stopped.

"You can't touch it. I said, there are security measures. These plates," Jake said, finger extended in the direction of several floor tiles, "are all calibrated to a specific weight. If you step on any one of them, the case will explode." He looked pointedly at the tile directly in front of Ferrinogean's leading limb.

The Gexcorian backed up, clacking his teeth together as he did.

Jake continued. "And the case is on a pressure sensitive plate, itself. The lid is rigged to blow if anyone but me accesses it." He swallowed, glanced at Lexa, and hurried on. "Which I can't do when there are other people in the room. It's set to explode the case if there is more than one life form in the room when it's opened." He crossed his arms and gave Ferrinogean a winning smile, his teeth all showing. "It's well-protected. And until we reach the system, that's how it's going to stay."

Lexa clenched Elani's hand and glanced at her from the side of her eye.

Elani smiled at Jake, so wide it looked like her cheeks might split.

That feeling was easy to relate to. Lexa was bowled over at Jake's confidence explaining the whole intricate fake to Ferrinogean. Gexcorians could be pretty threatening and imposing on their own. Add to that Jake's innocence and lack of interaction with non-humanoid aliens, and it was downright unbelievable how cool he was right now. Which, thank goodness, because Lexa's insides were a wreck. She needed to lie down.

Limbs still curled around his face, Ferrinogean backed out of the room, stepping only where he had stepped when entering.

Jake followed and urged Lexa and Elani out of the room, a hand on each of them as they left.

After that, Ferrinogean went willingly enough to his berth. Jake put him at the far side of the petals, where he'd have to go through several doors Jake locked behind them before he could reach "the Cynosure."

Lexa still wasn't at all sure what they'd do once they reached the system, but at least Jake had bought them some time. Again.

And when the three of them stood outside Ferrinogean's door, waving goodnight to him, Lexa hardly contained herself long enough to let the door close. When it finally eased shut, she grabbed Jake's hand and drug him down the hall, Elani following.

Once they'd rounded a bend, Lexa threw her arms around his neck. "I could kiss you, you brilliant man."

He hugged her tight, leaned back, and lifted her from her feet a couple centimeters before setting her back down. "Then why don't you?"

And, universe help her, she almost did.

But Elani stood right there, a smile on her face to rival the sun, her golden eyes dancing and throwing soft yellow light into the dim hallway.

Lexa stepped back and held out an arm for her.

She joined the two of them and they closed the circle, laughing.

"I can't believe you came up with that so quickly, Jake," Elani said.

He laughed. "You don't have to sound so surprised."

She cupped his cheek with one hand. "That's not how I meant it." Her smile still stretched her cheeks to what looked like the point of breaking.

Lexa stepped back. She shouldn't intrude on such a moment. Like the healing.

But before she could let them go, Elani tugged her closer in again. "No, Lexa. Don't pull away again. Stay with us, enjoy the moment."

Warmth spread from Elani's arm to her, tingled through her shoulders, eased down the other arm, and flowed into Jake.

And for a while, how long she couldn't say, they stayed like that. A warm circle, complete and whole.

CHAPTER 24

Elani and Lexa dropped Jake off and walked toward their own berths. They reached Elani's first.

"Come in for a minute? Keep me company? Sleeping in strange places is sometimes hard for me. It's nice to have someone near."

How could Lexa say no to that?

They walked into Elani's darkened quarters, one bank of windows up near the ceiling, the starlight streaming in. Elani flopped on the bed and patted the space next to her without looking.

Lexa sat in a chair.

Sitting up on her elbows, Elani cocked an eyebrow. "Something wrong?"

Lexa lied and shook her head.

"I can tell you're lying."

"You're not supposed to be peeking."

"Shoe me."

"Sue." Lexa smiled. "It's sue me."

"Shut up and get over here."

She did as she was told.

Somehow, Elani's bed felt softer than the one in Lexa's berth. She slid her hand over satiny sheets. "How did you end up getting a nicer room than me?"

"You can stay here."

Lexa met her eyes. They cast beams of gold that mixed with the silver starlight falling through the window. Lexa fell into them, swimming in the magnetic sense of peace that flowed from Elani to her.

Elani lifted a hand and smoothed the energy over Lexa's head.

Tension fell out of Lexa's shoulders as Elani's hand moved down, sweeping across her chest.

"You have so much stress here." She pointed at her heart. "I've been seeing it ever since Kuarpa. What's wrong?" She kept sweeping, and the knots in Lexa's shoulders unraveled.

"Whatever you do," Lexa said, eyes closing, "don't stop."

Elani laughed through her nose. But she kept working, starting up her little hum. It was a song Lexa could listen to for the rest of her life.

"Did you know June's husband was a Shadow?"

"What's a Shadow?"

"A professional tracker. Best at what they do. Just before he died, he was on the trail of an Ambran who was abusing their power." She cracked her eyelids. "Did you hear anything about that? That's pretty rare, isn't that what you said?"

Elani nodded. "It is. I didn't hear about it, but remember I haven't been on Kuarpa in years. Now shh. I'm trying to get rid of stress, not cause more."

Lexa let her eyes close again. Eventually enough of the stress and tension wore out of her and she listed to the side. All at once, she hit a wall and her exhausted legs, abs, shoulders, brain, couldn't get her off that bed if she tried. She stretched out onto it.

Elani laid down next to her and curled onto her side. "Stay." Her hand caressed Lexa's cheek much like she'd done to Jake in the hall. "Stay with me tonight. If you won't tell me what's wrong, at least let me help you."

Lexa's eyes started to slip closed. But there was something…something.

It hit her in a rush, and she tried to sit up. "Cat," was all she could get out before hitting the mattress again.

"I'll get her. Be right back."

While Elani was gone, Lexa kicked off her shoes, stripped out of her pants, and slid under the cool sheets. Somehow the lower temperature of the ship didn't bother her. Warmth spread within her, from head to toe. From the circle in the hallway to the energy healing Elani just did, she tingled with comfort.

It was when her cat jumped on her side, digging into her kidney with her little paws, Lexa started with the realization she'd fallen asleep while Elani was gone. Should she really sleep in here? Look what'd happened with Jake.

Dammit, she wouldn't make the same mistake twice. She tried to get up, but Van curled up on her legs and started kneading while she purred.

Elani changed in the bathroom and nestled under the blankets with her, taking her hand. She lay on her back and stared up at the stars. "Can I ask you something?"

"That's a loaded question."

"May I?"

"Shoot."

"Why did your energy toward Jake change? His did, too. And you're both so blue. What happened?"

"I don't want to talk about it." Instead of staring at the side of Elani's face, thinking about Elani—about someone else's soulmate—in a way she shouldn't be, she took her hand back and crossed her arms over the sheets. "Maybe I should go to my own room." Not that she meant that, but she had to say something, didn't she? The truth was uncomfortably close to the edge of her lips. *I slept with your soulmate.* How would that go?

"You both mean a great deal to me. I'd like to know how I can make you feel better in the long term, not just for tonight."

With a gentle tug she pried Lexa's hand loose again and intertwined their fingers.

"You've barely known me a month," Lexa said, the will to pull her hand free again fleeing.

Elani shrugged, the sheets shifting against her skin with a soft sigh. "Doesn't matter. Some people are meant to change your life. It doesn't have to be a slow process." She chuckled deep in her throat. "Look at me. A garbage collector on a strange planet, just doing my best to make my way. Constantly unable to handle other people's bad energy." She smiled and faced Lexa.

Lexa met her gaze, drawing the scent of Elani's skin, her rose-petal shampoo, and the indefinable aroma of a feeling of home, into her lungs.

Elani went on. "I found Jake, and his energy is just so positive. I stuck with him, an easy choice, given…" She trailed off.

But Lexa didn't need her to finish that sentence. She knew.

"And now look at me. An intergalactic outlaw with the likes of Dr. Alexandra Dean."

A grin spread across Lexa's face, warming her nose and cheeks. "Likely to get yourself killed by tomorrow, if you stick with her," she said, knowing Elani wouldn't, at this point, consider leaving. No, Lexa was stuck with her. Stuck with them both.

Lying there in Elani's bed, staring up at the stars with her and holding her hand, her cat purring between them, she let that thought carry her into her dreams.

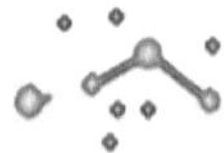

Lexa's head pounded. She slapped a hand to her forehead and squeezed her eyes closed. Breath short, she reached for the light button on the nightstand. Her other hand quested for Savannah, the anchor point she always used when she woke up afraid.

She found neither.

She couldn't hear Elani's breathing, either.

Eyes wide, almost popping from her sockets, she inched her fingers to the edge of the bed. Her head still pounded, occasionally showing her stars behind her eyes, especially when she moved. Finally finding the edge, she slipped her legs over and pointed her toe until it found the floor.

The lights came up all at once.

With a shout, her eyes stinging, Lexa fell off the bed and landed beside it with a thump. She grunted, trying to catch herself before her head bounced off the ground. She did, just barely.

Now that her eyes were open and somewhat adjusted to the light, she glanced at the bedside table. What should have been the bedside table. There wasn't one. There wasn't enough room in here for one. Had she gone wandering in her sleep or something? This was decidedly not Elani's room, nor her own.

She gripped the cover of the bed and pulled herself up, her shoulder sore from the fall. Using the bed for support, she stumbled to the door and pressed the open button.

It didn't budge.

She pressed it again, harder. As though pressing a sensor used to measure the voltage in your finger in order to open would react differently if you pressed harder.

Whatever, she tried it a third time, locking the joint on her finger and punching it.

Nothing. Again.

She stepped back and her legs hit the bed. Goosebumps ran all up and down her legs, and she sat. She gripped her sore shoulder. What had happened? Where was she, and why couldn't she get out?

Fighting the desperation attempting to settle in behind her eyebrows, she stood again and knocked on the door. "Hello?"

The radio speaker in the door panel crackled. A man's voice. "*Yes?*"

"Hello? Where am I?"

"You don't remember?"

"I…no. Who is that? Jake?"

He chuckled into the speaker, a little too close, and it crackled. *"You should have seen his face when you told him you were leaving with me. Poor guy, I almost felt bad."*

"Reid?"

The door slid open. In the cockpit of one of the *Auriga's* runabouts, he looked over his shoulder. "Come on up." He punched a few buttons on the readout in front of him. "It'll take longer to get there in this"—he gestured broadly at the ship— "but it was what you said you wanted and who was I to argue? A little alone time with you? Who says no to that?"

She stumbled through the door, holding her head, and gazed out the front windows at empty space. Her stomach did a trip to her toes and back. "Explain this to me slowly." She sank into the other chair in the small cockpit. "I said I wanted to leave with you? When was this?"

He glanced at her from the side of his eye, frowning. "Are you OK? Should I scan you? Did you hit your head when you fell out of the bed just now?"

She shook her head. "No. No. I…I remember Ferrinogean coming aboard, and I went to sleep…" Hesitating to finish the sentence, she stopped and tried to get her memory going. Showing Ferrinogean the fake Cynosure set-up and then going to sleep with Elani, that was the last memory she had. Then what? She tried to remember, tried to stand, tried to figure out where the fuck they were and where the *Auriga* was. Squinting at the panel in front of her, she started to call up a star map.

Reid laid a hand over hers and caressed the back of it with a thumb. "I have to admit, I was as surprised as Jake when you said you wanted to come with me. I thought you guys had a thing." He winked. "Made me jealous, I'll admit."

She shook her head, the fuzzy feeling not abating. "I don't understand. I didn't want to…I don't remember…where's my cat?"

"You didn't bring her."

Fuzzy feeling or not, now she knew he was bullshitting. "I think we should go back to the *Auriga*."

His lips pinched into a fine line. "Too late. They already went back through the wormhole, taking that horrid Gexcorian with them. Once you abandoned them, they said they had no reason to stay on this side of the galaxy and left. Your mom was only too happy to put tail to you. Again."

Bullshit or not, that hurt.

She sat back, air pushed out of her lungs. Her forehead tight, she riffled through her options. She was on a two-room runabout with a man twice her size, no weapons to speak of, no way back to her friends, nothing but outer space surrounding them. Not even a nearby planet that she knew of.

As slim as those options were, she couldn't just let him take her…wherever it was he was taking her.

A thought hit her.

"Where's the map?"

"In the back."

She stood on wobbly legs and shuffled her way to the bedroom again. Fuck's sake, had she slept with him again without remembering? She sincerely hoped not, for so many reasons. None of this made sense.

The map lay in an alcove above the bed, alone. No bag. Which meant no knife. Hell.

She grabbed it and headed back to the cockpit. "Let me plot a course," she said, going to pull up a star chart again. And search for the *Auriga*.

Reid stopped her, again. He turned the power off on her panel with the push of a button on his other side. "We already did that when we boarded. Wow, you really don't remember any of this?" He looked at her, spinning in his chair, and lay his hand on her forehead. "Maybe you did hit your head. Let's get you laid down." He stood and waggled his eyebrows.

"No, you're right. You're right. I remember." She waved him off.

He sat. Small favors.

"How long until we get there?" She leaned, looking at his screen instead.

The proximity alert beeped once, a soft intrusion in an otherwise peaceful cockpit.

"Oh, looks like we've got company," he said, smiling.

CHAPTER 25

R eid docked the ship inside the larger one that'd come up alongside it. It wasn't the *Auriga*, nor the Gexcorian ship they ran into earlier, which left about one possibility.

The door opened into a cavernous loading bay.

"If it isn't my thief. So nice of you to join us. Finally," Jenierien said, standing next to Qesson—who looked like he'd recovered as well as Lexa from their trip through each other—her long robe wrapped sort-of like an ancient Roman one and hanging off one shoulder. A large brooch held the layers of gossamer fabric pinched together on her other shoulder. "Welcome to the ISM *Sonne*, dear."

Lexa held a tight breath. She couldn't give Jenierien what she wanted. She didn't even have all her money.

Reid grabbed Lexa's arm. "Out." He paused, pressing his thumb into her bicep. "Please."

Though she climbed out on her own, he continued to push her forward until they both stood on the deck of Jenierien's ship. About a dozen people bustled inside the bay. The ship likely had a full complement. Lexa was more outnumbered than she could bother to count.

Map clutched in her hand, she tried not to sweat on it. Her head still pounded, Reid was a traitor, and only the universe knew if Elani, Jake, and Lexa's family were still alive. Not to mention her cat.

She spoke through clenched teeth. "What did you do with the others, Reid?"

Still gripping her arm, he propelled her toward Jenierien and Qesson. "You're in a bit of a predicament yourself, Lexa. Why worry about them?"

"Because if you ratted me out to Jenierien, who knows what you're capable of." Not that she wanted to imagine it, but she couldn't stop the thought of him just pushing Jake right out an airlock, his frozen body floating through space. Alone.

Or of him twisting Elani's arm behind her back, separating them in their last moments, making her watch Jake as he froze to death faster than he suffocated, faster than the blood boiled out his eyes. Terrifying her first, and then subjecting her to the same.

He chuckled. "Last time I saw them, they were setting coordinates for the wormhole. I told you, they left. You told them you were leaving with me and that was enough for them. I can show you."

Half a smile lifted Jenierien's rose red lips. "I'd like to see that, myself. Ah, Reid. You've been just a doll this whole time."

Still clenching Lexa, he put the other arm around Jenierien like they were old pals. "It's been nothing but a pleasure, ma'am."

"This whole time?" Lexa tried to extricate herself, stomach in free fall. "What whole time?"

Jenierien, Qesson, and Reid laughed in unison. But it was Reid who answered. "She hired me months ago, dear. To spy on you. You're a hard one to get next to, but getting in with June and Paisley was nothing. Just be at the right place at the right time, bat my eyelashes, and they were like putty in my hands. In more ways than one." He dropped a grotesque wink.

Lexa fought to keep the puke inside her mouth. It was close. "So when you came to my house…"

"I was working for Jenierien. Yes."

Never once had Lexa felt shame for her sexual habits, or revulsion, but at this moment both surrounded her in equal parts with a tightening of her throat, a tingling flush spreading through her cheeks, and a slick feeling in her stomach. Her lack of real coping skills, and waking up from that dream about Gram, had put her in the wrong bed, at the wrong time, and it just kept coming back to bite her in the ass.

They walked her all the way to Jenierien's quarters—and it could be no other room with a large, four poster bed at the center, draped with as many gems and jewels as there had been in her home in PNY—and Reid sat her in a tall-backed gold-plated chair in front of a large screen. "Milady, Qesson, you're going to want to see this, too." He pried Lexa's fingers from around the map.

Lexa'd barely been aware she was still holding it. Her fingers numb, she let it go.

He handed it to Qesson and reached inside his jacket.

Which was when Lexa discovered where the Cynosure had disappeared to.

Jenierien took it with a smile that showed all her teeth.

Reid bowed and walked to the screen. He inserted a small drive into the port, tapped the screen a few times, and brought up files from the *Auriga*, scrolling until he found the one that satisfied him. He tapped it.

It filled the screen.

From over Lexa's right shoulder, it showed Elani, Jake, Paisley, and Juniper, e-bands still slapped across her forehead.

The Lexa in the recording spoke. "*Look, I'm going with Reid. You all can fuck off back to our sector if you want, I don't care. We're done here, though. I just want to go with him.*" She stopped long enough to stare at Elani and Jake in particular. "*It was fun or whatever, but enough is enough. When I woke up this morning it was obvious this had gone too far. Leave me alone. I want nothing to do with any of you, ever again.*"

She wanted to look away. She wanted to look away from Jake's face crumpling, from Elani putting her arm around him and using him to hold herself up as much as she held him up, her eyes dull and wet. Paisley and Juniper didn't look terribly surprised, although Mom had an expression on her face Lexa rarely saw. It took until the video cut out to place it on her.

Grief.

Like the day Gram died and Lexa had to tell her over the phone. Grief.

Lexa closed her eyes. Why would she leave Savannah with them, at the very least? And why couldn't she remember any of this? It had clearly happened, it was right there on the video. At some point after Ferrinogean came aboard, she'd abandoned her friends, her family, and her cat, to run away with a man she barely knew and who, as it turned out, had been working for Jenierien the whole time. And what would Ferrinogean do to them now?

"So, Lexa," Jenierien said, stepping up next to her and laying a cold, starkly pale hand on her arm. "Are you going to take us to the site?"

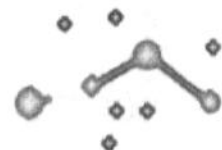

The next few days passed with more of the same. They brought Lexa food, tried to entice her to read the map for them, threatened her with torture, then led her back to her windowless room to brood.

For all the torture talk, they never seemed to have the spine to follow through. Too bad, it would have broken the monotony.

Falling asleep was its own special torture. With her eyes open in the dark, no Savannah nearby purring her off to dreamland, all she saw were Elani and Jake's faces crumpling. Their disbelief that she would come this far with them, only to dump them in a strange place and leave.

She couldn't imagine having done that. Not now. Even if pushing them away like that was par for the course for Lexa. It wasn't wholly unbelievable, just because she didn't remember it. Her feelings for both of them had developed to levels of discomfort she would normally have fled from long before she did. Long, long before. The unbelievable part really was that she hadn't done it sooner. What was she thinking in the first place, bringing them out here?

She should have left them on Earth.

Should have abandoned them on Birkishni.

Should have walked out of Elani's house on Kuarpa and never looked back, especially once she overheard that conversation between Elani and her mom.

The fact she couldn't forget their faces, the fact she couldn't let go of the grief on Mom's face, the surprise on June's was a thing she'd just need to admit and live with.

She hoped they were safe from Ferrinogean and well on their way back home. And equally as far on their way to forgetting her. Elani and Jake would get over it. She was a blip on their radar. Mom and June had already gone long enough forgetting she existed, it shouldn't be hard to go back to it.

After about five days of this, she rolled over when Qesson opened her door and spoke before he did. "Fine. I'll show you how to get there."

THE SITE

CHAPTER 26

If we go along this course—don't touch that." Lexa slapped Reid's hand away from the star map in front of her and went back to explaining how her map fit it. "If we go along this course, and enter the star system we're approaching, there should be a number of planets in the Goldilocks zone." She lay the map over the lighted panel. The light shone through, illuminating the lines crossing the map and the dot in the center. "Once I can get a better look at the lay of the system, I should be able to pick out a planet. This planet." She poked her finger into the map. Gently. No need to rile it up.

Save that for later.

The ancient leather soft on her fingertip, she rubbed the dot that stood for the planet. Was this it? The place where life was born?

She cleared her throat, staring out the window. The red star crept closer still. This ship moved at a good clip. "I'm not sure what we're going to find. Goldilocks or no, there may not be breathable air. All I've got on this map is a location, it doesn't tell me where on the damn planet to land."

"You're the best exoarchaeologist I know of," Reid said. "I'm sure you can find it."

She clenched her teeth. "Fuck you and your flattery."

He leaned into her ear, hot breath going down her ear canal. "We already played that game. You lost."

If she crushed her teeth together any harder, she might crack one. They squeaked inside her head. She wound up for another volley.

Jenierien slid the map off the console and rolled it up. "That's enough, you two. If you don't get me to the site, Lexa, I'll leave you on the planet farthest from that sun. Is that clear enough?"

Lexa nodded, her eyes on the map. She'd already lost sight of the Cynosure, though she might be able to weasel her way to it if she played her cards right. What she'd do once she had it was a different question, one she could mull after escaping on the runabout.

Although…

Seeing the site had its own pull. She might not live through all this, and she certainly wouldn't get the credit for the find if Jenierien and Reid had anything to do with it, but just to see it. Just to see where life began. Was it enough?

Enough to make her believe this ephemeral universe had something permanent in it besides death? Something that could carry on? Something that would mean life wouldn't just…end…without meaning anything to anyone after it was over?

"Mr. Weller," Jenierien said to the officer sitting at the conn, a man descended from the Indigenous people of North America if Lexa was any guess, "push these engines until you cannot push them any more."

Staring out the window, allowed to stay out of her cell for longer now that she was cooperating, Lexa concentrated on the growing red star. A star they wouldn't have been able to even see from Earth, it was too dim. Too old, too small. A red dwarf, capable of living for trillions of years. Even without cheating its DNA.

Gram lay on her bed, wheezing, holding Lexa's hand. Her grip wasn't strong, it barely clenched Lexa's fingers, and it was that weak grip that told Lexa more than anything else her Gram was slipping away. Paisley was out there, right now, living a life that would at least double, if not triple Gram's, and it meant nothing to Lexa. Not the way Gram's life did. And yet.

"It's OK little Lexa. I don't want to live forever." She wheezed between words, her breath labored. "If life has no end, what would give it meaning?"

She hadn't understood that at the time. And now, facing down the oldest site she'd ever thought about seeing, a site she wasn't sure existed but had hunted for her whole career, she wasn't sure she understood now, either. If life meant something, wouldn't it stick around? Wouldn't it be there for someone else to see? To say, "look at what we have done, remember we were something."

And if it didn't, what then? What even was the point?

Jenierien tapped her on the shoulder with the map. "What equipment will you need?"

Lexa jumped and refocused on the now. "Pressurized suits. Extra lights. Personnel. Brushes."

"Brushes?" She perched in the seat next to her and crossed one smooth leg over the other, her robe falling open where it was slit up to her thigh. The mellow scent of vanilla overtook Lexa.

She shook her head against its intoxicating aroma. "Yes. Like paintbrushes. Something small. Trowels. Shovels. Do you have heavy equipment?"

"I brought two exodiggers."

Lexa nodded, fingers on her chin. Exodiggers looked like those mech suits in all the late twentieth and early twenty-first century animations Gram loved, with hands made for digging instead of fighting. Though with their eight-foot steel frame, they could be deadly if handled right.

She filed that information away for later.

"Good. Good. This site is not likely to be sitting out in the open. Even if the Cynosure and map somehow pinpoint the location, it could be maybe months of digging to get to it."

"You have days. Not months."

"I can't control—"

"You have days." She stood. "Not months."

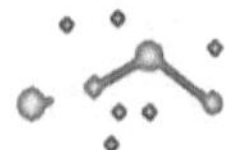

They may have relegated Lexa to a rear seat in the sizable cockpit of this ship, but she could still see some of the charts and equipment, and had a grand view out the front window.

A panel to the right of the co-pilot showed a UV detail of the system as it approached. The heliosphere was massive, the area around the red star completely blasted by its fierce solar winds. Some of the planets inside, if they were rocky, likely didn't have atmospheres at all. The heliosheath—the area where those solar winds rushed into interstellar space and met with interstellar plasma, a turbulent region and that was putting it mildly—was her biggest concern right now, as it always was when entering a new star system. And without any data on this one but what the instruments gave back, it could be a bumpy ride. Especially considering the cloud around the system that was full of comets, rocky debris, and space dust.

She buckled in and tightened the belts until they hurt.

At least the pain gave her something to focus on that wasn't Elani, Jake, and her family.

Mr. Weller made a PA announcement, asking the crew to ensure everything was fastened down and get themselves to their designated safety areas within two minutes.

Two minutes.

In two minutes, she might see, through that window in front of her, the planet on which life was born for the very first time. Just a couple million years after the universe was new. The first stars had already grown too large and melted down, spewing their newly-birthed heavy elements out into the black mass of space around them, and rocky planets were nothing but brand new babies getting sucked into orbit around red dwarfs that lived so long they would probably outlast everything.

Teeth gritted, she watched with breathless horror.

The pilots navigated the debris field, only one large comet coming close enough to give Lexa any pause. But the hands at the wheel were clearly experienced, and they cleared the cloud with ease. The heliosheath approached.

Lexa closed her eyes. The goosebumps began on the top of her head and radiated down, even covering her eyelids before moving to her chest, arms, and legs. The hair on her legs stood up, scratching against the inside of her pants.

The ship shuddered, and the air got greasy. Of course, the interior environment was contained, fully sealed from the harsh reality of outer space, but that didn't make the air feel any less slick. The turbulent plasma passed through the ship, seeming to collect around the corners and on the surfaces before continuing to move through.

That was all Lexa's imagination, really, but that didn't make it any less real to her mind.

She breathed through tight lips.

"You did this when we entered the Kuarpan system, too," Reid said. "We haven't lost *that* many ships going through the heliosheaths of the galaxy."

Though her desire was to stay quiet and not engage him in any way, her response was out of her mouth before she could stop it. "One is too many."

He chuckled. But at least he quit talking.

The bile climbed up Lexa's esophagus, saliva collecting in her mouth. She swallowed, trying to cut some of it down. It helped. A little.

Before she could think about it, Elani's face materialized in her mind. Lexa worked to make an image of smoke into reality, filling in the little lines and dimples around her mouth, the slight crow's feet around her eyes, even the hairs of her eyebrows. She focused on the swirling amber of her irises, her shining bronzed brown skin, and the way her mouth moved when she smiled, just the corners turned up toward her almond eyes. Reid spoke again, but by then, Lexa was with Elani, her fingertips brushing her cheek.

Jake materialized next to Elani, holding her hand, his full lips in a wide smile. Lexa focused seeing him the way he looked on Kuarpa; his skin deep brown with golden, sun-kissed highlights. She studied every millimeter of his twisted hair, the way it stuck out from his head and added joy to his enthusiastic aura. And his round brown eyes, how they scrunched up when he laughed, wrinkles forming under them. Dimples in his cheeks, facial hair buried inside them, his eyebrows high on his forehead.

She couldn't help but smile with him.

What a pair.

The shuddering of the ship stopped. Smooth space travel reasserted itself, and the pilot made another PA announcement.

They had arrived in the system.

CHAPTER 27

"Scans show five interior planets, all rocky, ma'am," the co-pilot said. "Two others are out here with us, both gas giants." Qesson hung over his shoulder, *tsking* his disapproval at how long it took the scan to complete. He slid over to Lexa where she still sat strapped into her seat.

She knew she would hardly be able to see the planets from this distance. Still, she stared out the window in front of her and tried to make them out.

Qesson stopped about a meter from her. "Tell me which planet."

Unbuckling, she held out a hand. "I need the map and Cynosure."

Jenierien cleared her throat. "Absolutely not."

Lexa stopped, halfway out of her seat, and smiled across the cockpit at the haughty socialite. "If you don't let me use the map and its key, we'll never find the site. Those are the only things that got me here."

"That and your mother's money," Reid said.

"And mine," Jenierien added.

Lexa sat. "Fine. We can sit here and rot."

Jenierien pursed her lips and motioned to Qesson. "Get them."

And once they were in Lexa's hands again, she was that much closer to feeling OK. The map and Cynosure were together again, and the only thing she lacked now was her friends. Lovers?

Whatever they were. She should never have left them. Not on Earth, not on Birkishni, not on Kuarpa, and certainly not in the far-flung reaches of the galaxy.

As she lowered the Cynosure to the map, watching them do their dance once again, she wondered if Elani and Jake would even want her back after the things she said. Just because she didn't remember saying them wouldn't make the words any less hurtful.

The map and Cynosure came together, settling onto the console where they lay, and she exhaled.

But then the two did a dance she'd never seen.

They literally floated, together, a few centimeters off the console. And they rotated as though the map was a spinning plate. A slow rotation, yes, but a rotation. Until they got where they were happy, and stopped.

Like before, the Cynosure exploded into bright light.

Everyone but Reid and Lexa covered their eyes and screamed. Looked like Reid had remembered as well as Lexa, and had closed his eyes against the initial flash just like she had.

He smirked at her. "Hope you weren't thinking that moment would give you a chance to take us off guard."

"Nothing of the sort." But she glared at the map. She had indeed been hoping it'd give her a few seconds to grab the two and head to the runabout. Not that she knew how she'd get out of the bay when she got there, but she could figure that out once she was locked inside, alone, with the map and Cynosure.

Since it hadn't, she knelt next to the map and looked at the image the Cynosure projected onto the ceiling.

It was this star system. She recognized it from the scan.

Three of the seven planets glowed as the Cynosure projected them orbiting their star in an accelerated illustration. And for the first time, the projection from the Cynosure was done in color. The four non-glowing planets were grey, but the glowing ones were three different colors. Closest to them was cyan, followed by magenta, and a deep shade of golden yellow that reminded Lexa of Elani's eyes. They glowed and twinkled hypnotically. All three looked to be within one AU of their star, give or take.

Lexa couldn't decide which to choose. What did the colors mean? Was there an order to them? Were they to land on each? Or would pulling up into orbit tell them what they needed?

She answered herself aloud. "I guess there's one way to find out."

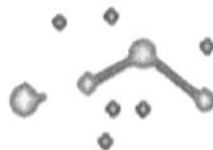

Once Lexa explained just what her statement meant, Jenierien very decisively chose the magenta planet on the impeccable logic it was one of her favorite colors.

At which point Lexa almost mentioned an old 20th century musical Gram loved to watch and how one of the aliens had been named Magenta. Serendipity, maybe.

Once they approached the planet, the map glowed again, this time a deeper magenta highlighting a spot on one of the smaller continents in its northern hemisphere. Which Lexa assumed meant, "land here."

Mr. Weller and his co-pilot guided the ship through the atmosphere with ginger care. Lexa didn't know what to expect down there, from unbreathable air to crushing gravity to flora, fauna—or both—that tried to kill them all, but Jenierien gave her the unbothered shrug of one with deep pockets.

When they arrived, one of the men got into an exodigger, his air-tight suit on under the metal frame of the exoskeleton, and stepped out of the airlock onto the surface of a planet Lexa had good reason to believe was almost as old as the universe itself.

CHAPTER 28

"Milady," Qesson said, snapping his feet together with a *clop*, "your men have determined the planet is hospitable and the area in which we've landed is uninhabited. We may depart."

Lexa peeked out a window in the large loading bay at the barren, rocky landscape, red sunlight baking into the sand and turning it red, too. It reminded her of Mars. Outside the domes, of course. "They're sure the air is breathable? We could put on the suits too, just in case."

Jenierien adjusted her flowing skirts and cropped top, all made of silk and chiffon with hand-embroidered flowers. "I am not putting a suit on over this, and the instruments we brought are accurate. My men do know how to read a simple air quality report."

Fighting to get a handle on her squirming stomach, Lexa stared out the window again. Despite what Jenierien's men said, this planet could turn against them at any moment. And what about wildlife? Microorganisms? Any manner of things could be out there. There could be people somewhere, coming to meet them now, treat them as invaders to their soil.

These kinds of things wouldn't normally go through her head, but all the places she'd been were places someone lived, or had lived, and the GHR had data on the local environment. You took your antibiotics, wore the protective layers they recommended, met with a local, what have you. Even the surprise on Birkishni was manageable. But this, this complete unknown…it hadn't hit her until she looked out the window.

They were alone in this. Isolated. Cut off from everything she'd known before this moment.

She had to get a grip. Jenierien would abandon her here or worse if she didn't deliver. That *and*, she'd never see the site.

Before asking, she climbed into the other exodigger and headed for the door.

Reid jogged to catch up. "Where do you think you're going in that?"

"I'm not going to let untrained personnel dig in the soil, potentially destroying fossils or other evidence that has waited billions of years to be discovered." She looked down her nose at him, something she'd never been able to do.

"Fine," he said, pacing her, his legs stretched wide with each step. "Just remember there are guns big enough on this ship to disintegrate you and that suit, if you get any funny ideas." He grumbled something else, but it wasn't loud enough for her to hear.

Given that he'd just been threatening her, it might be important. Otherwise, she wouldn't bother asking. "What was that?"

"I said you've been treating me really shitty. *You* wanted to leave with *me*, not the other way around. You don't have to keep being such a bitch."

She considered backhanding him with the exodigger. The hand with the oversize shovel on it. Disintegration or no, it might be worth it.

At the end of the loading bay ramp, she paused. Now that she was here, about to touch the sand on this planet for the first time, she almost regretted letting her fears get the better of her and strapping into this metal machine. Its feet would touch the soil before she did. Its feet would feel ground that was three times older than Earth's, not hers.

She stepped into the sand and sank a few centimeters. Not enough to make walking difficult for her, a positive of riding in the digger. The even better news was she left Reid behind in just a few steps as he struggled through the deep, loose sand.

"I'm wearing one of those things next time," he called to her back.

She kept walking, a self-satisfied grin curling up her lips. The air of this ancient planet filled her lungs, dust in her nose. It smelled of desert, of heat-baked sandy days and dark, frigid nights.

About a hundred meters away, she met with the crewman in the other exodigger. "What's your name?"

He grunted. "Smith." His voice scratched out through the speaker on the front of his helmet; still attached because he hadn't removed his air suit yet.

"First or last?"

He didn't answer.

What a friendly sort. But one friend on this ship might be useful. She tried again. "I once knew a man with a wooden leg named Smith."

He grunted again. With hardly a pause, he finished the joke, his Sierra Leonean accent becoming clear. "What did he call the other leg?"

She laughed so hard, she had to put one of the digger's legs out at an awkward angle to maintain her center of gravity and keep from falling over.

He chuckled with her and took off his helmet. The skin of his bald head was a darker shade than Jake's, almost midnight black, and he had a long, silvery scar running from one nostril, past the edge of his mouth, to his jaw. "What are we digging up?"

"I don't know yet." She looked over her shoulder. The rest of the group still struggled toward them, though Qesson had picked up Jenierien and now carried her in a cradle hold. His four legs slid through the sand with greater ease than the bipeds following him. "I need a core sample of rock. It'll be faster if we both work."

He slipped the helmet back on and lifted the left arm of the exodigger. At the end, the shovel folded in and a drill laser folded out. He clicked it on and nodded at her. The laser's motor hummed.

Lexa followed suit. She held one finger skyward.

On the strut over her head was a readout. She tapped it on and scrolled through the options until she found the ground-penetrating radar. Just like Jenierien's bubble bath, GPR would have meant something completely different to Gram. This one was lightning-fast, and would tell her accurately if there were fossils below, decaying tissue, bone, even plant matter. It was sensitive enough to reveal insect activity. Using it before digging would ensure they didn't drill through something important.

The scan revealed nothing until about five meters down, where it hit the first real layer of sediment. There seemed to be a few masses of decayed plant matter below that, but most of what was below them was rock. Convenient.

She nodded to Smith.

The drill lasers made quick work of the ground.

Before Jenierien arrived, they'd already drilled far enough to collect the kind of core sample Lexa needed for Potassium-Argon dating. A different tool, something she'd never learned the name of, brought up the sample from the deepest layer. She was halfway through the spectrometer scan of it when Qesson stopped behind them and sat Jenierien on her feet.

"Lexa, what is that you're doing?"

Lexa watched her readout, the scan almost complete. "Dating the rock."

"I thought his name was Jake," Reid said, finally catching up. He panted, breathing heavy from struggling through the sand all this way. Bright side, he'd have to struggle back to the ship, too.

She ignored him.

How on Earth could she have deserted them for him? How?

The scan finished with a soft beep. She glanced over and met Smith's wide eyes. He'd removed his helmet once again and almost smiled.

Lexa looked around at everyone else. When she got back to Smith, she spoke to him. "I'd like to welcome everyone to the oldest planet you've likely ever stepped foot on. We are standing on soil no less than eleven billion years old."

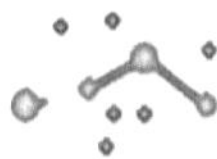

Back at the ramp of the ship, Lexa climbed from the suit and shot daggers at Reid. "Stay away from it."

He lifted both hands, palms out, his electric blue eyes twinkling nonetheless.

Lexa spread the map there on the sandy metal and held the Cynosure aloft above it. "I'm not sure what to expect now. We need a place to dig." She lowered the Cynosure.

Writing appeared on the map, fading into existence in the same shade as the planet had been. It filled the map, but it was written in a language not only did Lexa not know how to read, she'd never even laid eyes on it. Not on another planet, not in college, not in a textbook or library somewhere.

She sighed, disappointment filling her stomach, pulling her chin down into a frown so severe it hurt. The back of her throat bound up. "It's useless." She looked around at the group.

Jenierien frowned down with her, her youthful skin bunched between her eyebrows, around her mouth, and under her chin. Her eyes implied the threat she'd already spoken half a dozen times.

In desperation, Lexa leaned over the map. "Map, I can't read that. I can read dozens of languages, but that's not one of them."

The words rippled like they were coming to her from underwater. The alien letters faded, washing out until they were translucent white.

Lexa sat back on her heels. She considered picking up the Cynosure and heaving it into the sand before Jenierien killed her. At least if she was going to die, Jenierien wouldn't get her prize.

But she'd lost hope too soon.

The words began to fade back into existence, first one letter at a time, then whole words, then lines, until the page was filled again.

Lexa had hoped for English. She got Gexcorian. Must have been the Cynosure's doing.

She looked up, around the circle. "Anyone read that?"

Everyone shook their heads.

Excellent.

"I can. It's telling me where to go, using the mountains"—she pointed left, to the range nearby—"as a landmark." Holding the map and Cynosure together, she lifted them both and pointed them at the mountains. Their silhouette etched itself across the face of the map and if she held it at the right angle, she could see both the landscape in front of the map and the map's instructions.

She glanced around the circle again. "Smith, hold this." She handed the pair to him. "Keep the Cynosure on there just like that, hold it steady."

He removed his hands from the exodigger grips, took off his gloves, and cradled them. He gave Lexa one curt nod.

See? Friends were good to have.

A lesson that was new to her, but gaining traction fast.

She climbed into her exodigger and took the map and Cynosure back from him once she was settled. "Follow me."

They ended up at the base of the mountains, the map pointing directly at a pile of rubble that had to have been there for millennia.

Lexa stored the map and Cynosure in a bag she'd scrounged before coming out here. "Looks like we dig. You got more heavy equipment, Jenierien, or are we doing this by hand?"

"Are you certain this is the place?"

Certain it wasn't at all, Lexa nodded. "As best I can be." The more time they wasted, the more time it would give her to figure a way out of this. Maybe she could trap them all in a cave and steal the ship. It was worth a shot. Push came to shove, this laser would cut them all in half with one swipe. If she could bring herself to do something like that.

Either way, if they dug in the wrong place for the rest of the day, she'd have overnight on a planet to think about it.

And that's what they did, Lexa carefully calculating each move. Growing dismay, stress, even the little breakdown she had when she leapt from the exodigger and laid the map out again in front of an excavator with little warning. The poor guy driving it like to have had a heart attack when he almost ran her down. She'd have to get him something nice when they were back aboard. Have Smith apologize for her. Something.

At the end of the day, sweating and tired, the red sun painting the sky a brilliant orange, mixed with blood red and purple, Lexa threw up her hands. "I think I might have been wrong." She bit her lip and checked Jenierien's face.

Lady Jenierien had retreated under an oversized umbrella, protecting herself from the UV of the red star. It was less than Earth's sun, but Lexa wasn't about to tell her that. She was staying out of her hair for the time being, which was good enough.

Right now, though, the red cast a shadow on her face Lexa would have been afraid of if she had anything left to lose.

Jenierien spoke between clenched teeth. "You told me this was the right place."

Lexa shrugged. "I was wrong. I think."

"We will begin again tomorrow. Don't be wrong twice."

As Qesson carried Jenierien back to the ship, Smith helped Lexa gather up some of the hand tools they'd brought out and stuffed them in a bag. "Why did you do that?"

"What?"

"Have us dig in the wrong place. I'm not fluent, but I know enough Gexcorian to know we've been in the wrong spot all day."

Lexa flushed, uncertain if the red in her face would show against the red light filtering across the horizon. "I'm sorry. I'll make it up to you. I hope." She swallowed and met his eyes. "Thanks for not saying anything."

He nodded. "She pays me a lot, she pays us all a lot. But even that kind of money can't buy loyalty. Not from my crew."

"Your crew?"

One eyelid dipped in a wink. "Don't tell the lady. We all got our little secrets. My crew might be for hire—stealing, digging, building, whatever—but that's just our hands. My crew's hearts go where I tell 'em. Whose ship you think that is?"

Smiling, Lexa followed him back to the ship.

CHAPTER 29

Turned out, the *Sonne* had a rec room. Lexa found it by sheer luck as she looked for a way off the ship. Padding through the darkened nighttime hallways, she took a new turn, got lost, and was bowled over by a crewman leaving a bright, loud, and smoky room. At first, she thought there was a fire. But when the crewman caught her and steadied her on her feet with a gruff, " 'Xcuse me, Miss," the scent of beer on his breath was a giveaway.

She brushed him off and slipped through the door before it closed.

Inside was most of the crew, hard to be sure without counting, but she did see Smith back in the corner, facing the door, laughing and holding a cigar. He motioned her over when he saw her standing there with her mouth and eyes wide.

"Miss Lexa, have a seat with us." He shooed some of the crew members aside. At this table sat seven people, each with a few cards in their hand and chips in front of them. Smith made the count of men to women one over half, and Lexa joining them evened it up.

Smith went around the table and Lexa memorized one thing about each of them so that even if she forgot their names, which was likely since a drink was already in front of her, she'd remember they were on her side. Or at least, not on Jenierien's side.

They dealt her in and she played poker with them for the better part of…a lot of hours. More than she bothered to count.

The drinks flowed. The mellow cigar smoke curled in her hair, drifted up her nose, reddened her eyes. It smelled real enough to be actual tobacco, not that she'd ask where Smith got something so pricey.

On occasion, she'd meet the eyes of one of the women at the table and be forcefully reminded of what she'd left behind. Of lying in Elani's bed that last night, fingers intertwined with hers, their breathing in sync as she fell asleep under the stars with a woman she was fairly certain she'd been falling in love with from the moment she peeked over the top of that bucket.

And looking at Smith, after about ten drinks, was more than she could handle. She had to glance at him through her periphery. He looked nothing like Jake, but that didn't stop her from thinking of him and his wide smile. Lust was a hell of a drug, but she was pretty sure it'd edged into something more with him, too, and never in her life had she had these feelings for even one person. Let alone two.

It didn't matter that Jake and Elani were soulmates, there was no way she left them behind by choice. Add in her cat and something was going on she couldn't explain. Reid was lying. Had to be. That film was doctored.

Every time she started nursing a drink and thinking harder about that doctored film, Smith would nudge her and call her back to the game. She'd let it go and play for a while. But eventually she'd come back to it like a dog gnawing a bone.

Finally she leaned into Smith. Her breath probably stank of alcohol as much as his did. "Do you tink you could help me steal something?"

He grinned and took a puff off his cigar. Lips pursed, he exhaled a ring of smoke. "My specialty. What did you have in mind? That map? The pretty crystal thing?"

"A video drive."

He crossed his arms on the table. "From?"

"Reid."

He exhaled a laugh. "Your boyfriend? Why?"

She didn't punch him, but it was close. "He's not my boyfriend."

"Just teasing you, Miss Lexa. Does he keep it on him?"

"I don't know. Last time I saw it, it was in Jenierien's room."

Smith nodded, chin dimpled, that scar puckering next to his drawn mouth. "That would complicate things. But yeah." He nodded, slow. "We can do it."

"Name your price."

One eye wrinkled as he smiled sideways. "When it comes time to pay, you'll know."

She couldn't argue that.

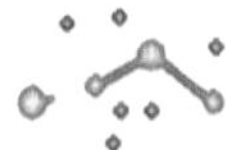

The second day of digging was much more productive, Lexa's hangover notwithstanding. They dug in the right place this time and soon began unearthing items and objects that took Lexa's mind off the alcohol dehydration and other chemical processes making her feel like ground shit. The red sun heated the sand, throwing the heat back up at her, and she sweated on top of her sweat, the smell of alcohol coming out with it. Each artifact was logged and recorded, Lexa insisted on it, and when they reached what looked like a short wall according to the GPR, Lexa had them all stop.

"We've found what looks like the outer wall of a building."

Jenierien called over from beneath her umbrella. "Is it an important building?"

Lexa clunked over in the exodigger. "I can't say. But we are digging where we're supposed to, so the odds are good. I won't know more until we uncover the building." She climbed down from the machine and sat in the sand at the edge of the umbrella's shadow.

"And how is that done?"

"We get out the shovels and do it by hand. If we use the exodiggers, we'll damage the structure."

"Remember what I said. You do not have weeks. You have days."

Lexa sighed out her nose. "Yeah, I remember. But if we damage the structure, we may destroy whatever clues we're here to find. We won't ever locate the final site if we do that."

Smith clanked over and disengaged from the exodigger as well. "Miss Lexa, allow me to help you with the sandshoes." He held up a pair of faux-wooden "shoes" that looked like tennis rackets. What Lexa could only think of as snowshoes. But Smith's crew were resourceful, and after a day of struggling through the sand, had come up with the idea of modifying snowshoes to work on the sand.

Which was both super helpful and disappointing. It'd been fun to watch Reid suffer.

As Smith helped Lexa strap on the shoes, he slipped a small piece of plastic inside her sock.

She said nothing, and didn't reach for it. How they'd gotten their hands on the drive so quickly was something she would kill to ask him later. When she stood, she wiggled her foot until the drive lodged itself between her ankle bone and the strap below it, where she hoped it would stay until she could either get it in a pocket or get back to the ship.

"Thanks, Smith. These were a great idea." She tilted the shoe back and forth. "And so stylish."

"Nothing but the best," he said, standing. With hand shovels, they and the crew continued to dig well past the afternoon and approaching evening. The site yielded a lot of walls but no signs of life. No pottery, old fires, no bones or any of the things one might expect from a dig that for all the world looked like an ancient settlement. More ancient than Lexa had ever imagined.

Maybe all that stuff had long since turned to dust and they were shoveling its ashes.

Stars began to pop out in the east and she stopped to look up.

The stars that popped out over the heads of the people who lived here would not be the same stars she looked at now. It was almost as if she had traveled to the past while staying in the present. And wasn't that what it was always like when she went on a dig?

Her foot shifted where she'd been standing on part of a wall still covered in sand. She'd told a white lie to Jenierien; they likely could have used the lasers for this, they could be tuned for this kind of delicate work, but hand-digging took longer. Not only that, it gave her a chance to touch the soil. To breathe the dirt up her nose and feel its granules pressing her knees where she crouched. It gave her a chance to connect with the site in a way the laser would never.

She shuffled to the center of the site. From her pocket, she dug out one of the paintbrushes Jenierien supplied her with. Its bristles were too soft, and inferior to her trusty brush in Savannah's bag, but that was one more loss she'd have to suffer.

For now.

She knelt in front of the center wall in the middle of what would look like a labyrinth if they had an aerial view, a puzzle they'd been able to just dig through instead of getting lost inside for hours, and teased away some of the sand there. A figure had been engraved in the rock. Lucky it hadn't been painted on. As shallow as this engraving was after all these billions of years, paint would not have existed anymore. It would have long ago fallen to sun, bacteria, and time. She took the moment she finally had to slip the drive out of her sweaty sock and into her pants pocket.

Jenierien called to her. "What have you found?"

She swallowed a startled jump and convinced herself no one had seen the video drive. "It's a rudimentary carving. Let me think."

Blocking out the sun, and the sand, and Jenierien's impatience, she dropped to her hands and knees in front of the drawing, her nose almost pressed against the stone. Whoever lived here, billions of years ago, carved rocks just like humans did. All this digital memory was great, like the drive in her pocket, but time would erase it. Completely. Stone was the only thing that stuck.

The figure in front of her held their hands around an object, aloft above their head, their legs spread on top of something Lexa couldn't make out. With the brush, she pushed sand away from the bottom of the carving and looked closer. She still couldn't quite see what it was.

She raised the lights in her arms and held her right forearm up to the stone. The light outlined it in sharper relief, and she bent over once again, muttering to herself. Everything faded away but the carving before her.

It looked like a biped of some kind. She'd have to date the stones making up these walls to figure out how old this civilization was, but it amazed and baffled and awed her that they'd come so far in so little time after the birth of the universe. Everything she knew about evolution quivered like a pile of boulders stacked atop a single, small pebble.

The important bit, right now though, was what the figure was standing on, what they were holding, and if she knew which direction to face.

She glanced over her shoulder.

Directly behind her was a mound of sand they'd not cleared. She rested one sweaty arm on her knee and pointed with her forehead. "Smith, could the men clear that mound right there, please?"

Without a word, they got to work. It didn't take long to uncover the pedestal hiding beneath the shifting sand.

As they worked, the sun slipped behind the mountains once again, marking their second sunset on Magenta. They hadn't brought overhead lights, so Lexa raised the lights in her arms as high as they'd go.

Once the men uncovered the ground around it and the whole of the round, flat pedestal, about a meter in diameter, Lexa inspected the carvings ringing it. She couldn't read any of it, though it appeared to match the language the map originally wanted to speak to her in. This must be its native tongue. The language of these ancients. Maybe the first language invented in the universe.

There were a couple pictures, and she studied these with the rapidly dropping temperature pressing her to move faster. The sweat dried on her skin and a cool breeze whispered against the stiff hair on her arms.

She shivered. This needed to go faster, or in the morning. But that symbol…that one, she recognized.

It was a star in the sky. Above a set of mountains.

She pulled the map out and compared.

The mountains on the map didn't match the ones on the pedestal. She glanced east and narrowed her eyes.

That range was further, but she could just make out their silhouette as the sun set across the horizon from them. They seemed to match the range on the pedestal.

Lexa exhaled through her nose and stood. "We need to be out here before sunrise tomorrow."

Jenierien had Qesson carry her over, and she stood next to Lexa, looking east. Orange light from the fading sunset glowed in her hair. "Why?"

"I'm not sure, but I think we have something else to uncover when it rises."

CHAPTER 30

"Thanks for letting me use your screen," Lexa said, following Smith into his quarters. Many of his men doubled or tripled up, but his room, though small, was empty, save for his furniture and trinkets.

She grinned at a statue sitting on a lighted pedestal. "A Dysling ceremonial mating statue. Where'd you steal that? I happen to know they don't just give them away."

Smith smiled, the scar riding up his cheek. "They do when you're dating them."

Lexa laughed. "You might want to be careful. They know how to break a human in about seventeen different ways with their hands alone."

"You're telling me."

She laughed again. "Where's your viewer?"

He motioned to the other side of the room. "The blue button." He flopped on the bed and removed his boots, shaking about a pound of sand out of each. "How much more digging in the sand do you expect we'll be doing?"

"As much as it takes." Finger bent, she punched the blue button with her knuckle. His view screen slid from the ceiling, the port for the drive on the bottom side.

She slid the drive in and stepped back. She scrolled through the same folder Reid had, a tad more slowly, and saw a few faces she recognized. Clearly he'd also used this drive to store Paisley and Juniper's vacation photos, playing the part of the perfect tour guide. She even came across—and as quickly scrolled past—some "intimate" photos of he and Juniper.

One file slid by with the colors blue and gold splashed across the thumbnail.

She stopped and looked at the picture.

Jake, Elani, and herself dancing. He'd recorded it.

Her finger hovered over the delete button, forehead tight. He had no right to watch this. It wasn't for him. It didn't matter they'd been in public. It wasn't for him.

She left it. If she went around deleting files—like this one he'd secretly recorded of she and Elani talking on the observation deck about the area of space they were in, Lexa pretending she didn't want to be holding Elani's hand the whole time—he'd know she'd gotten her hands on the drive. As it was, she hoped Smith could return it to where they found it and Reid wouldn't be the wiser.

Finally, she stopped on the file where she told everyone to fuck off.

Her heart hummed along at about 140 beats per minute as she pressed play.

The same scene replayed itself. Elani and Jake's faces crumpling, Mom frozen in grief, June sadder than Lexa remembered.

Lexa could hardly look at any of their faces. Which was good, because that's not what she'd stolen this for. She needed to see her own face.

"Damn, that's cold as shit, Miss Lexa."

She didn't look over her shoulder at him. "I didn't say that."

"It's right there on the film. Sure sounds like you."

"I don't care. I didn't say that." She joined him on the bed and met his eyes. "It's something I would do. It definitely is. Which is why it's so convincing a lie. But I didn't say that. I don't think…" She trailed off, staring at the wall, eyes glazed.

Smith prompted her to continue. "You don't think what?"

She snapped back to the room. "I don't think I could. I…well. They. I just don't think it's true."

He stared at her face for so long, she wondered if he'd forgotten what he was going to say. As she was about to ask him what he was thinking about, he stood. "Let me call one of my men in. We'll suss out if that video is doctored, and see what else we can find on this drive."

While she waited for Smith's man to arrive, she flipped through the rest of the files. In a separate folder, she found five encrypted files and wondered what it might take to break the encryption. She didn't have any code breaking software, that had all gone with her ship, so she asked Smith if they had any.

"We do, but if we use it on this drive and it's set to alarm, we're all cooked."

Idly, she nodded and turned back to the screen. None of the files showed her face. She wouldn't be able to see her own expression. She wouldn't be able to see if her mouth had actually moved to form the words, "fuck off." Without that, the only thing that could convince her she actually said that would be hearing it from any of the other people in the video, particularly Elani or Jake.

Smith's man came in to take a look at the files without disturbing any security programs attached to them, but by then Lexa was so lost in thought, she hardly noticed.

What had they done with Ferrinogean after she left? Surely he hadn't just been OK with turning around and going home unless they offered him the missing Cynosure. And that fake would only last so long. How long could Jake keep up the charade? Shame they hadn't brought any of the glass teardrops from Elani's collection. Some of them had been almost the spitting image of the thing, be it smaller or larger.

And why did she collect those, anyway?

That certainly wouldn't be the first question she asked Elani if she ever saw her again, but it would be one of them.

If the universe was kind, despite all evidence to the contrary, it would deliver Elani and Jake to her again. One more time, so she could make it up to them. Make everything up to them.

Smith tapped her on the shoulder.

She started. He'd been speaking. "Sorry. What?"

"It's not doctored. It's the real deal. We can't find any hint of manipulation of the file. I'm sorry Miss Lexa, but that's really you."

Mouth pinched in such a tight line it hurt, she held out her hand. "I'll take it back. Thanks for checking."

She ignored the pain crawling down her throat and into her chest, balled her fist around the drive, and stalked from the room.

Sleep before trudging out to the dig site in sandshoes would have been nice, but it hadn't happened for Lexa. She stood in the cold predawn, a thin jacket tight over her shoulders, breath pluming before her face, and scowled at the eastern horizon.

In the exodigger, Reid towered next to her. With no digging to be done, she couldn't talk him into giving it to her today.

No matter, she needed to be out of it. It wouldn't fit on the top of this stone pedestal. The sandshoes hung off the front and back where she stood in the middle of it. Before knocking off yesterday, they'd uncovered a dozen or so crystals embedded in the stone floor surrounding the pedestal. She stared down at them. What were they?

As the sun crept closer to the horizon, she held out her hand. "Cynosure."

He scoffed and began to speak.

She cut him off. "Don't give me that shit. Just hand it over. It's required, unless you want to wait and try again tomorrow?"

"I wasn't going to say no," he said, dropping it in her hand. "I was going to tell you to ask nicely."

Cold glass cupped in both palms, she faced east, her legs spread to the edges of the pedestal like in the carving. "Next, you'll be telling me to smile."

"You do look prettier when you do, now you mention it."

Her eyes rolled so hard she could see next week.

Luckily, the pink light from the rising sun deepened to red, a sure sign it was about to break the horizon. "Move back, please. Beyond the walls. I don't know what's going to happen."

Mumbling, he moved away, taking Smith's men with him, back to where Jenierien had set up under her umbrella again. When he stepped down from the exodigger, she handed him a glass of champagne and tilted her own at Lexa.

Lexa shouldn't be surprised she was a day drinker. Not that she'd never had her own liquid breakfast.

No room for judgement in her head but doing it anyway, she turned back toward the rising sun. If she had her guess, it would clear the horizon in less than a minute.

With both hands, again like in the carving, she held the Cynosure over her head and stared at the rising red ball.

The moment the entire star cleared the horizon, the pearls shifted in her hands and red light rained from above her head, hitting the crystals and reflecting back up into the sky. Everyone with Jenierien, including Smith, gasped, but Lexa didn't turn. Instead, heart racing, she called to them.

"Pictures! Get as many as you can! Mark exactly which crystals it's hitting. We cannot lose whatever this is trying to tell us, or it's another full day before we can see it again."

Which might not be so bad; she'd kill to be able to see what the area around her looked like. Did the Cynosure glow as well? She was afraid to move, even to look up, and lose the position from the carving. But the Cynosure warmed as though it was touching the map, and the warmth moved down her arms with a crawling sensation. Like a thousand small insects' feet moved down her skin. She wanted to drop the Cynosure to the ground and scratch, and until the sun finally got high enough to stop the show, she gritted her teeth and tried to ignore it. If someone wanted to torture her, though, this would be a lot more effective than what Jenierien and co had done during her first week on the *Sonne*.

Once the sun got high enough, maybe five degrees off the horizon, the Cynosure stopped glowing all at once.

Arms weighing about a thousand kilos, Lexa dropped them. She shuffled to Jenierien and handed the Cynosure back to her. "Did you get the pictures?"

Qesson snapped his feet together and answered for her. "We did everything you requested with utmost alacrity."

Lexa sat in the sand, some of it spilling inside her pants. Of course. "Good. Let's get back to the ship and analyze it."

Projected on the large screen in the cockpit, the photos astounded Lexa. From her position, it'd seemed like a red rain surrounded her.

From everyone else's position, she was almost lost in the center of that aura. The Cynosure's own reddish color mixed with the star in the same color magenta that'd been on the map. The pearls did indeed pick out several crystals on the ground, which returned the light and shot it skyward. Smith's men had dutifully marked each of them, and a drone had captured overhead pictures as well.

Breathless, she stared at the pictures for a lot longer than she should have. This living map and its mate-like key were like magic. Every time they showed her something new, she became less convinced anyone should possess them. They weren't possessions to be had, even by the museum.

"Miss Lexa?"

She tore her eyes away from the pictures and glanced at Smith. "I'm at a loss."

Jenierien sighed. "If we spend one more day on this godforsaken planet, I will leave one of you on it as a token gift to God."

Lexa shook her head. "The map showed us three planets, maybe this is just the first piece of a puzzle."

"Ready the ship for departure," Jenierien commanded.

No one moved.

She sighed. "Go! Now!"

Smith rounded up his men and Lexa started to follow them out.

Jenierien caught her with one finger as she walked past and leaned over. The smell of vanilla and lavender mingled and floated up Lexa's nose, the soft skin of that finger rubbing up and down her arm.

Lexa shuddered, her teeth clenched. Bile crawled up her throat.

"If you're wrong, my dear Lexa, it will be you I leave behind."

Lexa considered nodding and walking away. Ignoring the little threat. But she'd had about enough. Her depression—because that's what was happening here, no question—had kept her from speaking up for herself the way she normally would. But Elani and Jake wouldn't have wanted her to stay miserable. They'd have wanted her to tell Jenierien where to stuff it.

"If you leave me behind, no one will be able to help you find the site. And no one will deliver you the fame and fortune you obviously seek. And…" She smiled, the tips of her mouth curling up slowly. "Eventually the Gexcorians will come looking for your trinket and I won't help you get rid of them."

The blood drained from Jenierien's face as Lexa spoke. She snapped her mouth closed. Her nostrils flared. "What makes you think you can get rid of them when they've followed you to the edge of the galaxy? You could not get rid of me."

As repulsed as she was, Lexa leaned closer and lowered her voice like she was whispering to a lover. "If you don't stop threatening me, you're the one who'll end up getting abandoned in the sand. Like I did to you on that beach on Birkishni."

Out of the corner of her eye, she caught Qesson shivering. Clearly he hadn't forgotten that beach.

Jenierien turned to him, stared for moment, then faced Lexa again. "If you cross me, it will be the last thing you do."

"Oh I already know that." With a shrug, Lexa followed Smith and his men out.

CHAPTER 31

The ISM *Sonne* skittered across the system to the cyan planet.

They repeated everything, with a little less threatening and bullshit, and Jenierien allowed someone else could stand on the pedestal once they unearthed a site almost exactly like the one on Magenta. This time, Lexa watched with her mouth hanging open, 'catching flies' as Gram would have said, as the light surrounded Reid, who held the Cynosure. But this time, it was cyan light. When the Cynosure lit up the crystals, the light reflected skyward and surrounded Reid in a shaft of cyan and white that pierced the heavens.

After all the things she'd seen with this map, this still had to be one of the most breathtaking. The beings who birthed these items certainly had a flair for the dramatic. And for the poetically beautiful.

The yellow planet yielded much the same. This time, it was Jenierien herself who stood in the golden rain, and when it was over, Lexa was sure she caught tears streaming down her face. She handed off the Cynosure to Qesson and turned away from everyone.

Lexa made sure everything was documented and catalogued, and led them all back on the ship to decipher just what the hell it all meant.

But the mystery wasn't as forthcoming with its answers, this time.

As before, she lay the map on the console in the cockpit and lowered the Cynosure to it.

They warmed, as always, but nothing appeared on the map.

"It's got to have something to do with these crystals," she said, turning to the photos displayed on the screen. Nine photos lined up in a grid, three she'd picked from each planet. One from directly overhead, one from the west, and one from the east. The crystals lit by the glowing Cynosure weren't the same on each planet. Likely something to do with its position around the sun. Not for the first time, Lexa wondered if there was a timing to the positioning. Like if they'd have to wait for the solstice or something. They could run a simulation and figure out when that might be, but seeing as she didn't have any clue about specific dates or celestial events, she wasn't willing to ask Jenierien to corral any of Smith's men to program it.

Finally, eyes sandy from exhaustion, Lexa talked Jenierien into letting her get some sleep. Jenierien didn't bother to threaten her this time, maybe Lexa's own threat had stuck.

Shutting the door behind her, Lexa had just made it to flopping down on her bed when the doorbell rang.

She sat up on her elbows. "What."

The door slid open. "Miss Lexa. So sorry to intrude."

"Come on in, Smith." She flopped back down.

He inched through the door and closed it with a quiet sigh. "My men would like to know what we expect to find at this site, should we reach it? I told them it's no business of theirs but they are…"

"Pirates?"

"Motivated by money."

She smiled at the ceiling. "I know that feeling well, my friend. Very well." She sat up on her elbows again, abs tight. "It's what got me into this mess in the first place."

With a smile, he leaned on the small table she used for eating at. "I'd like to hear about that."

"No you don't." She sat all the way up and flapped her hand. Using the other one to wipe her face, she let her shoulders droop. "It was senseless. I just wanted a new ship. Something that could maybe take me someplace this far. Take me away from, well, things, on Earth. For good." She shrugged and gave him a tired smile. "Now I'm out here, away from those things. They're probably halfway back to the Sol system as we speak. I never have to speak to them again if I don't want, and I'm on the verge of probably the greatest exoarchaeological discovery in history."

"It sounds like it's turned out pretty well for your plans, then. You're getting everything you want." He held out the drive. The one with the non-doctored video on it.

She took it and turned it over in her hands. "I don't know when you took this back but why are you returning it to me?"

"It has a backup of all the photos from the labyrinth sites. You should hang onto it."

Her forehead tingled and she nodded. "Thanks." She clenched it in one fist.

He didn't get up to leave.

After they shared at least a minute of silence and he still didn't move toward the door, she glanced up at him, her brow raised, and asked the silent question.

"Why don't you look like a woman on the verge of making her career?"

Lexa shrugged again, a pitiful laugh slipping from between her lips. "Why don't I?" Small plastic drive clenched in her palm, she laid back again and covered her eyes with her arm. "Why don't I? Smith, that's the best question anyone's asked me in days."

When Lexa looked out the window on her way to the cockpit the next morning, she discovered the black blanket of diamond stars staring back at her. In the night, Jenierien had moved the ship back to space. Raised voices floated out of the cockpit when she approached.

"I told you not to trust her. Now look. We're lost with no clue which way to go. Chasing this site is a pipe dream."

"Reid, I will not be spoken to on my own ship like that. I don't care that you brought her and my trinket back to me."

Lexa stopped in the hall and backed up against a bulkhead so she could listen to the rest of the conversation.

"She is the best in her field, Mr. Stuart. I do expect she will guide us to the site soon enough."

Who knew Qesson would be the one to stick up for her? Certainly she would be the last one to expect it.

Jenierien lowered her voice, but the acoustics in the hallway still carried it to Lexa's ears. *"Do you think she's telling the truth? Is she really lost on what to do from here? Where to go?"*

"I don't think she's told me the truth a single time since I met her," Reid said, voice gruff. *"She's a hell of a lay but I wouldn't believe a word out of her mouth."*

Lexa grimaced, her throat clicking when she swallowed. The feeling was mutual.

Unwilling—unable—to keep listening to her fan club rave about her, she walked into the cockpit. "Morning everyone. Miss me? What are we doing in space?"

Jenierien waved her to the console. "Lexa, you will begin this day by telling me what course to set with my ship." She clutched the Cynosure in one hand. The map lay spread on the console in front of her. Her flaxen hair was twisted and pinned up with a long hairpin that reminded Lexa of those needles in the Librarian's hair back at Port de Playa. Forever ago. The true beginning for her, Jake, and Elani.

She swallowed, throat clicking again, and tried to boot them out of her mind. The first kiss with Jake. Elani watching from the shadows.

Maybe it was better if they were gone. Maybe they were better off withou—

The proximity alarm blared, a shouting klaxon that made Lexa cover her ears with both hands before they began bleeding.

Jenierien did the same, dropping the Cynosure.

Even with her ears throbbing, Lexa leapt to it before anyone else could notice, and snatched it out of the floor.

Jenierien's voice shrill over the wailing alarm, she shouted. "Mr. Weller, turn that blasted thing off!"

"I'm sorry, milady, the ship came up very quickly. The alarm responded accordingly." Weller flicked a switch on the board and the alarm cut in the middle of a screech.

Lexa unclenched her teeth and loosened the shoulders that'd somehow climbed up around her ears. And remembered the Cynosure was in her hand.

She slipped it into her pocket and eyed the map. How would she get out of here once she got them both? No answers came, but this was her chance, if she was gonna have one. She had the Cynosure, the pictures, all she needed was the map and she could find the site herself.

Before she got any further in her planning, the radio beeped.

"We have an incoming message, milady." Weller sat at the drive console, hand on the radio switch, and looked up at Jenierien.

She nodded. When he flicked the switch, she crossed her arms and threw her head back. "This is Lady Filhelmina Jenierien. I demand you reveal yourselves."

Lexa's stomach jittered. What if it was the Gexcorians? Could Jenierien hold them at bay?

She didn't have to wait long to find out who had invaded their little corner of space.

A woman spoke over the radio. *"Hello, Lady Jenierien. You have someone of ours."*

As if to back her up, a cat meowed in the background.

CHAPTER 32

outh dry, Lexa's lips flopped open and closed. She couldn't think to make words.

They came.

They came back.

They came back for her.

Stomach somersaulting, she didn't think about what she was going to do. Everything she did after hearing Elani's voice over the radio was instinct.

She grabbed Jenierien's shoulder. Before anyone could stop her, she gripped the long pin in Jenierien's hair, undoing Jenierien's hair in the process, and held the sharp point to her neck. With the hand on her shoulder, she reached around Jenierien's neck and pulled her close, pressing against her back. "Mr. Weller, if you would respond, please." Some of Jenierien's hair got caught in her mouth.

Weller flipped a switch. Before Lexa got a chance to form more words, mainly because her stomach was still up in her throat where it'd lodged when she heard Elani's voice, Jake's voice came over the radio.

"Lexa, are you there? We need to know she's OK."

Lexa swallowed, her eyes stinging, throat thick. She couldn't answer them.

Smith spoke from the back of the cockpit. "She is. What would you have us do?"

Jenierien twitched. "Let me go, Lexa. This will not work out well for you."

Lexa found her voice, pushing the tip of the pin into the soft skin under Jenierien's jaw. A bead of blood oozed from around it. "Why don't you come with me, huh? We'll get on the runabout and be on our way."

Qesson took a step. "If you hurt her again—"

Lexa pointed the pin at him. "Stop right there."

He stopped, his eyes on Jenierien.

With Elani and Jake waiting out there in space for her, it suddenly hit her. The answer to the question she'd asked Qesson the day she sold the Cynosure to Jenierien. *Why do you insist on working for Jenierien?*

The poor sap was in love with her. Who knew why he began working for her, but he stayed because he loved her.

Which meant he wouldn't do anything to get her hurt. But he might do something reckless to save her. Holding Jenierien hostage wouldn't be enough, she needed a distraction.

"I'm sorry," she muttered.

"Thank you," Jenierien said. "Now—"

"I wasn't talking to you."

She lashed out with the pin and gashed the map.

It leapt up, vibrating the air around it so hard the shock waves rippled Jenierien's hair directly into Lexa's face.

A strand stung her in the eyeball and she whipped her head to free it. She almost succeeded. Some of it stayed stuck in her lashes.

The others all surrounded the map, trying to get it to back down.

Lexa dragged Jenierien backward, the pin back at her throat.

Following her with his glowing red eyes, Qesson clenched his fists on the other side of the vibrating map, but he appeared unable or unwilling to phase through the men surrounding him.

Jenierien stood tall, pulling her head away from the pin. "You do not need me, Lexa. You've distracted them, you have time to get away and back to your own ship."

"Yeah. Not good enough. Plus, you have to open the door of the runabout for me. Don't pretend like it's not locked."

Jenierien scoffed, dragging her chin higher.

They traveled the length of the long hallway like that, Jenierien tugging her chin higher every few steps, Lexa digging the pin further into her throat. When they stepped into the open air of the cargo bay where the runabout was parked, men milled about around the edges. Lexa caught sight of some cards disappearing as they all stood.

The one who'd confirmed the video wasn't doctored stepped forward. "Milady. Is everything OK?"

"Does it look OK you feckless moron?"

Lexa dug the pin in.

Jenierien sucked air through her teeth.

None of the men moved toward them. In fact, a few sat and crossed their arms like they were watching a show. Lexa and Jenierien approached the ship.

"Are none of you going to lift a finger to help me?"

The one who'd spoken before sat. "To be fair, you paid us to help you dig. Not rescue you."

A laugh bubbled up Lexa's throat. She giggled, grabbing a handful of Jenierien's silky hair, her head spinning. Was she really about to get on this runabout and back to Elani and Jake? Did they really come to rescue her? After the horrible things she said?

She forced Jenierien to bend in front of the locking panel for the runabout. "Open it."

Jenierien punched in a code.

After forcing her inside, Lexa shut the door behind them. As it irised closed, the laughter of the crew came through the door.

"Never hire pirates," Jenierien said, edging around the bed. She entered the cockpit ahead of Lexa and flopped into the copilot chair. "Now what?"

"Now we fly back to the *Auriga* and find the site."

"And how do you plan to do that without the map?"

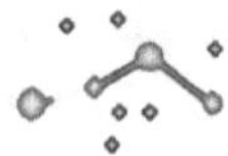

Lexa's knees almost went out from under her when the door opened on Elani, holding Savannah, and Jake standing in front of Paisley, Juniper, and Ferrinogean. The way Elani and Jake smiled from ear to ear, Lexa could almost do what Elani did and see a big, bright, glowing aura of energy surrounding them both. Even Mom and June looked happy to see her and Lexa floated off the runabout and down the stairs to them. Jenierien trailed behind her, silent.

Bypassing Elani and Jake for the moment, forgetting the absurdity of leaving the map behind, Lexa beelined to Ferrinogean and slid the Cynosure from her pocket. She held it up to him, throat tight.

Ferrinogean fell to his…well not knees but he bent over in supplication and muttered like he had the night Lexa met him.

"This belongs to you," she said.

Jenierien cleared her throat. "You cannot give away my—"

"This belongs to him," Lexa said, not turning. "I've thought about a lot of things the last few days. And one of them is that if this belongs to anyone, it belongs to the Gexcorians." She stared down at the bowing alien. "I'll give it to you. But I'm asking you to let me use it to find the site."

Ferrinogean quivered, his head shaking. "All that matters is the Cynosure. It must be returned."

"Will you let me use it? Just for a few more days?"

Elani took a step behind her. Lexa shouldn't have known that was her footstep but she did. She could even pick out Elani and Jake's breathing from the rest of them.

And it was Elani who spoke first. "Do you know where we're going?"

Lexa slipped the Cynosure back in her pocket and turned to them. Her stomach jittered and her knees shook. She tried to speak but nothing came out of her mouth. She cleared her throat and tried again, scared out of her mind for the first time in so long she could hardly remember. "I'm sorry. I don't remember saying those things." She glanced at her mother and sister. "I don't remember. I didn't mean it." Voice lowered, she dropped her eyes. "I'm so glad you didn't fuck off. I don't want that. I'm glad you came back for me."

She peeked at Jake and floated her eyes to Elani.

They both smiled and stepped toward her in unison. They each took a hand.

Their warmth coursed up both her arms. For the first time since Kuarpa and the conversation she overheard between Elani and Yrciel, she didn't worry about their bond. The only bond that mattered to her was the one she'd formed with them both. Individually, and as the three of them.

Her nerves abated. She wanted to kiss them. The two things combined in her gut like alcohol and adrenaline soup. She swallowed. "Thank you for coming back for me. I…I like being with you. Is that OK?"

Jake squeezed her hand. "More than OK."

Elani echoed him. "If it wasn't OK, we would have fucked off."

Lexa chuckled. "I have something I need to tell you when this is all over."

"Me too."

"Glad to see you, Lexa," Mom said. "But what are we doing?"

Before she thought about it too hard, Lexa dropped Elani and Jake's hands and spun to Paisley. She wrapped her arms around her neck. "I'm sorry, Mom."

For once, not a word escaped Paisley's mouth. After a moment of stunned silence, she hugged her back, arms squeezing Lexa's lungs. "OK. I, uh, me too."

Lexa chuckled and released her. Hugging her mom voluntarily wouldn't have been high on her list of things to do just a month ago. But the weirdness had abated by the time she'd gotten around to doing it.

Paisley smoothed the fabric of Lexa's shirt on her shoulder.

Leading them all to the bridge, Lexa spoke over her shoulder. "How did you guys find me?"

Elani paced her. "Juniper."

Mouth flopping open, Lexa stopped and turned on a heel. Jake ran right into her with a soft thump and an, "Oof."

He gripped both shoulders. "Sorry. Didn't mean to mow you down."

She smiled at him. Universe only knew what would happen after this was all said and done, but touching him again was something she'd hoped for without acknowledging until right now. She tapped him on the hip and stepped around, fighting back the rising tide of desire to grip his skin—any skin—and never let go.

"Juniper?" Lexa asked her. "How did you find me?"

June flushed, twisting a toe. "Doug was a Shadow. He taught me some things. Enough to trail the runabout's engine wake where it met up with a much larger one." She grimaced. "It took us a while to find you, because trailing isn't fast."

Lexa nodded, the thrill of touching Jake abating, the thrill of them coming for her subsiding. Instead, a cold twist began in her gut and socked her in the forehead like an ice cream headache. "We've got to get out of here. Give us some time to decipher the coordinates of the site without Reid on our tail." She started for the bridge again.

Elani caught back up to her. "What's with Reid? He didn't want to help you get back aboard the *Auriga* once you said you wanted to?"

Lexa jerked a thumb over her shoulder. "Excellent question. Why don't you ask Jenierien?" She glanced at the lady.

Jenierien grimaced. "He was, is, working for me."

Elani stuck her thumbnail in her mouth. "He's your employee? I thought he worked for some travel company."

"He does," Paisley said. She sucked air between her teeth. "How dare he lie to us like that. Why?"

"To get close to me, of course," Lexa said with a shrug. "Worked, didn't it?"

Paisley touched Lexa on the shoulder. "I had no idea. Had I, I would not have hired him. We may not have the best relationship in the galaxy, but I would not betray you in such a way."

Lexa stopped before walking onto the bridge's catwalk. "I know, Mom. Even before this trip, I wouldn't have thought you that evil. Daft, maybe. Evil, no."

Half a smile curved Paisley's lip. A smile Lexa had seen in the mirror more than once. "Thanks for that." She grabbed June's hand. "Let's go to the upper deck, let Lexa figure this thing out."

June nodded and started up after her.

Lexa watched them go. Ferrinogean followed, his eyes glued to Lexa until the deck plate got in the way.

Once they'd disappeared above, Lexa turned to Jenierien. "I need to ask you something."

Jenierien pressed her painted lips together. "If it's a favor, I'm not inclined to help you. You've given away my prize and stolen my freedom. Not to mention taken my money. Help is the last thing you'll get from me."

"Look. I can't give you the Cynosure. And I can't pay you back for it, either. But I can give you credit for the discovery. The wellspring of all life in the galaxy. You'll be famous for eons. Half of which you'll probably live to see, with your fancy DNAging treatments."

Jenierien's flawless cheek curved. "What do you expect in return?"

"I expect that when you're not locked in your room, you won't try to kill me or anyone else aboard."

Jenierien opened her mouth and began to speak. Lexa cut her off.

"And, you won't try to steal back the Cynosure and head for your ship."

Lips pressed together again, Jenierien narrowed her pale blue eyes and stared into Lexa's. "That's asking a lot."

"Yeah but do you have any idea how famous you'll be? Your face will be on the cover of every news report and gossip rag for years. The site will be named after you. Hell, the whole system probably." She fought chewing her lip. Much as she disliked the woman, going back on deals wasn't something she made a habit of, and she'd stick to this if Jenierien agreed, even if it meant losing the notoriety she'd been seeking when she started this trip.

Also, bribery was a method of control far more effective than simple shackles.

"I'll agree," Jenierien said slowly, "but not until you show me how you plan to find the site without the map."

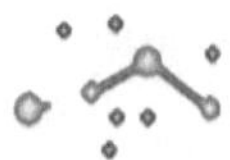

Elani and Jake piloted the *Auriga* high above the ecliptic plane of the star. Out of all the planets' orbits and above them. Their instruments essentially looked down on the plane of the system similar to looking down on a model kids would make for school of Earth and her seven sisters' orbits. Jake punched a few buttons and a simulation of this system popped up on the glass dome of the bridge, a twenty-foot-tall computer-generated illustration.

"Damn, that's nice," Lexa said, staring at it, gape-jawed, from tactical. "I honestly think even Nylah would be jealous of this display."

"It's beautiful," Jake said, the air punched out of his words.

Lexa grinned at him. In all her imaginings of men she might get attached to, she hadn't imagined he'd be so soft, gentle, comfortable. The attachment might not stick, given he was someone else's soulmate, but she wouldn't forget how he'd made her feel. Not if she lived two hundred more years.

"Look here," she said, pointing to the inner planets they'd visited. "Magenta, Cyan, Yellow."

Paisley called down from the observation deck. "I know this one! CMYK."

Lexa craned her neck. "Sorry, what?"

"CMYK," Paisley repeated. "It's the color combination of primary colors. In a perfect world, cyan, magenta, and yellow make black. Pigments are rarely perfect, though."

Lexa snorted. "How do you know that?"

"If you want perfectly-dyed clothing, you need to know something about color."

Lexa shook her head. The things she didn't know about her mother could probably fill a book, but that went both ways, didn't it?

Biting her lip, she looked back at the simulation. "Jake, could you color the planets?"

He punched a few buttons and the moving simulation changed hue. Now it resembled the smaller one Lexa'd seen on the map.

Elani leaned over the pilot's panel. "So, are we looking for black?"

Lexa nodded, staring out at the vacuum of space. Where almost everything was black. "Yeah. But how do we find it in this?" She waved a hand.

"I believe in you," Jake said.

"That makes one of us."

"Two," Elani said.

Unable to hide her smile, Lexa kept her face turned away from them. She plugged the memory drive into her panel and tapped a few buttons. The images from the sites popped up on her screen and she selected the top-down trio. A few more button-pushes and they displayed beside the system simulation in a vertical line.

"Great. OK. These are the photos we took at each site. The Cynosure shone onto specific crystals in the ground during sunrise. We need to know what those crystals correlate to." She settled her chin in her palm and stared at the big display, eyes darting between the photos and the simulation.

Elani spoke first. "Maybe they're coordinates?"

"You mean like, places we need to visit?"

"Yeah."

Lexa considered. It made sense, but they'd already done that with the planets. It didn't follow the precedent the map had set. "I don't think so. If that were the case, it would be leading us halfway across the galaxy again."

"Maybe it is," Jake said, tone gruff.

The bottom dropped out of Lexa's stomach. Maybe it was. Maybe these were star coordinates. Maybe she'd been wrong, and this wasn't the system where life was born. And maybe, maybe she'd never find it.

Ferrinogean trilled in Gexcorian. He stopped, cleared his throat, and tried again. "The Cynosure produced these beams of light? In the photos?"

Lexa twisted in the seat and nodded up at him where several of his tentacles wrapped around the observation deck rails. "It did. It was quite amazing. Where did you guys get it, anyway?"

His chin waggled as he approximated a head shake. "No one knows. It's as old as our civilization. Probably older."

"Definitely older." Lexa turned back to the photos. "Any idea what it's trying to tell us?"

He wiggled out onto the outer side of the deck. Hanging on with three limbs, he stretched toward the pictures. "Layer them."

"I'm sorry?"

A warble came from him again. He stopped, visibly switched to English, and started again. "Like cake. Layer."

Turning back to the pictures, Lexa wondered how he knew about cake. Gexcorians certainly didn't have cake. Whatever, she swiped the pictures on her display and stacked the three of them on top of each other, turning down the transparency on each of them so she could see all three at once.

On the big display, they aligned. The stars shone through them.

"What if—" Jake began.

She held a hand over her shoulder, her index finger partially extended. "Shh. Thinking."

No one else spoke.

Lexa's mind spun, staring at the alignment of the crystals. Three of them in each photo overlapped. Maybe a triangulation of a sort. Where to begin triangulating from?

Her eyes shifted to the star system map again, silently swirling.

Without taking her eyes from the large display, she lay one finger on the cool panel in front of her and slid the photos over as one, until the pedestal in the middle lay over the star.

It pulsed, crimson in the center of the puzzle. The crystals glowed white, each planet pulsing in its assigned color.

"Jake," she said over her shoulder, her voice barely breaking a whisper. "Speed up the orbits. Find me a time when these planets align with the lit crystals."

He did as she asked. The planets revolved hundreds, thousands of times, until they aligned.

When they did, Lexa gasped, pulling air in so quickly her teeth got cold. Pain shot though them, but it was distant.

Elani laughed. "There it is. You've found it!"

On the screen, big as life, a black sphere orbited directly in the center of the magenta, cyan, and yellow planets.

Lexa wanted to jump up and hug them. Hug everyone. She couldn't have done any of this without them.

But.

Her stomach floated back down to where it belonged and kept going, resting on her bladder.

She stared at the picture. "How to find its coordinates the way the planets are right now?"

Feet clanked down the stairs to tactical. Warm hands landed on her shoulders.

"You can do this, Lexa," Jake whispered in her ear, his breath warm on her neck. "I've watched you decipher an impossibly old, unreadable map. This, you got."

Fingers tingling, she put her right hand over his left and squeezed.

"He's right," Elani said, from above them.

"Ships leave a trail in space, like a wake," June called down from the observation deck. "That's how we found you. Do you think planets do too?"

Lexa narrowed her eyes at the system. June had a point. Planets displaced a major amount of space dust as they revolved around their stars. Their magnetic fields, if they had them, interacted with the star's, and they left small amounts of magnetic castoffs in space.

Not that astronomy had been her thing, but when you spend thirty years in college, you pick up a thing or two about a lot more than your major, even if your core classes are years long. She punched in a few calculations with one hand, reaching up with the other to twirl some hair in her finger as she did. Jake's hands left her shoulders but she was too deep in thought to give it much notice. If she could add its wake, its magnetic field—dear universe let it have a magnetosphere—and its projected orbit together, she should be able to run this simulation back to now and still be able to find it.

She programmed it all in and hovered her finger over the button to run back the sim.

"Oh hell," she whispered, under her breath, "what's the worst that could happen?"

She punched the button.

The simulation spun and spun and spun, dizzying as it ran backward in time. The black planet disappeared from sight, somehow hidden entirely from their eyes. What could it have been made from, to disappear so completely? Was it pure obsidian from the heart of the star?

All at once, the simulation stopped. The planets floated in space, their real-time orbits rotating so slowly Lexa almost couldn't perceive the movement.

She frowned. "Elani, take us back to the ecliptic plane at these coordinates." She punched them into her panel and transmitted them to Elani's.

"Is it there?"

Lexa bit her lip and clutched her stomach. That adrenaline dump like she'd gotten in Maridoxia's tomb resurfaced, the one she got before uncovering something new. That seemed like such a long time ago, now. A lifetime. "I want to see something."

They dropped slowly, Elani checking with Jake every few minutes to be sure the valdar was clear and they weren't going to accidentally run through an asteroid or bounce into the mystery planet's atmosphere. They were the only ones who spoke. She adjusted course twice in the silence, moving around some larger rogue objects. Once the ship's movement stopped, Elani spoke, her voice barely above a whisper. "We're here."

Lexa gazed out the front window. She stepped around the panel and stood in front of it, staring out, straining her eyes for what she knew was right in front of her.

For a few breathless moments, only the bright red star shone through the window. But then, as anyone who'd ever watched a solar eclipse knew, a small bite was taken out of the side of it.

Then the bite got larger. And larger. Larger still, until the light bent around the curve of something that was more than shadow.

When the sun shone around it like a halo, Lexa thought she'd never remember how to breathe again.

The black planet, outlined in red, floated in front of them, dark as night and blended perfectly with the space around it.

If this was a natural phenomenon, Lexa would eat her hat.

She stared at it so long, her mouth dried out. When she tried to speak, she had no spit left. She closed her mouth, worked her tongue until she got some spit again, and turned to face the rest of them.

"Now all we need to know is where to land."

Jenierien snorted. "We need the map."

CHAPTER 33

Lexa paced the long hallway at the rear of the ship, what looked something like a rose's stem from outside. She wished she could ask Reid where he found this uniquely gorgeous ship, until reality set in again. Arms crossed over her stomach, she paced the hundred-meter hallway at least three times.

On her way toward the rear again, footsteps sounded behind her. Whoever it was, they weren't trying to hide their presence.

She stopped and turned just the side of her face, so she could catch them in her peripheral.

"When we met, I don't think I would have been able to handle the energy coming off you."

Lexa smiled and resumed pacing. She walked in a circle until Elani caught up.

When she did, Elani linked her arm through Lexa's and set her pace a little less breakneck.

Leaning into her, Lexa sighed. "I saw a video of what I said to you guys. I feel horrible. I don't remember saying that at all." She stopped and met Elani's eyes. "When we met, I would have said it in a heartbeat. I did. But not now." She grimaced and tried to tell Elani what sat so heavy on her heart—that she never wanted to be apart from either of them again. But it just wouldn't come.

"Your energy is so pink right now," Elani said, smiling. "Did you know that when we're searching for our soulmates, we can sometimes see…what's the best way to phrase this?" She paused and stared at the ceiling. "Future residuals."

"I don't follow."

"Sometimes, when a bond is strong enough, we can see the people you're *going* to touch. More often it's people you already have, but sometimes you haven't met them yet. Energy is unpredictable that way."

"That makes no sense to me, but then I'm not the one seeing all this." She stared into Elani's eyes, the bright amber in them swirling. "I do see you, though."

As slow as the planets out there orbiting, Elani leaned her forehead until it touched Lexa's. She whispered onto Lexa's upper lip, her breath warm and wet. "I would like to finish that kiss now, Lexa, if you want to, too."

Lexa didn't give herself a chance to think about it and fuck it all up. She rolled her forehead over Elani's and met her mouth with barely a breath of hesitation. She gripped either side of Elani's waist and pulled her hips until they touched hers. Her center warm, she was sure if she looked down, she'd be able to see bright pink energy the way Elani could. But she wasn't for a moment about to let go of this bliss.

Elani slipped both arms around her and tugged her closer, the kiss heating from pink to fire-engine red in a moment. Her tongue slipped into Lexa's mouth and explored before slipping back out and then returning in a tease. She inhaled through her nose against Lexa's cheek and let out a small moan.

It was all Lexa could do to keep her feet at that. She gripped Elani and pulled her as close as she could get her, feeling for all the world like the floor no longer existed and they floated in the inky black of outer space together.

Before she sank deeper into the kiss, and hoo-boy, there were layers of deeper to get into, something bumped her gently on the top of the head.

She started and broke the kiss, looking up.

Her nose bounced off the ceiling.

"Elani." Her voice shook.

"OK, it's fine," Elani said, sounding more confident than she looked. "Sorry. It's uh…whew. That was. I hadn't expected it to be like that."

Lexa tried to glance down and decided against it. The ceiling and the floor were separated by at least 15 meters. If they fell from this height, even Elani's skill at healing might not help. She trembled, and buried her face in Elani's neck.

"Yeah, don't look." Elani's arms tightened around her waist. "I'll get us down. Hang on."

Without looking, Lexa had to just imagine what Elani was doing. Her perfect brow was probably creased, her eyes narrow, the golden light falling on her eyelashes as her irises pulsed bright with concentration.

Something touched Lexa's toes. She didn't open her eyes.

"We're down. You can let go."

Lexa dug in deeper, squeezing Elani until she was sure it was uncomfortable for her. "What if I don't want to?"

Elani chuckled. "I'm sorry about that. It's, uh, it's not easy to explain, but I guess there's no time like the present."

"Can I tell you something first?" Lexa disentangled her arms and backed up a step. That kiss had been exquisite, but it almost felt like taking advantage, when she knew she wouldn't be able to do it again. She had to head herself off at the pass and make sure she didn't fall victim to that overwhelming need. Because the desire to do it again was building already. "I need to tell you something."

"I get a turn after you, then."

"Fair enough." Lexa frowned. "I don't know how to tell you this so I'm just gonna say it. I slept with your soulmate."

Brow wrinkled but this time in confusion, Elani stepped back. "What?"

"When you uh"—Lexa cleared her throat—"when you went with your parents to the store, me and Jake, um." She frowned. "Please don't be mad at him. I overheard you and your mom talking and I know he doesn't know it's him. He told me he wasn't your soulmate and I believed him, even though the way you two are together…" She peeked up at Elani's eyes, little as she wanted to see what was in them right now. The hurt, anger, disappointment.

But there were none of those things in them. A small smile crossed her lips and her brow smoothed. "Is that what happened? You can't imagine all the things I thought, when your energies turned blue. I thought you'd had a fight or accidentally killed someone or something. It's not like Jake to keep things from me."

"I cut it off as soon as I found out," Lexa said, the words rushing as fast as she could get them out. "I told him not to tell you. You should tell him about your soulmate, though. He needs to know."

Elani nodded, her head bobbing up and down slowly. She poked out her lower lip, but her eyes still smiled. "He does need to know. And so do you. I never said anything, because it wasn't the right time. Sometimes…people don't react well to the news, especially humans." Her cheeks flushed. "I see now I may have done more harm than good. Listen—"

An alarm blared, lights in the hall strobing white and red.

Lexa's eardrums vibrated. Eyes wide, she met Elani's gaze.

"We better get to the bridge." She grabbed Elani's hand without another word and took off at a sprint.

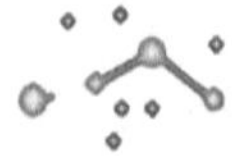

Jake stood at the tactical station, bouncing from foot to foot. When Elani and Lexa's feet hit the metal catwalk, his head jerked up. "Sorry about the racket. I set the proximity sensors a little more sensitive after our last encounter." He punched a button and the klaxon died. The lights kept flashing.

"Not gonna lie, Jake, I thought it was maybe the second coming. Holy shit, that's loud," Lexa said, gripping the stair railings and sliding down them. She landed next to him. "Good job, though."

He grinned, his sunny smile #1.

Damn, but it was good to see.

"You're welcome." His smile slid sideways a tick. "It does mean somebody's approaching, though. We should get ready."

Lexa shouted up to the observation deck. "You guys should strap in, just in case."

Someone's pale thumb stuck out over the railing. "Don't worry about us."

"You guys have Jenierien? Or should I send Jake up?"

June peeked over the rail. "I think we have her."

Lexa nodded. "Keep quiet." For a wild moment, she considered there was some kind of welcoming party to this mystery planet, maybe someone who could help guide them through the strange atmosphere. What was making it effectively invisible?

Elani spoke from her station. "Transmission coming in."

Jake pecked Lexa on the cheek and jumped up the stairs in one leap.

Cheek warm, Lexa slid into her seat at tactical. One hand rested on her cheek where he'd kissed it. She'd not invited that but she didn't hate it, either. If only there were some way...

Now was not the time for that. If they survived, there'd be time to figure it all out later.

She glanced over her shoulder. "Who is it?"

Elani's eyes, still glowing brighter than usual, met hers. "Your favorite person in the universe."

"Impossible when they're sitting right behind me," Lexa said, eyes bouncing between them.

Jake's sunny smile #1 resurfaced. Elani dropped her eyes, cheeks redder than the sun out there, and tapped the radio. "ISM *Auriga*. Who do we have the pleasure of speaking to?"

Reid's voice boomed over the speaker. *"You know who this is. Where's Jenierien?"*

"She's comfortable," Lexa answered. "What do you want, Reid?"

The proximity sensor went off again, klaxon blaring.

"Fuck, now what," Lexa muttered. She tapped the button to get the klaxon to stop.

Reid chuckled. *"I see your proximity alarm has alerted you to our friends' presence. They've been so anxious to see you again."*

Lexa glanced out the window. As the *Auriga* sat in space in front of the mystery planet, two ships came into her view.

The *Sonne*, and a ship she'd hoped to have put tail to forever. Couldn't win em all.

The Gexcorians just wouldn't quit.

She seethed through her teeth. "How do they keep finding…" It hit her in a rush. She turned back to the comm panel and brought up the video.

Reid sat in front of the camera, his face taking up most of it, and smiled. His blue eyes twinkled, but the smile was rotten on the edges. Too wide, too much mouth.

"You son of a bitch. It's you."

He nodded. "I had heard you were smarter than this. It sure did take you a loooong time to get it." He drew out the o, his eyes wide and voice mocking. "It's been me this whole time. Getting you on the cruise was a trick, but I have my ways. The Gexcorians offered a very pretty price. Prettier even than Jenierien's cheap ass."

Jenierien scoffed but said nothing, which both impressed and surprised Lexa.

"Great, OK, so you sold me out to every bidder in the galaxy. What do you want now?"

"It's not what *I* want, Alexandra."

Lexa shuddered. The son of a bitch gave Jenierien and the Gexcorians everything they needed to track her down at every turn, and now he sat there and called her by her full name like he knew her? Fuck that.

But. Shit. He was right. It wasn't about what *he* wanted, was it?

She pinched her lips together. When she spoke, it came out more like a growl. "What do you want for the map?"

"What will you give me?" He lifted it up. A string had been tied—tight—around the middle, constricting it. "It was hard to get this thing tackled when you left. It almost killed one of the men. Luckily he already had a scar on his face, so what's a few more?"

Damn. Damn, damn, damn. Of all the people on that ship, Smith was the one she wanted to hurt the least. She'd have to make it up to him, and his crew.

She clenched her teeth. "I'll offer you the same deal I gave Jenierien. We'll put your name on the discovery. You'll be in every archaeological zine from here to the other end of the galaxy. History will remember your name long after it's forgotten mine."

He chuckled and lowered the map again. "It's a good start."

"What else?"

That rotten smile crept onto his face again. "Guess." He lifted the map back into frame and waggled it violently as if to promise harm would come to it if she refused.

Rage—at being used for sex and money, at being lied to for his own gain, at the way he took advantage of Paisley and June, even—boiled up Lexa's throat and into her mouth, burning as it went like stomach acid. Her mouth filled with saliva and the urge to puke overwhelmed her.

She swallowed it back, staring at the projection of his face on the screen. "I'll only meet you on neutral ground."

"Where in the hell will you find that?"

Lexa glanced up at the observation deck. "Call your people, Ferrinogean. It's time to talk."

CHAPTER 34

Ferrinogean led Lexa and Jake across the airlock he'd come from in the first place, only this time there were less guns. Elani stayed behind with Savannah and the others. The last thing Lexa wanted to do was be separated, but she couldn't bring them both, and she couldn't come alone. Besides, Elani was the only one Savannah liked who wasn't Lexa.

Once aboard the Gexcorian ship with the airlock closed, the atmosphere changed. On Gexcor, the relative gravity and atmosphere were similar to Earth's. But water living the way the Gexcorians tended to prefer came with some changes.

When her feet left the ground after her next step, Lexa flung out a hand and caught Jake's.

He clutched her back. "Been a while since I was in zero G."

"It is not zero," Ferrinogean said, limbs floating and pulling him through the air like he was in water, "but more like your moon. A bit less than one-sixth of Earth's gravity."

Lexa tried to pedal and ended up almost spinning a circle before Jake got the hang of it and helped counterbalance her. They pushed off as a team and followed their host deeper into the ship, working together in a way that both exhilarated and frightened her. When the walls closed in and the hallways got slimmer, Jake and Lexa crowded each other. Jake's arm floated in the air behind her.

"Sorry," he said, "I don't really know what to do with this arm."

She slid one arm around his waist and caught his floating hand. Wrapping it around her shoulders, she smiled up at him, his body heat not the only thing warming her up. "There."

His skin was too dark to blush, but there was definitely a change in the hue of his cheeks. He bit his lip. "Sorry about kissing you on the cheek earlier. I felt foolish the second I did it. I was excited, but that's no excuse."

She tightened the arm around his waist. "If we survive this, I want to have a good, long talk with you and Elani both. OK?"

He smiled, mouth stretched wide. "OK."

They squeezed through a door together. Entering the cockpit, their toes scraped the ground. The gravity reasserted itself in gentle waves like washing up on a beach.

Reid already sat in a chair in the corner, scowling. "Thought we agreed on a neutral meeting."

"Sure, is that why you brought strong-arms?"

Two of Smith's crew stood to either side of him. Lexa thought she remembered them from poker. Benson and…Sandoval?

Reid grimaced. "You aren't to be trusted. You've gone back on so many promises in the few weeks I've known you, it's a wonder anyone even takes you at your word anymore."

Rather than engage, she drew the Cynosure out of her pocket.

A gasp flitted around the Gexcorians in the cockpit.

Ferrinogean stood tall. Maybe he was becoming immune to the effect it had on them from having seen it so many times. As far as Lexa knew, he'd been the first Gexcorian to see it in eons. He held out two limbs. "As sworn arbiter of this meeting, I will now take both artifacts and lay them here, on this pedestal."

As he spoke, a table-like pedestal rose from the floor without a sound.

Lexa gripped the Cynosure with a sweating hand. Gexcorians were good for their word, and breaking an oath to arbitrate a meeting was a death sentence to them. She'd used that to her advantage when she and Devin had gotten permission to search for Maridoxia's diadem, and she used it now. Staring Reid in the face, she held the Cynosure over Ferrinogean's outstretched limb.

Reid sucked through his teeth, eyes hooded, and brought out the map. "If I untie this string, I can't be held responsible for what it does." He started to tug the bow.

"Wait." Lexa narrowed her eyes. "Map. We mean you no further harm."

Where the map had been visibly straining against the string, it now relaxed, flattening as though it had been paper all along.

Damn this thing was amazing.

They laid the two objects in Ferrinogean's curved limbs at the same time. With another limb, he uncurled the map and laid it on the pedestal. He went to lower the Cynosure with a third shaking limb. You could have heard a pin drop.

"Wait," Lexa whispered.

He stopped, eyes wide, and stared at her, not breathing. His pointed tongue whipped out of his mouth and touched his upper lip.

Out of sheer force of needing to hold onto something to stand in the face of that expression—equal parts reverence, fear, and anger—Lexa grabbed Jake's arm. "Lower it slowly. They don't like it if you're rough with them. And…well…I guess you'll see. Just, be gentle."

The sac below his chin waggled in his approximation of a nod. He turned his head back to the map and lowered the Cynosure with two limbs. Slowly, reverently, as though it was a newborn child.

The heat baking off them as they approached each other warmed Lexa's skin from here. Her mouth dried out, and the memory of all the times she'd done this overlaid each other like a mashed-up slide-show. She thought about her own skin heating at Jake's touch in the hallway, at the way she'd floated with Elani into a world all their own.

How many eons had the map and the Cynosure spent apart? How many eons more would they have to after this was all over?

The map and Cynosure came together in that loving touch and tears collected in the back of Lexa's throat and spilled, instantly forgotten, down her cheeks.

Springing to life, the map projected its secrets into the entire room, covering every surface in a smoke-colored fog so dense, Lexa couldn't see anyone else.

Boy was she grateful to have been holding Jake's arm.

With his other hand, he clutched her, and they stood together, watching the secret of the planet below them unfold.

The spherical scene surrounding them began to hum. Not a song, just one note. It reverberated through Lexa's chest like a bass drum in a marching band. Those big, resounding *booms* as the drums approached, signaling to everyone it was time to feel music as much as hear it.

Her breath caught somewhere up near her teeth, she stared with her mouth open as the scene in front of them cleared.

The note continued, now vibrating the panels in the room so hard, screws began to pop out and *tink tink tink* to the ground around them. If it went on much longer, the panels above their heads might end up crushing them.

She gripped Jake tighter, and he did the same.

But as the note continued, the smoke began to lighten. Where it started as a fog almost as thick as the black shroud covering the planet, now Lexa could see the pedestal again. Now she could see Ferrinogean, and now Reid. And as they appeared again through the smoke, the projection around them began to shift into blue and green. It surrounded them and Lexa could swear she almost smelled freshly-cut grass and wet earth. Before the smoke cleared entirely, the scent of rain filled the air so completely, Lexa's face was left wet.

Or maybe those were the forgotten tears resting on her cheeks.

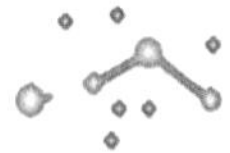

"Someone tell me that got recorded."

Most of the Gexcorians quivered on the ground, unable or unwilling to look at the Cynosure.

Lexa let Reid take the map while she grabbed the Cynosure again. The glass was still warm.

Clutching it in her palm, she wiped her cheeks with the back of her hand. "Anyone? What frequency was that?"

Ferrinogean managed to stop shaking long enough to trill a few whistles and clicks. The computer panel behind him sprang to life and spoke in Gexcorian.

Lexa knew the words, but not what the frequency estimation meant. She asked Ferrinogean to translate.

He shook his head. "I am familiar with your culture but not that much." He waved a limb at someone else and spoke to them in a low voice. They nodded, plugged some things into the computer, and showed him the readout. They wouldn't make eye contact with Lexa, and instead kept sneaking glances at her clenched fist.

Ferrinogean faced her again. "87 Hertz."

Jake squeezed her other hand. "What do you think it meant?"

She considered. The smoke filling the room at first, almost as black as the planet out there in space, had to have represented the atmosphere surrounding it, hiding it, protecting it. The note played and the longer it held, the lighter the room became, until it disappeared into air. "I think it means we need to project that note into the atmosphere long enough to get our ships through. The note is the key to opening it."

Reid grunted from his chair. "How the hell are we supposed to do that?"

"Damned if I know." Lexa shrugged. "I've certainly broken into easier tombs."

Ferrinogean cleared his throat.

She flashed him a tight-lipped smile. "Not now."

He gurgled out a laugh before turning serious again. "Is there a way to play the note through the hull?"

Lexa frowned and nodded. "I think you're on the right track, there." She stared out the window at the planet, eyes unfocused. They had parked in its closest Lagrange point and rode with it around the star, so that it continued to block the red light. The crimson ring around it flashed from time to time, maybe the light from solar flares. How could they match the frequency? How could they get the air around them to match a frequency? How could the energy surrounding them…

Oh, that was it.

"I need to talk to Elani. Jake, let's get back to the *Auriga*." She tugged his hand.

He followed, but Reid stood. "You're not leaving us here to go land on the planet by yourself."

She stopped. "And you're not setting foot on that ship again."

"It's not your ship," he sneered. "You don't get to make that call."

"We can ask my mom if you prefer. Everyone on the ship, Jenierien included, heard your little speech last time we spoke." Her lip curled in a self-satisfied grin. Let him start trying to weasel out of that.

He hung his head. "Great." He glanced between Smith's men and grimaced. "Doesn't matter, you can't leave me here while you run down there and find whatever it is. I shared the map with you willingly."

Ferrinogean stepped between them. "He is right. You gave your word."

From beneath heavy lids, she stared up at him. "Fine. Get her on the radio, then."

Ferrinogean nodded at one of the others.

They turned around and made a few taps. A sound like static filled the speakers. "Speak," they warbled.

"Elani, can you hear me?"

Elani's face popped up in the video feed. "Lexa, is everything OK?"

"It is." Lexa sagged with relief. Not that anything would have happened to her but…it was still a relief to see her and hear her voice again. "I need your opinion on something."

"Anything."

A smile hit Lexa right in the belly. She clutched Jake's hand harder and leaned toward the radio. "Could you make energy form a musical note? Like 87 Hertz?"

"I…hm. I think so. Music is just an energetic vibration. Why?"

"We might need to do something like that."

"What's the scale?"

Lexa swallowed and looked around. "Big enough to encompass these three ships?"

Elani scoffed, her voice hissing through the radio. "I've never tried something that big. Can you explain it better?"

Reid stood and walked to the radio. "Why doesn't everyone come to my ship and we'll take it down. It should be easier if it's just the one ship."

A voice called from the background of the *Auriga*, "Your ship?"

Lexa suppressed a grin. She'd love to see the outcome of all this between Reid, Jenierien, and the Gexcorians, if she didn't get killed in the process. Biting her lip, she shook her head. "And give you the high ground? No thanks. Anybody else got an idea?"

Seconds ticked by in silence like minutes.

When no one answered, Lexa started talking before she knew she was going to. "I changed my mind. I think it's a wonderful idea, Reid. I'll come alone and we'll go down together."

"Good." He reached to shut off the radio.

Lexa's knees went out from under her and she fell into the nearest empty chair. There was a lot of exclaiming going on around her—Elani, Jake, Jenierien, even Ferrinogean—but she couldn't wrap her head around any of it. The color drained from the room, and a tingling hit her everywhere—from the crown of her head, through her chest and around her thudding heart, out to her fingertips. She blinked over and over, trying to keep her eyes open and failing.

Jake dropped to his knees next to her and grabbed her hand. "Lexa? Are you OK? What's wrong?"

When she didn't answer him, he repeated her name with one hand on her face.

She tried to focus on him, she tried so hard.

Now she couldn't hear the others in the room. A moment ago, it'd been all fighting and voices and cacophony, and now it was all cotton balls in her ears. In the moment before she was sure she was about to lose consciousness, Jake wrapped her in a tight hug.

All at once, it was like her sinuses cleared, and she snapped back. Eyes open wide, she gripped him. "What the fuck just happened?"

He squeezed her tighter. "I don't know but you scared the hell out of me." Hands on her shoulders, he leaned back and took in her face, a line between his brows. "You lost all your color. It was like when you left the ship with Reid…" He trailed off and his eyes unfocused. "Huh."

"Huh?"

Elani interrupted from the radio. "Lexa!"

Lexa faced the screen. She thought about responding but all she could do was stare and wonder why she'd say she'd go alone with Reid? That made no sense whatsoever.

"Listen to me very closely, Lexa. You and Jake must return to the *Auriga* immediately. I don't care what happens to the map or the Cynosure or any of it. You have to get back here. We um"—she looked over her shoulder—"we have an emergency."

Lexa stood, Jake supporting her when her knees shook, and spoke to Reid. "We'll finish this conversation later."

CHAPTER 35

Reid slammed his hand on the radio, cutting Elani off. "You're coming with me. Now. Bring the thing." He shoved the map into the hands of one of the strong arms and reached for Lexa.

She wobbled, still not entirely certain on her feet. Jake's arm wrapped around her waist, steadying her, and she gripped him. "I am not coming with you. We'll go see what Elani needs and figure it out from there."

Without warning, Reid's balled fist connected with Jake's nose.

Jake howled and stumbled back, blood spurting past the hand he clapped to his face. It dripped onto his shirt, covering it in splotches that looked like paint.

Reid pushed him, causing the blood gushing from Jake's nose to splash onto Lexa's arm like warm rain.

"Jake!"

He fell to his ass in the floor; wide, round eyes bulging up at Lexa. "The hell, Reid?"

Reid didn't answer him. Instead, he gripped Lexa's arm and began to tug. "If you won't go with a little persuasion like you did last time, I'll just drag you." He shook her.

"Persuasion? Last time?" Her feet skidded in the blood with a loud squeak, leaving a trail of thick red across the deck of the Gexcorian's ship. Her head was still fuzzy and making sense of Reid wasn't happening. But she pulled back on her arm as he stepped forward, throwing him off balance enough for her to free her arm and skip backward to Jake. "I'm not going with you."

He huffed and rolled his eyes. "I had tried to be nice about this." He sneered at Jake. "Ever since you met this guy and that chick, you've been impossible to deal with. I hate to be so crude, but you leave me no choice."

One moment, his hand was empty. The next, he clutched an old-fashioned, projectile gun. Not only equally deadly to its more modern energy counterparts, but infinitely more painful to be shot with. At least a blast from an energy gun didn't rip your flesh apart in a ragged hole and break your bones on its way past. There was something a lot more civilized about being left with an instantly cauterized wound—at worst—instead of a lead slug buried under your skin.

Lexa grabbed the arm Jake wasn't using to press his nose and hauled him to his feet, her other hand raised in the air. "Where did you get that?"

Reid stared at her, the blue of his eyes changing, going deeper, like the ocean from space.

She'd never experienced a deeper blue, and the feeling that overcame her was more than awe. It blew right past that into acquiescence. She nodded, mouth dry. The words came out of her mouth like someone else spoke them. "Just don't hurt Jake."

He nodded. "Why don't we all go? It'll be a fun field trip." He glanced at Ferrinogean, a smile curling his lip. "Why don't you come, too? Love me some fresh calamari."

Lexa barely felt the feet at the end of her legs as they followed Reid out of the cockpit and toward the *Sonne* parked outside. She didn't really want to go—though the black eye of that projectile gun scared her on a level she hadn't accessed in a long, long time—but the compulsion to follow him was too strong to ignore.

Jake and Ferrinogean clearly felt the same. Jake continued to clutch her, and she clutched him back, her guts quivering when she thought about his bloody nose.

Ferrinogean followed behind and Smith's men brought up the rear.

But there was a moment, just before they boarded the *Sonne* that Benson leaned into Lexa's field of vision and winked.

Oh, that could be useful.

Before she could take advantage of the knowledge she had more than one ally here, Reid had closed the door behind them. They stood in the cavernous cargo bay and Reid lowered the gun. "Welcome aboard, first timers. Lexa, welcome back." He pinched her chin between two fingers.

Scowling, she jerked her face away. "What's your plan now? Are we just gonna sit here?"

"Follow me," he said, leading them through the bay and into the hall that would take them to the cockpit.

Jake leaned into her ear. "Why the hell did we say yes? I didn't want to come. I didn't want *you* to come."

"I don't know," she whispered leaning into his ear. A twist of his hair brushed her cheek. "It was like I couldn't help myself."

His breath warmed her ear. "Me too. What do you think it means? Do you think—"

In a quiet voice, Reid said, "No talking," over his shoulder.

It would have been better if he'd threatened in a booming shout, but in a way, that quiet, controlled calm was that much more frightening. Lexa shivered and stood straight, following Reid into the cockpit.

What had Jake been about to ask? Was it what she was thinking? Had she been lied to this whole time, believing Reid was human?

"Move," Reid said to Weller.

The man slipped out of his chair and stood to the side.

Lexa sidled closer to him, desperate to ask about Smith's injuries. But what Reid did from the conn made her forget all about, well, pretty much everything.

CHAPTER 36

Reid leaned forward and tapped a few keys on the drive panel. The ship began its descent toward the pitch-black planet.

Lexa held her breath. Was he going to crash them all into it, kill them instantly? If he couldn't have it, no one could, kind of thing?

She didn't have to wait long for the answer.

Large hands gripping the arms of the chair, Reid sat back and closed his eyes.

The hum started so low, Lexa felt it more than heard it.

A vein stood out on Reid's forehead. The humming intensified and climbed in frequency.

It was easy enough to pinpoint the epicenter of the hum.

"Lexa," Jake said, breathless. "He's—"

"Manipulating energy. Yes."

The corner of Reid's mouth curled, but he said nothing. Clearly couldn't break his concentration by speaking right now.

Lexa considered it. For a moment, she really did.

But the ship was hurtling toward the blacked-out atmosphere, and who knew what would happen if they hit it before it cleared? Also—and it wasn't like she wanted to admit this but it was the truth—she wanted to see the site. She needed to see it. Her life's work had led to this moment; more than that, her entire belief system needed this. Needed to know life itself was inextinguishable. That it couldn't just be snuffed out like a candle on a windy day and never heard from again.

A brief moment of doubt struck her at that, remembering that the map and Cynosure were proof enough. She'd already experienced life's indefatigable persistence.

Maybe that was enough.

But before she could decide, the note reached the right pitch. It buzzed inside her chest, inside her teeth, inside her head. It surrounded them all, penetrated them all.

The black marble in space ahead of them began its own vibration. Like ripples on the surface of a still and glassy lake, the atmosphere trembled. Its color shifted.

More than one vein stood out on Reid's forehead now. Sweat drenched his brow, large circles of it seeping into his shirt under his arms, and his teeth clenched so tight Lexa thought they might break. The joint where his jaw met his skull was a solid mass. He panted through his gritted teeth.

Lexa tore her eyes away from the Ambran in the driver's seat and stared, transfixed, out the front window.

The atmosphere reacted just the way the map had shown them.

It lightened by degrees and as they approached, and Reid strengthened the note, looking for all the world like he was about to cause an aneurysm inside his own brain, it shifted from opaque to translucent. They crossed the terminator from night to day.

The outline of a continent came into being, sunrise brightening its glistening shores.

A continent, with water outlining it. Maybe methane, but what if it was good, old-fashioned, H2O?

If it was, did that mean the people who made this map still lived here?

Lexa caught her breath and gripped Jake's hand so hard he flinched.

"Sorry," she mumbled. But she didn't let up.

The atmosphere went fully transparent.

Earth. She may as well have been looking at Earth.

It shouldn't have been a shock. A lot of rocky Goldilocks planets had water. A ton of them looked passingly like Earth. She'd just never expected to see it staring back at her this far from Sol.

"It's beautiful," Jake breathed.

All she could do was nod.

The copilot murmured. "We're about to enter the atmosphere. I'll try to make it smooth, but everyone should grab a seat."

Reid's hands, knuckles white as paper, continued to grip the arms of the chair. He'd frozen, his face a rictus. The note persisted, though, so, sadly he was still alive.

The ship rocked, running into its first bit of atmospheric turbulence.

Lexa's pocket all but ignited in flames.

She screamed and dropped Jake's hand, digging into her pocket with both of hers.

She tugged the Cynosure free. The glass was nearing molten. "Fuck!" She dropped it.

It never touched the floor. Ferrinogean, who she had almost forgotten existed, leapt and outstretched every limb. He caught it before it hit the ground and his skin sizzled. To his credit—or maybe his detriment—he didn't let go. He cradled it instead, thick tears falling from his eyes and gooping on his face.

Lexa looked away from the scene, and the planet below fast approaching, and caught Benson's eye. "Where's the map?"

He held it up.

Reid twitched but it didn't look like he could let the note go. Not yet.

They had a few seconds before clearing the atmosphere. Would it be enough?

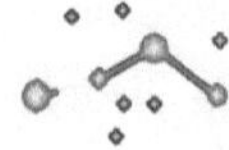

Smith stepped through the door to the cockpit, holding his side. His scarred, and now bandaged, face turned to Lexa. One side of his mouth turned up. He looked at Benson holding the map, to Reid, and then back at Lexa. He jerked his chin in Lexa's direction, eyes on Benson.

Benson tossed the map to Lexa and stepped aside so Smith could continue into the room.

Lexa hadn't been expecting the map to come sailing through the air toward her and she fumbled it. But it never hit the ground, and she softened her grip so she wouldn't damage it, or piss it off. What it had done to Smith's face wasn't going to heal pretty. Her stomach clenched at the realization that was her fault.

Before she could make a move on Reid, Qesson followed Smith through the open door.

"Where is Lady Jenierien?"

Of course that would be his first question.

"Tell you what," Lexa said, sidling closer to their captor, "I would have brought her with me, but your boy here didn't want her coming. So I guess you should ask him."

Qesson turned to him and tilted his head. "What is he doing?"

Reid's slitted eyes turned to Qesson for the barest of seconds. His jaw was still practically welded shut, and he said nothing.

"Did you know he's Ambran?" Lexa fingered the edges of the map and watched Ferrinogean press some of his limbs together where they'd been singed. The Cynosure still all but glowed from heat, but he seemed to be handling it better. Maybe his nerve-endings had gone dead.

Qesson slid around Reid, eyes never leaving the back of his head, and edged closer to Lexa. "I did not. We assumed he was human, but now that you mention it, he never said that explicitly. What is he doing?"

"Right now, he's getting us safely through an atmosphere I'm pretty sure would try to kill us if we didn't have the password." She pointed the end of the map at him. "I think we should be ready for when he's done, maybe take him into custody?"

Smith's men all shifted, almost imperceptibly, hands closer to their weapons without seeming to move.

Reid growled through clenched teeth. "Do that, and I'll close this atmosphere over all of us. Be hard to land the ship if it was in two pieces. Or more." His eyes slipped sideways enough to meet hers. "That what you want?"

She wanted to zip back a snarky answer, tell him hell yes that what she wanted if it meant he didn't get to see the site, either.

But it wasn't, and she knew it. She was too close now. It was land the ship or bust.

One flick of her eyes at Smith and his men stood down.

Smith limped to her and held a hand out. "You can sit here and watch us land. Do you know where we should be landing?"

With a start, Lexa faced him. "Shit. No." She slid into the chair next to Jake and unrolled the map.

The ship hit some turbulence again, and sparks flew past the front window as the friction of flying through the atmosphere lit the bottom of the ship on fire. Nothing unusual. Built-in heat shields were a lot more reliable now than they had been when Gram was a kid.

Lexa snapped her seat belt and leaned over the map again.

Jake leaned to take a look too.

She reached over and gripped him with one hand, an anchor to hang onto. Something—someone—solid enough to ground her. An unusual feeling swept through her like a wave and it took her more than a moment of staring blankly out the window to figure out that it was gratitude for him being here with her. Her head spun.

The smile on her face unbidden, she went back to the map. It didn't show anything. "Ferrinogean," she called, "bring the Cynosure."

He whimpered but made his way over, crawling across the floor and putting as little weight as possible on the end of his limbs.

Lexa grimaced. "You need the doc to take a look at that." She glanced up at Smith.

"He's experienced," Smith said. He gestured at the bandages crisscrossing his face. "This could have been a lot worse."

Ferrinogean's head wobbled. "Not until the Cynosure is safely back with my people. Until then, I will guard it with every breath left in my body." He trilled and the limb holding the Cynosure trembled.

With nothing to say to that, Lexa turned back to the matter at hand. "Point it at the map. See what happens." Knees together, she lay the map on her thighs and waited. Probably not the best idea, considering the spot of fused sand on Birkishni, but she had nowhere else to put it.

The map seemed to know that. It settled over her legs with a gentle caress, wrapping over her thighs like a small fleece blanket.

Ferrinogean raised off the floor and stretched out his limbs as best he could, holding the Cynosure close.

They both began to resonate with the note Reid still held. They didn't play the same note, but each played a different harmony.

Lexa had never in her life heard a more pleasing symphony. Something inside her, a coil she'd never known was wound so tight it was always ready to snap, loosened. The way she floated inside the wormhole came back, that moment of knowing every secret of the universe and its complete and overwhelming peace, and she settled back into the chair with a smile on her face that should have hurt from being too wide.

A picture appeared on the map. A dense forest and a building set on a hill above enormous stands of trees. Numbers appeared in Gexcorian and floated in the sky above them.

"Ferrinogean, can you read that?"

"You cannot?"

"I can, but it's easier for you, isn't it?"

His chin wobbled in that peculiar nod of his. "It is. They appear to be coordinates."

"Good. Tell the copilot."

He trilled and turned to do so.

Reid stood behind him, that projectile gun in his hand again. He shoved it into the sac below Ferrinogean's head. "I'll take that, thank you." He held out the other hand.

Ferrinogean trembled. "I cannot give it to you. I am sworn—"

Reid pulled the trigger.

Lexa had never seen a Gexcorian struck by a bullet. Hell, she'd never seen a human struck by one. It tore through the soft flesh of his organs in a blast of sound that left Lexa's ears ringing, sending grayish blood mixed with bits of his stomach, heart, and probably brain, all over her, Jake, and Smith.

They all shouted in unison and Lexa wiped bits of organ off her face as the now-dead Gexcorian slid to the ground. The Cynosure rolled out of his grasp and clinked to the floor.

Without giving her any more time to mourn the life of a being that, yes, had tried to kill her, Reid swung the black eye of the gun to her for the second time today. "The map."

Staring at the gun's neverending darkness, she handed the map to him with tingling fingers. She tried to take her eyes off the hole at the end of the barrel, but it was hypnotic. She couldn't stop staring at it if she tried. And she willed Reid not to point it at Jake. If the universe had any kind of fairness, despite evidence to the contrary, he wouldn't point it at Jake.

When he disappeared it back up his sleeve or wherever he was keeping it, Lexa exhaled through lips so tight, they'd gone numb.

She stared at Reid as he sat back at the conn. "Now what?"

"Now we get me that fame and fortune."

CHAPTER 37

It took all Lexa had to anticipate landing at the site with excitement. What Reid had done—not just today but since before the day they met—had sucked all the enjoyment out of it for her. Not that she was in love with the fact that this asshole could ruin what should be the greatest accomplishment of her career, maybe her life, but it was what it was. She was terrified, angry, sticky with black blood, and heartsick. She'd never truly considered killing someone, but Reid had just about pushed her over that threshold, and she couldn't wait to get a chance to see if her resolve held.

He stood behind the men piloting the ship, arms crossed, and grinned out the window. "Your energy is all tangled up with his," he said, over his shoulder.

Lexa glanced at Jake and shrugged. "OK?"

"I tracked you from Earth—easy enough since Qesson knew what ship you were on and you filed your flight plan with Light Speed Control. When I saw this weak-minded one wandering down the beach on Port de Playa, your energies all entwined, I didn't even break a sweat convincing him to bring you aboard the cruise."

She bit the back of her hand, swallowing bile.

Reid kept smiling out the front window but said nothing else.

Smith leaned over and spoke to Jake. "Smith," he said, hand out. "My ship. You are?"

Jake shook, his infectious smile surfacing like a miracle. "Jacoby Harris." He glanced at Lexa.

She nodded.

"You can call me Jake," he finished.

Smith gave him a firm up and down pump. "Good to meet you, Jake. Any friend of Lexa's."

Reid glanced over, lip curled, looking for all the world like he wanted to tell them to quiet down. Instead, he paced to the engineer's station and leaned over the chair. He spoke loud enough for Lexa to overhear. "Can you mask our trail?"

The man, white and almost as battle-scarred as Smith, silvery scars running across his neck and down the side of his face, glanced over his shoulder. "Our trail?"

Reid smacked him, the gun reappearing. "Don't play coy. The ship's signature. If those people out there somehow get through the atmosphere"—he gave Lexa a leer, like he knew Elani wouldn't be able to pull off what he just had—"I don't want them to be able to follow our trail."

The engineer grimaced, lips pulled tight, and faced his panel again. "Yeah. Yeah I can do that."

"I thought so. No pirate ship is complete without being able to obfuscate." He paced back to the pilot and stood, arms crossed. He gave Lexa a wink.

She swallowed bile again.

Jake leaned over. "That's how June found you before. I guess he learned?"

Lexa shrugged. An idea had begun forming in her head and if she was right, killing Reid might be a good option after all.

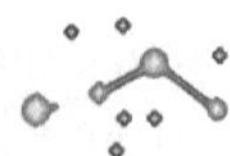

The ship hovered over a canopy of trees thicker than anything Lexa had ever seen on Earth. Some illustrations they showed in school of the time before the dinosaurs—when the planet was nothing but rain and trees—rivaled it. The pilot whispered that the surface was at least two hundred feet below the crown of the smallest trees, and Lexa pulled a breath in and held it. Even the babies of this forest were likely half a millennia old, if they aged at the same rate as Earth.

Most of them looked something like pine, though a few with broad leaves grew scattered throughout.

She fought to break a whisper. "Find a place to land that's not going to hurt them."

Weller shook his head. "There's nowhere. Scans show not a single square meter not covered by trees."

Reid leaned over him. "Our landing site should be as close as possible to the coordinates the map gave."

"No," Lexa began, "you can't—"

Ignoring her, Reid pressed a few buttons. Cannons blasted into the trees, ripping them to shreds and disintegrating large swaths of them.

Lexa watched in horror, unbidden tears streaming down her face, until a landing zone larger than the ship had been cleared. The murdered trees lay inside and around the ragged hole in the forest, smoldering. Their delicate bark crisped and blackened.

Jake hugged her shoulders and turned her toward him.

She wanted to look away from the slaughter, but it was too late, and in any case, she couldn't. Her own folly was responsible for this, in the end, and she had to watch what it had wrought. "You just destroyed thousands of years' worth of growth."

Reid shrugged. "Just trees. Land," he said to Weller.

He did, bringing the ship in gently over the trees so that no more of them were damaged by the ship's hull. When they settled unevenly atop the corpses, he pushed a few buttons and the landing skids beneath them compensated for the uneven forest floor until the ship sat level. He shut down the engines and glared up at Reid.

With a wide smile, Reid clapped him on the shoulder. "Thanks, pal. Nice, soft landing." He turned to Lexa. "Let's go on down." The gun reappeared and waved toward the door. "After you."

Dragging Jake with her, Smith and Qesson following close behind, they headed down the hall. "We need to test the atmosphere before we go out there. It might look like Earth but that doesn't mean the atmosphere has the same composition."

"Sounds like a perfect job for you."

She sighed. She wanted to tell him that without her, he'd never be able to decipher what he was looking at when they reached the site, and that he might not even reach the site at all. But that would sound too much like wheedling, and she wasn't about to beg for anything from him. In silence, she let Jake and Smith help her into a suit and stepped into the airlock.

Jake lay a hand on the window between them and mouthed *be careful.*

She nodded and blew him a kiss. Not that he could see her face through the darkened face shield on this thing, but she was pretty sure he could understand the pantomime.

He smiled, lips wide. His #1 A+ smile. What a nice sight.

She held that with her as the bay door hissed open and she turned away to follow the ramp down. If it was the last thing she saw, it was at least a good thing.

Her first step on the planet where life had begun was like any other. The ground was slightly springy and when she got both feet under her, she looked around the landing site. There had been ferns, too, and probably some lichen. She spotted a few fungi sticking out over the decimated trees, and wild grasses here and there. It looked so much like Earth, she could hardly believe her eyes. How could this be? They'd met so many species, explored so many Earth-like planets, but none of them had been this close.

It astounded her. In college, she'd learned not to look for Earth in the stars, and never expected to see it.

"Hey." Reid's voice echoed inside her helmet.

She jumped, stomach tight, and twisted to look over her shoulder.

Reid looked through the window to the airlock and pointed to his wrist.

Fine.

She punched a few buttons on the wrist unit and the air test began.

Something moved out of the corner of her eye.

She turned toward it. The last thing she needed was to get eaten by an alien carnivore of some kind. Frozen, she stared into the trees.

Nothing moved.

Starting to relax, she looked down at the wrist readout and caught movement on the ground.

A lizard no bigger than her foot zipped by, its scales a shifting iridescent, and it had six legs. It ran under a smoking tree trunk beside the ship and disappeared.

She grinned. Small lizards she could handle. But she said a quick prayer to creation they wouldn't get to "thunder" size.

The air tester beeped.

She took a look.

Well then. Not exactly like Earth.

Trudging back to the ship, she toggled the radio on. "It's not toxic, but there's not enough oxygen for us to breathe. We can convert what's there, but we're going to need to bring oxygen purifiers with us if we want to survive for more than an hour or so."

Reid replied through the radio. *"This many trees, you'd think there'd be O2 to spare."*

"They might not work like Earth trees. They might just look like them."

"Whatever. Stay out there. We'll bring supplies and get going."

She sat at the bottom of the ramp and removed the helmet. A few minutes wouldn't kill her, and she wanted to breathe in the air of this world. Smell the fresh soil and the green scent of the trees, hear the movement of the forest and breath of the wind. After inhaling deep through her nose a few times, the air cool and refreshing, she removed a glove and lowered her hand to the ground.

Her fingers sunk into the charred soil of the forest floor and slid through it, digging in up to the third knuckle, moist on her fingertips as they penetrated the ground. She pulled her hand out and rubbed it over a small patch of lichen that had somehow escaped Reid's onslaught. It was fuzzy like Earth's, but it moved beneath her fingers of its own accord. When she pulled her hand back, it reached up for her the way the map reached for the Cynosure.

She lowered her hand again and it brushed her palm like she would pet her cat. It tickled and she laughed, so engulfed in the feeling of a plant petting her that she didn't hear the others tromping down the ramp until Reid stepped next to her and crushed some of the lichen beneath his foot.

He twisted his heel like he knew what he was doing and gripped her shoulder. "OK, show me the way."

She stood and again considered killing him. It'd probably be doing everyone a favor.

Eyes narrowed, she glared at him. "You're really something else."

"Something you know all too well."

Stomach churning, she took the oxygen purifier he held out and stuck the nasal cannula up her nose. The unit itself, no bigger than a button, clipped easily to her suit, and after checking it was set to "O2," she clicked it on. "Follow me. Please watch your step." Something she said more for the benefit of the others than Reid. She set off to the north.

The group—Lexa, Reid, Smith, Jake, Qesson, and half a dozen of Smith's men—cleared the devastated circle of forest quickly and tracked deeper into the woods. Animal trails led off in several directions, telling Lexa a few things. One, there were more than just little lizards living here. Two, the planet was teeming. And three, they were bound to run into something if they continued this way. Hopefully if it was a large carnivore, being loud as they walked would scare it off, rather than call it closer. Even still, she turned to Reid. "I hope you let some of those men behind you bring weapons. I don't know what lives here, it might try to eat you. It'd regret it, you probably taste like sewer sludge, but still. I'd hate to give it heartburn."

He gave her a weak chuckle. "Good point." He waved two of Smith's men to the front. "Keep your eyes peeled."

They nodded and took point. Lexa stayed close behind them, giving directions. When they reached a point where they still needed to go north but the animal trail led off to the west, she told them to break through the brush—gently—and keep going.

The grade increased until they were forced to put the guns away and grab onto trees and vines to pull themselves up the hill. It put Lexa in mind of trekking through the forest above the Amazon, looking for ancient Mayan sites buried in the jungle. She'd hoped to have a clear view of the site, but if it was covered the way those sites were, they might walk right past and never see it. It could be completely buried in forest growth.

At least there was less mud than in the Amazonian Forest.

Something rustled in the trees above them.

She gripped the two men in front of her and pulled them to a stop. The others stopped behind her, the rustling of their progress quieting to nothing.

Reid broke the silence. "What—"

"Shh."

Miracle of miracles, he shushed.

From above their heads, a sound emanated from the throat of something Lexa imagined to have a mouth full of pointed teeth and maybe pointed claws below it.

She looked up just in time to see it sail from the top of the tree, at least a hundred feet in the air, extending its legs into flaps of skin that worked like a sort-of parachute the way a flying squirrel would. "Look out!"

It landed on the back of one of the men in front, its claws and teeth even longer than Lexa imagined. Small, pointed ears laid flat against its head and whiskers the length of baseball bats extended from its snout. Besides the whiskers and flying squirrel skin, it looked like a jaguar, only its spots were green and gold instead of black.

Its long, puffy tail twitched, trying to balance it atop its flailing prey.

Smith and Jake shouted in concert with Lexa and the man trying his damnedest not to be eaten. Reid squealed like a stuck pig and retreated behind the closest tree.

Lexa picked up a stick lying on the forest floor next to her, gripping the rough bark in her palm, and swung it at the jag-squirrel's back. It glanced off when the wailing man turned and stumbled downhill, reaching over his shoulder to try and grab the creature whose body was easily as long as his own.

Jake ran toward it with a large rock in his hand, while Smith pulled out an energy rifle and took aim. Before he could get the shot off, the man swung around again, facing the gun, and Smith lowered the barrel. Jake danced around the man and swung at the creature with the rock, hitting it in the ear.

It yowled at him and took a swipe at his face.

Lexa screamed, heart bound up around her teeth.

Jake ducked it, but the claws stuck in his cannula and tore the purification unit from his face. He slipped out of it and slid to his knees.

Deafening in the dense forest, Reid's handgun blasted.

The creature relaxed all at once and fell to the forest floor with a flat *thwump*.

CHAPTER 38

Oesson hauled Lexa to her feet. Before letting her go, he leaned into her ear. "Promise me you'll help me get back to Jenierien and I'll give you any help you require to make it happen."

She gave him an absent nod. Tears spilled over her bottom lid, her eyes wide and staring at the dead creature. They'd been on this planet less than ten minutes and had done nothing but destroy whatever they encountered. Maybe they should get out before they destroyed the site itself. She tried to swallow but her throat wouldn't let the spit go down. Sucking through her nose, she gritted her teeth and tried again. Her throat loosened enough to let her.

She crept past the corpse and knelt next to Jake. "You OK?"

He held up the purifier. "Yep. But this?" It dangled from one of his fingers, the cannula useless and the unit cracked down the middle.

Lexa turned and found Reid creeping out from behind the tree, his gun stowed once again. "We have to go back and get Jake a new purifier."

Reid shook his head. "Hell no. We go forward. No one goes back."

Helping his man to his feet, Smith grimaced and gestured at him. "We need to take Enjoula back. He's injured."

That projectile gun made its appearance again. "We go forward. If he can't make it, he can get left here." He pulled back the hammer and aimed.

The man, Enjoula, snuffled, and addressed Smith. "I can go on. It's OK, Sir."

Smith nodded. "Jake, do you want to share my purification unit?"

Lexa pulled her own off. "He can share mine. Jake, two minutes, then back to me."

"You got it." He tugged it on and stuck the cannula up his nose. "Thanks." He gave her, if not a thousand-watt smile, at least half that.

She found an answering smile on her face before turning back to Reid. "Let's go, then. It should be dead ahead."

He pushed past her and scanned the forest. "That mound above us?"

She nodded. "I think so."

He plunged past the men in front and swiped at the vines ahead of him. They moved without being touched.

Now why wouldn't he have used that power to fight the jag-squirrel? He could have saved them all a lot of trouble. Said a lot about him that he chose to hide behind a tree then, but used his power now to get himself to the prize first.

Sweeping both hands in front of himself, the trees and vines covering the mound cleared, leaving the mound open to blue sky.

Lexa charged up the hill behind him and looked down onto it. Before she could focus on what she was seeing—a large, flat, round table etched with carvings all across the top of it inside a depression at least six meters wide carved out of the top of the hill—a note sang out from Reid's pocket. Light shone through the weave of his pants.

"Holy shit," she breathed. "The Cynosure knows it's home."

Reid slid it out of his pocket and held it up.

The light emanating from it had never been this peaceful. It radiated through all colors of the spectrum, fading from one to the other in a smoothly pleasing pulse.

Lexa began to drift with it, her consciousness floating away from her body in a way similar to what had happened when they went through the wormhole. Something about this was different, though, and her brain tried to tell her she'd forgotten something. But it didn't matter; the sense of peace descending over her was enough to make her want to lie down in the center of that table, or right here in the soft grass, and fall into the deepest sleep she'd ever known.

Someone grabbed her by the shoulders, their rough hands shaking her, and something tickled her nose. She tried to paw it away from her face, but the person's other hand gripped her wrist.

"No, Lexa. Breathe," Jake said, voice husky.

Unable to really process what he was saying, but trusting him enough to stop fighting, Lexa lowered her hand and inhaled a few times.

Her vision cleared like coming up from underwater, her lungs suddenly suffocating as though she'd been under too long. She began gulping breaths, the cool air rushing down her throat and burning as it went.

Jake rubbed her back. "Easy. Easy, OK? Don't hyperventilate on me."

She nodded. "Maybe two minutes is too much," she croaked.

"Maybe."

"Thanks." With a grin, she kissed him on the side of the mouth.

He turned into her, the arm around her shoulders sliding down to her waist.

Reid cleared his throat with a gross, wet hacking sound. "Whenever you're ready, *Doctor*."

Mouth pinched, she stepped away from Jake and re-settled the cannula. "Hand me the Cynosure."

Reid scoffed and said nothing.

"Fine." She huffed out a breath. "Stand in the center of the table. Be prepared."

"For what?"

"Anything."

He skidded down the gentle slope toward the table on his heels.

They'd climbed to the top of the canopy without Lexa really realizing it, and the trees cleared to give them a view of the valley they overshadowed.

Trees. Trees as far as she could see.

She'd often wondered what would become of Earth after people had gone. Here, the trees had taken back over, and if that's what happened to Earth, she wouldn't be sad about it. They'd seen the rise and fall of the dinosaurs, the passing of an untold number of forgotten species, and they'd oversee the rise and fall of man, too.

Reid called from about two meters below her. "Now what?"

Lexa opened her mouth to say she didn't know.

The silence surrounding them hit her. Until this moment, the forest around them had been teeming. Bird whistles, something that sounded like frogs croaking, the rustling of leaves in the wind. Now, a thick silence had descended on everything and she found she didn't want to break it. She raised a hand to Reid to try and keep him quiet, for all the good it'd do.

She needn't have worried.

Before he had a chance to speak, a great cracking sound came from the sky, like the crash of a hundred lightning bolts slamming into the ground at once. Her ears rang.

The clouds above them rippled as though they floated in a pool of water. Behind them, the blue of the sky paled.

Jake broke the silence before any of them. "No fucking way," he whispered. He whooped and jumped in the air, fist extended. "That's my girl!"

Lexa jumped and started to ask him what he meant. Before the words were out of her mouth, she looked into the sky again.

It continued to ripple. A small shape appeared in the sky; the runabout, its heat shield bright orange.

She covered her mouth. Elani had done it again. Had come for her, again.

Reid climbed out of the hole, Cynosure still clutched in one hand, and grabbed Smith's collar. He shook the man. "I thought you said you covered our trail."

Smith held up his hands. "We did. I don't know how they followed us."

Growling, Reid threw him to the ground. He grabbed Lexa's shoulder and twisted.

The twisted skin on fire, she gritted her teeth and spun to face him. "What. What do you want?"

"You're going to show me what this thing does"—he held up the Cynosure—"if I have to melt your brain to get it out of you." He stared into her eyes, his own turning that deep shade of ocean blue.

A violent twist traveled down her spine and into her legs, her feet going out from under her. If it weren't for Reid's hand holding her up, she'd be flopping on the ground like a fish on land right now. Unable to resist, she followed him back down the slope and stood on the table with him.

At least she got a good look at the carvings beneath her feet. She took in as much of it as she could, hoping she'd still be alive later so she could capture a few pictures.

Reid threw her down but she didn't hit the stone. After letting go of her shoulder, he stretched his hand toward her, his mouth drawn and forehead creased.

The way the energy kept her afloat in mid-air was similar to the way she'd felt when Elani had floated them to the ceiling like Charlie Bucket and his grandpa drinking magical fizzy soda. This was somehow not as pure as that, though, and her stomach turned at the slick, greasy feeling surrounding her.

"You're a hell of a trickster, Reid," she said, teeth clenched. "I admit I had no idea who you really are, and I'm usually a pretty good judge of character."

He bowed. "We all make mistakes, my dear." He lifted his other arm and on his outstretched palm lay the glowing Cynosure. "Never mind your intrusive family. Tell me how this works."

Her family. Had they come down, too?

No time for that right now.

She stared down at the carvings beneath her. There was a line of text circling the table, the language the map tried to show her at first, and she wished for time to learn what it said. Time she didn't have. Instead, she studied the illustrations and did her best guessing. Which was admittedly not as good as she liked to believe but still better than a good number of people. On this subject, at least.

"You put the Cynosure down and step back. It's the key to the site, just like it's the key to the map, and I don't think we want to be standing here when it activates."

Reid dropped the energy surrounding her.

She crashed to the stone with a grunt, her teeth biting through the side of her tongue and filling her mouth with coppery, slick blood. She spat some of it on the stone. She stood, eyeing Reid as he laid the Cynosure in the middle of the table like she told him to.

When she tried to grab it, a lot happened all at once.

CHAPTER 39

The runabout dropped in altitude so quickly the occupants must have floated for a few seconds. It stopped above the hill and its back door irised open.

At the same time, Reid clenched his fist.

If Lexa had been buried alive in a coffin form-fitted to her skin, it might have been more comfortable than the energy squeezing every millimeter of her.

Elani poked her head out the door of the runabout. "Reid, stop!"

He grinned. "You're going to make me?"

She put a leg through the door, balancing with one foot out and one foot in, and lifted both hands. "Whatever it takes."

Lexa tried to inhale. Her lungs barely moved. At least when she almost passed out from oxygen deprivation a few moments ago, it had been comfortable. This was like being pressed with bricks. Her eyes wide, she watched Elani take aim at Reid.

The hand not holding Lexa pointed toward Elani. "Try it. See what happens." He twitched the other hand.

Red pain shot up the sides of both lungs and into Lexa's head. A vise settled over her temples and squeezed. Bone creaked.

She tried to keep it in, but the pain was too sudden, too sharp, too much. She screamed through her teeth.

Elani and Jake shouted in unison. "Lexa!"

Elani lowered her hands. "We'll land and let's talk. Don't hurt her any more."

Reid chuckled. "See? I don't need to rely on mind control. You people are so easy, I can do it without hardly lifting a finger." He released Lexa.

Again, she fell to the table. This time, she knocked her head. Everything went white for a few seconds and she bit down on her tongue where she'd bitten it before, trying to focus and stay conscious.

Jake ran over and dropped to his knees next to her.

Lexa wasn't sure where the runabout landed, but by the time she sat up and handed the purifier off to Jake, Elani and the others had joined them.

Jenierien slouched behind Elani, Paisley, and Juniper, her hands bound. Qesson started to lope toward her.

Reid turned. "Stop. No one move. Qesson, get back over here."

Brow furrowed under his nostrils, Qesson slid back half a meter. He didn't take his eyes off Jenierien.

Elani stood at the top of the hill, holding Savannah in her arms and looking down at Lexa. Her eyes glowed the color of gold in the seam. Not bright and effervescent like usual, but rock hard. She stroked the cat. "Reid. You're Ambran. You hide it well. But I should have known, when you took Lexa off the ship. I knew she wouldn't have gone with you."

He scoffed, hands raised toward her. "Please. You can't even tell her the truth. I'm frankly shocked you got through the atmosphere. Your ability is weak. Why have you come here? To threaten me? A whole planet full of Ambrans couldn't stop me. You don't stand a chance."

"It's you," June said, stepping around Elani. "You. You're the one. You're *the* Ambran. You're the one Doug was shadowing."

"Lot of good it did him. I learned a couple tricks though, like how to block our trail. But I guess what they say is true. Can't hide an Ambran's soulmate from them." He glanced at Elani again. "But I can rob you of them. Just like I did for June."

Lexa's head whipped in her sister's direction, and she stood, she and Jake holding each other up. They took a step toward Reid. "Wait a fucking second. It was you? You killed June's husband and daughter?"

He didn't do her the favor of looking at her. One hand raised behind his back and clenched.

Lexa and Jake squeezed into each other, their bones crushing into one another.

Reid laughed. "It's more fun to break the bones by hand, but this will have to do. Say goodbye, everyone." His eyes flashed over his shoulder, the smile curled on his lips wide and showing all his teeth.

Lexa couldn't make out who shouted. It seemed like everyone did. But all she could hear were her eardrums trying to collapse and for a moment, she wished Jake was Truscian so they could flow through each other instead of be crushed together.

Jake breathed fast through his mouth, panting and trying to fight the energy crushing them. "S…s…sorry," he said, with what sounded like everything he had. Like this was his fault or something.

"N…" It was all Lexa could squeeze out. The vision in her left eye went red as it pressed into his shoulder, the pain sure to rupture the eyeball soon.

Savannah yowled.

Reid screamed.

The energy released.

Gripping each other, Lexa and Jake lowered to the table in a slow, somewhat controlled fall. On the way down, Lexa glanced at Reid.

He howled, struggling with a very pissed-off cat attached to his face by all twenty claws.

Lexa couldn't help but smile. Ruthless cat. She deserved a raise.

Elani fell to her knees next to them and inspected them both. "Are you two OK?"

Jake grinned as well as he could and nodded. "Think so. I'm so proud of you."

She met his smile and shifted her eyes to Lexa. "And you?"

One hand over her throbbing eye, Lexa shook her head. "You came back. Again."

Elani leaned in and slid one hand behind Lexa's neck. "Of course I did. You're my soulmate."

Mouth falling open, Lexa dropped her hand. "I…what? No, it's. No. What?"

"It's you, Lexa," Elani said, meeting Lexa's forehead with her own. "That's what I wanted to tell you when we kissed. You weren't ready to hear it before then."

Well, shit. That changed things, didn't it?

Without time to worry about it, she held onto both Jake and Elani and stood, just as Reid won the fight with Van and flung her away from him.

"Savannah!" Lexa started after her.

That damn projectile gun appeared again. "Not so fast. Show me what the hell to do here." He held up the Cynosure with the other hand. "Now." The end of the gun floated toward Elani. "Didn't think you had the juice to get through the atmosphere, but now that I know you do, I also know you should probably be put down like they tried to do to me when I was a kid."

He fired.

Elani threw up her hands in front of her and the bullet stopped in mid-air.

Qesson took the opportunity while Reid was distracted and wrapped two legs around his ankles, taking them out from under him. The Cynosure skidded across the table.

Smith's men all produced guns and aimed them down into the depression.

At the crest of the depression, Smith knelt and grinned sideways at Reid. "You were saying?"

But Reid said nothing. His fists clenched, he seethed at Smith and kicked out at Qesson.

His foot went through the red-eyed Truscian, who re-solidified before Reid could pull his foot back and grabbed him once again. "I would advise you to remain still."

That vein popped out on Reid's forehead, and his throat bulged. His face went so red, Lexa thought his head might genuinely explode.

Elani hadn't lowered her hands, and she spoke over her shoulder. "I think you should get away. Find Van, get back on the runabout, and get out of here."

"Why?" Lexa gripped Elani's shoulder. "What's going on?"

Reid's skin turned as red as a chili pepper. His neck continued to bulge and that vein looked ready to enter orbit.

"I've only read about it, but I think he's going nuclear."

"Nuclear?" The word alone was enough to get Lexa to move her feet. She grabbed Jake and pulled him with. "What does that mean?"

"It means he'll decimate the whole area when he explodes."

"Literally?"

Elani peeked over her shoulder. "Yes. And I don't know if he can stop it. You go. I'll try to hold him together."

Jake squeaked. "Elani, no. You can't."

"I can." She smiled at him. "You're the very best friend I've ever had." Her eyes flicked to Lexa. "I'll see you the next time around, love."

And all Lexa could see when she looked at the hair stuck to Elani's sweaty brow was Gram, lying in her bed, taking her last breaths before she left Lexa forever.

Paisley stepped to the edge of the depression and held out a hand. "Lexa. Please."

Mouth dry, heart racing, Lexa stared up at her mother. "What?"

"Come on. You heard her. We have to leave."

Grabbing Paisley's hand, she put one foot on the incline and stopped. "I can't. I can't let her—"

June whacked Reid in the back of the head with a branch as big around as she was.

He dropped like a sack of bricks, the Cynosure rolling out of his hand.

Qesson grabbed it.

Reid's skin returned to a normal color.

Lexa just stood with her mouth open, her hand in Paisley's, and one foot in the dirt. "Damn, sister. Hell yes."

June grimaced and reached for Reid's face. She tore off the purifier and spat in his unconscious face. "Choke." The purifier crunched beneath her heel.

Elani sidled up next to Lexa. "Now what?"

"Can we handcuff him?"

"That won't do anything. When he wakes, he'll be just as dangerous as before."

Lexa nodded. Her gut sank to her toes, but what choice did they have? "Exile it is."

Jake stared at him. "Won't he die without the purifier?"

"I don't think we're that lucky." Lexa climbed the hill and looked down at the table, memorizing as much as she could about it. She clicked her tongue. "Savannah? Vanny-fanny? Where'd you get to?" It took all the will she had not to think the cat might have broken her back when Reid tossed her.

She approached the runabout, holding Elani and Jake's hands. "Smith," she said, angling toward him. "You need to get out of here. Thanks for your help, let me know how to repay you."

He smiled. "I told you. You'll know." He raised a hand and whistled through his teeth. His men disappeared into the forest behind him.

"Can someone help me out of these cuffs?" Jenierien held out her wrists.

"Qesson." Lexa angled her chin. "Give me that Cynosure back and let her loose."

He glanced at Jenierien.

Lexa'd never seen her so disheveled, nor as sweaty and dirty as she was now. This forest, even for the few minutes she'd spent in it, hadn't been nice to her. It was refreshing, somehow, to see her so…human. She smiled.

Jenierien met her grin and nodded.

Qesson nodded back and handed the Cynosure over.

It was still warm, but at least it was manageable. Lexa slipped it into her pocket and kept searching for her cat.

"You still owe me, Lexa," Jenierien said, rubbing her freed wrists. "We will need to settle up in the very near future."

Lexa hardly heard her. A jag-squirrel cleared one of the trees below the mound, limp Savannah in its jaws.

Breath caught in her throat, the top of Lexa's head pounded. All this, and she lost her cat, too? No.

The jag-squirrel lay Van on the forest floor, saliva dripping from its maw onto her sleek coat.

Van stood and twittered. She arched her back and rubbed her head along the bottom of the jag-squirrel's jaw.

The creature purred and returned the head rub. Before it turned and left, it glanced at Lexa.

More than animal instinct flashed in its eyes. Lexa would have bet her life on it.

Van sauntered over and curled around Lexa's ankles.

"Ready to go now, Ma," Lexa said, voice raised. She reached down and snatched up the cat, holding her warm little body close to her chest and covering them both in that creature's saliva.

"That's a good idea, Van," Elani said. "He could wake up at any moment."

Before climbing aboard the runabout, Lexa gave Reid one last look.

"Exile, it is."

CHAPTER 40

On the crowded runabout, Lexa stared out the window and watched the Wellspring get smaller until they passed back through the protective atmosphere. None of her questions about these people—or whatever they called themselves, whoever they were—had been answered. She didn't know how long they'd been there, what they'd been about, or if they had been watching them from the distance the whole time.

Elani leaned over from the pilot's chair. "We could bring the Kuarpan authorities back. They'd know what to do with him. Then you could look all you want."

Lexa shook her head. "Look what Reid did in just a few minutes. Look what he could do if we hadn't stopped him. No. I don't think bringing more people here will fix anything. I didn't get any of the information I wanted, not even a souvenir. But I saw it, I know they existed, and I think that's enough."

"Your call," Elani said, going back to the controls. "Docking at the *Auriga* in a few moments."

"It's a nice ship, Mom," Lexa said over her shoulder. She spun so she could look through the door into the room where Jenierien, Qesson, Paisley, and Jake all crowded on the bed. Van had gone under it as soon as she got a look at all those people. "I can recommend some good pilots when we get back to Earth."

Paisley slipped off the bed and squeezed around the others. She leaned in the door. "Do something for me."

"Sure."

"Take Mom's house off the market."

Staring out the window at the stars now in front of them, Lexa nodded. "Yeah. I think that's a good idea." Taking a breath deep into her lungs, she let the feeling of exhaustion wash over her. It'd been a long day, and—

"I want you to have the ship, honey."

That kicked her in the ass like a pot of steaming coffee. "You what?"

"Take the ship. I'd like to stay at the house for a while, maybe settle for a bit, but you don't have to say yes. My offer still stands. You're the *Auriga*'s new owner, if you want it."

Lexa exhaled and sat back. "You're giving me a ship? You could see the whole galaxy in that thing."

"I know. And I want you to have it."

Chest tingling, Lexa spun back around and met her mother's eyes. "I don't know what to say."

"Say you'll think about starting your treatments again."

A smile curled the side of Lexa's mouth. "Don't push it."

Dust crawling up her nose, again, Lexa stepped through the sand with soft feet. "OK, look out for the Gex-rats. They're not nice. Savannah is pretty good at taking care of them, but those claws are sharp." She patted the bag slung across her body.

Elani sneezed. "That where you got those scratches I saw on your back when we first met?"

"That, and the broken mirror."

"I think you should tell us that whole story sometime," Jake said. "You left out a bunch of details. Like, how exactly did you end up naked?"

She grinned over her shoulder. "You would go straight to me naked."

"I'd like to."

Elani and Lexa laughed.

They moved into the room with the carved relief, the top of it still open where Lexa had liberated the diadem that now sat on a shelf at the Galactic Historical Record's museum. It did look better all polished up and shiny with its own little spotlight.

The map was there now, too, in a Lucite display case. She hoped it would be happy in the museum. It probably missed the Cynosure. The next time around, maybe they could get together again.

Something shuffled in the shadows.

She unsnapped the bag. "Go get em, girl."

Van oozed out of the bag, landed on the ground with a quiet thump, and stretched.

"If you let one of them eat me, I'm not going to forgive you."

Tail straight up in the air, Van wandered into the dark.

"OK you guys, follow me," Lexa said, angling for the pedestal where Devin and the Gex-rat had become one with the tomb. They still lay there, likely until the end of time, unless someone came along and broke them. Devin's legs had already begun the process of being mummified by the arid desert. She stopped and stared at the two of them, and a moment of doubt fluttered near her heart. She never wanted to regret bringing Jake and Elani with her the way she regretted bringing Devin. Besides the fact it'd be ten times worse if it was one of them. She pointed out the unfortunate man and tried to understand why she was grateful to have Elani and Jake there to see and understand her failure. Maybe she could forgive herself, maybe this was the first step toward a life where she didn't have to hate every decision she'd ever made.

"Don't step on the pedestal. There's a pretty nasty surprise if you set off the trap."

"You never said there were traps involved," Jake said, squeezing closer to her.

She squeezed him back and gave him a reassuring kiss. Which turned into a longer kiss, one that lit her up better than the lights in her arms. When she let him go, his thousand-watt smile had returned and her guilt had been subsumed by acceptance of her mistakes.

His smile, always good to see, sealed the deal.

"We have to get through that door," she said, pointing up.

Jake craned his neck. "You wanna stand on my shoulders and maybe…I dunno. Hm."

Elani chuckled. "Please. Let me." Her eyes flashed gold, bright in the dim tomb. "Though this is easier if you help." She took Lexa's hand.

Lexa's feet left the ground. She laughed. "That'll never get old, I swear." She took Jake's hand with her other one.

The three of them floated up to the ceiling. Elani planted a kiss on Lexa that not only lit her up the way Jake's had, but made her forget completely about floating. All that existed in that moment was the woman she was in love with, the man she was in love with, and the energy between them all.

When she'd walked into this tomb the first time, the thought it'd end like this simply would never have entered her mind.

They landed on the floor in the upper chamber. Lexa let her lovers go and looked around. "I accidentally shattered their queen." She bit her lip. "I don't know how to repay them for that."

Jake's hushed tone fit the room. "I think returning the Cynosure is a good start."

She nodded and climbed the dais. Maridoxia no longer reclined on her throne, so Lexa lay the Cynosure in the seat and stepped back.

It flashed red, once, and was still.

None of them spoke for several minutes. Lexa stood between them, one of their hands in each of hers, and considered what Gram might have to say about all this.

"Thanks," she whispered.

Elani whispered back. "For what?"

"Rescuing me."

Jake chuckled. "For the record, I wanted to throw you back out in the rain."

"Probably the better choice."

He laughed. "So what now?"

Lexa grinned. "Check this out." She raised the lights in her arms and knelt, careful to avoid the sharp pieces of shattered queen. She pulled a paper out of her hip pocket and flattened it on the floor. "I didn't get any pictures of the table, but I remember this portion."

Elani knelt next to her. "I didn't know you could draw."

"It's just a rough sketch."

Jake knelt across from her. "What is it?"

"I think it might be a gateway. I've read about them, but never seen one."

"A gateway?" Elani's delicate brow wrinkled, her eyes bright. "What is that?"

"There's lots of theories, but the predominant one—and the one I believe—is that it can transport us to another galaxy in minutes, and I think the people of the Wellspring knew where to find one." She looked up at them, smile stretching her cheeks wide. "You wanna help me find it?"

THE END

ACKNOWLEDGEMENTS

Special thanks to those of you who not only beta read, but answered all my silly little questions about this book. It wouldn't be the book it is without you.

Thanks as always to my family for throwing food and affection at me as I hunched over my computer, muttering to myself about the precious and whatnot.

Big thanks to Drew and the Cloaked Press team for giving my space book a go. And as always thanks to Carmilla for the more than gorgeous cover. You never fail to impress me right into tears.

Thank you, reader, for coming with me, Lexa, Jake, and Elani on this journey. I hope you're ready to see where they go next!

ABOUT THE AUTHOR

Bethany (she/her) has been writing since her first-grade teacher said, "this is pretty good," if not before. She's had several poems published, taking after her father in poetry. In 2019 she published her first book, a poetry chapbook in which she shared some of her late father's poems as well. In early 2020, she published her debut novel. In hindsight, publishing a book in February of 2020 about the world recovering from a virus was probably not the best timing, but she loves that book and the series with her whole heart. She has always had a soft spot for horror, sci-fi, fantasy, and zombies. Check out her other books and socials by going to https://linktr.ee/bperrywrites. Sign up for her mailing list and purchase autographed copies and swag at bperrywrites.com.